CARRIER

These are the stories of  *a force including a superc... cruiser, and destroyer. Ar... blistering reality of inte... Explosive.*

CARRIER...The smash debut thriller about the ultimate military nightmare: the takeover of a U.S. Intelligence ship.

VIPER STRIKE...A renegade Chinese fighter group penetrates Thai airspace—and launches a full-scale invasion.

ARMAGEDDON MODE...With India and Pakistan on the verge of nuclear destruction, the Carrier Battle Group Fourteen must prevent a final showdown.

FLAME-OUT...The Soviet Union is reborn in a military takeover—and their strike force shows no mercy.

MAELSTROM...The Soviet occupation of Scandanavia leads the Carrier Battle Group Fourteen into conventional weapons combat—and possibly all-out war.

COUNTDOWN...Carrier Battle Group Fourteen must prevent the deployment of Russian submarines. The problem is: They may have nukes.

AFTERBURN...Carrier Battle Group Fourteen receives orders to enter the Black Sea—in the middle of a Russian civil war.

ALPHA STRIKE...When American and Chinese interests collide in the South China Sea, the superpowers risk waging a third world war.

ARCTIC FIRE...A Russian splinter group has occupied the Aleutian Islands off the coast of Alaska—in the ultimate invasion on U.S. soil.

book ten

CARRIER
Arsenal

KEITH DOUGLASS

BERKLEY BOOKS, NEW YORK

CARRIER 10: ARSENAL

A Berkley Book / published by arrangement with
the author

PRINTING HISTORY
Berkley edition / March 1998

All rights reserved.
Copyright © 1998 by The Berkley Publishing Group.
This book may not be reproduced in whole or in part,
by mimeograph or any other means, without permission.
For information address: The Berkley Publishing Group,
a member of Penguin Putnam Inc.,
200 Madison Avenue, New York, New York 10016.

The Penguin Putnam Inc. World Wide Web site address is
http://www.penguinputnam.com

ISBN: 0-425-16345-8

BERKLEY®
Berkley Books are published by The Berkley Publishing Group,
a member of Penguin Putnam Inc.,
200 Madison Avenue, New York, New York 10016.
BERKLEY and the "B" design
are trademarks belonging to Berkley Publishing Corporation.

PRINTED IN THE UNITED STATES OF AMERICA

10 9 8 7 6 5 4 3 2 1

CARRIER

Arsenal

ONE
Saturday, 22 June

0300 Local (+5 Greenwich Mean Time)
Cuban Fulcrum 101
17,000 Feet, 50 Miles South of Cuba

Cuban Air Force Colonel Emilio Santana banked his Soviet-built MiG-29 Fulcrum to the left, skirting the air defense perimeter of the American battle group. The fighter twisted through the sultry night air as though the mechanics of airspeed, altitude, and control surfaces were mere formalities in the relationship between man and machine. The advanced composite struts and fuselage were extensions of his own body, the howling jet engines an echo of the blood rushing through his arteries and veins. The single-seat fighter seemed to read his mind, translating the smallest twitches of human muscle and nerve into tactical maneuvers that would have been impossible in any other aircraft in Cuba's inventory.

Tonight he was alone in the sky, suspended between the heavens and black water, surrounded by hard points of light that bit into the dark without dissipating it. Spattered overhead, the stars. To his right, Cuba, city lights clustered into hard gems set in velvet. Directly below him, fog seeped up from the ocean and mixed with broken cloud cover to obscure patches of water. Water and land, night and stars—

the world below him seemed remote and untouchable, changing in response to universal rhythms that man could neither understand nor alter.

Reality isn't that simple. First the Soviets, now the Libyans.

In both cases, the first seemingly harmless offers of technological assistance and money had led to an ominous military presence that pervaded every facet of daily life. The military advisors weren't so easily ejected once they'd established a military presence eighty miles south of the United States.

More than just a mere presence. They are an infestation, a plague. As long as we can control them, we benefit. But as with any parasite, there is a danger that the host may suffer.

He nosed the fighter up, aiming directly at a star. The maneuver bled off airspeed, slowing his rate of travel around the latest of many American intrusions into Cuba's sphere of influence.

Forty miles to the north, clearly visible under the full moon and through the light haze, the USS *Thomas Jefferson* and her covey of escorts were finishing up the last phase of their workup operations prior to deployment. The Cubans had been watching carefully for the last two weeks as *Jefferson* fought a mock opposed transit through notional landmasses charted in the middle of the Caribbean. Flight operations had ceased at 2200, and the Cubans had had sole possession of the airspace surrounding their island nation since then. From his altitude, on a moonless, slightly overcast night, the only indications of the American presence were the phosphorescent green lozenges on his aircraft's radar.

Santana sighed and shifted his attention away from the stars and to his duty. As commander of the Western Air Defense Zone, he'd wanted a personal look at the armada assembled off his coast. American battle group workups were a normal part of life, but this one was particularly irking. This battle group included the first operational deployment of an Arsenal-class cruiser, and both Cuba and her allies were desperate for intelligence on the platform.

That the Americans had no compunction about conducting military maneuvers so close to the coast of his nation irritated him. Had the situation been reversed, the Americans would have strenuously objected to a foreign power conducting war maneuvers off *their* coast. Why was it that the Americans were unable to understand Cuba's objections?

Not unable—just unwilling in their arrogance to even entertain the idea of Cuba as an equal, as a leader in the Caribbean basin. Yammer as they will about self-determination and democracy, the Americans understand power, only military power. They have chosen the weapon in this duel, but we will choose the time.

A new speck of light on his RP-29 coherent pulse Doppler radar caught his attention. Code-named Slot Back by NATO, the MiG-29's radar had a search range of fifty-four nautical miles, and was collimated with laser range finder and infrared search/track sensors. Using data supplied by the radar, the MiG was capable of launching AA-8 Aphid infrared air-to-air missiles or AA-10A Alamo medium-range radar-guided antiair missiles. A GSH-301 in the port wing root carrying 150 rounds completed its armament.

The new contact—what was it? He studied the radar screen carefully, noting that it was growing stronger by the minute. Not a military aircraft. The pulse size was too small, and the wavering edges of the lozenge indicated that the radar was having a difficult time maintaining any resolution on it. The first tingles of adrenaline tickled his senses.

A light aircraft, then. Possibly civilian, or a small reconnaissance or spy aircraft deployed from the Florida coast, only eighty miles to the north. At 130 knots, the contact could be either a helicopter or a fixed-wing aircraft. Whatever it was, it warranted further investigation.

His orders were to maintain radio silence pending identification of any threat or an indication that a contact was proceeding into within twelve miles of the Cuban coast. Santana rolled the MiG out of its turn and vectored off toward the contact.

He glanced down at the SO-69 electronic countermeasures display. Aside from the normal search radars from the carrier and her escorts, as well as the familiar signature of the Cuban land-based air search radar, there were no new contacts. Odd, that. But understandable. Only an aircraft wanting to avoid detection would make the journey toward Cuba without radar. His level of excitement ratcheted up another notch.

The new contact was still sixty miles to the north of his position. He shoved the throttles forward slightly, accelerating to 520 knots. At that speed, he was only minutes away from obtaining a visual. He swore quietly at the layer of low clouds at five thousand feet and checked the altitude of the unknown contact. As he'd suspected, it was right in the middle of the layer, using the clouds for cover. Again, more suspicious conduct.

Madre de Dios! What were the Americans thinking?

Anger shattered the traces of his earlier mystical contemplation of the sky and the sea. Exercise operations, however odious, were expected. But expanding the routine into an open affront to Cuba's domestic airspace—such arrogance! Did they really think they could make a covert approach on the Cuban coast without being detected?

If so, it was time to teach them a lesson.

0305 Local (+5 GMT)
Combat Direction Center (CDC), USS Jefferson

The tactical action officer frowned and spun his track ball cursor over to the new contact. He clicked once, calling up data on a small secondary screen. Airspeed, altitude, IFF— International Friend or Foe signal—were all indicative of a small civilian aircraft.

CDC was the carrier's nerve center. Sensor data from every radar and ESM—electromagnetic sensor—detection suite in the battle group was relayed to the carrier's computers, analyzed, compared with other sensor data, and projected onto the blue large-screen display in the forward part of CDC.

Hardly a threat to an aircraft carrier, but where the hell did it come from?

The new symbol had popped into being on his screen without any prior warning from Tracker Alley, the long array of air search and correlation consoles that took up a quarter of the CDC spaces. He keyed the microphone to his headset with the foot pedal. "Track supervisor, what is this?"

The tinny voice sounded bored. "Don't know, sir. We just gained contact a few moments ago. It's off any commercial air routes, and it's not one of ours."

"Any ideas?"

"No. That's why I've got it designated as unknown. There's no IFF squawk from her, and no flight plan for the route."

The TAO sighed and jotted down the details in his watch log. He turned to the CDC watch officer, the person normally responsible for the operations of CDC. "Let's do the standard challenge and reply. That contact's course puts him well to the west of us, but he's transiting our area. Could be drug runners, could be a civilian pilot who's lost. My bet is on the former rather than the latter."

The CDC officer nodded and reached for the microphone. "I bet we don't get an answer."

"No bet—I'd say you're right. We'll notify the Coast Guard."

"Unidentified air contact at"—the CDC officer glanced at the latitude-longitude readout on his screen—"thirty-two north, seventy-two west, altitude five thousand feet, speed one-three-zero knots, this is USS *Thomas Jefferson*. Over." He waited for a few minutes for a reply, then repeated the call-up. After the third time, he turned back to the TAO. "No response, sir. Big surprise."

"Notify the Coast Guard in Miami. We'll let the normal law enforcement handle this." The TAO turned back to the briefing sheet before him, wondering whether his summaries of the previous day's flights and engagements would take long enough to kill the rest of the watch.

"Keep an eye on it," the TAO said. "If its course puts it within ten nautical miles of the battle group, we'll talk to Tach'cal Flag Command Center about what to do. Until then, just be sure the data is relayed to SOUTHCOM. We'll let them worry about it."

0310 Local (+5 GMT)
Commander, Southern Forces, Miami

"New contact," the operations specialist at SOUTHCOM announced. "My bet is it's a drug runner."

The watch officer at SOUTHCOM, the composite commander responsible for all areas south of the continental United States, glanced at the big-screen display. "The Coast Guard knows about it?"

The operations specialist nodded. "They're checking into it, but there doesn't appear to be a flight plan. Not much we can do about it now, but they'll be alert for a contact on the return from Cuba."

The watch officer frowned. "Could be another one of those rescue operations. We had two last month, you remember. American activists trying to evacuate relatives from Cuba. Let's make sure INS is in the loop."

"Already on it," the operations specialist announced smugly.

0315 Local (+5 GMT)
Fulcrum 101

The small contact was now five hundred yards in front of him and one thousand feet below. There was still no visible contact, and the Fulcrum was closing rapidly on the slower target.

"And if you had honorable intentions, my friend, you would be showing your running lights," Santana said aloud. "Since you aren't, I suspect you don't want me to see you."

The contact was not painting brightly on his radar scope. Santana was certain he hadn't been detected in return, since the contact was emitting no radar pulses. He waited until he was only five hundred feet behind the small contact and, still without visual contact, put the Fulcrum into a steep climb. If he judged correctly, the wake from his two Klimov-Sarkisov RV-33 turbofan engines would buffet the smaller aircraft, letting him know that he'd been detected. Just to be sure, Santana slammed the throttles forward and kicked in the afterburners.

He ascended to ten thousand feet, smugly certain that the civilian aircraft knew it was no longer alone in the skies. He stood the Fulcrum on its tail, then executed a sharp turn downward. He watched the radar scope carefully, judging his approach angle. If this worked correctly, he would cut directly in front of the small contact.

When the scope indicated he was almost in front of the smaller plane, Santana flipped on all of his external lights. He watched on the scope as the small aircraft executed a hard turn to the right, and grinned. Whatever the contact was, its maneuverability and speed were no match for the Fulcrum, and he was willing to bet that the other pilot would need a change of underwear as soon as he was back on the ground.

Wherever that might be. He frowned, wondering why the Americans had decided to pull such a stupid tactical maneuver.

"Perhaps another pass will dissuade you from your plans," Santana said out loud. He gained altitude and prepared to repeat the maneuver.

0320 Local (+5 GMT)
CDC, USS **Jefferson**
Combat Direction Center

"A nice little game of chicken?" the TAO asked. "That's our Cuban shadow that's been watching all day, isn't it?"

"Or his relief." The CDC officer looked amused. "Do you know what would happen to us if we tried to harass an inbound aircraft like that to turn it back from the coast? We'd all be facing a court-martial."

The TAO frowned. "Not something I'd want to do even in relatively clear weather like this," he remarked. As an F/A-18 pilot, the TAO was well aware of the range inaccuracies that could creep into any radar system. "He's getting so close to that contact that we're getting a merging of the two blips on radar."

"I'm not sure which would be worse—to be in the Fulcrum trying to pull it off, or to be in the small plane he's harassing."

The CDC officer shook his head. "Either way, it's a hell of a way to make a living."

0328 Local (+5 GMT)
FULCRUM 101
10,000 Feet

Santana was not pleased. Despite two buffeting passes, the light aircraft continued inbound on Cuba. At first he'd assumed it was just a smuggler plying the regular route between Florida and Cuba, but it hadn't reacted like any drug dealer he'd seen yet. He glanced back to his left at the battle group. Was there some other reason for its foray into Cuban airspace or was it mere coincidence that the American battle group was in the same vicinity? He toggled the comm circuit to relay his observations to the Cuban controller.

For the last five months, the area around the western end of Cuba had been closed airspace. It had only taken a couple of weeks before the word had spread throughout the close-knit smuggling community, and it had been months since there'd been an unauthorized intrusion into the area.

The Fuentes Project—he grimaced in frustration. Protecting it from outsiders had been his highest priority as Western Air Defense Zone commander, and it wouldn't do for the first unauthorized intrusion to occur during one of his personal surveillance missions.

"Continue maneuvers as briefed." The ground control intercept officer, or GCI, sounded bored even over the circuit's static. Santana smiled. Perhaps he should have consulted with the GCI before the first warning maneuver, but this permission, in effect, granted retroactive absolution for the maneuver.

"Commencing second run," he said as he toggled the circuit mike. "Estimate contact is forty minutes from the coast."

"Do you require assistance?" the GCI asked.

"I don't think so," Santana said. He rolled his eyes in disgust. As if the Fulcrum were incapable of handling one small, turboprop aircraft. Even the mighty F-14 Tomcats on the carrier's deck were little match for *this* fighter.

At ten thousand feet he tipped the nose of the Fulcrum down, heading for the deck at five hundred knots. He watched the airspeed indicator slowly creep to the right as the Fulcrum traded altitude for speed. A little closer this time, perhaps, with full lights on blazing the entire way.

"Fulcrum 101, GCI!" The controller's voice was taut with tension. "Contact's course indicates it is on an intercept course with the Fuentes Base. Imperative that no overflights are allowed. If the contact cannot be turned back, take with missiles."

Santana sucked in his breath. Weapons-free permission? Now that was something new.

The briefing he'd received indicated that some form of military research was taking place at the small naval base, but no details had been forthcoming. Rumor had it that a new, powerful, land-based intercept radar site was being installed, but he hadn't found anyone to confirm that yet. It irked him. As the officer responsible for enforcing the no-fly zone, he should know exactly what was down there, particularly if it could pose a problem for his own squadrons of interceptors.

He watched the radar scope and considered his options. When could he legitimately claim that he'd tried to turn back the aircraft? By leaving the decision of when to fire up to him, the GCI officer was effectively transferring responsibility for the engagement to the pilot.

The Soviet-trained GCI controllers were not noted for their boldness in combat. Nor were they often willing to disturb their superiors for direct orders. They walked a fine line between maintaining tight control over their assigned intercept aircraft and doing everything possible they could to avoid responsibility for anything that happened.

Well, this time they'd made a mistake, as far as he was concerned. His orders from the GCI required him to keep the contact away from Cuba. Even if a later tribunal decided that the attack was not authorized, he could be relatively certain that the blame would be fixed on the GCI officer rather than on him. He reached out and touched the small recorder he'd taped to the instrument panel, glad he'd begun taking the precaution of recording the transmissions on his own.

A little closer this time. He eased the Fulcrum to the right, instantaneously calculating the intercept angle and the relative airspeeds of the two aircraft. This pass, and then—he gasped as the contact suddenly accelerated on the screen, then twisted the Fulcrum into a hard, braking turn. Too late. Santana had two seconds to wonder just how the other aircraft had managed to eke out another fifty knots of airspeed and make one frantic grab at the ejection seat handle. Before the fifty-six-foot Fulcrum could even begin to twist its thirty thousand pounds of mass through the turn, the Fulcrum slammed into the smaller aircraft. The fireball blotted out the full moon's light.

0330 Local (+5 GMT)
CDC, USS Jefferson

"What the—where the hell did they go?" The TAO's voice ratcheted two notes higher. He turned to the CDC watch officer. "Get your ass back to Tracker Alley—find out what the hell is going on here."

The CDC officer bolted out of his seat and trotted toward the two parallel rows of consoles. The TAO turned back to the large-screen display. Two seconds earlier he'd held hard paint on both the Fulcrum and the civilian aircraft. Now the screen showed empty airspace.

0332 Local (+5 GMT)
40 Miles West of Cuba

The surface of the ocean slammed into Santana like a brick wall. The force drove the air out of his lungs. He sucked in a breath reflexively, then erupted into choking and spasmodic retching as seawater coursed down into his lungs. He twisted his head back and stared up at the surface so far above.

Five seconds later, the automatically inflating life preserver did its job. Santana bobbed up to the surface, coughing, sputtering, and gagging. Warm night air poured into his lungs like a blessing.

Burning debris from the mishap spattered the ocean

around him. A large chunk hit near him, floated for a few seconds trying to scorch the water, then sank with a burbling swirl of bubbles. Santana gasped, finally able to concentrate on something besides his own desperate need for oxygen.

He fumbled with the pocket on his flight suit and drew out his portable air distress radio. Ten seconds later, he was talking almost calmly to the sea-air rescue station ashore. GCI had already passed them his last location, and the watch officer assured him that a helo was launching at that moment for his location.

Santana let the radio slip out of his fingers, leaned back in the warm water with the life jacket buoying him up, and waited.

There was no doubt in his mind now as to the identity of the other aircraft. No smuggler would have been so careless.

The Americans would pay for this. He would make certain of it.

TWO
Saturday, 22 June

0345 Local (+5 GMT)
TFCC, USS Jefferson

"This better be good." The noise level inside TFCC dropped immediately as Rear Admiral Edward Everett "Batman" Wayne strode into the small compartment.

The Flag TAO, still wearing his modular headset, stood up and turned to the admiral. "Admiral, approximately fifteen minutes ago, a Cuban MiG-29 apparently downed a civilian aircraft forty miles north of Cuba. The contact was inbound at one hundred and thirty-five knots, no IFF, no Mode 4. We designated it as a contact of interest and maintained a watch on it, pending a change of course toward the battle group."

"Shit," Batman said softly. "Did we interrogate the contact on International Air Distress?"

The TAO nodded. "No response. And no distress call now on either civilian air distress or military air distress."

Batman rubbed his hands over his face, then scratched absentmindedly under his left arm. The flight suit he'd slipped on as he crawled out of his rack naked was still new, and the stiff fabric chafed. "Is anybody saying anything?"

He jerked his thumb at the right bulkhead. "What about the spooks?"

"That would be me," a short, blond-haired, blue-eyed officer said as he stepped through the hatch leading into TFCC. "There was a brief, encrypted transmission from GCI, probably to the Fulcrum, immediately prior, Admiral." Commander Hillman Busby, known as Lab Rat to the other intelligence officers, shrugged. "Not unusual. They keep their land-based air patrols under close control. We knew the MiG was there, of course, but there were no indications of hostile activity."

"Did the MiG take a shot at it?" the admiral asked. "A small contact like that, maybe he's just too low and dropped off our radar."

Lab Rat shook his head. "We can't tell. Immediately before the contact disappeared off radar, we were holding targeting transmissions from the MiG, but there was no contact on an actual missile launch. They both just dropped off the screen."

Batman suppressed a yawn. "Any indications where the aircraft launched from?"

"The track seems to correlate with a civilian aircraft launched out of Miami forty-five minutes before. No flight plan, but that doesn't mean anything. It's entirely possible that he launched from a private airfield. That, or the paperwork just got mixed up. The Coast Guard is checking on it now."

"Has SOUTHCOM been notified?" the admiral asked.

The TAO spoke up. "Voice report five minutes ago, and the message is almost ready to fly." He held out a single sheet of paper. "Any comments to add, Admiral?"

Admiral Wayne studied the message, then shook his head. "No, we don't know anything at this point. Just what the message says." He scribbled his initials in the upper right corner of the paper. "Go ahead and send it."

The admiral climbed up into the high-backed, elevated leatherette seat located in the middle of TFCC, his thoughts hundreds of miles away from the carrier. Ashore, the watch staff would soon be waking the SOUTHCOM admiral, just as Batman's staff had awakened him. He grinned, wondering if his old running mate, Admiral Matthew "Tombstone" Magruder, would like it any better than he had.

Tombstone and Batman had spent practically every tour in the Navy together on one carrier or another. Together they'd seen most of the nastiness the world had to offer, fighting wingtip to wingtip. First, as junior nugget aviators, they'd chased MiGs in all parts of the world ranging from Norway to the South China Sea. Later, as more senior officers, they'd fallen into a now predictable pattern. Tombstone, two years senior to Batman, blazed the trail. In his last two tours, Batman had relieved Tombstone in his billet while Tombstone went on to scout their next duty station. What had first begun as an odd coincidence had been elevated to a standing joke within the tight-knit F-14 Tomcat community.

Distracted, Batman stared at the left-hand seat in front of the TFCC. He stared for a moment, then grinned. Odd that he could recognize the back of her head, when she'd spent most of her time in the air staring at his. He stood up and walked over to the console. "Tomboy?"

The diminutive naval flight officer turned around, looked up, and stood. "Yes, Admiral. Can I help you?"

Batman shook his head amusedly. "As I live and breathe, Lieutenant Commander Joyce Flynn. What the hell are you doing here? I thought you were still playing test pilot out at Patuxent River in Maryland."

Following their last cruise, the radar intercept officer, or RIO, had been ordered there to operationally test the latest flying machines the Navy had to offer. Foremost among them was the JAST bird, an advanced avionics F-14 Tomcat that featured an augmented look-down, shoot-down Doppler pulse radar.

Tomboy had flown as Batman's RIO during a conflict two cruises ago in the South China Sea when Batman, as program manager for the JAST project, had persuaded Tombstone, then commander, Carrier Group Nine, to use the test platforms in actual combat.

"Just catching up on the changes," she said, gesturing to a large-screen display behind her. "A few things are different."

"More has changed with you than has with TFCC," Batman said, looking down pointedly at her left hand. "So you finally did it?"

Even in the semigloom of TFCC, he could see her blush. "Las Vegas. Neither of us felt like a large wedding."

"You could have at least told me. Me, of all people," the admiral huffed. "As many aircraft as I have on board this ship, I would have found a way to get there."

"My apologies, Admiral. The next time—"

"There'd better not be a next time. So what are you doing on board?"

"PXO, of VF-54." The small naval flight officer couldn't hide her grin. "Who'd have thought?"

"I saw your name on the list, but didn't realize that was so soon. You're relieving Henry?"

"Yes. He fleets up to CO in two weeks. I talked Tombstone into letting me come aboard a week early, just so we could start turnover. Besides, I need a FAM flight in the B-bird." She shook her head ruefully. "After the birds I've been flying, it takes some getting used to. At least I've got Gator in the squadron to keep me honest."

"That's right—he's the VF-54 operations officer, isn't

he? Good man." The admiral glanced up at the tactical display, then turned back to her. "If I didn't know better, I'd swear that Bird Dog was in the air. This is just the sort of situation he'd be involved in."

Tomboy laughed. "He's your problem now, Admiral, not Gator's, since he's on your staff."

"Since this is old-home week, let's just get his young ass up. How about it?" The admiral turned to a messenger. "Go wake up Bird Dog. I think he'll want to see this."

0355 Local (+5 GMT)
Stateroom 03−135−03−L,
USS *Jefferson*

For some reason, Callie Lazier was trying to wake him up. Her hand was on his shoulder, shaking gently but insistently. He could feel her snuggled up spoon fashion in back of him, her nipples gently pressing against his back, his butt nestled into the taut hardness of her belly. He smiled, wondering if her other hand was already snaking around his waist, reaching lower to caress him, waking him up in what had already become a delightful morning tradition in their relationship. If so, she'd find out just how ready he was, asleep or not.

Lieutenant Commander Curt "Bird Dog" Robinson moaned and rolled over onto his side. Why not make it easier for her? He pulled her hand off his shoulder to guide it down, feeling the urgency and anticipation build as he—*since when did Callie have hairy wrists*?

"Sir. Sir!" The voice was low and insistent.

Bird Dog tried to twist away, then paused to think. *Sir? Why was his fiancée calling him that?* It didn't make sense.

The only time he was awakened with that was when he was—

His eyes snapped open and he stared into the plain, honest—and now, horrified—face of the Flag messenger. "Oh, shit." With a sigh, Bird Dog shoved the pillow away from his face. "I'm back on *Jefferson,* aren't I?"

The admiral's messenger gulped, then nodded. "Sir?"

"Never mind." Bird Dog released the man's wrist and shoved himself up into a sitting position. "This better be good."

The messenger smiled. "That's just what the admiral said, sir, about ten minutes ago. He thought you might want to see this."

Bird Dog sighed. "The admiral, huh? Okay, I'll be right there."

As the messenger scuttled out of his stateroom, closing the door quietly behind him, Bird Dog flipped on the small light mounted immediately over his head, casting a dim glow over the entire room. No point in waking up his roommate if he didn't have to.

Heavy snores cut through the compartment from the rack above him. Bird Dog glanced enviously up at his roommate, wondering why he deserved to sleep another four hours.

Well, no help for it. When the admiral wanted his staff assembled, it happened, and happened now. He reached for his flight suit, paused, then sighed and pulled his khaki pants and blouse out of his locker, trying not to make any noise. His days of living in the soft, comfortable green jumpsuit were over. At least until he got back in a squadron. And that wasn't the only disadvantage to being a staff puke.

In his last two cruises, both on board *Jefferson,* Bird Dog had seen combat in the Spratly Islands and helped thwart a Russian invasion of the Aleutian Islands. Based on his extensive operational experience, he'd been promoted early to lieutenant commander, then selected to attend the Naval War College in Newport, Rhode Island. Attendance at the demanding college of staff and command courses was reserved for only 10 percent of naval officers service-wide. During his year there, he had been exposed to the most advanced techniques in tactical and operational art, rubbing shoulders daily with the top officers from every other service and civilian agency in the U.S. government. Somewhere along the way, he found out that he'd done the right things during his previous two cruises, if sometimes only by mistake.

And that wasn't the least of it. He pulled on his blouse, smiling as he thought of Callie. Of all the great things in Newport, she was the best. And if tonight was any indication, she was indeed the girl of his dreams.

Callie Lazier, Navy lieutenant commander surface warfare officer. He smiled. If ever there'd been an officer that looked less like a warrior, it was her. Long, honey blond hair, deep blue eyes, and, at five foot ten inches tall, only two inches shorter than he was. Her soft, luxuriant curves couldn't mask the fact that she spent an hour in the gym every morning before classes and ran five miles every evening. The woman was a jock, an absolute jock. The last time he'd tried to keep up with her, he'd fallen out on the side of Thames Street, made his way into the Brick Alley Pub, and was happily half drunk by the time she'd finished her run. Callie had been disappointed and mockingly stern.

A woman who drives ships for a living. Bird Dog shook his head. How could someone be satisfied with a life in which top speed meant about thirty-five knots? He'd tried to explain to her the sheer glories of naval aviation, the heady exuberance of catapulting off the front of the carrier, the sheer joy of flying the world's finest aircraft, the F-14 Tomcat, under any and all circumstances, but somehow he had the feeling she'd never really understood. In fact, Callie had displayed a noticeable disdain for the exploits of the F-14 in combat.

Bird Dog crossed the small compartment in two steps and rummaged around in the debris on a small ledge over the sink for his wings. He found them, and jammed the two metal spines on their back through the well-worn holes on his khaki shirt. Well, she'd feel differently once she had her first flight in a Tomcat. He didn't know yet how or when he'd arrange it, but it would happen. Had to happen, if he were ever going to explain to her why it was so important that he keep flying.

Five minutes after he'd been awakened, Bird Dog slipped quietly out of his compartment and headed for TFCC.

0355 Local (+5 GMT)
TFCC

"Sir, I recommend we put CAP—Combat Air Patrol—up." Tomboy's voice was confident. "We probably won't need them unless we don't. Then it'll be too late."

Batman frowned. "Any other indications of hostile activity?"

"No, Admiral. I simply think it's a reasonable precaution."

Batman nodded. He turned to the officer seated in the right-hand TAO console. "Why didn't you think of that?"

"I'm sorry, Admiral." The assigned TAO looked uncomfortable. He *had* thought of it, but hadn't felt comfortable interrupting the admiral's conversation with Tomboy. He shot the small female officer an irked look. It was one thing for her to hang around TFCC, catching up on the changes that had occurred, another entirely for her to trash out her fellow officers in front of the admiral. If Mrs.-Admiral-Commander-Flynn/Magruder wanted to get along with this staff, she'd better learn to fit in.

"We have two VFA F/A-18s on Alert 15, Admiral," the TAO continued. "The Marine pilots are in their Ready Room."

"They don't do me much good there, do they? Come on, man, let's get moving." Batman turned back to Tomboy. "Not so long ago, it would have been you and me scrambling for those aircraft, wouldn't it? I sure do miss it."

"Anytime you need a backseater, Admiral, you just let me know." The two exchanged a look of mutual admiration.

0400 Local (+5 GMT)
Flight Deck, USS Jefferson

Marine Major Frederick "Thor" Hammersmith shivered slightly as he stepped out onto the flight deck and pulled the heavy metal hatch closed behind him. The night was warm, sultry, but the flood of adrenaline that had hit him when the phone rang in the Ready Room had not yet subsided. The quick five-minute brief in TFCC had done no more than crank it up an extra level.

Around him, the flight deck buzzed with activity. Sailors tumbled out of their racks and were now streaming across the deck, visible only in the glare of the giant floodlights mounted on the tower. Green shirts, red shirts, yellow shirts, each color denoting a separate function in the intricate ballet that made up the flight deck operations.

His F/A-18 Hornet was still parked in the center of the

flight deck, a location befitting its assignment as Alert 15 aircraft. A few minutes to run through the checklist and power up, and he could simply taxi straight forward to the catapult.

He groaned and rubbed his eyes. Pulling Alert 15 was a pain in the ass during training exercises, but this was something real. A MiG-29 shooting down a civilian aircraft— what in the hell was that about?

Sure, tensions between the United States and her southern neighbor had ratcheted a notch higher since the U.S. had nationalized some of Cuba's American-held assets, but that had never disturbed the Navy's operations in its traditional training ground to the north. And why shoot down a civilian aircraft? Bullshit, that was. Why fight somebody who can't fight back?

Moments later, he was standing next to his aircraft. He walked around her carefully, checking for loose fittings and undogged compartment access panels. He ran a hand over her nosewheel gear, checking carefully for any signs of looseness or excessive wear on the tires. The Marine enlisted technicians who maintained Hornet 301 were fanatics, but it was one thing to take responsibility for an aircraft on the deck, another thing entirely to trust your life to it while getting off of the pointy end of a carrier.

Finally satisfied, he stood and stretched, feeling the last vestiges of fatigue seep away. He glanced up at the tower, already illuminated with red light. Inside, the Air Boss and Mini Boss would be settling into their seats, staring down at Thor and his aircraft and waiting for the report from the steam catapult operators that all was ready. A thin wisp of steam was already rising from the narrow gauge track in front of him, evidence of power to the system.

Thor grinned. The Air Boss held certain misconceptions about Marine pilots, prejudices that Thor liked to tweak at every opportunity. As the flight deck teemed with activity around him, Thor dropped down to the nonskid, assumed position, and whipped out a quick fifty push-ups. The exercise flushed the last traces of fatigue out of his body. Invigorated, he jumped to his feet and trotted over to the port side of the F/A-18. Clambering up the handhold and steps, he quickly settled into the cockpit. A technician followed him up, pulled the safeties on the ejection seat, and double-checked his harness.

"You're good to go, Major." The Marine Corps technician nodded solemnly, barely visible in his bronze shirt on the moonlit deck. "Good hunting, sir."

Thor nodded. "Anytime, anywhere, Marine."

0410 Local (+5 GMT)
TFCC

"There he goes." Tomboy pointed at the plat camera that showed the flight deck. Two JBDs, or jet blast deflectors, had popped up from the deck and were partially screening the raging afterburner fire spewing out of the Hornet's tailpipes. They could see the dark figure of the catapult officer standing near the Hornet's nose, the other technicians carefully clear of the red line delineating the flight deck area.

As they watched, the overhead ceiling panels resonated with the harsh roar of the fighter's engine. The sound built, then climbed an extra notch, rattling monitors, computers, and bulkheads alike. Finally, when it seemed impossible that the noise could get any louder, the Hornet started moving, slowly at first, then quickly accelerating to minimum airspeed of 135 knots. The catapult dragged the fighter down the flight deck to the bow, spewing a trail of steam behind it. Finally they heard the gentle thump, always too soft, that signified the shuttle had reached the end of its run.

The Hornet disappeared from view for a moment as it lost altitude at the end of the carrier. It reappeared immediately, barely climbing as it struggled to remain airborne. As soon as it reached three hundred feet, it banked away from the carrier in a sharp right-hand turn.

"I always feel better having CAP on station," the admiral said. "If I know the Cubans, they're going to blame this on us and put up a full combat spread. If they do, we'll be ready for them."

0500 Local (+5 GMT)
Southern Command Watch Center, Miami

"You've got the feed from LINK?" the watch officer asked.

The operations specialist nodded. "*Jefferson* just launched CAP. Two Hornets, on station in approximately ten minutes."

The watch officer nodded. He reached for the telephone. Whatever was going on down in the Caribbean was far above his pay grade. As much as he hated waking the admiral up, he disliked taking sole responsibility for it even more.

0800 Local (+5 GMT)
Coalition for Cuban Liberty, Miami

Jorge Leyta watched the crowd surge and eddy around him. The protest was taking shape without any effort on his part.

Word traveled quickly in the Miami Cuban community. Within the next hour, everyone who was anyone would be there, up to and including his own rival, Emanuel Aguillar.

Leyta savored the moment, listening to the murmur of the crowd intensify. It took on a deep, almost imperceptible cadence as the voices grew louder, until it seemed to merge with the beating of his own heart. Even Aguillar couldn't have topped this, not on his best day.

Leyta's aide tugged at his elbow and nodded discreetly at the far right-hand corner of the crowd. "There. In the white BMW."

Leyta let his gaze drift back, seeking out the edges of the crowd. There. He'd known Aguillar would have to show, just not how or when. "*Muy cerca de los carros de televisión,*" Leyta said quietly. "*Por que,* no?"

"*Sí,* and what else would you expect?" his aide answered, slipping easily between English and Spanish. Like most members of the Cuban community, both were fluently bilingual.

Leyta shrugged, an expressive gesture. "To use such an occasion for personal gain—it sickens me. But the Coalition must come first. My brother would have wanted it that way. He was a man of great courage, great honor. He flew to Cuba that night knowing he faced both American and Cuban weapons. He would have done it every night, if he could have, to free our country from Castro's Communists and American imperialism." He let his voice choke off.

"*Hijo de puta,*" the aide muttered. "*Si tiene cojones,* Aguillar would confront us directly. But no, he does not dare."

Leyta shook his head. "*De nada.* Anything he does now

will only help us, even if he does not wish to. The people, you see," he said, gesturing to the growing throng, "they know. Only the Coalition has taken action—real action— and made sacrifices. Aguillar merely postures and talks. If he had his way, Cuba would become the fifty-first state." He glanced sideways, noting how his words settled his aide's thoughts. It was always so when he put his mind to it. That's why leadership of the community was rightfully his, not his rival's. "And the Americans, they have shot down a peaceful civilian aircraft. *They killed my brother!* Where now is this wonderful 'normalization' that Aguillar wants?"

His aide turned his head sharply toward Leyta. "How sure are we? Can we be certain? The news reports say it was the Cuban government that shot down our aircraft."

Leyta's mouth curled into an ugly arc. "And you believe what you hear on the news?" He shook his head. "No, there is no doubt in my mind. My brother"—his voice caught for a moment; he drew in a deep breath and shivered slightly before it steadied—"knew the risk he was taking. He is a hero, a martyr to our cause. And I will make certain that this government understands just how badly they have fucked up this time."

From the back of the crowd, Aguillar studied the swaggering man on the makeshift podium. How much did Leyta really understand about what had happened? Not much, not if this demonstration was any indication. Leyta had never understood political realities, never been able to accept that Cuba must—*must*—turn to America for support and security.

He heard a high-pitched squeal as the television van to his right started its engine, the fan belt complaining loudly. The vehicle ground into gear, then edged slowly forward, parting the massive Hispanic crowd like the bow of a ship through water.

"Senor Aguillar, any comments?"

Aguillar turned toward the microphone waiting demandingly to his left. "Senor Leyta has my deepest condolences on the tragic loss of his brother," he began smoothly. "It is right that our community should turn out to mourn such a tragic—" *and unnecessary* "—loss of life."

The reporter holding the microphone edged closer. "Senor Leyta claims that the American government is responsible for his brother's death. Is it your position as well that the government is lying to him about this tragedy?" The reporter lifted one bronzed hand to her face and smoothed the hair back from her eyes. "Or are you going to support his version of the facts as a gesture of solidarity?"

Aguillar looked somber. "Miss Drake, this is hardly a time for politics. The Leytas, however ill-advised their political views, are a close family. Despite our differences, I mourn with them. This need not have happened, and how much greater their grief must be for knowing that they are in part responsible for their brother's death."

Pamela Drake regarded him sardonically. She made a motion to the cameraman following him, then handed an assistant her microphone. "Off the record now, if you please. And," she added, "that was about as smooth as I've ever seen you slide the knife into his heart, making it clear that Leyta's political ambitions are responsible for his brother's death." She shook her head. "And the public thinks that reporters are callous."

Aguillar glanced at her equipment with a look born of long familiarity with publicity. Satisfying himself that her recording devices were indeed turned off, he turned back to her. "You wouldn't understand, Miss Drake. For all your experience with ACN, you don't have the slightest knowledge of what it really means to be involved in the middle of a struggle such as this. To you, it's just another story. But to them," he continued, pointing at the crowd, "it's our future. Every one of us has family still in Cuba, still under Castro's harsh yoke.

"Leyta and I agree about one thing—they must be freed. He, however, chooses violence and terrorism and claims that Cuba must take its place as a leader among nations. A nice dream, but I prefer reality. I work within the law; I know that relationships with the U.S. must be normalized. All we agree on is that Castro and his pigs must go. Castro knows that—he uses me to spy on Leyta and vice versa, all the while perpetuating his regime. But do you and your colleagues understand the difference?" His voice rose angrily. "No. In every report, we're both branded as some form of evil, cultish separatists, while you ignore the very real differences between us. If you understood what was at stake—" Aguillar stopped abruptly. "No, you can't, can you?" he continued more quietly. "To you, it's just another story. That's all it will ever be."

Pamela Drake edged closer. "Perhaps if I understood the dynamics better, I could make sure the public understood the difference," she said softly. "Get me access, Mannie. You know you can. You do, and if what you're telling me is the truth, I'll make sure everybody understands it."

Emanuel Aguillar studied the small white woman in front of him. For over ten years now, Pamela Drake had been a star on ACN, her face a familiar sight against the background of every major world conflict of the last decade. Under the harsh southern sun, he could see the small lines at the corner of her eyes artfully disguised with makeup, the slight looseness along the line of her jaw. Passion still backlit her dark green eyes, and not a trace of gray speckled the shining cap of sleek brown hair. An attractive woman, indeed a beautiful one, even at her age. He let his eyes drift down from her face to the thin silk blouse strained taut over her breasts and found himself speculating what it would be like to make love to her. Abruptly, he made his decision.

"You'd like the real story, would you?" He laid a hand on her shoulder, digging into her skin lightly with his fingers. "It is possible, you know. I have many friends in Cuba still. The guerrillas would talk to you if—"

"If what?" Pamela's voice was hungry.

"If you went to them," he finished. He smiled slightly. "I understand that battlefields and rough conditions are not new to you, but Cuba is a world unto itself. Are you ready for that world, Miss Drake?" His voice was low and caressing.

"Just get me in there, Aguillar," she said softly. "Get me in there, and I'll show you how ready I am."

"I will. But first, there is something you must do for me." Aguillar's smile broadened into a grin.

1300 Local (+5 GMT)
Commander, Southern Command, Miami

"You'll have to talk to the media, Admiral. There's simply no way to avoid it." The public affairs officer's voice was urgent.

Rear Admiral Matthew "Tombstone" Magruder ran a hand through his unruly dark hair. Even clipped short, it managed to look mussed. His dark eyes were somber and unreadable. "Your job."

"Admiral, I can handle all of the smaller affairs. And, after your initial statement, I'll handle the routine briefings as well. But this is major news—it's getting prime-time coverage on every channel and station in the United States, as well as considerable overseas interest. I can try, Admiral," he added hastily, seeing the look of displeasure on Tombstone's face, "but they're not going to be satisfied with my statement. Especially not with Admiral Loggins spearheading the debate over the *Arsenal* ships right now. You've heard what he's saying already."

Tombstone leaned back in the chair and sighed. Why, oh why, had he ever accepted this assignment? Ever since his last at-sea tour, life had gone downhill. Aside from his marriage to Tomboy, there hadn't been a damned thing he'd liked about this tour. His thoughts drifted back to *Jefferson,* one of the United States Navy's most potent supercarriers. Commanding her battle group had been his first Flag tour, and the most professionally challenging assignment he'd had since he was in command of a squadron. And he'd done well at it, he thought—no, he was certain.

Somehow, he'd managed to keep the explosive tensions in the Spratly Islands from escalating into a full-scale war the United States was not prepared to face. With China trying to stake a claim to every inch of the oil-rich seafloor in the South China Sea, only the USS *Jefferson* and her cadre of escort ships had stood at the brink of war to prevent a new China hegemony. And their last mission had been the most challenging one of all.

"I've prepared some remarks for you, Admiral." The PAO's voice took on a softer, almost wheedling, note. "At thirteen hundred, you read them. Take a few softball questions, then I'll hustle you out of there. Really, sir, it won't take long at all."

Tombstone stood up abruptly, unfolding his long frame

from the comfortable chair. "All right." He sighed. "I guess this is what they pay me for. Five minutes of questions and that's it, though."

Tombstone walked to the door. If this was so routine, why did he feel like he was walking to his own execution?

THREE
Sunday, 23 June

1000 Local (+5 GMT)
United Nations

Ambassador Sarah Wexler studied the faces across the table from her. The Cuban delegate to the United Nations had an explosive temper on the best of days, and this was hardly that. For a moment, she thought almost longingly about the cold, taciturn Asiatic delegates she'd so recently faced down in the Spratly Islands. There'd been treachery there, certainly, but at least it had been masked behind the careful facade of diplomacy.

Not so this time. She sighed, inwardly steeling herself for the confrontation.

The Cuban question was never an easy one, and even less so in the last two years. With the collapse of the Soviet Union, she had hoped that the United States could take measures to bring its southern neighbor back into the community of democratic nations, but the decades of distrust had been impossible to overcome. Since then, other nations had courted the tiny island for most-favored-nation status. The latest intelligence reports indicated that military advisors from Libya appeared to have taken up permanent residence in Cuba, no doubt intending to take advantage of the political turmoil orchestrated by a cadre of old Che Guevara supporters.

Behind her, a small bevy of aides and assistants murmured amongst themselves. Finally, the Cuban delegate paused in his tirade. The small conference room sounded deafeningly silent after having been filled with his angry rampage for the last fifteen minutes. How, she wondered, did he manage to speak so continuously without pausing for a breath?

"The United States did not shoot down your aircraft. Did not shoot down *any* aircraft," she amended quickly. "As you well know, any aggressive action was taken by your country, not mine."

"So you say! But when have we ever been able to trust the word of the United States in reference to my country? Conducting armed military maneuvers off our coast at this very minute—a deliberate insult to Cuban sovereignty." The Cuban ambassador took a deep breath.

Ambassador Wexler winced as she watched him gather strength for another filibuster. When, oh when, would the nations of the world learn to solve conflicts by talking? Never, she decided, not if this was Cuba's definition of a diplomatic discourse. "Ambassador," she broke in sharply. "I granted you the courtesy of sitting quietly while you made your position plain for fifteen minutes. I insist that you return the favor." She glared at him.

The Cuban ambassador seemed to swell up. While he was barely an inch taller than she, it was clear that very few women of any size had rarely had the audacity to challenge him so directly. "I demand to be heard!" He banged his fist on the table.

Ambassador Wexler felt the yellow pine table quiver under her fingers. "You will have your turn when I am done," she snapped. She turned to the chairman of the

Subcommittee for Caribbean Issues. "Sir, I insist I be allowed to finish my statement."

The chairman, a rotund, dark black man from the Bahamas, stirred uneasily. His island nation was caught in the difficult position of arbitrating the conflict between its two large neighbors, neither of which the Bahamians wished to offend. He'd dreaded this moment since the day he'd been elected chairman of the subcommittee.

"I think," he said slowly, his gentle island accent rising questioningly, "that perhaps the United States—"

"More lies! Always lies!" The Cuban ambassador jabbed an accusing finger at the Bahamian. "You are bought and paid for, my friend. Do not deny it. Without American aid, your little lumps of volcanic ash would still be hard down under the British crown. Someday you'll realize that the only reason the United States provides money to you is to use your island as a staging point for aggression against your neighbors."

The Bahamian chairman stood. "You are so fast with words. But we are not in Cuba, where everyone bows down to your dictator. This is," and his voice took on a note of pride, "the United Nations. Even a tiny nation such as mine has a voice here." The chairman turned to Ambassador Wexler. "Your statement, madame," he said with grave courtesy.

She nodded her thanks, then turned to face the rest of the delegates. Cuba, Barbados, Puerto Rico, Antigua, and the Virgin Islands—the combined landmass of all these nations put together was not even half that of Florida's. Yet, for all their lack of size, they had an equal voice in these proceedings.

"As you all know, the USS *Thomas Jefferson* and the USS *Arsenal* are on routine naval maneuvers south of Florida," she began. "A number of smaller ships are also operating in the area—again on routine operations. A little after three A.M., a Cuban MiG-29 shadowing these ships conducted an intercept on an unidentified contact approaching the battle group. Shortly thereafter, the unidentified contact disappeared. Later correlation indicates that it was a civilian aircraft that was apparently en route to Cuba for what has been termed rescue operations." She spread her hands expressively. "The full data tapes from that battle group are available for any nation that wishes to examine them." *Not that any of you have the equipment to play them back,* she added silently.

"Lies! As you all knew it would be," the Cuban ambassador broke in. "Their aircraft carrier shot down a group of Cuban tourists touring the island."

"At three o'clock in the morning?" Ambassador Wexler let the question hang in the air for a moment, saw doubt and fear flicker across the other representatives' faces. "And what evidence do you have to support this conclusion?"

"You position an armed battle group in our waters and ask my justification?"

"This from the nation that let thousands of refugees die at sea between our two countries?"

He shook his head angrily. "No, Madame Ambassador, this time the United States has gone too far. The attack on a civilian aircraft was your doing." He placed his hands flat on the table and leaned forward toward her. "Effective immediately, Cuba is declaring a no-fly zone fifty miles around her coastline. Tell your pilots, Madame, that they violate our sovereign airspace at their own risk. They may find that our MiGs are not quite so easy to shoot down as an unarmed civilian aircraft."

1155 Local (+5 GMT)
Hornet 301
30 Miles North of Cuba

Thor yanked back hard on the yoke, shoving the throttles forward to full afterburners in the same moment. The Hornet responded almost before he'd completed the move, pitching nose up in the sky and standing on her tail. Gravity worked with the force of the afterburners to shove him back in his seat, pinning him against the lumbar support panel with five Gs of force. Thor felt the flesh pull back from his face, try to creep around back to his neck, and smiled. God, there was nothing like it! Open sky, plenty of fuel, and a Hornet strapped to your ass—it didn't get any better than this.

He shut his eyes for the briefest second, letting the thundering waves of noise wash over him. The afterburners were fully engaged now, adding the peculiar, deep-throated roar of their fire to the normal, solid, reassuring howl of the engines. He enjoyed the brief sensation of danger with his eyes shut, then looked quickly back down at the altimeter.

"Bet that'll make them sit up and take notice," he said out loud, noting that his instruments indicated an SOG—speed over ground—of zero. "You check that altitude, boys, and you'll see what a Hornet can do. Straight up, no forward movement. Now *that's* a fighter."

Sure enough, the voice of the operations specialist from *Jefferson* sounded anxious in his left ear. "Hornet Three-zero-one, say state?" The routine inquiry into his fuel status masked the real question: Now, just what the hell are you doing, Hornet 301?

"Eight thousand pounds," Thor said, forcing the words out of his throat. He grunted and tensed his abdominal muscles, driving blood from his extremities back up into his brain. "I'm fine, Flasher," he said, using the air intercept controller's nickname. "Don't worry about me—just puttin' her through her paces."

"It's a postmaintenance check flight," Flasher noted calmly, "not a tryout for the shuttle program, sir." The enlisted technician's voice was just barely tart.

Thor toggled his mike and let the OS hear him laughing. "I know, I know. Someday I'm going to strap a backseat on this baby and let you see what you've been missing, Flasher."

"I'd like that just fine," the AIC said immediately. "Just fine." The words were slow, and rich with a southern drawl. "But you keep this up, sir, somebody's gonna be noticing. You know?"

"Okay, okay," Thor muttered. He shoved the yoke forward slightly, dropping the Hornet's nose down from straight vertical. "That better?"

"Almost, sir. Now you just look like a helicopter on the scope, instead of a balloon."

"You find me a balloon with this much armament on it and I'll ride backseat on you." He eased the Hornet forward farther, into level flight. "Okay, Flasher, I'm heading back to the pattern. You happy now that you've destroyed my fun?"

"Fun's not over yet, sir." The operations specialist sounded amused. "Your tower flower just called down and said you're short one formation flight this month. He'd like you to get it over with now."

Thor groaned. "With who?" Flying close formation with another Hornet was a routine qualification for all pilots, but it was not his idea of fun. Traveling a little under Mach 1 that close to another airplane required a pilot's constant attention, not only on his instruments, but on the eight thousand pounds of flying metal just yards away. No screwing around, no unexpected maneuvers, just a careful ballet between two giant dragonflies.

"Fly in with the Tomcat, sir. Tomcat Two-zero-eight is airborne for formation flight in five mikes. You've got time to scamper over and get a drink, then back to Marshall to join on him."

"Who's flying her?" Thor demanded. If anything was worse than a formation flight, it was working with a Tomcat. While the F-14 had an extended range and could carry more armament than a Hornet, it was markedly less nimble. It was, he reflected, not a damn sight much better than driving a surface ship. He shuddered at the thought.

"Staff wienie, sir. Call sign Bird Dog. That okay?"

Thor grinned. "Sure, send the young lad on up. We'll let him get a look at a real aircraft."

Thor heard muffled voices just below audibility come out of the headset. Finally, the operations specialist came back on the air. "Tomcat Two-zero-eight will be on button three for coordination. And, sir, he asked me to tell you that you'd better suck on some fuel before he gets up there. He doesn't want to be waiting outside the rest room for you every five minutes. He said," and Thor could hear the smile in the OS's voice, "that you should've gone before you left home."

1205 Local (+5 GMT)
Tomcat 208
Flight Deck, USS **Jefferson**

"You ready?" Bird Dog asked. He twisted in his seat to look back over his shoulder at Lieutenant Commander Charlie

"Gator" Cummings, his backseat radar intercept officer. "Just like old times, huh?"

"I don't know how the hell I let you talk me into this," Gator muttered. "It's not like I have to get five traps a week to stay current."

"Come on, you know you love it. Besides, no one else wants to fly with me." Bird Dog's voice took on a plaintive note. "They think I'm getting rusty."

"You *are*. That's why you're scheduled for FAM flights every week." Gator's voice was tart. "And I'm not so sure that playing grab-ass with a sponge of MiGs is my definition of a FAM flight."

"I'm *entitled*—I'm on staff," Bird Dog responded. "Jesus, don't you think I'd fly every second if I could? But somebody's gotta keep the big picture around here."

Gator snorted. "You?"

"Yeah, me. What, you think that's funny? Considering that the Cubans have gone from a couple of lookie-loo surveillance flights every day to full-scale combat patrols, I don't find anything at all amusing about the situation."

"Considering I was teaching you to fly not three years ago, I damned sure do. When I first met you, you were as raw and fresh-caught as Skeeter Harmon was a little while ago," Gator snapped, referring to the young pilot who'd been their wingman cruise before last. Skeeter was currently attending Top Gun school, honing the combat skills he'd learned on their last Med cruise. "Now all at once you're a military genius?"

Bird Dog sighed and turned back to face forward. He ran through his prelaunch routine automatically, consciously tensing and untensing his muscles, giving his ejection seat harness one last tug to make sure it was secure. Was he that rusty? No, he didn't think so. And he'd never been as raw as Skeeter—the young black pilot might have shot down a missile in flight, but so what? Bird Dog had more time in the cockpit than Skeeter had in the chow line.

Still, the notable lack of enthusiasm among the RIOs on staff had irked him. "Just like riding a bicycle," he muttered.

"No it's not," Gator said sharply. "And if you think it is, you just let me out at the next stop."

Bird Dog signaled to the yellow shirt on the flight deck and tensed himself for the catapult shot. "It's damn sure not. You can't do this on a bicycle." He snapped off a salute and waited.

The Tomcat jolted, started rolling forward slowly, and quickly gathered speed. About 150 feet later, it was hurtling down the flight deck at 134 knots. Bird Dog heard Gator's sharp intake of breath and grinned. His backseater always had been a nervous Nellie on cat shots, even on routine flights. And if he couldn't answer a simple question about whether or not he was ready, then he deserved what he got.

Seconds later, the aircraft shot off the pointy end and Bird Dog felt the familiar lurch in the pit of his stomach and his ass floating away from the seat as the Tomcat lost altitude. The sea rushed up at him, smooth and glassy.

His balls contracted as a small flash of terror shivered through him. The first few microseconds after launch, this fight for altitude and safety, were every pilot's worst nightmare. If *Jefferson* lost steam pressure unexpectedly on the catapult shot, the Tomcat would dribble off into the ocean. A soft cat shot meant dead aircrews. Moments later, he felt the G-forces press him back into his seat as the Tomcat clawed for altitude.

"Good shot," he announced. "Airborne once more."

Behind him, he heard Gator groan.

1206 Local (+5 GMT)
Hornet 301

"Button three for coordination with tanker," Flasher said.

"Roger. Got a visual on him. Making my approach." Thor
eased back on the throttles, slowing the Hornet's forward
speed imperceptibly. Of all the evolutions a carrier pilot had
to master, refueling in midair was one of the most dangerous, second in his nightmares only to landing on the carrier
deck at night during a storm.

"Hey there, Thor," the female KA6 tanker pilot's voice
echoed in his ear. "You dirty-winged?"

"Hell, no. This is a PMFC, not CAP. Why, you want me
to kill somebody for you, sweetheart?"

"Maybe later, big boy. It's just that there's a cluster-fuck
of MiGs milling about smartly in the middle of Tanker
Alley. Thought we might sneak off somewhere that we
could be alone for a while."

Thor grinned at the lascivious note in the other pilot's
voice. The Marine Corps forced him to be politically correct
on the ground. In his estimation, the paranoia that over-
reacting politicians generated did more to harm the morale
of both men and women than it helped. This was more like
it—the good-natured banter between two pilots who re-
spected each other. "I'll follow you anywhere, Striker," he
said, using her call sign instead of her name. "You got some
particular dark and secluded corner in mind?"

Striker rapped out a quick series of vectors defining a
piece of airspace well away from the MiG herd. She led the
way, with Thor darting around her in his faster fighter. Ten
minutes later, they were in clear airspace.

"Now, how can I make you happy, Thor?" Striker asked finally.

"Five thousand pounds will do it. Burned up some on afterburner, and I need some legs to play patty-cake with a turkey," he added, using the common aviator's nickname for the Tomcat.

"Cozy on up to momma, Marine. I gots what you be needing."

Thor focused on the drogue extended in front of him from the back of the KA6. The basket bobbed and weaved in the air as it streamed out behind the other aircraft. "Steady, steady," he muttered, talking himself through the approach. If the Tomcat pilots thought tanking was tough, let them try it in a Hornet without a RIO to act as safety observer for them.

He watched the drogue grow larger and bled off a few more knots of airspeed. "There," Thor said, satisfied. He tapped the throttle forward and increased speed just enough to thump gently forward into the drogue, seating his probe firmly inside the refueling apparatus. "Got it first time."

"Good seal," Striker agreed. "Ready to pump."

"Receiving," Thor reported. "And Striker, it's only polite to ask—was it good for you, too?" He grinned and waited for the rude reply he knew he deserved, all the while watching the fuel transfer indicators for signs of trouble.

The insistent beeping of his ALR-87 threat warning receiver filled the cockpit. Thor's head snapped up and he scanned the sky, urgently trying to find the source of the fire control radar illuminating his Hornet.

"Settle down back there," Striker snapped. "What do you think you're—"

"Emergency breakaway!" Thor throttled the Hornet back, jerking out of the basket. Raw fuel streamed out of the drogue before the tanker's back-pressure sensors terminated

the flow. "Striker, get the hell back to the carrier! We're
being illuminated by—" The two aircraft were separated by
barely fifty feet when he saw the missile.

*Too low, too slow! I can't maneuver, I've got no airspeed.
There's no choice.* Thor reached for the ejection seat handle.
"Striker, punch out. *Now!*" As his fingers closed around the
yellow and black ejection bar, the tanker disintegrated into
a fiery, expanding ball. Metal shrapnel tore into his Hornet
as he yanked down on the bar.

A massive force slammed into his ass. Thor blacked out
milliseconds later as he cleared the shattered canopy.

FOUR
Monday, 24 June

0600 Local (+5 GMT)
50 Miles North of Cuba

I'm drowning. Thor's body realized it before he was fully conscious. He emerged from a warm, dark unconsciousness to the feel of water searing his throat, the taste of salt filling his senses. Instinctively, he began flailing his arms and legs, pushing himself toward the surface twenty feet above. The same survival instinct clamped his mouth shut and made his lungs strive to extract every last molecule of oxygen from the air still trapped inside.

Hours later, it seemed, he broke the surface. He drew in a deep, shuddering gasp, as he only then started to realize how close he'd come to buying it.

With sudden clarity, the details of the accident came flooding back. The tanker, jinking violently to avoid a missile. His own response, the hard diving turn of his Hornet, the water glistening below, looking soft and inviting. He remembered the flameout—vaguely, just enough to wonder how he'd managed to pull the ejection seat before the massive G forces had drained the blood from his brain and thrown him into oxygen-starved unconsciousness.

The life jacket. Why wasn't it inflated? Thor swore,

coughing up seawater. He quickened the rhythm with which his feet beat at the water as he felt for the manual inflation tube. There it was, on the left side of the life jacket. He screwed the retaining valve apart, put his lips around the hard plastic tube, and blew.

Immediately, he felt the swell of expanding plastic around him. With each breath, the life jacket started contributing to his buoyancy rather than weighing him down. Finally, when it was fully inflated, he turned his attention back to his surroundings. Sea state three, maybe four, with whitecapped waves obscuring his line of sight. He caught a glimpse of an unnatural fluorescent yellow fifty, maybe seventy-five feet away, and started stroking doggedly toward it. It bobbed into view, then disappeared behind the growing swells. The wind was in his face, blowing spray and wavelets up his nose.

From the summit of the next wave, he caught sight of it again. If anything, it was farther away than it had been when he'd started swimming toward it. At this rate, there was no way he could get to it. He paused, treading water, the full impact of his situation starting to sink in.

The rough water around him was blood temperature, and survival time without slipping into hypothermia was almost unlimited. But warm water brought hazards of its own, the ones that downed aviators feared more than almost anything else. This part of the ocean was host to a wide variety of sharks, all of which were more at home in the water than Thor. Their senses of smell and their acoustic ranging abilities rivaled that of any submarine.

He touched his face with a hand, then held the limb in front of him. Thin streaks of blood trickled down from his fingertips to his wrists. Thor groaned. Even more than the rhythmic motion of a panicked swimmer, blood attracted sharks. The scent traveled for miles, enticing every natural predator with the prospect of an easy meal. Wounded prey—the sharks would know it immediately.

Despite his years of training, panic crowded the back of his throat. He forced it down, concentrating on remembering countless survival lectures and ample practice in open ocean.

Thor stripped off his flight suit, knotted the legs, and flung the garment over his head while holding the legs to inflate the rest of it with air. He tied the neck portion shut, along with the arms. The flight suit swelled satisfyingly as the cotton fibers soaked up water and held the air in.

Thor gathered up his strength and lunged onto the inflated flight suit. According to what he'd been told, floating instead of treading water accomplished two things. First, he could conserve his strength, extending his stay time in the warm water. Second, by relying on the natural buoyancy of the flight suit, he could avoid the frantic flailing motions of treading water that attracted sharks.

Was there anything else? Of course. He turned the flight suit over, unzipped one leg pocket, and drew out the standard Navy-issue shark repellent and dye marker. He cracked both open, spilling the contents into the water. A sickly yellow tint spread through the water, highlighting his position for the sea-air rescue helos that he hoped would be overhead shortly.

But would they? He considered the matter, his heart sinking.

He and the tanker had been far off course when the collision occurred, well outside of the group's flight pattern. While *Jefferson*'s radar had undoubtedly held them, it would take some time to get the helos vectored over.

How long? Too long.

The tanker crew—could they have made it out? Not likely—he'd seen the fireball, and no chutes. For better or for worse, he was the only passenger the SAR helo would have.

He glanced nervously at the water around him, imagining sharply raked dorsal fins lurking behind every swell, and started stroking for the life raft.

0610 Local (+5 GMT)
USS Jefferson

"Where the hell is he?" Batman slammed his hand down on the TAO's desk. "Damn it, what was he doing inside the no-fly zone? And why didn't you give him a vector back to Tanker Alley?"

The TAO was pale and shaken. "Sir, they didn't look that far out-of-bounds." He gestured at the large-screen display covering the wall before him. An ominous stick figure marked the spot where Thor's Hornet had last been detected. The estimated location was being transmitted to every ship in the battle group, along with the air assets overhead.

"He's not too far out of area, Admiral." The TAO tried to sound confident. "We should have him back on deck in ten minutes."

Batman stared at the TAO, cold anger lighting his eyes. "You better, mister. You damned well better."

0615 Local (+5 GMT)
50 Miles North of Cuba

Maybe the tanker crew had gotten out? Thor felt a moment of irrational hope. Maybe they were just over the next wave, drifting in closer. He tried to believe that they'd ejected in time, but the memory of the massive fireball he'd seen just as he ejected kept intruding.

Just at that moment, he would have given virtually anything not to be alone in that warm, churning water.

He tried the PRC-70 one more time, speaking slowly and loudly into the small handheld radio tuned to military air distress frequency. "Home Plate, this is Hornet Three-zero-one. Do you copy?" He held the radio to his ear, desperately concentrating on the hissing static.

Had that been a small, extra crackle, an indication that someone was keying a mike on the other end? He felt a surge of hope, followed immediately by despair. No, it hadn't been. Whether the problem was the notoriously unreliable batteries or some malfunction in the radio from the force of ejection was impossible to tell. The only thing that mattered was the end result—no communications. And without that, trying to vector *Jefferson*'s SAR assets to his location was an impossibility.

He turned the radio over and studied the back. The tough casing was partially shattered, and he figured he must have hit it against the canopy during ejection. The radio might have even saved him from breaking a leg. But just now, it seemed like a bad trade-off.

The life raft looked farther away than when he'd started swimming toward it. He set out for it again, alternating between keeping it in view and searching the sky for the SAR helo.

0700 Local (+5 GMT)
USS Jefferson

"As of two minutes ago, there was still no contact on Major Hammersmith." The Marine Corps colonel's voice was grave, but professionally detached. "All six helos are engaged in a standard expanding square search pattern around the last data. Additionally, S-3 Vikings and E2C Hawkeyes are quartering the area, searching for any visual or electronic traces of him."

"How the hell could they miss him?" Batman burst out. "Jesus, it's not like we don't know where we lost contact on him."

The Marine Corps colonel stiffened. "I don't know, Admiral. That's a question Major Hammersmith will have to answer for us, when we find him. *When, not if.*" The Marine's tone of voice brooked no disagreement. "The admiral will recall that there are seven MiG-29s in the immediate vicinity. The Cubans are in targeting mode, so my fighters are having to cover the SAR assets and keep the MiGs off the slow-flyers. The seas aren't helping any, either."

"Just find him, Colonel," Batman said wearily. "We'll sort out what happened later. Right now, all that matters is we have a man in the water and we don't know where he is."

The admiral took a deep breath and turned to his chief of staff. "What's next on the agenda?"

The chief of staff pointed at Bird Dog. "Preliminary CONOPS—contact of operations—for integrating the Arsenal ship into battle group operations against Cuba under the current scenario. Arsenal is too new to be covered in the standard scenario. Until we have Major Hammersmith back on board and air superiority established, we need to consider a full range of options."

Batman nodded. As distasteful as it was, the tactical situation demanded that he and his staff put aside their worry over one pilot in the water to focus on the big picture. If the MiGs kept swarming, odds were that Washington would feel obliged to execute one of the contingency plans developed for this area. It was up to him to make sure the carrier battle group used every asset as effectively as possible, and that included the USS *Arsenal*. "Go ahead."

Bird Dog stood and moved to the podium, gesturing at the enlisted technician manning the computer at the back of the room as he did. His entire presentation was integrated with intricate graphs and charts, a briefing skill he'd been especially adept at at the War College. Not that anyone in this crowd would notice, not with their attention riveted on Thor's fate. Bird Dog felt a ripple of anger, then pushed it away, ashamed to be considering the impact of Thor's mishap on his staff work.

After the standard greeting to the admiral and senior officers, Bird Dog said, "All war, of course, is political in nature. All operations here are merely the extension of politics by other means." He paused, surveying the room, assessing the impact of quoting Clausewitz to officers so senior to him. "With that in mind, our targets against Cuba must be carefully chosen in order to maximize American national security objectives." He clicked the mouse in his hand, flashing a detailed topographical map of Cuba onto the screen. "Indeed, given the delicate issues at stake, I've taken the liberty of preparing a precise list of target locations and the estimated impact on Cuban national strategy for Joint Chiefs of Staff approval. I've also detailed areas that we must avoid, where the danger of collateral damage is too great. Here, for instance." He flashed his laser pointer up on the slide, privately pleased at the professional look it gave his presentation. "This is the central medical complex on the base. Three buildings to the west is the Cuban command post. We must insure that—"

"Didn't they teach you anything at War College?" Batman said coldly.

"Sir?" Bird Dog's confidence fled.

"We've had plenty of experience with detailed input on targeting objectives with political purposes in mind. In fact, as a War College graduate, you ought to know that. The individual targeteering and weaponeering management of that conflict significantly prolonged the entire war. Additionally, it led to tragic results." Batman's voice took on a somber note as he remembered how many classmates and friends he'd lost in bombing runs supposedly targeting truck farms. "Targeting must be a military function, first and foremost. Yes," he continued, waving aside Bird Dog's attempt to comment, "whether or not we enter into conflict is a political decision, I'll grant you that. But micromanagement of targets will lose this conflict faster than anything we can dream up on this ship."

"Admiral, if I could just—," Bird Dog began desperately, seeing his newfound career as a staff officer slip away.

"No, I don't think so." Batman shoved his chair away from the table and stood. "I understand what you're trying to do, but you have to take the War College with a grain of salt. Out here, mister, your job is to keep pilots from going into the water for no reason and to no military advantage. Try again—and make sure you understand the difference between using assets to achieve a desired result and muddling about in decisions way above your pay grade." Batman looked around the room slowly, catching each officer's eyes. "All of you keep that in mind. This briefing is over." Batman strode quickly to the door of his private cabin as the other officers scrambled to their feet in belated courtesy.

As the admiral's cabin door slammed shut, the chief of staff turned to Bird Dog and regarded him gravely. "In my office in five minutes."

1100 Local (+5 GMT)
Washington, D.C.

Senator Williams, the junior senator from Virginia, shook his head gravely. "Keith, you can't live in a vacuum. What happens down to the south has a big impact on operations." He glanced across the table to see if the admiral was paying attention, then he turned his attention to his meal. "People are starting to talk—the wrong people."

Admiral Keith Loggins, deputy AIRPAC, gazed down at his Cobb salad in disgust. "The hard-boiled eggs aren't done all the way through. I hate it when they do that."

"Pay attention, damn it, I'm trying to help you earn that next star." Senator Williams's voice was viciously sharp.

"I *am* paying attention. Can't I do two things at once? Besides, the idea of using an aviation mishap for political advantage turns my stomach."

Senator Williams sighed and pushed his plate away. "You didn't tell those pilots to get loaded on testosterone and do stupid stunts with those aircraft, did you?"

"Of course not. We didn't shoot down the civilian bird, and they're not playing *Romper Room* out there." Admiral Loggins pointed his fork at the senator. "That's one thing you people have never understood. We're in a dangerous business out there, and there's bound to be mishaps. There's no way to prevent them."

"Reality makes damned poor politics. Listen, Keith, you ought to know that by now. Everything has a slant to it, a twist, an angle. These F-14s of yours and Hornets that keep falling out of the air—well, the taxpayers start wondering what their tax dollars are going for. The average Joe, the one who gets out and votes, starts asking me why he can't buy a new car and we can afford to replace your toys. It's a problem."

"But not mine."

"Not yet." Senator Williams motioned to the steward. "You got any of that pecan pie from yesterday left?"

"What do you mean, not yet?" Admiral Loggins said uneasily. With the selection board for vice admiral meeting in only two months, this just might make a difference. "I wasn't at sea on that carrier; I wasn't commanding that squadron. I took my turn in the basket, and I survived that tour. They can't hold me responsible for those mishaps."

"We most certainly can," the senator replied as he watched the steward walk away.

Admiral Loggins noted the shift in pronouns with growing apprehension. "Hey, wait a minute. . . ."

Senator Williams returned the gaze of the senior officer. "I work for the people, Keith. And the sooner you learn that, the better."

Damn it, I wish he would stop calling me Keith. Nobody in this building gets away with that. "Just what do you mean?"

"Just what I said. You're deputy AIRPAC—people are starting to wonder why you're not doing something about this."

"Like what? Fly every flight myself? I spent twenty years in the cockpit and I never had a mishap."

"Like do *something*—for God's sake, Keith, exert a little leadership." The senator quit talking as the steward approached bearing his pie. He waited until the white-jacketed mess man had set the plate down and carefully repositioned the fork nearby. As the steward left, Senator Williams continued. "The Navy's gone through this spate of accidents before. You usually shut down operations for a while and try to figure out why, right? A safety stand-down?"

"When we can. But *Jefferson*'s in the middle of operations down off Cuba. I don't have to tell you what's going on there."

"And what else is near Cuba?" the senator pressed. "Damn it, don't you see what this means? It's a golden opportunity—you piss this one away and you'll not get another one like it anytime soon."

"The Arsenal ship?"

"Oh, the light finally goes on," the senator said sarcastically. "The one project you and I have been working on for a year and a half now, and you finally think of it. Nice. I like a team player, Keith."

"Quit calling me Keith," the admiral said, his temper flaring suddenly.

A cold, still silence settled on the table. The senator carefully and meticulously placed his fork down on the tablecloth. "Fine. *Admiral,* then." The venom in his gaze left no doubt about his opinion of the formality. "Well, Admiral, let me just recap the situation for you, if I may, sir. In case you don't realize it, a large part of your future is riding on the successful performance of that Arsenal ship."

"I'm an aviator." The statement was almost an anguished cry. "Besides, you're the one who—"

"I'm the one who what?" the senator snapped. "Helped you get that second star? Shoved your nomination and promotion through committee? Made sure nobody asked any nasty little Tailhook questions? That guy?"

Admiral Loggins suddenly realized how far he'd gone over the line. Everything Senator Williams had said was true—the politician had been a major influence on the admiral's career. "Look, I didn't mean anything by that. And come on, we've known each other too long—I was out of line. Call me Keith."

The senator leaned back in his chair and assessed the man opposite him with a cold stare. "Make up your mind. Which side of the fence are you on?"

"I want what's best for the Navy. I've always said that."

The senator sighed. "And we agreed when we started this that the Arsenal was what was best for the Navy. A lightweight, easily built ship packed to the gills with every kind of advanced weaponry and with a skeleton crew on board. Hook up the electronics that allow for remote control of the firing, and you've got a perfect political platform." The senator's voice was low and urgent. "At least that's what you told my committee when you were testifying as a member of the research and development team. You remember? It was your first political move, your maiden appearance in front of the Senate."

"I remember," the admiral said gruffly. And a pleasant experience it definitely had not been. Yet, despite an extensive grilling by the senators, who understood so little about the military, the project had gotten their blessing. Ten Arsenal ships were to be built in the next three years, and Admiral Loggins's name and reputation were firmly riding on each one.

"This is what you do," the senator said, speaking quickly and quietly. "Things are going to get worse in Cuba real soon—no, don't ask me how I know. I just do." He grinned. "As you would, if you paid any attention to your fiancée."

"Pamela?" the admiral said, confused by the sudden change of subject. "What's she got to do with this?"

"Everything—and nothing."

Admiral Loggins frowned. Eight months ago, he'd finally screwed up his nerve and asked the luscious Pamela Drake for a date. They had quickly established that they had more in common than either had thought. Loggins found her sharp, analytical mind refreshing, and Pamela had never been shy about sharing her political acumen with him. It had been through her connections that he'd met Senator Williams, as well as a host of other powerful men and women in both the House and the Senate. Suddenly, another star on his collar was looking a whole lot more probable.

For her part, Pamela seemed to appreciate the insights he sometimes gave her into military affairs. She'd told him more than once that he helped her convey a more balanced picture of the military to her viewers.

On a more personal level, they were equally compatible. Last month, he'd finally asked her to marry him, and she'd accepted. Now if she would only stay in the country long enough for them to finalize the plans.

"What do you suggest I do?" the admiral asked, pushing aside the thoughts of his fiancée to concentrate on the senator. Pamela had warned him several times that Williams had the power to make him—or to break him.

The senator sighed. "Let me spell it out for you. As deputy AIRPAC, you're concerned about pilot safety. And about the F-14 Tomcats—some of those airframes are getting old. You decide to call a safety stand-down and major responsibility for any strike prosecution shifts to the USS *Arsenal*. Hell, you can even tell that admiral of yours to shift his flag to her. That would be even better."

"And the USS *Arsenal* gets to be the hero of the Cuban confrontation," the admiral said. "I don't know. You're talking about a major shift in policy, pulling our carrier off the front lines."

The senator's voice was suddenly harsh and vicious. "You won't think so when I get that pilot's grieving widow plastered across every major network, complaining about how the Navy's not taking care of its people. How will that look?"

"You wouldn't."

"I would." The senator began attacking his pie, glancing up only once to assess the impact of his statement on the admiral. "Do it, Keith."

"What's in it for you?" the admiral asked suspiciously.

"Subcontracts," the senator said promptly. "Every small business in my state is going to have a piece of this. Building them at Newport News was a masterstroke."

I don't like this man, Admiral Loggins thought suddenly. Don't like him, don't trust him. Even if what he's saying makes sense. But a safety stand-down isn't that off an idea. It's what we might do anyway.

"I'll think about it," the admiral said finally. "No promises."

"Think fast, Keith," the senator said, his voice almost a whisper. "There are plenty of admirals where you came from."

0600 Local (+5 GMT)
Admiral's Briefing Room, USS Jefferson

Batman's face was colder than Bird Dog had ever seen it before. Something savage lurked just under the surface of the admiral's dark brown eyes, the harsh, demanding look. "Any idea why he called the meeting?" Bird Dog whispered to Lab Rat. The intelligence officer shook his head and motioned for the pilot to keep quiet.

"The chief of staff is passing around a message I want each one of you to see. You'll notice it's marked P4—a 'personal for' message for me from AIRPAC. I think once you read the message, you'll get the gist of it." Batman paused, watching twenty sets of eyes glance quickly at the text of the message. "This is bullshit."

"A safety stand-down?" Bird Dog blurted out. "Sure, we've had some mishaps, but—" An angry glare from the ACOS Ops—assistant chief of staff for operations—made him break off in mid-sentence. Batman's eyes pinned him to his chair.

"That's exactly what it is—an order to stand down. Evidently, AIRPAC is concerned about the way I'm leading this battle group and decided to give me rudder orders. It doesn't set too damned well with me, I can tell you that." The admiral sighed. "But, of course, we'll comply. There's no choice in the matter."

Lab Rat cleared his throat pointedly. The admiral glanced across the table at him. "You have something to say, Commander?" the admiral asked.

"Yes, Admiral. I understand the need for safety first, but things in Cuba are going to get a lot worse before they get better." The intelligence officer shook his head. "I don't understand why Washington would stand down an entire battle group for at least one day of training in the middle of this. Too many desk drivers, if you ask me." Lab Rat flushed as he belatedly remembered how many Washington assignments the admiral had under his belt.

"He *suggests* I shift my flag to the Arsenal ship. Out of the question, of course," Batman continued as if the intelligence officer hadn't spoken. "No space, and not enough communications-band width." An odd smile crossed his face momentarily, replaced immediately by the anger churning under the surface. "Sometimes I think a battle group runs more on antennas than it does on aviation fuel. Nevertheless, effective immediately, every aircraft in this squadron is grounded. No logistics flights, no mail runs, nothing. And tomorrow we start bright and fresh with a safety stand-down. I want to see those NATOPS manuals in every aviator's hand for at least eight hours tomorrow. If Admiral Loggins thinks this will keep people from getting killed, then I'll go along with it."

The admiral surveyed the room. Apparently satisfied with the response he saw in every officer's face, he turned a cold glare on Bird Dog. "We've also been directed to develop a targeting list for D.C. that will maximize the use of the USS *Arsenal*. There's some thought back there that the president may wish to exploit *Arsenal*'s remote control capabilities to allow more direct control over any potential conflict."

Bird Dog felt a surge of vindication. Maybe his own admiral didn't agree with him, but evidently somebody in D.C. saw the true potential of the Arsenal ships. Hell, with them in the battle group, a number of logistic and resupply problems were solved. An *Arsenal* ship carried more missiles—and of more different kinds—than any three surface ships combined. And if the admiral didn't see that, then thank God somebody in D.C. did.

"Admiral, I—" Bird Dog broke off suddenly, remembering the unpleasant session he'd had with the chief of staff earlier. COS had made it plain that what the admiral expected was results, not some esoteric bullshit theorizing from a junior officer with too much education and not enough experience to make use of it.

"You have something on your mind, Bird Dog?" Batman asked softly, warning in his voice. "More wisdom from Clausewitz to share with me?"

"No, Admiral, it's just that—sir, with the *Arsenal* ships," Bird Dog plunged on, trying to feel the raw confidence he always felt in the air, "maybe part of our problem is simplified. This conflict with Cuba—it's a *political* issue, not a military one. If JCS—hell, even the *president*—does the actual launch planning and weapons firing, doesn't that take us off the hook for some of this?"

Batman stood, his face livid. "Ask Major Hammersmith if this is a political problem." He strode out of the room and slammed the door behind him.

COS glared at Bird Dog again. "You just don't listen, do you?"

1620 Local (+5 GMT)
Wreckage of Hornet 301
50 Miles North of Cuba

Thor was riding low in the water, his body sprawled out across the barely inflated flight suit, his face just out of the water. After six hours of trying to catch the life raft, he'd given up. He was floating on his back, the hard summer sun beating down on it as it had earlier on his front. Saltwater licked at the cuts on his face and body, the sting now fading below the level of perception.

The sea was still boisterous, throwing him up and down in a sickening seesaw over broad, flat rollers—not the angry lashing of a storm at sea, but more like the exuberant playfulness of a child much larger than its peers.

He heard it before he saw it, a harsh, mechanical pounding at odds with the natural sounds of the wind and the waves. He tried to prop himself up, plunging his hands deep into the sinking flight suit, straining to see over the swells. A ship, it had to be. For a moment, he felt an irrational surge of hope that it was one of the American destroyers, detached from the battle group. It was possible, wasn't it? Surely they'd been looking for him for at least twenty-four hours.

Even as he thought it, he realized it couldn't be. A destroyer close enough to hear would have been easily visible, even for a man plunging from trough to crest over the waves.

A smaller boat, then—any boat, he didn't care. Anything to get out of the ocean. In the last four hours, he'd seen a dorsal fin pop up at irregular intervals in the surrounding water. Once, he'd thought he'd felt something brushing at his leg, and it was only by the most forceful act of will that he had not panicked.

One moment the sea was empty, the next he had company. The fishing boat was hardly impressive by any standards, but to Thor it was the most wonderful sight in the world. The hull had been white once, although it had faded to some colorless shade speckled by seagull droppings and scars. The superstructure looked rickety, as though it were shifting back and forth independently of the hull. Two large booms trailed out from behind, supports for the massive fishing nets the boat would be dragging behind it.

"Hey! Hey, over here!" Thor raised himself as far out of the water as he could and started waving his arms frantically, pumping his legs to lift his upper torso out of the water. Damn the sharks—if he didn't get this boat's attention, in another couple of days it wouldn't matter.

At first he thought they hadn't seen him. The boat continued on a steady course, the noise of its diesel engines growing louder. Thor sucked air into his lungs, took another deep breath, and then screamed with all of his might, "Over here!"

Some vagary of the wind picked up his words and wafted them over to the fishing boat. Just before he slid down into another trough, Thor saw one of the men look up sharply, then approach the rail to scan the ocean in his direction. The seconds before he slid up to the top of another wave were the longest ones of his life.

When the boat came into view again, he saw that it had changed course. Its silhouette had shortened and narrowed, indicating that it was now bow-on to him. Thor was too dehydrated to cry, but he'd never felt more like it in his life.

Five minutes later he was on the deck of the fishing boat staring into four brown, impassive faces and wishing he had taken Spanish in high school instead of Latin.

1900 Local (+5 GMT)
Fuentes Naval Base

"Muy interesante," Santana murmured. He tapped a message with his finger, then glanced across the room at his companion. Libyan Colonel Kaliff Mendiria showed no reaction. "It could be that this is the final element of our plan. God flies, does he not?" Santana said, intentionally goading the devout Muslim.

Tall, too tall for a Cuban, reaching almost six feet in height, Mendiria was a peculiar dusky color. Brown without looking Cuban, dark without looking black—Santana tried to place the coloration and drew a blank.

The Libyan's hair was short and dark, straight from the looks of it, and clipped close to his head. A few gray patches showed through in odd spots on his head. Not gray from aging, but the peculiar patterning of hair growing back in after a war injury. The Libyan's face was pockmarked, dominated by a massive nose slightly off center, and a too-full lower lip. The eyes were a startling yellow-green, almost luminescent under anything other than bright sunlight.

The skin around Mendiria's mouth whitened slightly as his muscles clenched. "As Allah wills," he said sharply. "It does not matter what happens with this pilot. Our plans are already in place."

"But don't you see?" Santana pressed. "The Americans have an obsessively sentimental attachment to their military personnel. Remember the forces that were downed during their Desert Storm fiasco? Their pictures were in every newspaper, on every television station for hours on end. They will be very interested in the fate of this one pilot."

Mendiria snorted. "If they find out you have him. If you had a proper security program in place, that would not be possible. Now, however, your headquarters leaks like a sieve."

Santana bolted to his feet. "A sieve that Libya has found more than useful in the past," he thundered. "Remember, my friend, it was your country who approached us."

"As though you could have survived without the Soviet money," Mendiria responded sharply. "Look around you. Every bit of this building—and most of your people—were bought and paid for. After centuries of sucking the Soviet's tit, you *needed* us. Needed *us* more than we needed you. Without us, you have two choices: anarchy under your good friend Leyta's leadership or lapdog of the Americans."

"Bah! Having Libyan troops on Cuba poses more risk to us than it does to you. And the stupid fools on that fishing boat—if he heard them talking, there's every chance that he knows they're not all Cubans."

Mendiria raised a lazy hand at the agitated Cuban. "It

matters not. Your next shipment of farm equipment is on schedule, just as we planned."

"And the only crops it will ever grow are graveyards," Santana said. He fingered the sling holstering his right arm, a reminder of the ejection that had saved his life. It was time America took Cuba just a bit more seriously. "By bringing those missiles to bear on the U.S. just eighty miles away, we can force the President to lift the trade embargoes that now cripple us. With a fair opportunity to sell our agricultural and crop products, Cuba will enter the next century as a great island nation." He saw the look of amusement on Mendiria's face. "Do not laugh," he said, pointing one finger at the Libyan. "England ruled almost half of the known world at one time. A nation not so much larger than Cuba ruled your own people, as a matter of fact. Have you forgotten so soon how powerful an island nation can be, protected from enemies by the sea?"

"My people will not be the problem," the Libyan said softly, cold rage growing in his eyes. "But you—you little fool. At least next time consult me before you do something rash. Like shooting down any American planes."

"That was not rash. That was merely payback." Santana smiled. "And more will follow before I'm satisfied."

FIVE
Tuesday, 25 June

"You're holding our pilot." Ambassador Wexler's voice was calm and level, deadly. She held the Cuban ambassador's gaze, forcing him to meet her eyes.

The man spread his hands apart, palm up, and shrugged lightly. "So you say, Madame Ambassador. You have become uncharacteristically boring on this point. Yet you have no evidence. Do you? Just your bald assertion that Cuba is somehow responsible for this pilot." He half turned away from her and gestured to the stack of messages on his desk. "I would know, would I not?"

"We have sources, too," she replied levelly. "I know you have him." The satellite imagery she'd seen earlier that morning was conclusive. "And you do, too. Let's quit playing games with each other." Without waiting for him to offer, she took a seat on the large leather couch dominating one end of the Cuban ambassador's office. "Tell me why you're doing this."

He hesitated for a moment, then followed her to the small seating area. He chose an armchair at right angles to the couch and lowered himself into it slowly. "I will play your game. For the sake of argument, just why would we want to keep your downed pilot from you? I assume you do have a theory, one no doubt involving a massive conspiracy by my small nation." He eyed her sardonically.

Ambassador Wexler leaned forward. "This is your third strike. First, downing the civilian aircraft. Second, holding our downed pilot. And third—" She paused and gazed at him steadily, looking for any reaction. "I think you know what number three is."

He shrugged. "We are in disagreement as to one and two as well. How can I read your mind and know what fantasy you have contrived as reason number three?"

"I think you know all too well," she answered softly, steel underlying the smooth words. "And it costs nothing for me to confirm what you already know. In a word—no, make that two words. Libya. And weapons." She leaned back, a grimly satisfied expression on her face.

The Cuban ambassador held the pleasant, charming expression on his face at some cost to him. He could feel the muscles quiver, the mouth threaten to twitch into a scowl. It was just the confirmation she was looking for, he was certain. If, in fact, she needed it at all.

"What would you like me to say?"

"Nothing. At least then you won't lie to me." She eyed him sternly. "What Cuba does as a sovereign nation is her own business. But you know better than to push us too far. And you have this time. That pilot had better be back in American hands by the end of the day or you'll suffer the consequences."

"A threat?" he snapped.

She paced slowly across to the door, paused with her hand on the knob, and turned back to him. "Consider it a promise."

"Release me now." Thor kicked at the man holding his arms behind him. "Damn it, you have got no grounds to—"

"We can do anything we feel necessary." The guard easily evaded Thor's foot and jabbed him sharply in the kidneys with the muzzle of his pistol. "You are no longer in the United States, my friend, but on our soil."

"We're not at war!" Thor wheeled around to face Santana. Thirty-six hours of kick-floating in the warm ocean, no food, no sleep—the movement made him dizzy. But he held on to consciousness, straining to look solid and steady on his feet.

Santana regarded him blandly. "Oh, indeed we are. You're to be tried for war crimes, sir—on behalf of the nation that downed an innocent aircraft in our airspace and then violated our no-fly zone."

"*You* shot those aircraft down, not us. And you damned well know it. And as for this supposed no-fly zone, what makes you think your nation has the right to cordon off international airspace unilaterally?"

Santana shrugged. "The rest of the world believes otherwise. As for the exclusion zone, you should understand that well enough—America is the first to declare one in any part of the world. Iraq and Bosnia are just the most recent examples. I suggest you cooperate fully with my friends when they ask you questions—it may help to mitigate your sentence after your trial."

Two of the men standing against the wall stepped forward. The first one slammed his fist into Thor's gut, then brought his knee up to smash the pilot's face as he doubled over. Thor hit the deck, bleeding.

The second stranger muttered a questioning comment to the first. Even through the pain, Thor heard enough to cause his balls to contract.

He may not have taken Spanish in school, but Latin had at least given him a familiarity with some of the root words, and what they were speaking was certainly not Spanish or any other Romance language. He stared up at the two men, now more afraid than he'd been when the first shark had brushed up against him in the warm ocean.

1130 Local (+5 GMT)
VF-95 Ready Room, USS Jefferson

"And that concludes this discussion of rough sea ditching procedures. Are there any questions?" The VF-95 safety officer looked around the room inquiringly. Not an aviator twitched.

The safety officer sighed and shook his head. Not that he'd expected any. Still, it would have been nice to be certain they'd been paying attention. Deep in his heart, he knew exactly what they were thinking—the same thing he thought at that age. Invincible, invulnerable—no way they'd ever need to review rough weather ditching procedures, not a chance. Maybe the guy in the next seat. But not me. He supposed it took turning thirty and putting that first oak leaf on the collar to convince a pilot that the unthinkable could happen to him.

"Okay, let's break for chow. We'll reconvene in the Ready Room at thirteen hundred. At that time, I'll give the quarterly NATOPS quiz. Those of you who are current have to take it, too," he added quickly as the surly muttering arose from the back row. "That's part of safety stand-down."

He watched from the podium as the aviators filed out, some in shipboard washed cotton khakis, others in faded flight suits. He heard the comments drift toward the front of the room.

"Goddamn Marines. If they could just . . ."

"I don't know why we need to . . ."

"And then she wrapped her legs around . . ."

He placed the pointer carefully on the narrow lip at the edge of the podium. Well, there was nothing that said they had to be enthusiastic about the safety stand-down.

If truth be told, he wasn't so wild about the idea himself. Parking the world's finest naval aviators in a classroom—all right, a Ready Room, but a classroom for this day—while a pilot was missing at sea and tensions boiled to the south rankled all of them. Still, AIRPAC supposedly knew best. With the spate of recent mishaps and incidents, he could understand a renewed emphasis on safety. But a stand-down? Now, with so much unexplained in the area? He shook his head again, and scowled. The only aircraft airborne right now were the SAR helos still searching for the downed Marine pilot.

Like his fellow aviators, there was no requirement he like the safety stand-down—just that he do it. He followed the last aviator out of the Ready Room and headed for chow.

1200 Local (+5 GMT)
Admiral's Conference Room

"All right, what have we got?" Batman said as he strode into the conference room. "I want some answers, people."

The admiral sat down in his usual spot halfway down the table and glared at Commander Busby, who was standing in front of the room. Lab Rat met his gaze steadily. It was always like this, admirals demanding immediate answers and definitive explanations for every scenario. In an ideal world, Intelligence would be perfect and there would be no surprises.

But this world was far from ideal. Lab Rat clicked the mouse in his hand, flashing the first slide up on the screen. He saw the admiral shift impatiently in his seat as a topographical map of Cuba lit the front of the room. Lab Rat hastily punched the button again, cycling on to the next slide.

"Let me cut to the chase, Admiral." Lab Rat flicked the laser pointer on and centered the small red dot over the western tip of Cuba. "We have indications that Major Hammersmith is being held here. Additionally, I have satellite imagery that indicates the Cubans are standing up a new weapons system, probably long-range offensive land attack missiles." Lab Rat paused, guiltily enjoying the sudden sharp intakes of breath he heard around the room.

The admiral shook his head from side to side. "You don't fuck around when you say cut to the chase, do you?" he said, surprisingly mildly. "Okay, Lab Rat, go ahead and start the backing and filling I know is going to come. You intelligence types never make absolute pronouncements, do you?"

Lab Rat resisted the impulse to gloat. "We do when we can, Admiral. As of thirty minutes ago, this was the situation." He punched the clicker again, flashing the next slide up on the screen.

It was overhead imagery, a highly detailed and accurate photograph of the area produced by one of the U.S. national assets—a satellite. Everyone in the room, even those who had seen such imagery before, leaned forward almost involuntarily. The clarity, the detail—exceptional.

The photograph was in black and white. Centered in the rectangle was a man in an American flight suit surrounded by a squad of six armed Cuban army guards. They were walking toward a small cinder-block building. The American had his face turned up toward the sky, and was being jabbed in the kidneys by the rearmost guard.

"Thor appears to have remembered his SERE lessons well," Lab Rat said neutrally. Every pilot attended the Survival, Evasion, Rescue, and Escape course before being assigned to a carrier. "He was looking up at the sky at every opportunity. The Cubans seemed to know what he was doing, too—they nailed him every time. We've got six good photos of his upturned cherubic little face, this one being the best of the lot. It's him, no doubt."

Batman studied the photo for a moment before nodding sharply. "Concur. So we know he's alive and we know they've got him. Now tell me about these weapons."

"Here." The next slide was just as detailed, but not as immediately self-evident. Lab Rat traced around three rectangular structures on the screen. "For those of you who are familiar with the short-range Soviet land attack missile systems, you'll recognize this launcher. It's designed to handle either conventional or nuclear weapons. The satellite pictures picked it up first, and the existence of such weapons has been confirmed by HUMINT—human intelligence. Spies and informers, to give them their common name." Lab Rat paused to let them absorb the implications. "Let me remind you that all of this information is classified 'top secret.' Given the political instability in Cuba, with the fighting between factions over control and the presence of military advisors from Libya, we have warnings and indications that Cuba may be advocating the nuclear option."

"Nuclear?" Batman's tone of voice left no doubt as to the depth of his concern. "Is that a probability, or just a possibility based on capabilities?"

"A strong probability, unfortunately. While I can't confirm that there are nuclear weapons inside Cuba, examination of two freighters making port in the United States immediately after Cuba indicates small traces of radioactivity. The Coast Guard picked them up after they became suspicious during a routine drug search. Evidently they saw something they didn't like and ordered a full detention and search. After the first click on their Geiger counter, they called in NEST—the Nuclear Emergency Services Team. They confirmed that something radioactive has been in that container within the last thirty days. Unfortunately, they can't tell us exactly what. But the levels indicate"—Lab Rat spread his hands open before him—"that there's a strong possibility it was weapons-grade material."

Batman turned pale. "And I thought we'd solved this forever with the Cuban Missile Crisis," he said wonderingly. He shook his head as though to clear his thoughts. "So we can't be certain, but that evidence combined with the missile launchers gives me a really rotten feeling in the gut."

The room was deadly silent. Not an officer moved, and some barely seemed to breathe. Lab Rat glanced around the room, noting the pale, shaken faces. He understood completely—he'd felt that way himself not an hour before when the first satellite imagery had been faxed into the highly classified CVIC. He felt an odd, incongruous sense of relief. It was nice not to be the only one who knew.

"I think I'd better talk to SOUTHCOM right away," Batman said slowly. He stood up, dismissing the rest of the staff with a gesture. "Pull up the contingency plans. All of them, even Bird Dog's. Be ready. This is a surprise, but it's not one we can't handle. I want full reports from all

departments in thirty minutes." He turned and walked
rapidly toward the door leading to his cabin.

"A rotten feeling in my gut," Lab Rat echoed slowly. He
walked to the back of the room and took the floppy disk
from the technician who'd been operating the computer.

"Sir?" The young enlisted man's voice shook slightly.
"What does it mean? Do they really have nukes?"

Lab Rat clapped the man on the shoulder and forced a
smile onto his face. "I don't know, Benson. But whatever
they've got, we've got a cure for it. There's not a damned
thing they could possibly have that could get through the
Jefferson battle group—not a damned thing. Remember, if
they start pulling any shit on us, we can turn the whole
island into glass."

The man looked slightly less worried. "That's right, they
can't get past *Jefferson*." He paused for a moment, then said,
"But what about that major there? The Marine?"

And that, Lab Rat thought, *was the two million dollar
question. What about Thor?*

1210 Local (+5 GMT)
Flight Deck

The angry chatter of gunfire cut through the dull roar of
wind across the flight deck. Lieutenant Commander Bran-
don Sikes, officer in charge of the USS *Jefferson* SEAL
detachment, paused at the hatch leading out onto the hot
tarmac and surveyed the scene. The forward portion of the
deck was crowded with aircraft, wings-folded Tomcats nose-
to-nose with similarly configured Hornets, the bulkier E2C
Hawkeyes taking up the space just aft of the island.
Helicopters with their rotors folded like broken mimosa

leaves edged the deck, with the exception of two ready helos positioned slightly behind the rest of the pack.

Even with the hangar bay below crowded with aircraft, it was an impressive display of weaponry and force. Almost a football field away, a small group of men clad in tattered khaki shorts and faded brown T-shirts stood in a line facing aft. Even from here, he could make out the outlines of the different types of weapons they carried—45s, M16s, and AK-47s. Had they not been U.S. SEALs—his men—he would have been worried.

Sikes trotted down the tarmac. The safety observer spotted him immediately, and with a sharp motion terminated the exercise. He could hear the men grumbling good-naturedly, a sound that faded away immediately as they saw his face.

"What's up, Skipper?" Senior Chief Petty Officer Manuel Huerta asked. He motioned toward the broad wake behind the ship with his free hand, carefully keeping the AK-47 in his other hand pointed aft. "A no-fly day—figured we'd get in some weapons practice. Never can have too much."

Sikes drew to a halt. "You may have a chance sooner than you think. Quick, huddle time. I need some fast thoughts." He motioned for the men to close around him.

Within the elite SEAL community, rank made little difference when it came to planning an operation. Even the most junior man might have some valuable insight to contribute. He looked around the circle of faces like a quarterback, noting the keen interest on each one of them. A good team—hell, maybe the best team. His team.

"Here's what's going down." He briefly outlined the strategic scenario, then settled into the business of discussing tactics. "As I see it, there are two main objectives. First, we find our man. Get him out if we can. Second, we disable the weapons systems." He saw a few frowns across faces. "I know it may not be reasonable, particularly if they've got nuclear weapons on there. Still, I want to plan for it. Failing that, we can at least bring back the admiral some hard info on them. We've got the gear?"

"Sure, we've got everything we need. Radiac equipment, the new version—fits in the palm of your hand, it does." The man who'd spoken smiled. "I've been wanting an opportunity to field-test them."

"You've got it. Any thoughts on how to get the pilot back?"

"It will depend on where he's being held," said Felipe Garcia, a petty officer second class and SEAL for three years.

"Garcia, you may be the whole key to this." Sikes studied the man carefully. He was shorter than most, a fact Sikes noted simply for its reference value. In the SEALs, size made no difference. He'd had his own ass kicked by men far smaller than Garcia. "You grew up in Havana, didn't you?"

Garcia nodded. "And I've been back there since then. Five times in the last two years. To different parts of the island."

Sikes nodded sharply. Given the diverse and dangerous nature of the SEALs' normal missions, he had a good idea of what Garcia might have been doing in Cuba. Not that he'd ask—he wouldn't have to. Only Garcia knew how highly classified his mission had been, and what details he could release to his fellow SEALs. Even if Garcia couldn't give them a blow-by-blow account of his mission, he'd factor every available detail into the planning of this one.

"Good. I expect you to vet every step of this." Sikes looked around the circle again. "How do we get in? Helicopter and HALO would be my preference," he said, referring to a high-altitude low-opening parachute drop.

"But that's not going to be practical, not with those radars ringing the island."

"Small boats might be better, but still not entirely safe," Garcia said thoughtfully. "The whole littoral area is patrolled regularly by Cuban gunboats. We might be able to outrun them, but there's a good chance we would be detected."

"How much of a chance?" Sikes pressed.

"Maybe fifty-fifty." Garcia shrugged. "I've had worse odds." He looked up and met his skipper's eyes. "A submarine and lockout in an SDV—a swimmer delivery vehicle—is better."

Without asking, Sikes knew that was exactly how Garcia had gotten in last time. It made sense, too. The few remaining U.S. diesel submarines would be particularly valuable for this mission. Quiet and undetectable while operating under battery, it carried a docking station bolted down onto the conning tower that contained the small swimmer delivery vehicles favored for team insertion in an operation such as this. "That would be my preference, but I don't know if we have time to get one down here. Any other thoughts?"

"We could swim." The SEAL who suggested it looked displeased. "I don't favor it, though."

Sikes shook his head. "Me neither. Sure, we could do it, but we'd be dragging ass when we got ashore." He looked at the men's faces and saw them harden. "Not that we couldn't do it," he added hastily. "It's an option. But not the best one."

"Helicopter or a boat, then," Garcia mused. He shrugged again, a peculiarly Latino gesture of resignation. Then his face brightened. "Our odds go way up if we use the Army's Stealth helos. Think we could get the carrier to send us back to Miami and deploy from there?"

"No doubt. Even on a no-fly day, we ought to be able to arrange that sort of transportation." Sikes grinned, a wolfish expression crossing his face. "I surely do love those Special Forces helicopters." The other men nodded.

"I don't think so," Huerta said, speaking for the first time. "Too much radar, even with Stealth technology." He shook his head. "We go in with what we're best at—small boats, then swimming. Less chance of a casual observer seeing us that way, too. Go with our strengths."

A grizzled veteran, ancient at the age of thirty-five, Huerta was still in superb physical condition. Sikes had watched him outrun, outswim, and outshoot almost every man in the team. He might be beat occasionally at one of those particular skills, but never in all three categories by the same man. Overall, he was the strongest, most indestructible-looking man Sikes had ever met.

As he looked at Huerta, a familiar feeling of pride flooded him. *Don't ever think about being a SEAL*, he told himself. Not unless you are worthy of commanding men like this.

A quick shorthand discussion of equipment and timing followed, the men thinking as one team and each contributing his own comments on particular capabilities and assets they would need. Less than ten minutes after he'd first walked out on the flight deck, Sikes had his answers. And a plan.

He motioned back toward the ocean. "You kill a whale, you file the environmental impact report. Other than that, shoot the hell out of it." He made a brief gesture, then turned and trotted back toward the island.

1015 Local (+5 GMT)
Admiral's Cabin

Batman stared at the overhead speaker as he spoke into the handset. The COSMIC circuit was the most secure form of radio communication available on the carrier, and this call from Tombstone was hardly unexpected.

"So you think we'll be ordered to conduct the strike?" Batman asked. He ran a hand across his forehead, feeling the deep grooves that the pressures of daily living were cutting into his forehead. Even after commanding a squadron and two tours in D.C., nothing had prepared him for the awesome weight that fell on the shoulders of a carrier battle group commander. "Come on, Tombstone, I need some answers."

Admiral Magruder's voice sounded tired. "I've seen the same pictures you have. If it were my call, you know what my answer would be. Damn the political consequences—just get the mission done."

"But it's not. It's not mine, either." Batman felt the beginnings of a headache start at the base of his neck. "Jesus, Tombstone, how much of this would we have believed when we were still flying? Back then, we thought the admirals had the easy jobs."

Tombstone chuckled, his voice thin and reedy over the secured circuit. "Not laughing at you, my friend, laughing with you. At least you're at sea—you could be stuck flying a desk, like I am."

"Yeah, yeah, yeah. I know that. So, how long will it take to get an answer?"

"Your guess is as good as mine."

Batman could hear the resignation in his friend's voice. "Hell of an answer, Tombstone."

"Sometimes it's like that, Batman. As soon as I hear from the eight-hundred-pound gorillas, I'll let you know."

Batman knew Tombstone was referring to the Joint Chiefs of Staff. "But when? I've got preparations I need to make out here, you know."

"Of course I know that," Tombstone said sharply. "Look, as soon as I hear anything, I'll let you know. It shouldn't be long, though. I understand the President's in conference on the matter right now."

Batman sighed as he hung up the telephone. The President might be consulting his top political and military experts, but it didn't take a rocket scientist to figure this one out. Weapons poised on Cuba could have only one target— the continental United States. And, when a decision was finally made, it would be up to Batman to walk that thin line between defense and aggression, between preserving the integrity of the United States and provoking war.

1220 Local (+5 GMT)
The White House

The President stared down at the photos strewn around his desk. In his past twenty-five years as a political animal, he'd seen satellite imagery often enough—never before, however, in such telling detail.

He leaned back in the custom-built chair, feeling the sinking sensation of resignation. Around him, his staffers and aides fell silent. The President steepled his hands under his chin and thought. Finally, he glanced back at the man standing in front of him. "So it comes down to this? Again?"

The chairman of the Joint Chiefs of Staff nodded. "Yes, I'm afraid so, Mr. President."

The President sighed. "Kennedy thought he had the problem licked forever," he said reflectively. He gestured at the photographs. "We should've known better. They won't stop—not really. Even with the fall of the Soviet Union, there will always be power-mongers and terrorists in the world. Whole nations, even."

The chairman shifted uneasily. "We have some options."

The President spun his chair around to stare out at the Rose Garden. "Oh, I'm certain we do. We always do. There's not a spot on the world that we haven't projected out as a terrorist or rogue state and tried to figure out what we should do about it. But in the end, what it comes down to is American men and women setting foot on foreign soil, doesn't it?"

The roses were in full bloom, each bush carefully and lovingly tended by the White House gardener. Some of the plants were decades old, he guessed. There was no garden on earth that got finer care than this collection of roses. "We should take care of other things just as well," he said out loud. He heard the uneasy scuffle of feet behind him. *And now the President is talking to himself. Wonder if that makes them feel any worse—as if it could.* He spun his chair back around to face the group.

"One of the reasons I was elected," he said slowly, organizing his thoughts as he went, "was my commitment to a strong defense policy." He grimaced, shrugged slightly. "You all know I've seen all ends of this, from the ground up as a young Army officer in Vietnam to the crises I saw as vice president. I know what I'm about to do, more than any President since maybe Eisenhower. The other military men that have held this post came from some of the more refined fields of warfare—submariner, fighter pilot, that sort of thing." He gestured dismissively. "But it takes an old Army dogface to understand what fighting's really about. It takes men—hell, and women, too, now—on the ground, face-to-face." He finally came to a decision and looked up at the assembled group. "Cuba is a sovereign nation, but this is our part of the world. I won't have a land strike capability in Cuba—I won't. And I'm not going to sit in this office and watch the spectacle of an American fighting pilot being dragged through the streets of Cuba and tried for war crimes." His voice got louder and stronger. "It will not happen on my watch—am I absolutely clear about that?"

The chairman seemed to stiffen. New conviction and pride filled his voice. "As you say, Mr. President—not on my watch. On our watch, sir."

The President nodded sharply. "We understand one another. Thank you for coming, General. I'd like to see you again later this afternoon—with answers, this time."

"I'll have them for you, Mr. President. You can count on that." The general saluted, executed a smart about-face, and left the room.

"The rest of you, start getting the other pieces of the packages together. I want everything—public affairs coordination, a conference call with the governor of Florida . . . no, Louisiana and Texas, as well—and the rest of the staff immediately available for the next forty-eight hours."

And that's all it should take: forty-eight hours.

2200 Local (+8 GMT)
Caracas International Airport, Venezuela

Aguillar reached out and patted Pamela's leg lightly above the knee. He let his fingers linger a moment, feeling the smooth silk of the stockings rasp against his well-manicured palm. He trailed his fingers up ever so slightly, lifting them reluctantly away only when she glanced sharply at him. The more he saw of her, the more he thought that the possibilities might be . . . ah, well, perhaps another time. He sighed, thinking what a waste it was that the woman's mind could be so firmly fixed on her job. "You are not nervous, I hope?" he inquired politely.

"Of course not," Pamela said calmly, anger barely edging her tones. "I've been to Cuba before."

Aguillar chuckled and leaned back in his chair. The aircraft was already taxiing for departure. "Never this Cuba, Miss Drake. And never with a native guide." A nostalgic look crossed his face. "There's nothing like it, nothing in the world." A strong wave of homesickness shook him, still a surprise after so many years away.

He felt her eyes on his face, studying him, dissecting him in the coldly calculating way he'd seen her operate before. "Never this Cuba?" she inquired, letting the question trail off to invite response.

"Oh, no, I'm sure you haven't seen my Cuba. Not the one I grew up in."

"Under Castro?"

He nodded. "Castro was part of it, but hardly the thing I remember most." He fixed her with a stern look. "You must remember, Miss Drake, for us, this is normal."

"Assassinations? Purges? Genocide?"

"That's not what I remember—not what I miss," he said, surprising himself slightly. For all her brittle prickliness, there was something about Pamela Drake that made him want to talk, to explain to her the sheer luxuriant sensuality of his homeland. The rich, warm nights, the endless beaches, the pure, clean water around her, though the latter would change now, since the advent of heavy industry along the coastline. "It was . . ." He searched for exactly the right words to convey to her. "Paradise," he concluded finally.

He saw her doubting look. "Oh, I know what you've been told. There's disease, poverty, and oppressive political regimes—but really, remember, we grew up with all that. There was nothing unusual, nothing abnormal about it. Life went on. We had families, we had children, and we had . . ."

Again, words failed him. It seemed impossible to convey to her the simple rhythms of life in Cuba, the feeling of rightness and oneness with nature. And the women—ah, the women. He glanced over at her again, contrasting her with Cuban women he'd known. Too many angles, he decided, too many sharpened little edges poking out of her. A classical beauty, yes, yes, every inch of her refined and somehow pure. But there was none of the raw sensuality he remembered from his island days, none of the exuberant passion for life and making love that he missed perhaps most of all. The American women, so far removed from what was important in life that they were virtually sucked dry of all of the joy of life—now that, that joy, was what he missed. "I will show you some places," he decided suddenly. "Yes, the guerrillas, the freedom fighters—you know they're there and that's where your story is." A small trace of bitterness crept into his voice. "But there is so much more, so much more that Cuba has to offer to America. There must be cooperation, you see. Not only for our survival, but for America's as well."

"And that's why I decided to come with you," Pamela said decisively. "To show the American people both sides of the picture. You claim there's a difference between your objectives and Leyta's. Fine, well show it to me. Show me why America should be a friend to Cuba instead of a suspicious neighbor. Show me how much we have in common, where our true future lies. If you can show me, I can show the rest of the world." She leaned forward, stared past him out the window. "That's why I came."

"I know." He resisted the impulse to reach out and trace his fingers up her thigh, groaned inwardly as he imagined how it would feel to reach the top of the delicate hose. *But that's not why I have you with me.*

"From here we will go by seaplane, then by small boat," he continued, regretfully suppressing the ripple of lust she always caused. "And something else as well—despite our differences, Leyta and I cooperate on a number of issues. His people will be guiding your tour. I believe he may himself be in Cuba at this very moment."

"Leyta? But why?"

Aguillar shrugged. "You've seen most of what I do. I work through existing organizations and channels in Washington. Leyta has other connections." He frowned for a moment, remembering that his public adversary had even gambled his own brother's life on an overt mission— gambled and lost. "While I disapprove completely of his methods, unfortunately he is the better equipped to show you our homeland. He will be rendezvousing with us off the coast of Cuba. I think you will find his planned tour itinerary most enlightening."

More interesting than you planned on, my sweet American bitch. If you knew how we are using you, my chances would disappear entirely.

2200 Local (+5 GMT)
The White House

"So this is it?" the President asked. "He gestured at the battle plan drawn on the chalkboard. "Why the *Arsenal* ship?"

"It's time for an operational task, Mr. President," the chairman of the Joint Chiefs of Staff said calmly. "With the rash of accidents we've had on board *Jefferson*, I'm afraid . . ." He let his voice trail off delicately.

Vice Admiral Thomas Magruder snorted. "There's absolutely nothing wrong with *Jefferson* and her battle group," he snapped. "Mr. President, with all due respect to the chairman, that ship is as ready as she's ever been. She was ready when my nephew Tombstone commanded her, and she's ready now." He leaned forward and jabbed angrily in the air with a forefinger. "If you want a strike on Cuba, *Jefferson* is the best bet. Using anything else is a mistake."

"The question of assets has already been decided," the chairman said shortly. He turned to the President and added smoothly, "Subject to your approval, of course, sir."

The President leaned back in his chair and looked puzzled. "Aircraft carriers have always been the primary platform for force projection," he said slowly. "I'm not sure why we should deviate now."

"The *Arsenal* ship can do the same job at a fraction of the risk," the chairman pointed out. "Totally independent, capable of putting massive amounts of ordnance onshore— smart weapons, Mr. President, specifically tailored to reach each target we want, without any collateral damage. Without *any* collateral damage. More importantly, every step of the battle can be controlled personally by you. The ability to order the attack while you're still talking to the Cubans on the telephone gives you a superb bargaining position."

The President glanced up at him sharply. "You're going to guarantee that?" He shook his head. "Impossible. There's always collateral damage."

"And how much did you see during Desert Storm and Desert Shield?" the chairman asked politely. "There were stories, allegations—but you have to admit, the smart weapons performed superbly. The weapons on the *Arsenal* ship are a generation beyond that. We have a target impact area of no greater than one meter, Mr. President. Less than thirty-six inches, and from a range of over eighty miles away. There's not an aircraft on that carrier that can match that kind of targeting precision. And there's one other factor," he continued. "Something that will make it the ultimate political war weapon."

"The targeting?" The President frowned. "I don't know that it's such a good idea."

The chairman stepped forward until he was standing three feet away from the President. "The entire *Arsenal* ship is capable of being remotely targeted. Mr. President, based on your experiences on the land, you know how critical unity of command and avoiding blue-on-blue engagements is. One screwup between the aircraft and we take out a friendly land force. But with the Arsenal ship, all movements can be controlled directly from here, from this very room if you wish. You will truly be the first commander in chief able to act immediately in response to changing battlefield conditions, making sure the war is fought exactly as you wanted it. Even the most advanced communications suite in the world can't give you that." He pointed at Admiral Magruder, who now stared down at the floor in disgust. "The admiral can't promise you that, not with flights of

Tomcats and Hornets filling up the sky and getting in each other's way."

The President looked over at Admiral Magruder. "Well? What about it? My predecessor seemed to trust you. You and I don't know each other that well yet. Let me hear what you think."

"I think it's a big mistake, maybe the biggest one you'll make during this term," Vice Admiral Magruder said bluntly. He stood and walked briskly to the front of the room. "Targeting decisions belong in the military arena, Mr. President. No disrespect intended, but you simply do not have the time to develop the in-depth targeting and weaponeering capabilities here that that battle group commander already has. Has, and practices regularly." Vice Admiral Magruder shook his head. "You get into micromanagement from the White House—or even from the Joint Chiefs of Staff—and you put lives at risk. Conditions change too quickly, and the battlefront is too fluid to allow that. You must remember that." The admiral's voice took on an urgent quality.

"That's exactly the point that you always miss, Admiral," the chairman said angrily. "We *can* bring that technology to the President's office. He can make every decision, just as though he were on the scene. And, more importantly, he can make this conflict what it truly is—a political statement. An extension of his foreign policy, a demonstration of his individual will. How do you think that will affect the Cubans, knowing that the man on the other end of the hot line has his finger poised exactly over the fire control circuits?"

"They'll think he's a fool," Vice Admiral Magruder said quietly. "Because even the Cubans remember Vietnam." He turned back to the President. "As do you, sir. You were *there*. You know what happens when Washington makes individual targeting decisions on a daily basis. How could you forget?"

The President nodded slowly, then frowned. "We spent an awful lot of money on the Arsenal concept, though. And what the chairman says is true—war is an extension of political objectives. Although sometimes I think it's the other way around—politics is a continuation of war by other means." He looked back and forth between the two men. "Install the equipment, General." He raised one hand to forestall Magruder's protest. "I'm not saying we'll use it. For now, the battle group commander remains on-scene commander. However, I want detailed plans from him regarding his proposed use of the Arsenal ship. And make it clear to him that I view this as an excellent opportunity to use our advanced technology, and to demonstrate its usefulness in any battlefield scenario." His voice took on a firmer note. "This will work, Admiral—if your people give it half a chance."

The chairman nodded sharply. He turned to Admiral Magruder. "I'll expect to see the plans later this evening."

Twenty minutes later, Admiral Magruder was on the telephone to his nephew. Over a highly secure circuit, he outlined the gist of the President's request. "Make it work, Stoney," he concluded. "You don't have to like it, but make it work."

SIX
Thursday, 27 June

With the Washington-mandated safety stand-down over, *Jefferson* immediately returned to full flex-deck operations. The Cubans continued to clutter up the sky around the ship with sponges of Fulcrums, but popular opinion had it that Admiral Wayne was not likely to allow that state of affairs to continue. The admiral had made it clear that current operations had two main objectives: to locate and retrieve Major Hammersmith and to obtain up-to-date eyeball intelligence on Cuban air defense capabilities.

No one had to tell the VF-95 Viper squadron what the latter information was for. They were going in. It was just a question of how and when. The demands on the flight schedule allowed even the staff pilots to grab some stick time.

"You have any idea what we're doing up here?" Bird Dog asked. His index finger was beating out a staccato rhythm on the throttles.

"I know as much as you do." Resignation tinged the normally taciturn RIO's voice. "They say launch, I launch.

They say go north of Cuba and look tactical, I give you fly-to points. What else do we have to know?"

"What the hell we're doing here would help," Bird Dog snapped. He yanked the Tomcat into a sharp right-hand turn without warning, shoving Gator hard against the seat back.

"Hey! What the hell was that about?" Gator's words were slightly muffled as he forced them out between clenched teeth. "Give me some warning next time, asshole."

"Sorry, shipmate, just thought I saw something up ahead, that's all."

Bird Dog eased quickly out of the turn and turned gently to port, putting it back on its original heading. Why the hell had he done that? If he was honest with himself, he had to admit that Gator didn't deserve it. He'd known the unexpected turn would subject the RIO to massive G-forces, and might even have caused him to black out.

There was no reason to take it out on Gator. It wasn't his RIO's fault that he was being treated like a less than completely essential part of the battle group. Hell, he ought to be grateful that he was flying, although his orders to proceed from *Jefferson* to north of Cuba and to orbit on a CAP station with two other F-14s seemed a waste of gas and time. Time he could have better spent sleeping, dreaming about the beautiful Callie. He sighed as images of his fiancée—well, almost his fiancée—rose in his mind, as they were wont to do at the slightest provocation.

Who would've ever thought he'd be torn between dreaming about a woman and flying? A year ago, flying would have won hands down.

"We're a diversion," Gator said. "There are four Tomcats and four Hornets on Alert Five right now. Since when does the carrier roust that many aviators out of bed simply to support a grab-ass mission?"

"A diversion? Why? There's nothing going on around here."

Gator sighed. "Of course there's not. It's a diversion, stupid. A diversion happens somewhere besides the main action. Didn't they teach you that at the War College?"

"The War College was a bit more sophisticated than that," Bird Dog said stiffly.

The yearlong curriculum concentrated on operational art, with many theories contrasted to old-style campaign planning. Students at the Naval War College looked at the big picture: how best to use military force to achieve political objectives, what composition of large-scale forces were most appropriate to applying pressure to an opponent's center of gravity. They didn't get down into the grass, as the professors there were fond of saying. Individual platform capabilities, weapon ranges, and tactics were the province of more junior courses, such as Tactical Action Officer School or even Fighter Weapons Course—Top Gun—at Naval Station Miramar. The War College students were expected to be beyond that, to concentrate on the high-level planning they'd be expected to do as members of a deployed staff or ashore at the Pentagon. In Bird Dog's case, he'd had a chance to apply his new skills even before he graduated. He'd wangled his way out to *Jefferson* in the Med just in time to take part in the Black Sea conflict.

"Well, maybe they should have," Gator said. "If I had to guess, I'd say there's a reason the admiral wants Cuba's air assets worried about the north. We're already getting I and W—indications and warnings—that they're launching more of them and vectoring toward us."

"If I'd been planning it, I would have waited until the weather was better." Bird Dog glanced overhead, looking for any patches of clear sky. No luck. "Where are our

playmates, anyway? The ones we're supposed to be diver-
sioning. If we're gonna boogie, we might as well do it."

"I hold a MiG on two-seven-zero at fifty miles," Gator
answered. "About time you switched into targeting mode,
don't you think?"

"Too far away."

"The bad guys won't know that, will they? No, they
won't," Gator continued, answering his own question. "Get
it through your thick skull, Bird Dog—the point of being up
here is not to engage another aircraft, it's to make someone
on the ground think we're up to something interesting. That
spells targeting illumination, simulating every electronic
and radar signal we generate when we're actually attacking.
Get with the program."

Bird Dog sighed and switched the powerful AWG-9 radar
into illumination mode. The ESM sensors arrayed along the
coast of Cuba and perched on its highest peak would
undoubtedly detect it within seconds. "There. Are you
happy?"

"I am. The question is—are the Cubans?"

0310 Local (+5 GMT)
Fifty Miles Southwest of Fuentes Naval Base

The small RHIB—rigid-hull inflatable boat—slid smoothly
up the side of one swell, picking up speed as it descended
into the trough. The eight SEALs on board held grimly to
the ropes around its hard rubber sides. Their bodies had
gotten accustomed to the rhythmic movement thirty minutes
earlier, and even the greenest of them was well past
worrying about seasickness.

Not that SEALs got seasick. Or that they'd ever admit to
it if they did.

A cold front had moved into the area yesterday, increasing the difference between wet-bulb and dry-bulb temperatures to less than two degrees. Consequently, dense fog was forming on the surface of the ocean, wafting up and enveloping the Special Forces platoon in a cloaking mist. Overhead, low clouds were rolling in, spitting short bursts of rain that left their wet suits gleaming in the low ambient light diffused about them. Each man held his weapon with his free hand, close to the chest. Not that they'd need them—at least, they wouldn't if everything went well.

"Three miles," Huerta said softly. He stretched his legs, twisted his torso to loosen the muscles growing stiff from the cold and damp. "Be ready."

One by one, the team members flashed a silent hand signal in acknowledgment. As if it were needed. SEALs were always ready.

The brief mission was relatively simple in planning, with the potential for unexpected complications in execution. They were to go ashore and take a quick sneak and peek at the Cubans' facility on the southwest corner of the island. The overhead imagery revealed new construction on the base, as well as the possibility that the downed American pilot was being held hostage there. Their orders allowed them to take action, if they could do so without compromising the unit's safety, to free him. Every one of them had firmly resolved to do just that if at all possible.

In addition to the normal bag of tricks, Huerta carried a few extra goodies. A low-light camera, capable of concentrating the ambient light to take pictures even under the worst of conditions. Two small, portable motion detectors, each barely larger than a small tape recorder, for mounting at the entrances to their areas of surveillance. And finally, the piece of gear responsible for the particularly grim expression on their leader's face—a microcircuitized Geiger counter.

The muffled hammer of the specially silenced engine attached to the RHIB soaked into the fog around them. Barring exceptionally poor luck, the team was undetectable.

"Shore," Sikes said finally. He pointed forward in the fog. Barely discernible was the dark outline of land. The SEALs made their final preparations for disembarking, careful to keep metal from hammering against metal and alerting a randomly patrolling sentry.

The boat ground ashore with a harsh rasp, small pebbles and rocks digging into the thick rubber bottom. Minutes later, the boat was dragged out of the water and safely concealed under a clump of brush in a small grove of trees.

The eight SEALs broke into two teams of four, the first headed for what satellite imagery showed as the new construction area. The second group slanted away from them toward the highly fortified encampment that intelligence specialists suspected contained the captive pilot. They would meet back here in two hours, with or without the pilot—and with or without the information they were after.

0320 Local (+5 GMT)
Fifty Miles North of Cuba

The insistent beeping of the ALR-45 radar warning and control system shattered the silence of the cockpit. Gator moved quickly to silence the alarm, then called out the identification. "MiG—just watching."

Bird Dog swore quietly. At this range, the MiG could be on top of them in ten minutes. His orders were to avoid an actual confrontation with any Cuban aircraft. It ate at his gut to have to run, but if he allowed the Cuban to approach them, the other pilot would quickly see through their deception. Still, to let the Cubans think that the mere presence of this MiG could make the Americans turn and run was distinctly distasteful.

"Bird Dog, get us the hell out of here," Gator ordered.

"We could have some fun with him," Bird Dog suggested. He held the Tomcat steady and level.

"I mean it. You know what our orders are." The RIO's voice notched up two notes on the octave. "There's no point in being a diversion if we blow it the second they come out to take a look."

"But what would be a more realistic deception than to go toward the MiG? The rest of the flight can turn tail and run, but the presence of one aircraft lingering around here is bound to get 'em interested. Besides, there's only one launching, right?"

"As far as I can tell," the RIO admitted grudgingly. "This is one of your worst ideas ever."

Bird Dog reached forward and flipped off the radios. "*Jefferson* will see what we're doing," he continued blithely. "If they want us to RTB—return to base—they'll let us know."

"Not with the radios off."

"Who says the radios are off? Communications problems are not unknown in the Tomcat, you know." He could hear the RIO's disgusted sigh over the ICS—the interior communications system.

"You're going to do this no matter what I say, aren't you?" Gator said finally. "To hell with your career, my career—let's give it all up so you can play grab-ass with the Cubans. You've been missing that ever since we were on patrol in the Spratlys."

"Think of it as a diversion within a diversion," Bird Dog suggested. "The rest of the flight turns away, and I'm the diversion that lets them go. It makes sense—perfect sense."

"There's only one thing wrong with this plan. A really critical factor." The RIO's voice was harsh.

"What's that?"

"Somebody forgot to tell the Cubans it's just a diversion. What if they take it a little more seriously than that?"

0325 Local (+5 GMT)
Fuentes Naval Base

The SEALs slipped silently through the vegetation, invisible in their woodland-patterned cammies and face paint. They moved slowly, brushing vegetation aside carefully to prevent inadvertent rustling of leaves, watching where they placed their feet in order to avoid twigs and branches underfoot. Not that the woodland debris would have cracked under their feet—the entire area was as sodden, and as dark, as a rain forest.

Ahead of them, the wire-mesh perimeter fence barely reflected the ambient light in a regular pattern. The SEALs crept up to within six feet of it, still hidden by the underbrush.

The SEAL leader motioned to his second in command, using only hand signals to convey his intentions. The other SEAL nodded, reached into his belt, and withdrew a heavy-duty set of wire cutters. Intelligence had indicated that the fence was electrified, but not alarmed, and that the Cubans lacked even rudimentary pressure sensors and motion detectors along the perimeter.

The SEALs waited. Their luck held—within a couple of

minutes, a bulky Cuban patrolling sentry came into view, his presence announced five minutes earlier by his clumsy, stumbling progress along the perimeter.

The SEALs held their breath, watched him pass by them on the interior of the fence and then disappear in the dark. They waited a little bit longer, until they were certain he was out of earshot. Then Sikes motioned sharply—*Move out!*

Garcia scampered up to the fence, slipping on his heavily insulated gloves as he moved while holding the heavy wire cutters with their rubberized handles in one hand. He crouched low, blending in with the low vegetation already struggling to reassert its domination over the trimmed area.

He worked quickly but carefully, snipping away the heavy strands and finally tossing aside a semicircular portion of the fence. Grinning, he held it aloft for a moment for his compatriots to admire, then laid it carefully on the ground. He scuttled back to join his teammates and resumed his normal position in the formation.

Sikes led the way, moving quickly across the open area. Behind him, at two-minute intervals, the rest of the team followed.

They regrouped at the rear of a ramshackle wooden building. The short, hundred-meter dash had driven the last traces of stiffness and cold from their muscles. They paused for a minute, regrouping, then employed the same silent dart-and-wait maneuver to move steadily across the rest of the compound.

Their target was the open field to the north of the main cluster of buildings, the one the satellite imagery had shown as under construction.

0330 Local (+5 GMT)
Tomcat 201

"I need altitude," Bird Dog said as a warning. He slammed the throttles forward, kicking the massive jet into afterburners, and yanked back on the yoke. The Tomcat rotated in the air to stand almost on end, its nose pointed toward the one clear patch of sky Bird Dog had found. Rain still spattered the canopy, the drops driven quickly aft by the jet's wind speed to leave most of the forward part clear. Five hundred knots of airspeed was better than any windshield wiper ever designed.

"They'll think you're getting into firing position," Gator warned.

"That's what I want 'em to think. Let's see if we can get him to play our game." Bird Dog tightened his stomach and torso muscles, forcing blood up from his extremities into his brain to prevent graying out. "I'm staying in search-right radar mode, so he shouldn't have any reason to get excited."

"Cubans don't need a reason," Gator grunted.

0345 Local (+5 GMT)
Fuentes Naval Base

The construction churned up the vast field to their north, raw, black dirt furrowed and rent, bearing an odd resemblance to the sea they'd just crossed. Past the square of disturbed earth, the field resumed its green march to the hot horizon, low shrubbery and tall grass surrounding the construction.

Sikes nudged his partner and pointed. Black iron girders jutted out of the ground at improbable angles. To the right, a yellow crane sat silently waiting, poised at the edge of the disturbed surface like a praying mantis. Just to the right of the crane, a stack of neatly arranged metal and wooden boxes rested. The metal ones were at least forty feet long, and bore the scrapes and gashes Sikes associated with shipping containers. The wooden boxes were smaller, measuring merely six feet in length. Associated equipment, he supposed. Based on their intelligence, there was little doubt in his mind as to what the larger crates held.

The girdered structure had the look of something almost complete, as though the addition of a few more support members would transform the collection into a stark, meaningful machine, one capable of handling the missiles he was certain were nestled in the longer boxes.

He glanced to his right, and saw his partner had already extracted the portable Geiger counter from his carryall. Huerta pointed the probe toward the field.

The light on the face panel, which glowed a barely discernible zero-zero-zero in the dark, shivered, the movement then picked up by the other two digits. Figures mounted rapidly, rising well above the threshold of what Sikes knew was regular background radiation.

He shivered despite the warm night. The trip to shore on the boat, the silent creep through the quiet compound, hell, even his last operation in the Middle East—none of it chilled him more than those three green digits staring at him now out of the gloom.

0350 Local (+5 GMT)
Tomcat 201

"He's onto us!" Gator twisted around in his seat to try to maintain visual contact with the approaching Cuban aircraft.

"Got a VID—visual identification?" Bird Dog queried.

"No." Gator rapped out the word more harshly than he'd intended as a twinge of pain spasmed through his lower back. Turning around to look over his shoulder in the cramped confines of the cockpit probably provided more business for chiropractors than he liked to think about.

"Doesn't matter. We know who he is."

"And he knows who we are."

"That's the whole point of it, isn't it?"

"Not if that puts him in a shitty mood."

Gator gave up trying to see through the clouds and mist and turned back to the radar display. The other aircraft was plainly visible on the scope, a fluorescent green solid mark against the scattering of returns generated by the thicker storm cells in the area. Solid, its edges well defined—and moving toward them at six hundred knots. He tried one last time. "Bird Dog, we need to rethink this."

"Ain't nothin' to think, Gator. He's close enough now, I'm going to turn tail and let him chase us."

"Missile lock!"

Bird Dog swore. Without responding, he tipped the nose of the Tomcat back toward the water and began trading altitude for speed and distance. Distance most of all—with the MiG, he needed at least another five miles of separation before he'd feel even relatively safe.

"Still no visual—too much haze," Gator said rapidly, his fingers flying over the peculiarly shaped knobs and buttons around his seat. Each one had its own special shape, one that no RIO could forget, even if there was no illumination. Bird Dog might be able to fly the aircraft by the seat of his pants, but Gator could launch weapons by the feel of his fingers.

"We're out of range," Bird Dog announced. "Especially if he's carrying—"

"It's not falling off, Bird Dog," Gator said urgently. "It should have by now."

"Jesus! What the hell? Hold on." The Tomcat's dive steepened, throwing both aviators against the ejection harnesses that held them in their seats.

"Watch your altitude."

"I am, I am! Get ready with the chaff."

Gator's world narrowed down to the small round scope in front of him; nothing else was important. A few small surface contacts. Fishing boats, probably, one part of his mind noted dispassionately. Then the one aft of them, the only radar contact that mattered. Indeed, unless Bird Dog was successful with his latest maneuver, nothing else would matter in the next five minutes except his view of the Almighty. Or, more important, how the Almighty viewed him.

He knew what his pilot was planning on doing, and the idea frightened him almost as much as the approaching missile. Get down low, get near the churning, violent sea below them, and try to hide within the spatter of radar returns generated by the ever-changing wave structure of the surface of the ocean. It was a chancy move, but that coupled with countermeasures such as chaff and flares might be enough to distract the weapon long enough for them to get away.

"Might be." With a regular missile, it would have been, of

that he was certain. But given the extended range on this one, a range he'd never even heard hinted at during intelligence briefs, who knew what else was new? An improved seeker head? A more accurate radar capable of distinguishing between sea clutter and the sweetheart metal contact that the Tomcat would generate on its sensors? He shook his head, shuttling the fear back to some small dark compartment of his mind. He couldn't get distracted now, when his primary task was to serve as a second pair of eyes and make sure the Tomcat stayed out of the water.

It would really suck if we lost the missile and slammed into one of the masts on the fishing boats. He frowned, knowing how close to the water Bird Dog was likely to get and how high the antennas and booms extended from some fishing boats.

A brief thought of his wife, Alicia, flitted through his mind. He allowed it to stay there for a microsecond, then compartmentalized it as well. No time for danger, no time for thoughts of love and family—all that mattered was getting away, now.

Bird Dog, he had to admit, was one of the best. He'd proved it repeatedly during the Spratly Islands conflict. But this scenario, with the young pilot, slightly rusty from his tour on staff duty, playing grab-ass with a missile of unknown capabilities, was more than either of them had bargained for.

0355 Local (+5 GMT)
Fuentes Naval Base

The second SEAL squad had followed the same peek-dart-peek transit maneuver that the other one had, with less success. Their target was still over 150 feet away, and under the circumstances, it wasn't likely that they'd be getting any closer.

"That's it," Garcia said quietly, careful to turn the *s* into a *th* sound. It was a habit born of long training, turning sibilant consonants that carried for long distances into fricative soft sounds. "Got to be."

The other men nodded. They were crouched down in landscaping shrubbery surrounding what appeared to be an administrative building, complete with flagpole out front and decorative bricks around the steps leading up to it. Due east from their position, a two-story cement block building without windows was surrounded by two storm fencing perimeters. The outer one was topped with razor wire. Bright lights on tall poles cast a harsh glare down on the building and the land a hundred feet around it. They could see two armed men patrolling just inside the perimeter, displaying none of the uncertainty or clumsiness that had characterized their compatriot by the outer perimeter fence they'd already passed through. These were men with a purpose, and with the training to accomplish it. Their steps were swift and sure. They glanced continually into the darkness around them. Sikes saw night-vision goggles mounted insectlike on top of one of their heads, evidently shoved back to allow him better visibility in the bright light. The guards would still be able to see them even if the SEALs were to shoot the lights out.

Not that they would. No, marching orders for this mission were simply to ascertain the location of the prison building and bring the pilot out if possible. Shooting out the lights would put the whole camp on alert immediately, complicating not only their own egress from the compound but compromising the other team as well. They would be lucky to escape with their own lives, much less that of the pilot.

Huerta ground his teeth in frustration. The rescue mission would have to wait for the next intrusion into the camp, if then. But for now, getting the American aviator away from the Cubans was going to prove tougher than his superiors had thought.

He motioned to his team, a quick, sharp hand movement, then faded back into the shrubbery. He strained to hear them moving through the brush, and a grim smile crossed his face when nothing met his ears but silence. They were good, very good.

Unfortunately, this time, it wasn't enough.

0400 Local (+5 GMT)
Tomcat 201

"Pull up! Pull up!" Gator's voice was frantic. And about two seconds too late. He could already feel the Tomcat starting to nose up, see Bird Dog gently easing the yoke back. Would it be in time? He hoped to hell the young fool knew what he was doing.

Gator craned his neck around to stare down at the water below them. It was now visible, since they were under the cloud cover and fog that had plagued their mission on the way in. Two thousand feet, maybe less, he decided, staring in horrified fascination at the churning wave tops white-capped with foam. Not enough.

The Tomcat was almost in level flight now, but still descending as its inertia carried it forward. Gator stared in silent horror, knowing that nothing he could say or do could change the aerodynamic equation now being worked out between the airframe and the atmosphere. Either Bird Dog had judged it right, or he hadn't. Either way, Gator was out of the loop.

He shut his eyes, not wanting to watch, then opened them immediately. As soon as he quit looking, every nerve ending in his body seemed to become preternaturally alive, extending out past the skin of the aircraft to feel the warm, hungry sea below him. Better the demons he could see than those he couldn't.

Finally, fifteen feet above the waves, the Tomcat pulled out of its steep dive. Gator felt a slight shudder, and wondered if the reckless pilot in front of him had nicked the surface of the ocean with the tail of the Tomcat. Still, the reassuring roar of both engines reassured him that nothing was wrong with their propulsion. He felt relief flood him, and waited for the moment when Bird Dog would start grabbing altitude again.

It didn't happen. The Tomcat streaked on northward, still fifteen to twenty feet above the waves. Gator remained silent, not wanting to cause the slightest distraction to the incredible concentration such low-level flying required. He stared at his radar scope, willing the missile away from them.

"Flares. Chaff." Bird Dog's voice was almost mechanical.

Gator automatically punched the buttons, watching in wonderment over the fact that his hands still knew what to do while his mind stared at the sea. He felt the gentle thumps on the airframe as the two countermeasure packages shot out from the undercarriage, and wondered what the hell good they would do. They were so close to the sea, both were likely to hit the water before the missile following had any chance to acquire them.

Just as the first thump shook the aircraft, Bird Dog wrenched the Tomcat into a tight roll. The countermeasures, housed on the underside of the aircraft, shot into the air, detonating one hundred feet above the water.

The ocean was now only twenty feet above his head, as

sky and water reversed themselves in his perspective. He experienced a moment of vertigo and a sudden tensing in his stomach. God, puking now, upside down—it would have been funny if it hadn't been so serious.

As the last of the countermeasures left the aircraft, Bird Dog rolled the Tomcat upright again and pulled back on the yoke. Gator felt the indescribably delicious sensation of moving away from the water, watching it recede until the hundred feet above it that Bird Dog appeared to settle on felt like a vast safety margin. In other circumstances it would have been far too low for his tastes, but now it seemed like the ultimate in safety.

As the aircraft regained altitude, the hard blip of the missile reappeared on his radar screen. It was now only five hundred feet behind him, far too close for another try at countermeasures. Or maybe it wasn't. He tried to remember the exact parameters of the countermeasures, calculated the possible maximum speed of the missile, and was still frantically thinking about it when he heard Bird Dog order another set.

Again, his fingers seemed to know what to do by themselves. He studied the scope. Just as suddenly as it had appeared, the missile's trace on the radar disappeared. Another, more amorphous bloom popped up, and seconds later he heard an explosion behind him.

"What the hell was that?" Bird Dog said.

"You know what it was." Inexplicably, Gator was now angry beyond all measure. "That fishing boat—your low-level stunt decoyed the missile right into it."

"It was an air-to-air missile—not an air-to-surface missile," Bird Dog said hurriedly. "It shouldn't acquire a surface ship. No way."

"How the hell do you know? It shouldn't have run as long as it did either. Comes in low, acquires the next best target

after us, and some sailor is fish bait now. How are you going
to like explaining that to the admiral?" Gator stormed. "This
is the last time, Bird Dog. I'm never flying with you again."

The two fishing boats were steaming together silently, all
lights extinguished. Their wooden structures were poor
radar reflectors, and absent the presence of a high-powered
beam, neither one was probably evident on any surface
radar.

Finding Leyta on board had been the first surprise—and
not the last, she suspected. Aguillar had turned her over to
him on the docks in Venezuela and told her he'd retrieve her
at the same location.

"We're safe?" Pamela Drake asked softly.

Leyta nodded. "As safe as we can be anywhere. I've done
this thousands of times—you are not to worry, Miss
Drake." His nonchalance gave her more reassurance than
his words.

She nodded and gazed off toward the bow of the boat. If
the chart was correct, the coast of Cuba was only five miles
ahead. Within twenty minutes, she'd be setting foot on
Cuban soil. Americans were still barred from visiting Cuba,
but the American government had conspicuously over-
looked the occasional presence of an American journalist
there. She decided not to think about the possible legal
consequences and concentrated on outlining the story she'd
soon present to the world.

The story—how much of it could she tell? More important, how much would her producers believe?

The more members of both Aguillar's and Leyta's political groups she met, the more disturbed she was by the
degree to which they were interconnected. While most of
her viewers would have given little thought to the differences in the two groups' political agendas, to astute observ-

ers on the international scene it had always appeared that
Leyta was a violently dangerous reactionary while Aguillar
was willing to advance Cuba's cause within the established
political system. Pamela was no longer sure either statement
was true, and she'd made that clear to Keith Loggins during
their last conversation.

Regardless of the political realities, she was finally on the
last leg of her journey, itself an experience in the degree to
which the two groups cooperated. Aguillar's people had
handled the seaplane flight from Venezuela to the Caribbean, while Leyta's people manned the fishing boat now
ferrying her into shore. As she understood it, her contacts
within Cuba were almost exclusively Leyta's people, a fact
that caused her some degree of concern.

Well, no matter. A story was a story.

She heard it before she saw it, a brief whine on the edge
of her consciousness, like a bothersome mosquito. In
seconds it crescendoed to a shrieking scream, and then the
boat in front of them exploded into flames. The captain of
her vessel had barely enough time to slew the small craft
violently to the right to avoid the wreckage and fireball.

A cacophony of swearing and exclamations, coupled with
screams, exploded on her own craft. She stared in horror at
the flaming wreckage, which was flung up into the air,
paused at mid-trajectory, then made its comparatively slow
descent back to the surface of the warm sea.

Her journalistic instincts kicked in, and she raised the
minicam in her hand and pointed it in the general direction
of debris, then passed back down to the burning spot on the
ocean. Flames everywhere, hurting her eyes as they seared
the night-adapted pupils, throwing oddly flickering shadows
of goblins over the bulkheads of her craft. She watched it,
caught it all on tape, and felt an absurdly inappropriate thrill
that she was present to do so.

"Get below." Leyta's hand clamped down on her bicep. He jerked her away from the railing and shoved her toward the cabin. "I don't know what's happened—who did you tell you were coming?"

"No one!" she said, with one eye still glued to the camera. "Shut up and leave me alone."

"No. Ten of my friends are dead, and you will not be the one to record it." He shoved her toward the cockpit hatch.

She swung the camera around to film him. "What happened? Why did it explode?"

He stared at her as if staring at an alien being. "A missile," he said finally. "The noise—I think it was. And where that one came from, there are probably others."

The prospect of being trapped belowdecks, waiting unknowingly for an attack, was unappealing. No, more than that—completely unacceptable. She twisted away from Leyta's grasp and ran to the stern of the boat, again aiming her camera at the burning wreckage. The vague outline of one side of the ship was now visible through the flames. The superstructure was completely gone. As her vessel drew away from it, secondary explosions—probably gasoline tanks, one part of her mind noted dispassionately—shook the air.

"We have to get away quickly. The authorities will be coming to investigate." Leyta stared at her. "You will stay there—no other parts of the boat, you understand? And no movement."

She nodded, still filming the burning wreckage. What a scoop.

After the last flaming bit of wreckage disappeared from the sea, Pamela hunted down her equipment bag belowdecks. She carefully stowed the camera, then extracted her second

most critical piece of survival gear. She punched in Keith
Loggins's telephone number from memory.

0700 Local (+5 GMT)
Washington, D.C.

"And your fiancée saw it?" Senator Williams demanded.

Admiral Loggins moved restlessly in his chair. "So she
said. She was calling from her cellular phone. I believe she's
off the coast of Cuba as we speak." He didn't believe that at
all—he knew exactly where she was: on land in Cuba, a far
different matter, and one he wasn't willing to disclose. "She
says she has tape, too, at least of the aftermath."

Senator Williams groaned. "That's all we need, a full
picture of this U.S. mishap on ACN in the next hour. I'd
better brief the President.

"You realize this supports the position I've held all
along," Williams continued. "Using a carrier in close like
that is just too dangerous. Accidents happen. Pilots get
downed, and collateral damage is excessive. The carrier is a
battle-ax, not a delicate political instrument. All we need
there is the Arsenal ship. The mere threat of that valiant
firepower will be sufficient, and it will be far less likely to
cause international mishaps than a group of testosterone-
laden aviators playing grab-ass in the sky."

Admiral Loggins wheeled on him. "You don't know what
the hell you're talking about. I do."

Senator Williams regarded him sardonically. "Once a jet
jock, always a jet jock. We all know about your exploits
during Vietnam, your career as a fighter jock, the times you
were shot down. But that was then, this is now. The public
is determined there will never be another Vietnam, and that

means no screwing around with our nearest neighbor to the south. The Arsenal ship is the answer."

"Didn't you learn anything from Vietnam? I sure did. The first lesson is that D.C. can't be in charge of targeteering. It's micromanaging and it won't work. The on-scene commander has got to be free to choose his weapons, and that means having somebody with enough savvy to know how to do it. And that, in case you don't understand it, means the carrier battle group. Besides, the Arsenal ship provides little capability to make the kind of instantaneous decisions that are needed in the air."

"Like shooting down a fishing boat?" Williams let the question hang in the air.

"Our intelligence is better than it was in Vietnam," Loggins countered. "The on-scene commander can make the kind of decisions he needs to."

"Which so far have led to one missing pilot, probably captured by the Cubans, and one dead fishing boat. A pretty impressive catch," Williams responded sarcastically.

Williams stormed out of the room, heading for the Senate majority leader's office. A small worry niggled at the back of his mind. Sure, this was an international incident in the making, but why had Loggins not worried more about the fact that his fiancée was on the other boat?

SEVEN
Thursday, 27 June

1200 Local (+5 GMT)
Fuentes Naval Base

Pamela Drake glanced at the clock mounted on the cinderblock wall on the other side of the room. The minute hand quivered just millimeters away from the twelve. Good morning, she decided, not good afternoon. That would make her report sound all the more timely.

And timely it was. That they were here on a Cuban naval base had pissed her off at first. She'd blasted off at Aguillar, certain that he'd lied to her about getting the real story.

But his explanation had satisfied her—and not even surprised the cynical part of her mind that always doubted the sincerity of any military organization. That the Cuban navy—part of it, at least—had cordial relationships with both Leyta and Aguillar made sense.

She ran her fingers one last time through the shining cap of brown hair that topped the face more Americans knew than that of the vice president. She took a deep breath, concentrated on centering herself, the normal routine for appearing on camera. Finally, as the minute hand clicked over to the upright position, she nodded at the cameraman.

"Good morning. This is Pamela Drake, reporting from

Cuba for ACN. This is a live report from the westernmost Cuban naval base. In keeping with my agreement with my host, I will not divulge any further details other than to say that the location of this particular installation is well known to the United States government.

"This morning, at approximately four A.M., the American government sparked another round in the increasingly escalating tensions between Cuba and the United States. For the past two weeks, the presence of an American battle group allegedly conducting routine operations off the coast— almost within the territorial waters of our neighbor—has caused increasing concern on the part of the Cuban government. This day, those concerns were made real.

"As you know, American citizens are not allowed to visit Cuba." She gave a small, rueful smile. "Restrictions on our First Amendment rights have never prevented ACN from being the first to bring you every story around the globe. That dedication to our basic constitutional guarantees of freedom led to the American aggression this morning that almost killed me."

Pamela paused for a moment, and repressed an involuntary shudder that threatened to work its way up from the base of her spine to her shoulders. There was no need to show fear—with her command of her voice, every member of her watching audience was already experiencing it. She'd survived; that was enough. She took a deep breath and continued.

"I have no doubt that the American military establishment will try to deny their involvement in this incident. This murder, I should say. However, I will not let that happen. I was there—I saw it. An innocent fishing boat, transporting freedom fighters to a clandestine meeting, was intentionally destroyed by an American missile. Whether or not the

United States knew I was on board one of those ships, I refuse to speculate. However, you may draw your own conclusions.

"During a time when the American government has decided its national interests required a formation of a Trilateral Commission, extensive participation in a new world order, and recognition of the impact economies in other nations have on our own, it is particularly disturbing that we ignore our neighbors to the south. The circumstances are made worse by the fact that there are opposing opinions about the proper relationship between Cuba and America. The American government claims that political uncertainty may lead to the loss of investment capital if trade relations are opened with Cuba, and may be taken by the world community as a movement of support for this dictatorship. The U.S. appears solely concerned with dollars — these freedom fighters, these men and women, risk their lives. If we can spend fifteen years in a war to try to support democracy on the other side of the Pacific Ocean, how can we rationalize failing to support these people in their struggle against Castro?"

She paused again, to let her audience absorb the argument. She would have to repeat it several times, she knew. While television was the most compellingly immediate news medium in the world, its listeners were not always particularly attentive. Many of them wanted the story wrapped up in sound bites, in a sentence or two of intelligent commentary that would form their political views both at home and at the polls. She thought for a moment, then decided to go with it.

"I call on the American government to aid and support these precious freedom fighters, who are the Cuban equivalent of our constitutional founding fathers." She gestured off camera toward a group of people her viewers could not see.

"I wish that I could show you their faces as I see them. Proud, determined, reflecting the knowledge that they know they risk their lives every day for the freedom of their country. How many of us can say the same?

"Instead of supporting these people, our government this morning embarked on a determined campaign to destroy them. This is unconscionable, and we should not stand for it. Cuba is a great and historic nation, and her people are deserving of our support—and our friendship." She continued to stare at the camera as she recited her normal sign-off, then relaxed only after she saw the telltale red light over the video camera blink out. "How was it?"

Santana stepped away from his watchful position near her cameraman. "Beautiful."

1220 Local (+5 GMT)
USS **Jefferson**

Batman slammed his hand down on the conference table, making most of his staff members jump. "Damn it, one of these days, I'm going to break her ever-loving neck!" He glared at the assembled officers, although they had nothing to do with his current mood.

The staff, hastily summoned from their other duties to watch the breaking news story, were equally horrified. That Pamela Drake had once been Admiral Magruder's fiancée was no secret. Everyone in the tight-knit aviation community, as well as most officers outside of it, knew, and had followed the affair with interest. Their breakup over the Spratly Islands affair and Tombstone's subsequent marriage to Tomboy had secretly delighted more than one. Tombstone needed to be kept inside the family, and that included his love life.

Batman sighed and leaned back in his high-backed chair. He let the tension drain out of him as he stared at the still, watching faces around him. "Okay. She's done it. So now what happens? You'd better believe we're going to be besieged by requests for visits and briefings." He pointed one finger at the public affairs officer. "Get it sorted out. Now."

"Admiral, I—," Bird Dog began.

Batman wheeled on him. "You keep your mouth shut, mister. You've done more than enough so far this cruise." He let the rage flood back, and focused on the lieutenant commander in front of him. "What in all hell's bells gave you the idea of executing an *aggressive* decoy tactic? I'd bet my stars that Gator was trying to talk you out of it the entire time. Is that right?"

Bird Dog nodded, relieved that at least his RIO wouldn't suffer his own public execution. After all, Gator had tried to stop him. He just hadn't listened. As he hadn't so many times before. "Gator had nothing to do with it, Admiral."

"I'm surprised he didn't just punch out and make you explain why you showed back up at the carrier without a canopy and a RIO," Batman muttered. "Hell, I know I would have. Damned harebrained idea like that." He intensified his scowl.

Bird Dog wilted visibly in his seat. Batman let it go on two beats longer, then said, "You're grounded. You couldn't expect anything else, not after this incident. There'll be a full JAG investigation, at the very least."

Or a court-martial. Batman let the words remain unspoken.

"Yes, sir." Bird Dog started to say something else, then decided that anything he could or would say at this point would only dig his grave deeper.

"Now, for the rest of it—I'm tempted to say let's get our

story straight, but we don't have any story. We simply tell the truth, that's all. At this point, I'm inclined to simply treat Bird Dog's little escapade here as part of an overall plan of operational deception. You all know the reason why. That, of course, remains top secret." He turned back to the PAO again. "Figuring out how to put this all in one neat package is your job. Tell the truth—as much of it as we dare—but steer away from anything that could compromise the safety of that pilot. You got it?"

The PAO nodded. "Aye, aye, Admiral. I'll have the executive briefing on your desk in one hour."

"Make it thirty minutes." Batman suddenly felt fatigue flood his body. The next few hours—hell, the next few days—were going to be an unmitigated public circus. He'd rather be taking five night traps in a row in a gale-force wind than face the media storm that was about to erupt. Had erupted, he corrected as he glanced back at the television set. ACN commentators were already clamoring for attention, asking pointed questions that were really snide comments on the ability of the U.S. military to control its forces.

"Nobody talks on this—nobody but me and the PAO," Batman said grimly. "Everybody understand? I mean no cellular calls home, no talking to anybody."

Around the large conference table, heads bobbed.

Submerged in his own misery, Bird Dog barely heard the words. He remembered Thor all too well, and the possibility that he'd done something to endanger the man's life was all but intolerable. Pilots supported each other, worked as a team, not as loose cannons with their own agendas. Maybe Gator was right. He was rusty and dangerous in the air.

1230 Local (+5 GMT)
Fuentes Naval Base

"There's nothing more I can tell you, Jim," she said. She was on live feed to the noonday news, answering questions from the ACN anchor back in New York. She glanced at something pointedly off camera, then turned back to face the anchor she could not see. "I'm informed that we've spent too long in this location. We'll have to leave. To stay any longer would compromise my safety, and, quite frankly"—the rueful grin appeared again—"I've had enough of that for one day. I'll get back to you as soon as I have more details."

"Thank you, Pamela," the anchor said sanctimoniously. "Do make sure that you—"

The rest of his words were cut off as Pamela signaled to the cameraman to terminate the feed. Headquarters had a tendency to try to micromanage every breaking story. And while the missile attack on the fishing boat might not be the big story she was sure she'd eventually report, it would do for the time being.

She turned to Santana and asked, "Where are we now?" It had been dark, the sun at least thirty minutes from rising when they'd come ashore. There'd been a ride in a truck, bumping along concealed in the back of a deuce-and-a-half army vehicle, then a hurried trot into this building. She'd tried to look around when they arrived, but her hosts had kept her moving too quickly for her to absorb more than the vaguest details of the area around her, which was shrouded in predawn gloom. "I'd like to know." She made her voice insistent.

"You agreed to be covered by our operational security rules," Santana said shortly. He turned away from her and walked toward the door, moving quickly. "One of our first rules is that people know only what they need to know. If you are captured—or when you are returned to the United States—you will not be able to divulge this location if you don't know it."

"I've been here since six A.M.," she snapped. "Trapped in one building with no windows. Do you think it would compromise your 'operational security' if you gave me something to eat?"

Santana stopped at the door and gestured to an aide. "Get her some food. Keep her here." He shot one look at her, a small expression of minor annoyance, then left the room, banging the door shut behind him. Pamela heard a bolt slide home as he left.

She turned back to the other freedom fighter—her guard, she now realized. She forced her face to relax and produced a friendly smile. "Any choices on the menu? I'm a pretty fair cook, if you've got the raw ingredients. I'll bet you're hungry now, too."

The guard stared impassively at her, no expression of understanding on his face.

"You do speak English, don't you?" she pressed. She took two steps toward him. "Don't worry, I won't tell anybody if you commit a fatal sin by having some lunch with me." She smiled prettily. "I do so hate to eat alone."

Something in the guard's expression softened. While it would have been pressing it to call it a friendly look, at least it was a change from the cold, impassive face he'd shown before. "I promise, I won't even ask you any questions about all this," she continued, waving her hand at the surrounding area. "Not a word. It's just that I'm a long way from home, and I'm not used to people trying to blow me up before breakfast."

The guard nodded finally. "We have American MREs," he announced, a note of pride in his voice. "Very nourishing."

Pamela groaned inwardly, but maintained the agreeable expression on her face. It wasn't this fellow's fault, not at all. He couldn't know how many times she'd eaten MREs and the C-rats that were their predecessors while in pursuit of a story in some exotic locale. And as for the incident this morning—well, it had shaken her, but she'd had worse times. Like in Beirut. Like in Bosnia. Sure, physical peril always produced a sense of danger once it was past, coupled with a renewed realization of one's own mortality, but this certainly wasn't as terrifying as her experiences in Bosnia had been. There, pinned down by a sniper, she'd had to wait until the UN forces cleared the area. She and her cameraman had subsisted on the ubiquitous MREs then, mixing the instant drink mix with water they'd collected in their helmets. She shuddered at the thought.

"MREs? Why, that would be very nice." She reached out to accept the gray vinyl plastic bag the man handed to her. "Do you have a knife?" she asked. Seeing his expression, she continued quickly, "To open the bag, of course. Here, I can let you do it for me."

The man grunted, then ripped through the heavy container with his knife. He tendered the open MRE back to her.

She paused for a moment to study the writing on the outside of the plastic, then groaned. Egg and ham omelet. Her least favorite of all the varieties, almost as bad as the pork patties in the old C-rats. Only the small bottle of hot sauce included in each MRE made the omelet palatable.

Still, as she dug into the main entree with her fork, she reflected that it was better than being shot at. Barely.

Just as she was holding up a package of dried crackers for her guard to open, a bloodcurdling scream from the next room echoed in the air. She jumped and dropped the package. The guard bent over to pick it up. For a moment, she fantasized about slamming her hand down on the back of his neck, stunning him, and somehow escaping the building. No, that was wrong. These were her friends, weren't they? Her sources, at least. Whatever was happening in the next room was not a glimpse into her own future.

She hoped.

Thor lost consciousness abruptly, the tail end of his scream still fading in the room as he slumped down in the wooden chair. The ropes held him semi-upright.

"Very attractive," Santana noted. He walked around the chair studying the pilot from all angles. "Yet you still have no answers." He stooped down in front of the pilot and stared at Thor's crotch. The pilot's flight suit had been peeled off and lay in a crumpled pile at his feet.

"I believe the electrical lead to the left testicle is coming loose," Santana said finally. He stood up and walked back over to the table. "Have the Libyans check it."

1245 Local (+5 GMT)
USS Jefferson

"TAO reports small gunboats approaching the carrier," the operations officer told Batman. "None of the larger vessels, though. I suppose that's a blessing."

"Don't discount those small boats. It doesn't take a

military genius to figure out that they caused us some real problems." Batman's voice was tired.

The TAO frowned. "A twenty-four-foot attack vessel versus an aircraft carrier?"

Batman shook his head. "Don't think of it in terms of tonnage. Think of it in the big picture. What happens if we run over those boats? We simply lend credibility to Drake's story, that's all. Worse, there are some ways they can hurt us—slow us down, at least. What if they get in our way? We have to avoid them, don't we? Especially given this morning's events. Add the fact that they can carry Stingers on board, and we've got a real problem."

"How much trouble is one Stinger? They've got a range of less than two miles." The TAO frowned.

"Maybe, maybe not. Remember the speculation on the TWA downing, that it was done by a longer-range Stinger, an improved version of the one we're familiar with. Those little puppies are manufactured all over the world now, and who's to say there haven't been some radical improvements in them? Besides, what can you tell me about our hangar doors right now?"

The question caught the TAO off guard. "The hangar doors?" He shrugged. "Not much, I guess. They're open right now, I imagine. I have them open in this heat."

"Exactly my point. What's one Stinger shot into the hangar bay going to do to us? How many aircraft will be set on fire—and I assume it's still crowded down there—before we get it put out? How much fuel will go up in flames? And how many missiles are down there? Any? I know that they're not supposed to be, but—"

"I get your point." The operations officer looked thoughtful. "We may need to shut the doors anytime small boats come around."

"Then we end up with heat exhaustion. The temperature

in that space is gonna climb like a bat out of hell." Batman looked grim. "Not many good choices, are there?"

There were, he thought as he watched the operations officer stride out of the room, hardly any good choices left in the world at all. Not down here, not for the USS *Jefferson,* And not for one Admiral Edward Everett Wayne, in command of Carrier Group Fourteen.

1400 Local (+5 GMT)
Fuentes Naval Base

Leyta looked skeptical. "You're sure about this?"

Santana nodded. "Completely. I've got four people who saw that aircraft returning to the carrier, and there were no empty spots on its wings. It hadn't fired a weapon."

"How could they tell? In foul weather, at some distance?" Leyta looked doubtful.

"They could tell." The quiet confidence in the man's voice lent weight to his statement. "The background—you don't want to know, but they could tell."

Leyta tossed the folder he'd been studying across the desk, wincing as it collided with a pencil holder and spilled its contents all over the floor. "It's almost like the way we fight a war, isn't it? Tossing things around, wondering what they'll knock over? Never really any planning? So now what?"

Santana bent over and started to gather pencils up from the floor, leaving the report facedown where it lay. "It depends. We can continue to blame it on the Americans or we can use it against the current regime. Either option poses problems." He looked up at Leyta and lifted one quizzical eyebrow.

"Starting with dividing our own movement," Leyta said,

finishing the other man's thought. "Regardless of how much we disagree about methodology, Aguillar and I want the same thing—a free Cuba. He just wants it to be free under the United States' protection and I want it to be a part of the world. No more insularity; no more being a farm plantation for the United States, either. A free Cuba, our Cuba. What we always dreamed it could be." He paused for a moment, staring down at the report on the floor without seeing it. "But you don't care about that, do you? Not really."

Santana shrugged. "You might be surprised what I care about. If I had to pick sides, I'd be on yours, not Aguillar's. Although in this scenario—" Again, the shrug that resigned all their fates to an indifferent god. "I'm not really sure what's the right course. Maybe we wait. The Libyans are only a means to an end—securing our freedom with superior firepower. Outside of that, it makes very little difference to me who runs the government. As long as it's not Castro."

"We wait," Leyta echoed. It was something they were good at—they'd been doing it for decades, if not centuries. "Although I may drop a hint to look into the details of this in a couple of important places. You know the type I mean."

"I don't need to. You do what you think is best, my friend."

1420 Local (+5 GMT)
The Pentagon

"I saw the same report you did, Admiral," Tombstone Magruder said, his voice cold and emotionless. "I have no information other than that."

The chairman of the Joint Chiefs of Staff studied him

carefully. "You understand, I find that hard to believe." He left the rest of the thought unsaid—*because of your relationship with Pamela.*

Tombstone stiffened. "Miss Drake no longer clears her stories through me. Not that she ever did. The only control I ever had over them was when she was on my aircraft carrier and I had to transmit her reports." And that went over really well, he remembered quite clearly. The illustrious Miss Pamela Drake had not taken kindly to having her precious copy edited or redacted. While Tombstone had found it necessary to do that on occasion to protect the security of the operation, he'd never enjoyed it. Particularly not the aftermath. "And I certainly had nothing to do with her being in Cuba," he continued as a new thought struck him.

"No one said you did. But with your prior relationship, and with you now in command of the Southern Forces, it does look suspicious. You understand that."

Tombstone nodded, feeling his throat tighten. What was the chairman leading up to? Had there been a decision to relieve him of command because of events far beyond his control, simply based on his prior relationship with a reporter? Was that fair? And, he finally asked himself, would he really care? To his surprise, he did. As tempting as it might be to chuck his entire naval career—and not a bad one at that, finishing up with two stars on his collar—and simply relax into his marriage with Tomboy, start off on a new civilian career, he couldn't do it.

Part of it, he admitted, was the sheer headiness of command. As commander, Southern Forces, he had operational control of everything south of the Equator. That included the massively burgeoning continent of South America and liaison with all the foreign navies there. It was an opportunity to build on shaky relationships that were barely in their infancy, to create peace instead of making war, for once. It seemed like a fitting capstone to his career thus far, which had consisted mainly of fighting first the Soviet Bear and then the Chinese Mongoose that had sought to dominate entire parts of the world.

Am I power-hungry? He considered the idea for a moment, then shook his head. Yes, it was true that all the ruffles and flourishes that went with his current position were easy to get used to. And he was eternally grateful for the fact that his uncle had found him a posting in an operational force and not consigned him to a desk in the Pentagon. An expensive, highly polished desk, but a desk nonetheless. If you couldn't fly—and he was far too senior for that—then the next best thing was command of operational forces. And at his current pay rate, even command of a carrier battle group was beyond his reach.

"If the chairman lacks confidence in my abilities—," Tombstone began, finally having reached his decision.

The chairman cut him off with a sharp wave of his hand. "Don't be ridiculous. You'll be asked that enough times in the media. But never here. I'm just trying to prepare you for what's ahead."

"A public hanging?" Tombstone's voice was harsh. "I have that to look forward to?"

"Maybe. Maybe not." A speculative gleam lit the chairman's eyes. "There might be another option."

"And what would that be?" Tombstone asked.

"Send you back to sea." The chairman's face threatened to smile, but never really got quite that far.

"Back to sea!" Tombstone's heart thudded as he considered it. But how? And why? "You mean as a—"

For the second time in as many minutes, the chairman cut him off. "I mean that we might form up a two-carrier battle group to resolve this matter. Or, given the way Senator

Williams is talking, a carrier and an Arsenal ship battle *force*—not just a battle group. Seems to me that that rates more than one star in command." He waited for his astonishing proposal to sink in.

For one of the few times in his life, Tombstone was at a loss for words. To go back to sea—God, yes. He'd give anything to simply be around the aircraft that had been his life for the first twenty-five years of his career, to roam the flight deck again, listening to the hard thunder of finely honed jet engines and the squealing rake of catapult wires across the deck. "How probable is that?" he asked finally, not daring to ask the other questions hammering in his head.

The chairman leaned back in his chair. "From where I sit, very probable. You know the commander of the carrier group, don't you?"

Tombstone almost laughed. "Yes, Admiral Wayne is an old friend." *And you damned well know that, you sneaky old bastard. But why be so coy about it?*

"How do you think he'll feel about it?" the chairman asked. "Because what we'll want on this, quite frankly, is a positive spin. I don't need any disgruntled admirals squabbling over seniority arguments, not if we're going to rehabilitate you and resolve the situation at the same time."

"Batman won't be a problem," Tombstone said. But, for a moment, he wondered. How eager would he himself have been to have an old shipmate turn up to take over tactical command of this scenario? "He'd stay as CARGRU commander."

"Of course." The chairman stood up abruptly. "Give it some thought. What's best for you; what's best for this country of ours."

"I will, sir."

"Get back to me tomorrow. I should have more information then," the chairman said in dismissal.

1600 Local (+5 GMT)
Fuentes Naval Base

Santana walked across the open, muddy field. The thick black dirt clumped on his boots, moist and lumpy. Ahead of him, the partially constructed missile launcher was completely exposed, its sheltering shield of canvas pulled back.

He walked around the installation, two aides trailing in his wake. From the daily reports he'd been receiving, he would have expected it to be much more complete — much more looking like it was about to be operational. His gaze wandered to the long metal boxes arrayed next to the crane. An impressive achievement, to be sure, but without the launchers they would be nothing.

"When?" he asked. He saw his two aides glance at each other uneasily before the more senior of them spoke.

"Two weeks, I believe. According to our Libyan technical advisors."

Santana restrained the urge to spit in the dirt. "When have they been right about anything? Not the schedule, not the American operations, not anything." He stopped abruptly, gazing at the stacked weapons, his eyes caressing them. "The only thing they have managed to do correctly is deliver the weapons, and even those are worthless without the launchers."

"Sir, the American battle group—perhaps if we ignore them, they will leave us alone?"

Santana whirled on him. "You would allow them to continue to invade our territorial waters? To mock our very sovereignty?"

"No," the aide said in a shaky voice, "not at all. However,

I have an idea that might prevent further intrusions into our airspace. And I think you might find it particularly appealing, under the circumstances," he continued, his voice gaining strength. "May I explain?"

Santana bit back angry words and nodded abruptly. The aide was the son of one of his oldest friends, and showed occasional signs of astute operational thought. It would not do to let his own temper prevent him from hearing what must be best for his mission, not at all. "Continue."

Ten minutes later, Santana's earlier rage had vanished as quickly as the mist had over the water. "A fine plan, my friend," he said, and clapped the man on the shoulder. "I think that will work just fine."

1750 Local (+5 GMT)
USS **Jefferson**

"A week from tomorrow?" Bird Dog said, trying to keep the tremor out of his voice. "That's quick."

The ACOS Ops glared up at him from his seat at the desk. "You want to drag this out? I thought you hated being behind a desk instead of in a cockpit."

Bird Dog swallowed hard. "Of course I want to get it over with. It's just that—"

The ACOS cut him off. He spoke, his voice softer than it had been before. "Listen, son, it's never easy going to a FNAEB—a Fleet Naval Aviator Evaluation Board. I went once myself—made a couple of bad passes at the boat back when they were starting to downsize, and a guy who didn't like me decided he might try to railroad me. It was painful, but nothing you can't survive. The basic question they're asking is whether or not you're safe in the air." He stopped, and looked quizzically up at Bird Dog. "Are you?"

Bird Dog nodded. "Yes, sir. I'm a damned hot stick. It's just that the other day . . ." His voice disappeared to nothing.

"You weren't thinking," the ACOS finished. "You just pulled a damned foolish stunt, and now you're going to a FNAEB board. Okay, stand up and take it like a man. Maybe it will make you think twice next time you get a wild hair up your ass."

And maybe there won't be a next time, Bird Dog added silently. The FNAEB had the power to revoke his designation as a naval aviator, leaving him permanently grounded. Would he stay in the Navy if it came to that? Of course not—absent the sheer joy of flying the F-14 Tomcat, the rigors of military life held no real attraction for him. Then there was Callie . . . ah, Callie. He'd spend more time with her, maybe start a second career—no, he decided, none of that would make up for losing his designation as a naval aviator. To know that he would never again fly the screaming Tomcat at Mach 1 plus, buzzing around the superstructure of an Aegis cruiser to annoy the captain, chasing MiGs through skies so blue they looked translucent, or screaming over the tops of waves with the spray flashing to steam in his afterburner fire. No, nothing was worth losing that—nothing.

"I'll be ready, sir. And thank you.

The ACOS nodded abruptly. "Get out of here. And be ready—that's all I can tell you."

2200 Local (+5 GMT)
Fuentes Naval Base

The night sounds of Cuba drifted in the front door, finally reaching Pamela Drake in the back room of the building. The air was still warm, heavy and humid, scented with the exotic blooms and heavy vegetation around the base.

"How much longer?" she demanded of her guard. "I came here to report a story. I can't do that stuck in one room."

The guard shrugged. *"No sea."* He eyed her carefully. "You stay here," he continued, evidently the entire extent of his English language abilities.

Pamela sighed and resumed pacing around the room. Something to kick, she decided. No, maybe a scream. How did one say "rape" in Spanish? Surely that would bring someone with enough power to resolve this situation, she fumed.

Forty feet away, Mendiria was asking the same questions. "You can't keep her here forever." He touched his mustache, smoothing the stiff bristles down against his face. They sprang back up as soon as he released them, producing a bushy caterpillar on his upper lip.

"And why not?" Santana demanded. "We have control over everything she releases from here. And when she cooperates . . ." He lifted his shoulders in a gesture of resignation. "She travels without notifying her own authorities, no doubt. If something happens to her, who will be able to say that we are at fault? An illegal entry into our country, during a time of so much turmoil? The guerrillas—one cannot trust them. They are, as the Americans say, unpredictable." He smiled, too-large white teeth catching the light from the bare lightbulb overhead.

"But what is the point?" the Libyan persisted. "I see no advantage to us. The longer she remains here, the sooner she will figure out she does not have freedom to travel where she wishes. Her interest in supporting us will burn away as the sea mist in the morning sun. There is no gain to us."

Santana leaned forward across the table, resting his elbows on the rough wooden surface. He reached over, grasped the other man by the wrist, and pulled him toward him. The Libyan resisted slightly, but stopped with his brass button of his uniform rubbing against the edge of the table.

"No advantage? Think! The Americans understand this sort of situation now, after Desert Storm. There are Americans here, as you well know. They come—whether as news reporters or tourists, illegally sneaking into our country, still they come. You understand the implications from a tactical sense, at least?"

"I see no advantage," Mendiria repeated. "Simply more victims if—" He stopped abruptly and considered the matter. A slow smile, as large as the one on the face of his colleague, crossed his face. "Hostages."

Santana nodded. "Exactly. If it comes to that. Do you really think that they will target their smart bombs on this facility, knowing that their star television reporter is being held here against her will? Especially one so attractive as Miss Pamela Drake? While she might not have planned aiding our cause in this way, she will be instrumental in safeguarding us against cruise missiles."

Mendiria sighed. "I was wrong to doubt you. My apologies. On the surface it seemed—"

Santana cut him off with a sharp gesture of his hand. "It is nothing between friends. We have lived close to America for a long time now. Perhaps we understand them a bit better, yes? But you agree?"

The Libyan nodded vigorously.

2300 Local (+5 GMT)
Viking 701

"There she is, Admiral," the S-3 pilot said over the ICS. "Just where she's supposed to be."

Tombstone clicked a brief acknowledgment. Two thousand feet below them, as they entered the starboard marshal pattern, the USS *Jefferson* plowed through the seas like an implacable weapon.

He wondered if the Cubans knew just how much trouble they were in with *Jefferson* off their shore.

EIGHT
Saturday, 29 June

Computers atop the two rows of desks arrayed in the traditional horseshoe pattern beeped in sequence. The muted *chirrup* traveled from left to right, sounding at each computer terminal in turn until it leaped from the last desk in the semicircle, leaped past the long, now vacant anchor desk centered in front of the arc, leaped to the producer's console in the glass-walled control room—the bridge.

The alert immediately began making its rounds again, the circulating sound designed to jar even the most preoccupied reporter into attention. Flashing letters danced across the top of each monitor screen, identifying the incoming message as a breaking news bulletin from the Associated Press.

Only a few of the workstations were occupied at this hour. The two o'clock news program was a cut-in, and the anchors had already done their five live minutes of reading the news and fled the scene. So had the production crew, leaving the message alert to echo forlornly inside the dark, empty bridge. The instant the live portion gave way to the taped news rerun, giving them fifteen minutes of "free" time, nearly everyone ran for coffee, snacks, the bathroom.

Only a few of the writers remained in the quiet, sound-proofed newsroom, working on scripts for the next show, getting on the telephone to finish gathering information for their assigned stories, using their terminals to check facts.

The computer beeped insistently, demanding that the operator attend to the incoming message traffic. Electronic transmission had long ago replaced the old yellow teletypes that chattered away in newsrooms.

"Will you look at this?" the reporter whistled quietly, hitting the keys which scrolled the full text of the bulletin down his screen. "But I guess we should have expected it." He looked over at the producer who'd just walked in and motioned her over. "We're going into Cuba. And you won't believe who's going to do the shooting."

1525 Local (+5 GMT)
USS **Jefferson**

"Who the hell told the press?" Batman stormed. The conference room was deadly silent.

"All right, all right, I know it wasn't anyone here." He turned to the SEAL team leader. "Can you get them out?"

"We know where the pilot is—at least, we think we do. With the right support, we can extract him."

"When?"

The SEAL team leader shrugged. "We've been ready since Thursday."

1545 Local (+5 GMT)
Fuentes Naval Base

"We're going to have to move you, Miss Drake," the colonel said. He bowed slightly, and smiled. "Of course, with your permission."

"Why? What don't you want me to see now?"

"You miss our point entirely. I know you've been watching the television coverage of this little conflict. Your country is planning on launching an attack. Staying where we are would be inadvisable at best."

She glared at him. "You're moving me to safety?" Scorn dripped out of her voice. "Because if that's what you have in mind, forget it. I don't run from a story—not ever."

"Not at all," the colonel said smoothly, ignoring the tone of voice. "In fact, we're going to give you an opportunity to see the futility of it firsthand."

Pamela stared up at the maze of girders, trying to discern a pattern. The metal beams angled out in odd ways, no two exactly parallel. There must be major sections of it still missing, she thought, tracing out the pattern in her mind and trying to match it to any other military equipment she'd ever seen before. Nothing immediately sprang to mind except—

She turned to the colonel. "These are missile launchers, aren't they?" It was more of a statement than a question.

A small frown crossed his face. "What is it to you?"

"Large missile launchers," she insisted. "In fact, the only thing comparable I've seen was in Germany, the housings for the short-range tactical nuclear weapons aimed at the Soviet Union." She watched his face carefully, searching for the confirmation she wanted. She found it.

"You will tape the next report from here," the colonel ordered. "This will make a fine background, will it not?" he said, gesturing at the girders.

"They'll know you've got them. You know the United States will never tolerate this."

"They already know. Do you believe that we do not understand your satellite operations?"

"Then if they know, this will be one of their first targets." *In fact, I suspect that this little trick you're trying to pull off is behind the whole conflict. That Cuban plane that was shot down—it came too close, I bet.* She studied the colonel, new respect in her eyes.

"Your report," he said, his voice harsh.

She nodded to the cameraman, stepped away from the girders, studied the scene to find the perfect position to report from, then nodded her head. "There, over by those boxes." With the girders on one side of her and the boxes on the other, it would make an impressive show of military readiness. Besides, her report might provide additional confirmation to the U.S. intelligence sources on the nature of Cuba's weapons. She gestured for the cameraman to follow her.

Ten minutes later, they were ready. She took a deep breath, made the last cursory pass of fingers through hair, and nodded.

"This is Pamela Drake, reporting live from western Cuba. We have just received notification that the United States intends to execute a tactical strike on Cuba. While no doubt one of the factors that figured into its planning was minimizing collateral damage, my sources here tell me there is little chance the United States will be able to achieve that objective."

She took a deep breath. Her voice felt unexpectedly shaky—this was going to be harder than she thought. She looked upward, wondering if a satellite was staring down on her as she taped this scene.

"This missile installation will undoubtedly be first on the United States' target list. As you can see, I am standing only fifteen yards away from what is probably the aim point. My sources here inform me"—she paused, taking a moment to make eye contact with the cameraman and nod at him, putting him on alert that something unexpected would happen—"that I will not be allowed to leave this area until the attack is over. Isn't that correct, Colonel?"

She smiled approvingly as the cameraman swung around to get a shot of her seniormost guard.

The Cuban officer appeared startled, and his face contorted in a flash of fury. "This was not part of—"

From off camera, Pamela persisted. "Isn't that correct? You're leaving me here as a hostage—or as the first civilian collateral damage. How can you justify that, given your party's consistent insistence on human rights policies in Cuba? Doesn't using foreign nationals as hostage shields, as was done in Desert Storm, cast doubts on the legitimacy of your claims to represent the real Cuban interests?"

The colonel covered the distance to the cameraman in five quick steps. He yanked the videocam out of the man's hands and threw it to the ground, then stomped on it. Pamela could hear delicate mechanical structures twisting, cracking, and snapping.

As though nothing had happened, she held the microphone back up to her mouth. "This is Pamela Drake, no longer reporting live from Cuba."

"Come!" The colonel walked over to her, grabbed her roughly by the upper arm, and started steering her back toward the battered jeep.

"What? You're not leaving me here?"

He smirked. "And this is why women should not be

involved in military planning. There is no further need for that. Your live report convinced them that you were here, and the satellite undoubtedly confirmed it. They may see us move you, but they won't take the chance that it's permanent. If they shoot now, they must do so believing that they will kill you."

1800 Local (+5 GMT)
USS Jefferson

The ocean churned against the carrier, disrupted in its orderly sea state two march toward the coast by the presence of the massive gray hull. While the carrier barely deigned to acknowledge the long, slow swells, the SEALs Special Forces boat tethered to the aft landing platform was another matter.

"Catch." Sikes heaved his backpack down into the boat, flexed his knees, and leaped lightly from the stable carrier into the pitching boat. He took the impact mostly in his knees, consciously keeping his body loose and relaxed as he hit, sticking the landing like an Olympic gymnast.

"Catch, yourself," Huerta snapped, thrusting the pack out toward him. "Back in the old days—"

"I know, I know—you weren't sissies back then," Sikes interrupted, taking the pack. He slipped his arms through the strap, buckled the waistbelt, then turned back up to face the admiral on the platform. "We're ready, Admiral."

Batman nodded. "Get some good pictures. I want to be able to send something home besides postcards from the ship's store."

"You've got it, sir." Sikes turned to the rest of the boat crew and assessed their readiness one last time. Everything was on board—it had to be. There was no running back to camp during the middle of a mission to retrieve forgotten batteries or repair parts for neglected equipment. Satisfied with the still, taut readiness he saw in his teammates, he made a sharp hand motion to the coxswain.

The low thrum of the engine increased slightly, but not much, since every orifice was sound-muffled. The engine noise was barely audible over the sound of water slapping against the carrier, but that would change all too soon. As soon as they put some distance between themselves and the massive mother ship, every decibel of noise would increase the possibility that they would be detected.

Sikes turned back toward the carrier, snapped off a last sharp salute at the admiral, then settled into his seat. There was no need for further orders. The mission had been thoroughly briefed, just as thoroughly talked through and committed to memory. The team was working like a well-oiled machine.

Twenty minutes later, they were four thousand yards off the coast of Cuba. The sky was just starting to darken in the east, and shadows were creeping away from the buildings he saw ashore. A few guards walked the pier, and there was little chance that they hadn't seen the gunboat. Would they do anything about it? That was the key question. Their best estimate had been no. The Cubans weren't likely to want to provoke an incident just then.

Fine. So much the better. As soon as he established for certain that the Cubans had seen them, they'd head back to the carrier.

And if the Cubans began mobilizing to repel a SEAL force coming ashore on the southern coast of Cuba, even better. Because coming ashore there was the last thing any one of them intended.

2300 Local (+5 GMT)
Fuentes Naval Base

Pamela had just started dozing when the sound of her door opening snapped her awake. She resisted the temptation to rub at her eyes, tried to discipline her face into an expression of watchfulness. The last thing she wanted was for the Cuban men to suspect she was tired.

But, oh, Lord, wasn't she? The last few days, the constant travel at night, the confrontation with the colonel earlier today at the missile launcher—it had all taken its toll. After the brutal execution of her cameraman, she'd slipped into a state that wasn't quite insanity or rationality. It was somewhere in between, a state that mostly consisted of waiting for the world to deal out its next brutal shock.

The colonel stepped into the room, as sharp and nattily dressed as he'd ever been. The hours that had passed seemed to have had no effect on him, hadn't even darkened his jaw with a five o'clock shadow. She felt his eyes roam over her, note the wrinkles in her clothes and the expression in her face, and she saw a trace of amusement.

"The waiting is almost over, madam." An odd note of formality was in his voice.

She stood, ignoring the odd popping in her left knee. "You're shooting the missiles?"

He shook his head. "No, certainly not. I've told you before, Cuba is a peaceful nation. No, it is your countrymen— they're planning on coming ashore. I want you to be there to witness it."

"How—?"

He stepped into the room, walked slowly to her side, and

grasped her gently by the elbow, his fingers brushing across the bruises he'd left there earlier that day. "You'll know when we get there. Not before."

"My camera—," she began.

"Has been replaced, with a more reliable operator." A small sneer tugged at his lips. "You, my dear, are professional enough to work around any technical flaws, I hope."

"But where are we going?"

"You'll see soon enough."

"Here it is," he said as the jeep ground to a shuddering halt. "Move quietly. No more surprises."

Covering ten miles along the rough, potholed roads in an ancient jeep without any apparent suspension had taken its toll on her. Every muscle in her body felt as if it had been stretched past any reasonable limits, and her legs felt shaky as she tried to stand. She held on to the side of the jeep, took a deep breath, and tried to gather her strength before attempting a few steps.

"Our conditions are too rough for you?" he inquired solicitously. "But surely you can continue another hour or so? Especially since this is the most significant story since Desert Storm." He put one hand out to steady her.

She jerked away. "I'm fine," she said. Her voice was strong, belying her weariness. "But you still haven't explained what we're here for."

He turned away from her, pointing out to sea, deliberately exposing his back to her. "There. They'll come ashore from that direction."

"Who will?"

"SEALs, I think. Or maybe Rangers. Either one—it will be Special Forces of some sort."

"How do you know?"

He turned back to her. With an air of infinite patience, he

spread his hands out in front of him, palms up. "Because they were sighted to the south earlier this evening," he said slowly, as though explaining to a child. "All of our forces on alert there saw them."

She shook her head, trying to clear out the cobwebs and make sense of his words. If the Special Forces had been sighted to the south, then why were they expected here? It didn't make—she nodded as a trickle of adrenaline energized her thought processes. Of course. What had Tombstone always told her? That the best operation begins with an effective deception.

"So they won't come ashore there," she said finally, starting to follow his reasoning. "Because they're very, very good at what they do. And if they intended to approach from that direction, they would not have been seen. Is that it?"

He nodded. "Perhaps you understand more than I believe. I will have to remember that." He turned back to his soldiers and rattled out a harsh stream of commands, the words barely understandable for the speed. She saw men move quickly in response, unpacking an array of equipment from the back of a deuce-and-a-half that had followed them down the rutted road. Metal stanchions, a bar of—lights, she realized suddenly. They were an older, less sophisticated version of the very setup she used when reporting from the field. But surely they wouldn't—

"I think you will be able to get some exceptional footage of this encroachment on Cuba's sovereign soil," he said, motioning to his aide. "Now let's get you in position. After all, what do they say in America? The show must go on."

2315 Local (+5 GMT)
SEAL Team RHIB

"Hurry up and get back before I run out of gas," the SEAL at the aft end of the boat grumbled.

Sikes glanced up at him from his position in the water, clinging to the side of the RHIB. "You know what the plan is. If we're not back in three hours, you scoot back to the carrier. You got that?"

"Yeah, yeah." The assent was perfunctory. Both men knew that, despite his orders, the SEAL would no more leave his station before the team returned than any one of them would leave a comrade ashore. Giving orders was one thing—making sure they were obeyed was another. And Sikes wouldn't have wanted it any other way.

"Let's go, then." Sikes slipped his mouthpiece into his mouth and let himself slip below the surface of the water. As the sea rushed up over his mask, he saw the dim forms of the rest of his squad forming around him. The only light was from dim stars overhead and the glowing combination watch and compass on each wrist.

They formed up quickly, each man conducting a last-minute check for safety on his partner, then broke into a single-file line to make their approach to shore. After the first few minutes, Sikes settled into the gentle rhythm. It was barely two miles inland, an easy swim in these waters with flippers and masks. The oxygen tank on his back would be more than enough. Getting in wasn't the problem—getting out was.

2345 Local (+5 GMT)
Fuentes Naval Base

"Colonel, I have them." The Cuban enlisted specialist spoke quietly, a note of excitement in his voice. He motioned toward his screen. "A heat spot."

Pamela followed the colonel over to the equipment mounted on the ancient jeep. "What are we looking at?" she asked.

"One of the latest advances in technology, my dear." He pointed to the small screen, which displayed various shades of gray. "It's a thermal imaging sensor. Superb for noting differences in the heat surface of the water."

"You can see swimmers?" She hated herself for asking the question as soon as she asked it. Of course they could—that was the purpose of this whole evolution.

The colonel reached out and gently touched four white spots on the screen. They almost looked like background noise, and it was only after extended observation that one became aware that they were consistently moving across the screen in a pattern and weren't part of the random noise generated in the moonless night by the cooling ocean. "Just one squad—more than enough for what they wished to accomplish."

"What are you going to do?" she asked calmly, dread trickling into her heart. She'd seen war, she'd seen conflict, and she'd seen death—and would again, if she ever survived this venture. But she'd never been on the other side, watching her countrymen cold-bloodedly murdered.

"You'll see." The Cuban colonel smirked. "It will not

involve casualties—not unless they provoke us by coming ashore. A peaceful, yet highly effective demonstration of Cuban military capabilities, one they will not forget quickly."

2355 Local (+5 GMT)
500 Yards off the Coast of Cuba

As the gentle swells turned to chop nearer to shore, the SEALs closed up again, pausing to take their bearings. According to each of their chronometers, they were exactly on course, creeping in toward land along the least guarded section of the coast. Another ten minutes and they'd be in.

Sikes motioned to his fellows to stay below water, and gently kicked himself up to the surface to take one last sighting. The landmarks were thoroughly embedded in his memory, as was every target point. Still, it never hurt to be certain.

He let his head poke up above the surface of the water, maintaining neutral buoyancy with gentle flicks of his flippers. He lifted himself up on the next swell and stared inland, trying to pinpoint the tall tower that was the first landmark. Within a few seconds, he knew he was fucked.

Lining the shore from one end of the insertion point to the other was light. Large headlights, as though a news crew were awaiting their arrival. And, after Grenada, he knew exactly what that was like.

Fifteen minutes later, they crowded back aboard the RHIB, tired, frustrated, and pissed beyond recovery. The peals of laughter and jeering from the crowd ashore just behind the lights still rung in their ears. Worse yet was the military band that had struck up martial music just as Sikes had poked his head above the water. And the fireworks.

They would hear the sound of laughter all the way back to the carrier, even after they were out of earshot.

NINE
Monday, 01 July

The morning was off to a bad start. Each one of the four men around the conference table had already heard from his civilian boss. The secretary of the Navy had been particularly unpleasant about the events off the coast of Cuba, since it was his service that was plastered across the early editions of *ACN News*. The live feed of the SEAL squad lurking in the shallow waters off the coast of Cuba, tracked by their thermal image and the blazing arrays of light along the coast, was already old news by the time most Americans were having their morning coffee. Personally, the secretary had agreed with the President—the marching band had been the worst part of it.

The reaction around the world had been immediate and vehement. There were too many small nations that had begged assistance from the United States, along with massive infusions of cash from the State Department, then immediately turned upon their supposed saviors as soon as a new, more repressive regime was installed. These nations' guilt over their inability to take care of themselves would transform itself immediately into righteous indignation that the United States would interfere with the political events of any country—their own included.

Still, the other chiefs of services refrained from commenting on the events. Each one of them knew that it could just as easily have been their own forces—the Army, the Rangers, the Marines, or even the elite Delta Force. That the SEALs, and by extension the Navy, were taking the brunt of world outrage was sheerly a matter of luck and timing.

While they might fight viciously among themselves over which service would win that high-visibility tasking, when the world united against them the Joint Chiefs of Staff stood firm. To admit to wrongdoing on the part of one service was to damn them all, and further jeopardized the fragile funding that kept a barely adequate core of forces in beans and bullets.

"They're there illegally," the Air Force chief of staff said finally. He looked off into the distance, avoiding eye contact with the chief of naval operations. "They've got no business being in Cuba."

"The First Amendment. I wonder if our founding fathers ever had this in mind," the Marine Corps chief of staff grumbled. "It's one thing to allow them to say anything they want in our own country, another matter entirely to be providing aid and comfort to the enemy."

The CNO nodded. "You won't get any argument from me. But like it or not, they're there. These days, the media's usually there before we are. You know that."

The Air Force chief of staff stirred restlessly in his chair. "Regardless, the question now is, what do we do?"

"We take the damned island! And keep it this time," the Army barked. "Damn it, if we—"

"Quit posturing, Carl," the Marine Corps snapped. "We tried that before, remember?"

"Hardly. The Army didn't head up the Bay of Pigs fiasco, the CIA did. Besides, this isn't at all similar."

"And why not?" the Air Force asked. "Missiles sitting on the ground, capable of striking the continental United States, foreign support for a repressive regime—if that's not similar, I don't know what is."

The four men fell silent, each lost in his own thoughts. All were well schooled in the history of war, and the parallels to the Cuban Missile Crisis could not be avoided. Each one of them knew in his heart that if the military had been in charge of that operation, the results would have been different. Indeed, the present situation might have been avoided altogether if the United States had just done the right thing the first time through.

"You know what we're going to have to advise the President," the Marine Corps chief of staff said, finally breaking the unpleasant, heavy silence that had descended on them. "We've got to follow through."

The CNO shook his head. "We'll endanger civilian lives. Reporters, even. How are we going to explain that to the American public?"

"We're not. The President is." The Marine Corps officer looked stubborn. "We've got to draw the line somewhere. We can't be protecting Americans in every rinky-dink rogue state in the world if they insist on going there illegally. Weighing the cost and the benefits and the correlation of forces, we can't allow those weapons to remain in Cuba. Not aimed at our cities."

The chairman glanced around the room, taking the measure of each man. He saw agreement on every face, coupled with reluctance and a knowing dread for the situation that would surely follow. "I see we're in agreement. You know," he added unnecessarily, "there will be civilian casualties."

The looks of resignation deepened. "How do you want to weaponeer this?" the CNO said. He sighed heavily. "We're on station, of course. And I think we'd all rather the shots weren't fired from the continental U.S."

The chairman stood suddenly, his mind made up. "I'll speak with the President this afternoon. My recommendation will be a surgical strike against those weapon sites. Rather than risk an aircrew and aircraft, I'm prepared to recommend that we use your Arsenal ship." He managed to eke out a wry smile. "It's about time it got an operational test, don't you think?"

"But not like this," the CNO said softly. "Not like this."

1400 Local (+5 GMT)
USS Arsenal
Fifty Miles North of Cuba

The ship cut cleanly through the light chop, making twenty-five knots with only one of her powerful gas turbine engines on-line. On both the fore and aft decks, sailors scampered over the hot nonskid painted-on steel, conducting weapons checks on the vertical launch hatches, dropping antennas and guardrails, and generally securing anything loose on the ship that might be damaged by the firing of a weapon.

On the bridge, Captain Daniel Heather paced back and forth, stopping only occasionally to take a hurried swig from the ever-present coffee cup perched on the ledge next to his chair. Captain Heather was a tall man, powerfully built, darkly tanned from hours of skiing and fishing. Dark blond hair, clipped short but still managing to look unruly, topped sharp features and ice blue eyes.

Captain Heather had tried sitting down, tried staying in

Combat, but found himself unable to stay away from the bridge. From his very first tours at sea, even before potent Aegis ships and combat control systems shifted the heart of the ship from the bridge to Combat, his station had always been here. Now, even under current combat doctrine, he found the familiar routines of navigating and conning the ship reassuring. All too soon, as the ship took station within her firing basket, he'd find himself relegated to controlling the operation from Combat.

It still seemed unnatural, even after his two tours on Aegis cruisers, to be so far from air and light and targets and to watch the battle take place on a large TV screen instead of along the horizon.

Besides, being on the bridge gave him room to pace, a way of working off the nervous energy he always felt at sea. His officers and crew encouraged it—it made him easier to live with.

He felt the bridge team getting nervous, could see it in the small movements they made adjusting equipment that didn't even need to be touched, in the snapping of a pencil point by the navigator on a chart, in the insistent queries to Engineering to reassure themselves that all was well with the main propulsion. He wasn't helping any, he knew. His nervousness was transmitting itself to them, adding on to the worries of the present tactical situation. With a sigh, he forced himself to slide into the large brown leatherette captain's chair located on the starboard side of the bridge, made himself prop his feet up on the window ledge and finish the cup of coffee calmly. It had an immediate effect on him.

"Thirty minutes," the officer of the deck said.

The captain finished sipping on his coffee, swallowed, and then made a point of not answering immediately. "Be good to see the ship actually work," he said finally, his voice determinedly casual.

"Yes, Captain, it will." The OOD seemed on the verge of unbending, of saying more, but then fell silent.

That's what we're here for, you know," the captain said, raising his voice without seeming to so that every member of the bridge crew could hear. "We're saving lives. No aircrews shot down, no SAR missions, just ordnance on target." He took another sip of coffee, silently assessing the impact of his words. "We don't want to do *too* well, though. The aviators will be after our commands."

The small joke, which referred to the requirement under law that an aviator be in command of an aircraft carrier, provoked a flurry of nervous chuckles from the crew. None of them would have put it past the naval aviators. Not at all.

The OOD cleared his throat. "Captain, they're asking for you in Combat. If it's convenient."

Captain Heather sighed. He drained the last of his coffee, climbed carefully down from his chair, and handed the empty ceramic mug to the quartermaster on watch. "Stick this in a drawer for me, will you? I'll be back up for a refill after we shoot."

The quartermaster nodded and wedged the cup between two volumes of *Dutton's Navigation* in the bookshelf behind him. "It will be right here where you can get to it, Captain."

It was odd, he thought as he strode back to Combat, how small things seemed to reassure the crew. The fact that he would soon be back on the bridge, having a refill on his cup of coffee, steadied them.

He wished it could do the same for him.

0900 Local (+5 GMT)
Fuentes Naval Base

The ancient Foxtrot diesel submarine moored to the pier was rust-streaked and battered. It had been five years since she'd last done anything more than turn over her engines on routine maintenance, longer than that since her last operational mission. A long-ago gift from the Soviet Union, she served mainly as a source of electrical power for other ships tied up at the pier, a naval war vessel in name only.

From the conning tower, a thick steel pipe rose ten feet in the air. In contrast to the rest of the submarine, it looked smooth and well maintained. Not unusual, given the fact that the rusted and corroded snorkel mast had been replaced the day before. As first one and then another of the Kolumna diesel engines kicked over, black smoke belched out of the mast, fouling the air around the submarine and settling in a fetid pool on top of the water. The line handlers standing along the pier choked and tried to cover their noses with wet cloths.

As the engineers warmed up the engines and adjusted the fuel mix feeding into them the exhaust gradually cleared. The gentle breeze wafted away most of the fumes, and the sailors soon grew accustomed to the smell of half-burnt diesel fuel.

Finally, three hours after she'd lit her first engine, with her batteries fully charged, the Foxtrot was ready. The sailors first singled up the lines, leaving only one set of Manila lines holding the Foxtrot to the pier. Then, following the orders of the officer in the conning tower, they cast off the remaining lines one by one. The roar of the diesel engines increased, vibrating through the steel mounts that bolted them to the decks, through the hull and the water around it.

Despite the noise, the fumes, and the somewhat unbelievable possibility that the Foxtrot would actually get under way and conduct a mission, each sailor watching her felt a stirring of national pride. No, it wasn't a Los Angeles attack class, not even a Soviet Union Victor SSN, but it was a submarine. And it was theirs. It didn't take a nuclear submarine to execute this most simple and ancient of naval missions—minelaying.

1430 Local (+5 GMT)
Joint Chiefs of Staff
Washington, D.C.

"The missile sites, obviously," the Army said decisively. "After all, that's what this entire conflict is about."

"Are you mad?" the Air Force argued. "Without proper satellite coverage, those civilian reporters could be right at ground zero. We'd never know it."

"We've been through this," the chairman snapped. "There are only two possible targets—the missile sites or the base itself."

"The missile sites," the CNO said. He pointed to the tactical display in front of them. The Arsenal ship, marked with its distinctive symbol, as well as the possible target sites were all cleanly laid out with distance vectors and estimated areas of damage shown. "It's a conventional weapon, not a nuke. With plenty of need for accuracy."

"The President wants to avoid killing our own people," the chairman said finally. "The only way we can be sure of that is to hit the ships and the pier. There's no indication that they're holding them there."

"They could be anywhere," the Air Force railed. "Our satellite—"

"It's the missile sites, of course," the Navy said wearily. He reached out one stubby finger and touched the red firing button. "And we'll do it from here."

0800 Local (+5 GMT)
United Nations

The room was decidedly frostier than it had been the previous week. Ambassador Wexler glanced around at the faces at the table, sighed, and tapped the note cards containing the gist of her speech on the podium in front of her. No, this wasn't going to be an easy sell. The broadcast from ACN had done its damage. Every nation there, even the ones that counted themselves as the United States' historical friends, was ready to believe the worst of the giant democracy to their north.

"I know you've all seen the broadcasts. What ACN has done is misinterpret the entire operation. What you saw was merely a reconnaissance mission, not the preliminary to a—"

"An invasion," the Cuban ambassador thundered. He shot to his feet as though rocket-propelled. He pointed a finger at her, righteous indignation blazing in his face. "You have wanted to for centuries, admit it. America covets Cuban soil. Well, you won't get it—not now, not then, not ever! You push us too far, Madame Ambassador, thinking we have no means to respond to your aggression. Well, the United States is not the only powerful country in the world. There are others who support our right to self-determination, our independence. Push us again—"

"Oh, stop this nonsense," she snapped, unable to contain herself any longer. "We know who your playmates are now. And if you think you'll find your new Libyan masters any easier to manipulate than your Soviet ones, you should reconsider carefully."

"Playmates! How dare you characterize an international diplomatic relationship such as ours as that of mere 'playmates'?"

The representatives of the other tiny nations glanced uneasily at one another. There was too much truth to what both sides were saying. None of them would have welcomed an armed, covert intrusion onto their own soil, and each could understand Cuba's outrage. Still, the presence of Libyan forces so near to their own soil had prompted more than one ambassador to call his or her sovereign. It was, at best, an uneasy waiting game—at worst, a powder keg rolling toward an open flame.

"You have long-range missiles in Cuba aimed at the United States," Wexler continued. "Don't think we'll tolerate this."

"If your missile strikes are as accurate and powerful as you believe, then there are no more missiles in Cuba," the Cuban ambassador shot back bitterly. "But I think such is not the case. Here," he continued, passing out enlarged photographs to the rest of the representatives, "this is what you hit. Armed men in painted faces coming ashore your country at night. Is that what we want from the United States?"

"And this is the reason!" Ambassador Wexler began passing around photos of her own. They lacked the dramatic intensity of the Cuban's, but they made a point. Even the representatives from the less sophisticated countries knew enough to identify the boxy structures captured in the satellite photo. "How many of you feel safe with these on Cuban soil?"

The meeting degenerated into charge and countercharge, with both sides claiming victory at the end of the argument. Really, it had been less a diplomatic effort than a barroom brawl.

As Wexler strode back toward her office, her entourage of aides and advisors trailing behind her, she thought back to the photograph the Cuban representative had flashed, and felt her anger grow again. There was a name for that sort of conduct, the media surprising military forces during the course of their operations in search of a story.

They called it the First Amendment. She called it treason.

TEN

Sunday, 30 June

0700 Local (+5 GMT)
The Pentagon

The Joint Chiefs of Staff gathered in the Tank, the strategic planning area into which every intelligence and tactical source provided direct feed. From the Tank, they could watch live satellite transmissions, tap into the database of any ship via high-frequency link, talk to the most remote two-man patrol in Bosnia.

The furnishings, luxurious by Department of Defense standards, couldn't disguise the tension hanging in the air. People moved quickly, rapping out orders and requests for information, studying green automated tactical displays, trying to anticipate what one piece of information their bosses would want. As the chiefs convened, the operational pace crescendoed to near panic.

The chiefs gathered at the round table, helped themselves to coffee or tea or their beverage of choice. A small refrigerator remained fully stocked. They exchanged pleasantries, trying to ward off the inevitable.

Even if they'd been inclined to, the fact that this was an election year made it almost impossible for the President to fail to act. Their only option at this point was providing the

President with a range of alternatives the military thought
they could win.

"Sunday. Why does it always happen on the weekend?"
the Air Force chief of staff grumbled. He stirred two sugars
into the heavy mug of black coffee. "What, no latte again?"

"I don't suppose we could persuade all of our enemies to
plan their operations around our schedule?" The chief of
naval operations was generally the most irreverent of the
group, capable of finding a wry or sardonic side to almost
every issue. Had his advice not always been so damnably
well thought out, the others would have been tempted to
ignore him.

"The Cubans aren't our enemies," the chairman snapped.

"Could've fooled that pilot," the CNO responded.

"And this isn't a war, is it?" said the Army chief of staff,
finally speaking up. "Could get a lot of people killed,
though, couldn't it? If we have to go in on the land, that is."

"Look, let's put the bickering aside for a minute," the
chairman ordered. "We can posture all we want to, but you
know we're going in. We have to." He scanned the table,
saw the agreement on each face—reluctant on the Army's
part, eager on the Air Force's, and decidedly neutral on the
Navy's.

"Any guidance from the boss?" Navy asked.

The chairman shook his head. "He wants options. That's
what we'll give him. Right now, I'm leaning toward using
the Arsenal ship." The expressions on the faces around him
mirrored the political maneuvering that continually went on
between all the services. The Air Force chief of staff looked
as if he was about to speak, to start lobbying for a significant
role for Air Force tactical bombers. Navy looked slightly
disgruntled. The Arsenal ship had been forced down his
throat over his protests that while it was a fine platform, he
had better uses for the money. Like training. Like aviation

fuel. Like diesel fuel to get his ships out of port and at sea, where they belonged, training and practicing for eventualities they hoped would never come. The Army simply looked envious. The lack of organic air support capable of carrying out the increasingly popular cruise missile attacks ate at him.

"Sounds like it's been decided already to me," the Navy grumbled. "I'll get my people started on a target list."

The chairman held up a hand. "Won't be necessary. Most of the target packages will be decided at the White House."

"The White—damn it, we can't go backward, not on this issue." The chief of naval operations stood abruptly. "You know what it did to us during Vietnam. Political control of military objectives simply gets men killed. Men and women," he amended quickly. "There's not a one of us sitting at this table that doesn't remember how it worked then."

"Bothers you to be out of the loop, is that it?" the Air Force asked. A slight smile crossed his face.

The CNO wheeled on him. "That's not the point and you know it. If it were *your* forces on the line, you'd be going ballistic. But you let this start now, with this ship, and you'll be fighting the same battle next time there's a ground war."

"The Navy's always been too damned independent," the Army shot back.

"Gentlemen!" The chairman's voice was the cold crack of a whip. "We stand united on this. Is that clear?" All of the other chiefs bristled. No one spoke to them like that, at least within their respective organizations. No one.

"The next thing you'll be telling me is that the President will be pushing the buttons himself," the CNO said at last, to break the deadly silence. "Is that about it?" He looked appalled as the chairman nodded in agreement.

"The President will be here for all the major portions of

the attack. It's the low-risk option." Every one of his audience could translate that. It meant that with the ship shooting the missiles, there was no chance of an aircraft being downed, no possibility of an American airman being paraded through the streets of Cuba as a prisoner. During this election year, that would be completely unacceptable.

"I've got a two-star out there," the CNO said. "Magruder—good man. Lots of combat experience."

"Let's hope we won't need that, but it's good to have him on-scene if we do," the chairman said. "For now, though, you can plan on most of the major decisions being made here."

As the meeting broke up and the men wandered back toward their respective evening offices, the CNO was grim. Why was it that his country felt compelled to repeat major operational art lessons they'd learned in previous wars? Couldn't they learn? And the chairman's easy capitulation when he knew—damn it, *knew* better. He felt a sick anger welling up again. Politics, the chairman's loyalty to the man who'd approved his appointment—where did you draw the line between honor and one's career?

And as for Magruder—well, he knew how he would have felt if he'd been the two-star on scene. This would have looked like a vote of no-confidence, not a political opportunity. He'd better call Magruder right away to make sure he got the news first. No telling how much damage one pissed off two-star could do during an election year.

0845 (+5 GMT)
The Senate Floor

"It's all set."

Dailey looked up to see Senator Williams leaning across

his desk, resting one hip casually on the corner. Behind them, a junior senator was lecturing the scattered crowd on the merits of easing restrictions on the processing of bee pollen. The only people paying attention were two bee pollen lobbyists seated in the upper tiers.

"I don't know about this," Senator Dailey said uneasily. "I remember it . . ."

"You remember which side your bread is buttered on," Williams said sharply. "Nothing else matters right now. You blow this, and every shipbuilder in your district is going to be screaming for your ass. You got that?" His voice was pitched low, and did not reach to bee pollen advocate who continued to drone on. "It's the Arsenal-ship show. JCS has already bought off on it, so get with the program."

Dailey nodded uneasily. He got it. And he hoped the only result would be the tarnishing of his own opinion of himself, that one more small compromise to political inevitability that he'd sworn he wouldn't make.

0900 Local (+5 GMT)
United Nations

Ambassador Wexler surveyed the faces arrayed at the round table. A wide range of colors were represented, ranging from the deep, purple-black of the Bahamian ambassador through the light, coffee-colored ambassador from Antigua to the barely diluted coffee color of the Cuban. So many cultures, so many nations—and all gathered with one purpose in mind. Or, she amended silently, at least the majority of them were. None of the small nations that dotted the Caribbean wanted conflict between their northern patron, the United States, and their cultural kin, the Cubans. If pushed, they would come down on her side, she decided. But the cost would be high. Too high, perhaps.

"We have two points to make. First, we must be allowed to inspect the wreckage of the fishing boat," she said firmly. Behind her, her aides rustled nervously, passing back and forth the reams of paper, documents, and incomprehensible multinational studies that were the lifeblood of the organization. "Our deep-diving rescue resources have the capability to recover parts of the wreckage if we move quickly, before the currents carry it too far away from the original site. Given the events of the last weeks, we are not prepared to accept Cuba's unilateral assertion that our forces were responsible for the loss of the fishing vessels, particularly not when we show that no weapons have been extended by any of our aircraft. Without independent verification, it is difficult to arrive at a final analysis of the situation. Second, we will not recognize Cuba's illegal and provocative no-fly zone and we require the return of the American pilot being held there." She paused and waited for the storm to break over her.

"Independent? You claim that role for the United States? *You* are the ones responsible. No one else." The Cuban ambassador paused to suck in a deep breath and glare at her. "The very audacity is—"

"Entirely within our rights," she interrupted calmly. "Under circumstances such as this, we have opened our records at all times to United Nations scrutiny. It is more than reasonable to expect you to do the same."

"As though you need to inspect it," he shot back bitterly. "How many years of study has the United Nations devoted to determining the best way to decimate our poor nation? We, who only want to be left alone to reach our own glorious future . . ."

And who desperately need new trading partners, she noted.

". . . to pursue our own great destiny and historic traditions of . . ."

Tyranny and oppression, building a nation of poverty by stripping out its national resources for the exploitation of the already rich.

". . . our role in the Caribbean is one of . . ."

Fomenting hatred and dissension among your neighbors.

". . . peaceful coexistence with the other island nations. We would extend that same offer of friendship to the United States, but your politics have . . ."

Prevented you from growing rich on the backs of your wretched workers while simultaneously providing sanctuary to the dregs of your society. Thugs, criminals, the diseased and insane. All dumped on our shores. There were, she decided, studying him carefully, advantages to having the United States as a close neighbor, no matter the posturing of Cuba's ambassador.

". . . a truly independent commission, one not tainted by American influences and interests. Composed, perhaps, of nations strong in the rest of the world, areas in which the United States does not bully and strut, thrusting herself into every affair as though anointed of God."

"And you would propose . . . ?" She let the sentence trail off delicately, knowing that the words were a mistake as soon as they left her mouth.

"Algeria, Libya, Iran, perhaps the Saudis. And, of course, our friends in South Africa."

"To summarize, any nation with whom we have had a conflict in the last twenty years," she said sharply. "No, I think there are better choices. The Swiss, perhaps."

The Cuban ambassador sneered. "The ones who hide so much of your money illegally?"

The debate, she knew, would continue for hours. Neither side would get what it wanted, and in the end, the truth would be hidden even deeper within layers of administrative demands, reckless proclamations, and finger-pointing. Cuba would continue to maintain that America had destroyed the aircraft, intervening in Cuba's sovereign airspace. The U.S., however, knew that it had been a strictly internal affair.

Furthermore, there was no way she could use the one trump card she'd already privately played with the Cuban ambassador. The presence of nuclear weapons on Cuban soil—she shivered slightly, then regained control of herself. To give details and provide proof would simply reveal too much about America's intelligence capabilities. Like many bits of intelligence, this one was simply too dangerous to use.

Was there any hope for this process? There were days when she wondered. But still, all in all, the United Nations beat hands-down other forms developed for resolving conflict. Answers were slow, cumbersome, and often unworkable, but they represented the best intentions of the nations brought to bear on difficult and insoluble problems. And for that reason, she stayed.

She turned to the Bahamian chairman of the committee and lifted one hand in a gesture of resignation. "We are open to any reasonable proposal, but none has been tendered yet. I ask you, Mr. Ambassador, as well as the other nations represented here"—she glanced around the table, catching each set of eyes in turn—"what you think we can achieve. I beg you to reason with your neighbor to the west."

Antigua and the Bahamas looked away, the blush barely visible on the Antiguan ambassador.

"You couldn't have been serious about it?" the British ambassador queried. "I mean, really," he finished, drawing the last word out in a patrician accent. "We know those people, of course. Colonies for years. Never should have let them declare independence—weren't ready for it, won't be for centuries." He shook his head. "You recall, the United States supported that."

"Cut the crap, Geoffrey," she said wearily. She reached across the table and fished another of the small, soft rolls out of the woven basket between them. "It won't help things now. What I need is answers, not more problems."

"Sometimes I see this relationship as strangely familial," he said. He pushed the small china dish containing the freshly churned butter toward her. "We're your older brother, of course, always there with advice and a bit of guidance when you chaps need it."

"Would you like me to beg?"

He shook his head, a smile twitching at the corners of his normally impassive mouth. "Not this time. But I reserve the right to remind you of this conversation later."

She nodded. "You know we didn't do it."

"Of course not. Play bloody hell with the rest of the world, though, convincing them." The British ambassador glanced around the room, as though looking for their waiter. "They're all watching now, you know. Every last bloody one of them."

"Tell me about Europe." She saw him stiffen slightly at her bluntness, and was amused. Surely he was used to it by now, after all his years in the United States. Still, Geoffrey never passed up a chance to be thoroughly and totally British in front of her.

"It won't be good," he said, matching her bluntness. "You may have embargoed trade, but many of us still enjoy the best cigar the world has to offer. Among other things— sugar, of course."

"It's in our backyard," she pointed out.

"And our backyard economically," he countered. "Naturally, you'll have our support, publicly and privately. I suspect Her Majesty wishes that you would just bloody well invade, solve the whole matter once and for all. Tiresome, this nattering back and forth. Ah, our food." His face brightened as he saw the waiter approach. "Famished, absolutely famished."

"What if we started giving you guidelines on how to resolve the Irish question?" she said quickly before the waiter arrived. She was silent while the waiter arranged her salmon salad in front of her, carefully setting a small flask of vinaigrette at the left-hand side of her plate. She waited until he'd left before continuing. "I suspect that we'd suggest that you simply quit forcing the issue, withdraw your troops, and let the status quo remain. Or even yield to Ireland."

"Never. To both your solution and your intervention." He looked up from the neatly boiled stuffed flounder to shoot her a piercing gaze. "You wouldn't dare."

"But the Cuba question is much easier than that, isn't it?"

Finally, she saw him give up. "You asked me for my advice, and I'll give you what I know. Europe will be most distraught. Do not count on automatic support from all the Allies. Cuba is an important trading partner to some, and there's a large reservoir of anti-American sentiment still fomenting about the Continent. The Cuban Missile Crisis, all that sort of stuff"—he dismissed it with an airy wave of his hand—"mere recent history. Nothing to compare with many nations' conflicts. You won't find much sympathy there, not with U.S. weapons still on European soil."

"So what do we do?"

"Proceed very carefully. Very, very carefully, and play this very close to the vest." His expression suddenly turned somber. "It's not all that difficult to damage a warship, you know. Learned that in the Falklands. Primitive mines and rusting diesel submarines are deuced cheap solutions to a pesky little aircraft carrier or two. The last thing the United States needs right now is international embarrassment over a successful attack on one of her warships. Bear that in mind, Sarah."

The unexpected use of her first name jarred her for a moment, then she assessed it for what it was—a diplomatic exclamation point, a way of insuring he had her total and complete attention, as well as conveying the close and personal support the United States would always enjoy from Great Britain. It was a familiarity that encompassed a compliment, as well as an expression of trust. "Have you heard anything?" she asked, suddenly suspicious.

He shook his head. "I don't need to."

0955 Local (+5 GMT)
USS **Jefferson**

"Welcome aboard, Admiral," Batman said, taking two quick strides toward his old lead. "Good to see you again, sir."

Tombstone grasped the other man's hand in a hard, warm grip. Life on board the USS *Jefferson* looked like it was taking its toll on his old wingman. A touch of gray, some lines around the corners of his eyes that hadn't been there a year earlier.

Still, the changes were more than physical; he could see it in Batman's eyes. There was a new air of security and determination, the kind of command presence that only comes from single-handedly wielding the most powerful assets in the United States military inventory.

Commanding the squadron—now, that had been sheer

pleasure. A chance to finally shape a group of disparate people from an array of backgrounds into a single fighting force. But command of a carrier group was different, both in purpose and in its span of responsibility. Batman would have had to make the same shift he had, from a tactical perspective concentrating on fighter furballs and enemy weapons' envelopes to a broader viewpoint. An operational viewpoint, one step above and encompassing tactics. It was a tricky transition, and some never made it. He'd known admirals who'd never gotten past that tactical focus, never been able to successfully integrate tactics to execute strategy, the heart of operational art.

And it was an art, not a science. It never would be, not as long as wars were started by people—and ended by them.

"We've set aside the VIP quarters for you," Batman said carefully. Tombstone felt Batman's eyes searching his face for any sign of disapproval. "Of course, my own quarters are always at your disposal."

Tombstone waved aside Batman's concerns. "No, you stay just where you are. You're still in command of this carrier battle group, Admiral Wayne. You remind me if I forget that." The corner of his mouth twitched. On any other man's face, the movement would have been meaningless, but it was as close to a smile as Batman had ever seen Tombstone sport in public.

Some tension melted out of Batman's face. "Maybe we'll have a chance later to discuss exactly how you would like this task force organized, Admiral. My people have a couple of ideas."

"I'd welcome their help," Tombstone said quietly. He let his eyes drift back to survey the faces arrayed behind Batman. "Bird Dog," he said. "You're still on board?"

The young lieutenant commander shifted uneasily. "I'm back, sir. I spent a year at the War College. Just reported back on board two months ago." He hesitated as though about to add something, then fell silent.

"This is right up your alley, then. You make sure you share that expensive education with the rest of the staff, understand?"

Two years earlier, when Tombstone had had command of this very carrier battle group, Bird Dog had been a nugget pilot. Events had thrust him into the thick of the combat in the Spratly Islands, and later he'd played point man in a careful game of cat and mouse over the Aleutian Islands. Yes, Tombstone thought, studying Bird Dog's face, still young, still feeling his way through this mess. His first staff tour, of course, and he's anxious to make a good impression. And, remembering his own tour of staff, not getting enough flight time. Tombstone let his eyes move on, careful to keep any trace of his thoughts from showing in his face. He greeted other staffers by name, reestablishing the bonds that had once drawn them together.

Finally, he turned back to Batman. "You got some time to talk?"

"At your disposal, of course, Admiral."

Tombstone took a quick step closer to him and spoke in a low voice pitched for his ears only. "Don't be polite, Batman, I know this job almost as well as you do. If you've got stuff that needs doing, let me know. We owe each other that much courtesy, don't we? After all we've been through together?"

The final traces of nervousness melted away from Batman's face. "Now would be very convenient, Admiral."

1130 Local (+5 GMT)
Five Miles North of Cuba

The small tugboat churned through the gentle waves like a thrashing, injured fish. She was bow on to the swells now, making steady headway but heeling from port to starboard in a rapid motion designed to discomfort all but the strongest stomachs. Waves battered her gunwales and the deck was slippery and damp from condensing spray and early morning mist.

It had been dark when she had left port, the sky obscured by the perpetual mist and fog. Later, as the sun had burned it away, the sailors had peeled off their shirts and donned hats, weathered brown backs giving evidence of their experience with this climate.

This mission was more important than fishing for tuna, or pursuing any of the myriad activities that they used to supplement the income generated by their legitimate occupation. Jaime Rivera, the master of the vessel, stood in the pilot house, staring aft at the small contingent of Cuban navy officers on board. So like them, the arrogance with which they'd commandeered his vessel. The drug running, the smuggling, or even the normal routines of trolling for fish were merely memories now. The officers had arrived at 0500, in a battered, rusted jeep. Two deuce-and-a-half trucks, on their last set of brakes and their suspension springs merely a distant memory, had followed.

Their cargo had been quickly loaded onto the aft of the fishing boat and then covered with canvas. What had been a surprisingly precise arrangement of mines was now a massive, dirty tan lump occupying most of the fantail.

"Now," the officer in the pilothouse ordered. "We are at the first position."

Rivera nodded. It would do him no harm to make friends with the naval officers, people who might one day in the future look the other way at just the most opportune moments. No, despite the loss of immediate profits, it was worth complying with these requests.

As though he had any choice.

He stepped outside of the pilot house to the aft weather deck and shouted down at his men. A Cuban military officer accompanied each one of them and carefully supervised the operation.

It should be more difficult than this, he thought, watching the massively muscled sailors wrestle a mine out of its wooden crate and onto the deck. From there it was a short heft, two grunts, and a groan to heave it off the back of the ship. He watched the first one throw up a gout of seawater, drenching the men near the fantail.

"Five hundred meters, then another." The officer's voice was curt.

Rivera nodded, smiled pleasantly. "Coffee?" he asked politely, gesturing toward the large thermos sitting next to the chart table. "My wife made it this morning. Very strong."

The officer seemed to unbend slightly, and a flick of annoyance was replaced by a more neutral expression. "Thank you. It would be appreciated."

As he poured two mugs, one for each of them, Rivera thought that getting along with people was not so difficult after all. They were the same almost anywhere you went. And after a cold, damp morning on the water, anyone would welcome a hot cup of coffee, especially the dark and bitter brew his wife made.

"Five minutes," the officer said. "Perhaps if you perform

this mission satisfactorily, there will be others in the future. Ones that are much more lucrative. I have an uncle . . ."

Rivera sighed as the officer launched into a tale of the excellent cigars produced by his uncle that could not be marketed in the United States. An enterprising man, one who was willing to take a few risks, one who knew the waters—well, there were always possibilities. The master smiled, nodded, and began counting his profits. Smuggling cigars and other illegal cargo into the United States was much more profitable than laying mines this close to an aircraft carrier.

1300 Local (+5 GMT)
USS Jefferson

Lieutenant Commander Charles Dunway, company operations officer on board *Jefferson* and senior surface warfare officer on board the ship, glanced nervously over at the glassed-in bridgeway on the starboard side of the ship. The captain and the XO, along with the most senior aviation officer on the ship, were gathered there discussing the intricacies of underway replenishment. Aside from flight operations, it was perhaps the most dangerous evolution the ship engaged in. Making the approach on the oiler, easing up on her from behind seen parallel, exactly matching course and speed with the smaller ship with only 180 feet separating the two vessels was never a routine operation.

At least not to the surface ship sailors. He snorted in disgust. The aviators, though—that was a different matter.

Aviation captains followed two career paths in their quest to accumulate stars on their collars. After a tour as a squadron commanding officer, they shifted their focus to being assigned as either the commanding officer of an aircraft carrier or as carrier air wing commander, both senior captain billets. Of the two, command of an aircraft carrier was the preferred track to the stars. But that meant completing the Navy's grueling Nuclear Power School, as well as prototype reactor training in Idaho. Along the way, the aviator was expected to become at least minimally proficient in ship handling, and that meant taking the conn of an aircraft carrier during underway replenishment.

For surface sailors, conning the ship through an underway replenishment operation meant careful coaching from their own commanding officer and close scrutiny every moment the ship was tied up alongside the oiler. The evolution was intricately orchestrated, and the surface warrior's tendency to sweat the details was profoundly in evidence.

Not so with aviators. They figured that if they'd managed to live that long during formation flights at Mach 1, they damned well sure could coach an aircraft carrier through an underway replenishment op at fifteen knots.

No memorizing the standard commands, turning radiuses, and knots per turn of the shaft. No, not for them. All of the important details were written down on a three-by-five card and passed from one to the other as each took his turn at the conn.

Generally, senior surface officers aboard the ship casually turned up on the bridge, keeping a close eye on the evolutions that their seniors in rank—but not in experience—strived to master. It was never an overt thing, no. The touchy ego of a jet jock would hardly tolerate supervision by a surface warfare officer, but Dunway damned well knew he felt better being belowdecks when his colleagues were keeping a careful eye on the Airedales.

At least it wouldn't happen on his watch. The underway replenishment was scheduled for 2100 that night, long after he would have gone off duty. This was merely a briefing session to make sure all of the jet jocks could find their way to the bridge and successfully locate the glassed-in area from which they would supervise the evolution. He sighed. Life just wasn't fair.

He looked forward and stared at the ocean in front of the carrier. The seas were running light today, maybe a sea state of two or so, he estimated. Just a few whitecaps, enough to make every detail of the swells visible. Not that heavy seas would have bothered *Jefferson*—she was capable of launching aircraft and fulfilling her missions in all but hurricane-force winds and seas. Even then, the ship would be in no danger, unlike her smaller brethren.

"Sir! Ready to commence flight operations." Dunway turned toward the conning officer, who had just received that notification from the air boss.

"Very well. Any contacts in the area?"

The conning officer shook his head. "A few small pop-up contacts to the south, that's about it. Our current course puts us with thirty knots of wind across the deck at zero-zero-zero relative."

Ideal winds for flight operations. The extra wind across the deck would give all aircraft the additional lift they needed to get airborne off the cat shot. Any more, and they might have control problems immediately after the shot; any less, and the heavier aircraft such as the Tomcats wouldn't be happy.

"Very well," he repeated, and turned back to the SPA-25G radar repeater located in the middle of the bridge. He was certain the conning officer had checked with Combat, but it never hurt to verify the tactical situation oneself.

It was as the conning officer had said. There were two intermittent contacts to the south, carefully annotated and being tracked by the junior officer of the deck, who was standing nervously at his side, white grease pencil clutched in his sweaty palm.

Up ahead, the sea looked clear. Excellent. While a fine ship, even if under the command of aviators, *Jefferson* was hardly as nimble and maneuverable as her battle group escorts. The 120,000 tons of steel took more than a few minutes to veer from her course. While she would be flying the Foxtrot pennant to indicate she was conducting flight operations, thus giving her the right-of-way over other ships on the ocean, it was common for smaller foreign vessels to ignore the danger signs. He wondered sometimes at the sanity of the other ships and boats, tracking nonchalantly and brazenly across her path. Didn't they realize that this ship could no more avoid them than a train could stop in time to miss a car parked on the tracks directly ahead? Something caught his attention on the screen, and he looked back down at it. What was it—there. A small fleck of green flickered dead ahead. He frowned and motioned to the JOOD—Junior Officer of the Deck. "What's that?"

"It's not very solid for a contact, is it?" the ensign said, nervousness in his voice. "Combat's not reporting anything."

"Don't rely on Combat," Dunway said sharply. "That's why we have a repeater here—two sets of eyes are always better than one. Get on the horn and ask them what they're seeing on raw video."

The JOOD nodded and reached for the toggle switch to the bitch box. He posed the question to the senior officer in Combat and waited for a reply, tapping his fingers nervously on top of the gray box that housed the interior communications circuits. Finally, he looked back at Dunway. "Combat says it might be a contact."

A shrieking roar rose from the flight deck nine stories below them. An aircraft—a Tomcat, by the sound of it—turning on the catapult. With a green deck and permission to launch aircraft, the air boss had moved ahead smartly. Dunway had only seconds left to stop it. He lunged for the bitch box.

It wasn't enough time. Just as his hand touched the toggle switch, he heard the roar increase, then the sound of an aircraft accelerating down the catapult. It was followed four seconds later by the gentle thump of the steel piston ramming against the stops in the bow as the aircraft broke free of the shuttle and was hurled into the air. He looked over the small ledge that ran around the ship immediately under the windows and saw a Tomcat dip down out of view briefly, then rise up to grab altitude and speed.

"Red deck!" He turned the toggle switch loose without explanation. That phrase alone would stop all flight operations until they had a chance to ascertain whether or not there was a contact immediately in their path.

He turned to look for the JOOD. The young man had disappeared from beside the radar repeater and was standing in the port bridge wing, binoculars glued to his eyes. Dunway saw his face turn pale. The JOOD dropped the binoculars, turned, and shouted, "Small vessel dead ahead, sir!"

"What's her course?" He hoped against hope that it would clear their path by the time they got to it.

"Bearing constant, range decreasing. She's bow-on to us, sir."

"Hard right rudder." Dunway whirled toward the conning officer. "Now, mister!"

The conning officer repeated the order, uncertain as to exactly why it had been given but instantly knowing this was no time for discussion. Dunway stepped behind the helmsman, saw him spin the giant wheel quickly to the right to the stops.

Dunway moved forward again, positioning himself immediately underneath the course repeater located in the center of the ship overhead. He watched the needle, praying for it to move faster, knowing it wouldn't. Turning the ship, even at maximum rudder, was like maneuvering an office building.

He looked back ahead again. There. Finally visible to the naked eye, the small, rickety craft came into view. It was no more than a dot, a black mark against the blue waves and whitecaps. Dunway reached for his binoculars and held them to his eyes. A rust bucket. She was riding low on the water, an open vessel with no powerhouse or other cover in her. Little more than a lake boat, he would have thought. But jam-packed with people, hanging all over each other and even spilling over the sides to hold on to the gunwales, their legs dangling in the water. Badly overloaded, hardly seaworthy, and directly in their path.

He glanced back upward, saw the course repeater notch slowly to the right, gave another order. "Starboard engines, back full. Port engines, ahead full." The combination of a backing bell on the starboard shaft and a full-ahead bell on the port shaft would steepen their turn. Not by much this early in the evolution, but perhaps by enough.

But even engine orders aren't instantaneous. They were given to the lee helmsman, who relayed the command down to his counterpart in main Engineering. Then, the steam valves were slowly rotated to adjust the speed of the turbine on that shaft, again introducing a delay. Furthermore, the giant turbines that drove the four shafts of the ship did not respond instantaneously either. It all took time. Too much time.

"What the hell's going on?" the CO of the ship snapped.

When had he left the bridge wing, Dunway wondered. How long had he been standing there? The man's face was now suffused with rage, his training session interrupted and emergency maneuvers taking place on his bridge without his having been informed.

"Contact directly in our path, Captain," Dunway said quickly. He ran through the normal litany of course and speed, pointing the contact out to the captain, his eyes still fixed on the course repeater as it clicked over one more notch. Maybe enough—maybe not. If it weren't, it didn't matter what the captain of the ship thought of him. His career was dead.

The captain snapped his gaze forward, finally spotting the small craft. His jaw dropped. Dunway noted the look of horror on his face with sour satisfaction. It was time the aviators realized that life at twenty knots could be just as dangerous as life at Mach 1.

Dunway could see the faces now, make out the details of clothing and expressions. The ship was still turning.

Finally, as it drew closer, the small ship disappeared from view, the line of sight to it blocked by the massive flight deck. Had it been enough? Maybe, just barely. If it had been, the ship was just now scraping down the port side of *Jefferson*, a tiny gnat against the giant gray wall of the ship.

He wheeled on the operations specialist maintaining the plot board at the aft of the bridge. "Reports from lookouts?"

"Port lookout reports that—oh, dear, sweet Jesus." The man's voice trailed off. "Sir, we hit them."

1500 Local (+5 GMT)
Fuentes Naval Base

"You'll send the message now." Santana glared at Pamela Drake, daring her to defy his order.

"I won't." She remained seated, staring up at him. Even if she'd been standing, he would have towered over her, and she had no intention of allowing him to feel one iota of superiority. Best to stand her ground where she was. "You can't force me to broadcast this report. Not while I'm being held hostage. Aguillar *promised* me that I could report the facts as I saw them. Quite frankly, I'm a bit fed up with being shuttled around under guard."

Santana slammed his hand down on the table. "You are not in the United States, Miss Drake. We agreed to allow you to come here, but you were informed there would be certain restrictions on your ability to pursue matters independently. You took advantage of our hospitality, yet refused to acknowledge those conditions. Is this your idea of integrity?" He turned angrily away from her, staring out the window.

"I'll report the story, but not some trumped-up fabrication you've prepared for me. And without access to witnesses, the ability to see the story developing myself, I have no way of judging the truth of what you're telling me. You want your story told, fine—I'll tell it. But my own way."

Santana muttered something to his aide in a quick, staccato voice, the Spanish too rapid for her to follow. The aide nodded, walked out of the room, and returned shortly bearing a videotape. He inserted it into the VCR, turned the power on, then turned back toward Santana.

Santana wheeled on her. He pointed at the television screen. "Perhaps this will be a sufficiently important story for you to reconsider." He gestured at the aide, who punched the play button.

The picture started out grainy, then gradually resolved into a clear pattern of light and dark. As the cameraman found his focal length, the dark shape in the middle of the screen became a small boat crammed with people. It plowed

up and down the waves, rolling from side to side in the
gentle swells and threatening to capsize even in the relatively calm seas. The camera panned to the right and
refocused, and a large aircraft carrier came into view.

The shot was taken from almost sea level, and the ship
looked like a massive, towering gray cliff. The cameraman
zoomed in, focusing on the number on the side of the steel
superstructure jutting up from the flight deck, the island.

Pamela recognized the number immediately. The USS
Jefferson. Even if she hadn't known that it was on presence
patrols in the Caribbean, the hull number was indelibly
ingrained in her memory.

The camera panned back to the small boat. The people in
it now were standing up, gesturing, and Pamela could see
their mouths opening as they screamed. Panic—and as the
cameraman zoomed back to include both the aircraft carrier
and the small boat in one frame, she understood the reason
why. *Jefferson* was bearing down on the small boat with all
the inevitability and imponderability of an avalanche. In a
battle between two ships for right-of-way, tonnage always
wins, and there was no doubt in her mind as to the outcome
of this encounter.

As she watched, the distance between the two ships
gradually decreased. The *Jefferson*'s aspect changed, becoming slightly more bow-on to her, but still Pamela could
see that there was no way it could miss the other ship. She
imagined the panic that must be taking place on *Jefferson*,
as frantic in its own style as the terror of the people in the
small boat. To die, or to be responsible for others' deaths?
She knew which was worse.

It was like watching the O. J. Simpson car chase, with the
white Bronco rolling slowly down vacant interstates. Minutes passed, and if it had not been for the impending
tragedy, it would have been almost as boring.

Finally, the inevitable. *Jefferson*'s clean-cut bow rolled over the midsection of the small boat, cutting it cleanly in half. The damage drove the small ship underwater immediately, dumping the horde of passengers into the sea. She could see a few of them churning up, tiny white flecks next to the skin of the ship; then those too disappeared. It was over just seconds after it began.

The aide punched the stop button, freezing the video on the last scene. There was no evidence of the encounter in the curling water around *Jefferson*'s hull, in the gentle arc of the bow waves that rolled off her steel sides.

"You wish to see it again?" Santana asked. The aide began to rewind the tape.

She shook her head. "When did this happen?" she asked, grasping for details to avoid acknowledging the horror of what she'd just seen. "Where?"

"Just north of our coast. And the time? About two hours ago, I think. Maybe more." He regarded her sardonically, evil cruelty in his look. "Is that timely enough to be newsworthy for you, Miss Drake? I assure you, there is no other network in the world that will have firsthand coverage of this event. And the United States Navy's own message traffic will support the occurrence of the actual event. If you would like to wait for that, for some other network to attend a stateside briefing and scoop you on this matter, we will be glad to oblige. We had just thought . . ." He let his voice trail off delicately.

"No. I want it. It's something—it's something the American public needs to see." Already the words were taking shape in her mind, the damning indictment of Tombstone's old ship callously running down a group of people seeking freedom. She would get three minutes, maybe even four— the lead story, at any rate. Excerpts from the videotape, along with her narrated coverage, would be replayed hourly at the top of the hour until some other critical world event bumped it off the schedule.

Some small part of her mind kept insisting there was more to the story than this. The American ship must have tried to avoid the small boat; she'd seen that from the way the angle on the bow changed in the course of those few minutes. Tried, but hadn't been able to.

She knew from Tombstone's long discourses on operations at sea that small craft were difficult to detect, even harder sometimes to pick out from the ocean by visual observation. That was why the rules of the road gave the larger, less maneuverable ship the right-of-way in most circumstances.

The truth, but a rotten story. Atrocities sell better than tragedies. She'd learned that lesson years ago in Bosnia, in Desert Storm, in a thousand other combat venues around the world. No, even if she didn't report it this way, her competitors would. And their ratings would outstrip hers in a New York minute.

"Who took this video?" she said suddenly. Santana smiled. Her gut churned as she considered the full implications of the matter. Not only had *Jefferson* plowed over the ship, but Santana had been somewhere within observation range, watching, and doing nothing to warn either the carrier or the small boat containing his countrymen of the danger.

She wondered whether the story she would report could ever begin to match the horror of the reality.

She took a deep breath. "Get my cameraman."

1530 Local (+5 GMT)
USS Arsenal

"Incoming signal," the operations specialist snapped. He kept his eyes glued on the screen and repeated the information over the secondary channel. "Captain, it's a firing order."

Seated in his tactical action officer chair, the captain stared at the display in front of him. It shivered, shifted, then resolved itself into a mirror image of the display in front of the Joint Chiefs of Staff. A red pip targeting indicator popped into view next to the missile site the carrier SEALs had found.

"Helluva thing, not having control over your own missiles," the chief petty officer of the watch said, his voice tight with disgust. "We're no better than a goddamned bunch of monkeys to them."

The captain turned. "Let's keep that quiet, Chief. We've done our job, getting weapons into the firing basket. If Washington wants to control the weaponeering themselves, we'll let them. It's not like we have a choice."

The chief pursed his lips and scowled. "Helluva way to run a war."

"Weather deck secure," the OOD reported over the bitch box. "Standing by to enable launching circuits."

"Enable the circuits," the captain echoed, nodding at the tactical action officer.

The TAO nodded, reached across the console, and gave his key one quick twist to the right. The captain did the same on his console. He sat back in his chair, sighed, and waited for the shot.

Moments later, he felt the dark rumble start down in the bowels of the ship, creep its way up the girders and strakes that made up the hull, and vibrate underneath his feet. The ship was ready; he could tell even without the weapons status indicators flashing warnings in front of him. The first shot fired by the *Arsenal* in anger, and it wouldn't even be at his command.

Suddenly, the hatches centered in the video camera popped open. Within seconds, a ripple of Tomahawk cruise missiles heaved themselves out of their vertical launch slots, seemed to hesitate above the deck in midair, then blasted the nonskid with fire. They gained altitude quickly after that, the noise and smoke from their propulsion systems blackening the deck and obscuring the picture on the camera. Even deep inside Combat, he could hear the missiles scream away from the ship and toward their target.

"That's it, folks," he announced as the noise finally faded. "Weapons away."

He saw the crew glance around at each other, puzzled looks on their faces. They'd all come from different ships, had been used to the routine of firing missiles, acquiring bomb damage assessments, and firing again. Many of them had served on the potent Aegis ships, working in Combat with a vast array of weapons under their direct control. There was something unnatural about this, giving up control of their very essence to someone they couldn't see, touch, or even be certain existed.

Yet, this was the very mission for which the Arsenal ship had been constructed. The captain stood and walked back out on the bridge to reclaim his coffee cup. As much as he might understand that, he didn't have to like it.

1532 Local (+5 GMT)
Fuentes Naval Base

A thin, high-pitched whine cut through the air like a buzz saw, at first barely audible, then quickly increasing in pitch and volume until it dominated the entire world. Pamela shrank back against the cement wall, panic overriding her trained reporter instincts, desperately wishing that she were anywhere in the world other than at ground zero for this attack. How many times had she been near military actions? Hunkering under bushes, darting around ruined buildings, following other freedom fighters on perilous missions against opposing forces whose ideologies seemed not too much different from that of the men she watched kill their relatives. Yet, never under any other combat conditions had she felt she was in imminent danger of dying. Why, oh why had she let her ego, her determination to get the best story before anyone else, lead her into this situation?

A Mach 2 missile gives its intended recipients barely enough time to appreciate the danger they're in. The precision guided munitions flashed into view, barely discernible gray-white streaks on the horizon, then became clearly visible almost before her terror could reach its peak. They moved too quickly for the eye to follow, streaking in over the gently rolling terrain to find their targets.

Two thousand meters away, the world exploded. One moment there was only the demanding keen of the missiles, the next a cacophony of noise and flame and fire. The earth blew up, shooting gouts of dirt and foliage into mushroom clouds of debris speckled with fire and metal. Shrapnel shot out at all angles, slamming into the structures and vehicles around the missile sites.

The compression wave from the explosion caught her first, even before the noise had a chance to deafen her. It slammed her against the concrete, smashing the back of her head against the rough-laid surface. She felt consciousness fade, and wavered on the edge of sanity. The microphone dropped from her hand unnoticed, and she paused for a minute, held against the building by the shock wave before sliding down to join it in a graceful heap.

Consciousness returned sometime later. She opened her eyes slowly, feeling raw and scratched, barely able to make sense of the images her eyes were transmitting to her brain. Around her, the world was silent. The green fields, the awkward and ungainly missile launchers, were gone. In their place, huge craters spattered the landscape, and a thick dust made the air almost unbreathable.

She groaned, tried to shove herself up on her knees with one hand. There was a sharp pain in her ribs, followed by the realization that every part of her body was dull and aching. She let it overwhelm her for a moment, then shoved it away, grim determination flooding her. Along with it came a strange euphoria, a gratitude that she'd survived. Life seemed sweet. Precious even, in a way it never had before.

The men scattered around her were starting to move as well, their groans and involuntary yelps of pain echoing her own. She felt along the ground, searching for her microphone, then looked for the substitute cameraman. She found him finally, still unconscious, his body wrapped around the old equipment protectively. She crawled to him, grabbed him by the shoulder, and shook.

"Get up."

The man moaned, then his eyes fluttered. He stared off

into the distance until finally his eyes focused on her. *"Qué?"*

"Get up," she repeated. "We've got work to do."

Ten minutes later, after gulping down tepid water from a canteen, she was ready. Her hair was pushed back out of her eyes, but she could feel it springing around her head in an unruly mess. She'd avoided looking in a mirror. It didn't matter, not now. If there were streaks of dirt and blood on her face, so much the better.

She waited until she was relatively certain that the cameraman was functioning enough to depress the transmit button on his equipment, then stared steadily at the camera. "This is Pamela Drake of ACN, reporting live from the western coast of Cuba. The United States has just completed a missile strike against this naval base not one mile from where I am standing." She gestured behind her, hoping the cameraman had enough sense to pan the damage. She saw him move, squint, refocus, and smiled. She let the time pass, waiting a few beats too long to increase the tension. Finally, she cut her hand down sharply and he snapped the camera back to frame her. "This is the area from which I made my last live report. As you can see, the effect of the missiles has been devastating. The structures that were here before, which I postulated were missile sites—a fact that was never denied by the present authorities in power—are destroyed. I have no word on casualties, but it seems—" All at once her voice failed. *I could have been one of them. Not minutes ago, it was* . . . "Casualties are yet to be determined," she finished finally. She stared at the camera, letting her image speak for itself.

1630 Local (+5 GMT)
USS **Arsenal**
Twenty Miles North of Cuba

Captain Heather paced uneasily back and forth on the bridge, staring out over the horizon at the barely visible land. Immediately following the launch the USS *Arsenal* had been ordered to assist other battle group assets in searching for survivors of the *Jefferson*'s collision with the small refugee boat.

Almost an hour after the attack, he still had no idea of how effective the attack had been. That was one of the problems of using cruise missiles alone, he reflected. At least when the battle group struck with aircraft and air-launched missiles, they had immediate feedback on the effectiveness of the attack. Not so with his ship.

He turned back to the OOD. "Any word yet?" It was unnecessary to ask, he knew even as the words left his mouth. The BDA—bomb damage assessment—would be conducted by the USS *Jefferson*. Two F-14s specially equipped with TARPS camera units were orbiting in a starboard marshal even as he spoke. Accompanying them would be two EA6 Prowlers armed with HARM missiles, capable of attacking any radar installations or any antiaircraft sites that were foolish enough to radiate their radars. Without knowing exactly how effective the attack had been, the aircrafts' mission was only slightly less dangerous than an actual bombing run.

"No, Captain." The OOD's voice was impassive.

"I guess we'll both hear at the same time, won't we?" the captain said. The battle group's circuit was wired into both the bridge and Combat. As soon as they knew anything, the carrier would let him know.

Or would they? He mulled the thought over for a moment. The political battle going on in Washington was making itself felt even down here. Admiral Wayne, commander of the carrier battle group, and Admiral Magruder, force commander, were both naval aviators. Would it be to their advantage to delay the BDA information's getting to the Arsenal ship? More important, even if it was, would they do such a thing?

From the few meetings he'd had with the two men, he suspected not. They were made of stronger stuff than their counterparts that he'd met, both fleet-seasoned aviators with a clear, sharp understanding of how a battle group worked, what it could and couldn't do.

"I'll be in Combat," Captain Heather said abruptly. He strode off the bridge, hoping that the dim light in Combat would mask his growing uneasiness.

1645 Local (+5 GMT)
Fuentes Naval Base

"A very effective report, Miss Drake," Santana said. His uniform was streaked and spattered with mud and dirt, and there was a haggard look to his face that hadn't been there an hour ago. "I hope they believed you."

Pamela flung out one hand and gestured toward the area of devastation to her left. "Why the hell wouldn't they? I sent them pictures, after all." Her voice was cold and bitter.

This was the man who'd exposed her to grave danger, who had made her a pawn—albeit a willing one—in this entire political struggle. In all the conflicts she'd covered, she'd never been used like this against her own country. Not intentionally, at least. Her mind wandered back over the other conflicts, to theaters around the world where she'd watched nations struggle for domination over soil. There'd been allegations, sure. The military never liked the press intruding, and was continually speculating that their very presence and reports influenced the course of the battle. The criticism had become markedly more raucous after Desert Storm and Desert Shield and Grenada. Especially Grenada, where a team of reporters had illuminated an incoming SEAL mission just as she had done earlier on the beach.

But the country had the right to know, didn't it? And how would it get information if the media didn't report it? Rely on the military officials?

She snorted. Not likely. The military's main concern was funding and power. Not so different from their civilian counterparts, but with even more at stake, what with the security of the nation entrusted to them.

All of them? An image of Tombstone Magruder flashed through her mind. She'd seen him agonize through tactical and operational decisions too often, felt the pain that tormented him over a mission gone wrong, and watched him suffering over the loss of life in his battle group. Somehow, when she put a face to it all, her distrust of the military's intentions seemed a little less solid.

"Now what?" she asked, suddenly tired of theoretical ethical speculations. She needed to focus her attention on what was next—on leaving this blasted country, she hoped. "With the missile launchers destroyed, that's the end of it."

A look of satisfaction backlit the weariness in the Cuban colonel's face. "I wouldn't be so sure."

She pointed again at the devastation. "I think the United States solved the issue once and for all." She was surprised to feel a sense of satisfaction at the statement. God, what had happened? Was she turning into a raving patriot just like Tombstone? No, her responsibility was to more than just one nation—it was to the world, to report accurately and precisely just what was occurring around the globe.

"It would be, if that's where the missiles were." He shook his head slightly, all at once looking more relaxed. "But they weren't."

"What do you mean? I saw—"

He interrupted her. "You saw a stack of shipping crates and some construction equipment wired together to look like something else. In other words, you saw what we wanted you to see. And what you wanted to see, if you will admit it. Isn't that so?"

Her mind reeled, trying to take it all in. The dangerous journey across the sea, the mistreatment in confinement, capped off by the very real missile attack she'd just witnessed—for what? As she looked up at him, his meaning became clear, sank into her mind with a dreadful clarity.

"I was part of the deception," she whispered. "You used me."

He sighed. "No more than you used us, Miss Drake. No more than you used us."

1700 Local (+5 GMT)
USS **Arsenal**
Twenty Miles North of Cuba

The ship finally finished the last section of its quartered search pattern. The special crew was starting to get tired, having started the evolution more than seven hours ago, frantically hunting for survivors of the collision between *Jefferson* and the small boat, their enthusiasm and hopes dimming over the ensuing hours. The crowds of off-duty sailors who had lined the weather decks, adding their eyes to the designated search teams', had started to drift away four hours into the search as the cruiser methodically quartered the ocean farther and farther away from the original collision. By now, they all knew, there was virtually no chance of finding any survivors.

"That's it, Captain. We're on the last leg of the pattern." The officer glanced down at the hastily scribbled sequence of course and speed used to bring the cruiser within visual range of any people in the water. "I wish we could have found one. At least one."

"Many times you don't." Captain Heather paused, deciding whether to launch into a discussion of some of the other rescue operations he'd been involved in, to place the whole event in perspective for his crew. No, he decided, better not to. They would learn in their own time and way the inevitability of death, how often the water that made up 90 percent of the earth's surface won in the battle between flesh and sea.

"Get us headed back toward the carrier. We'll take up our former station on her starboard quarter."

As the call went out to relieve the special team and set the normal underway watch, Captain Heather walked over to his brown leatherette chair on the starboard side of the bridge. Now that the sailors were being relieved—wearied men and women with feet aching from almost eight hours of standing along the lifelines—he felt he could at last sit down. It was one of the peculiarities his crew worshipped about him—his unwillingness to have them do anything he was not capable of doing himself.

He put one foot on the footrest and eased himself up into the chair, letting the hard-cushioned back support the small muscles in his back that were knotted and tense. He took a deep breath, watching the OOD guide the ship through the maneuvers to bring her back around toward the carrier, noting with one part of his mind that the young lieutenant was showing ever-increasing proficiency in his ship handling. Six months ago, there had been a certain tentativeness in his voice, a slowness in making critical decisions. During workups in the latest deployment, that had vanished, and what Captain Heather saw now was a more competent man, one surely and certainly on the track to commanding his own vessel someday.

Was he already seeing that? Did the young OOD look over at his captain now and wonder how it would feel to sit in his chair, feel the fear and eagerness that every captain felt in the pipeline? Heather hid a smile, remembering his own fantasies as a junior lieutenant officer of the deck, wondering how in the hell the Old Man managed to look like he knew what he was doing at every second, knew what was going on in parts of the ship he hadn't visited in hours. Those were other tricks of the trade that his OOD would pick up along the way, the captain showing him the ropes as he took more and more responsibility for the operation of the ship.

"All special teams secured and normal underway watch set," the OOD reported. "Captain, I've extended the chow hours below to allow the outgoing crew to get a hot meal before they turn in. Most of them will be back on watch at midnight."

"Very well." He acknowledged the OOD's decision neutrally, hiding the small rill of satisfaction it brought him. The man showed concern for his troops, another sign of good leadership to take note of.

1700 Local (+5 GMT)
Cuban Foxtrot Submarine

The submarine chugged along, operating at snorkel depth, sucking in air through its masts to power the diesel engines below. The captain was uneasy, and his mood was reflected in that of his crew. It had been too long since they'd put to sea, despite his insistence over the past years about maintaining some minimum level of proficiency in submarine operations. The crewmen on board were rusty; more than rusty—almost dangerous. Still, the mission was not terribly complicated. With any luck, they'd be back in port late that night.

"Captain, I have it." The sonarman spoke loudly, then immediately clapped one hand over his mouth to warn himself to be more quiet. "She's only a few miles away," he said in a lower voice.

"Bearing?"

"Three-two-zero true."

The captain wheeled to the conning officer. "Three-two-zero true, then. And warn the weapons crew to stand by."

"*Sí, Capitán.*" The OOD gave the new orders slowly, haltingly, desperately trying to refresh his memory for the mission that had been planned only the day before.

1740 Local (+5 GMT)
USS Arsenal

"Stand down from battle stations," the captain ordered, "and make sure the crew gets fed. It's been a long day."

The announcement sounded throughout the ship minutes later, securing the vessel from General Quarters. He could hear the tread of feet down the corridors as the minimally manned vessel stood down. Crewmen would be crowding into the galley, gulping down coffee, and chattering excitedly over the day's events.

"We're setting the normal underway watch now," the OOD reported. "Any special instructions?"

The captain shook his head. "Just the standard. And watch out for small boats—that's about all they could throw at us."

The captain retreated into his wardroom and sat down for dinner with the small group of officers manning the Arsenal ship. At least it was over, the first operational test of this awesome platform. Now they would wait.

1740 Local (+5 GMT)
Cuban Foxtrot Submarine

"Launch the first one," the captain ordered. He waited, growing increasingly impatient as the crew moved sluggishly to obey. Finally, he felt the pressure change within the boat, followed by a shudder as the first mine was shot out of the torpedo tubes.

Mines. Not the torpedoes that any self-respecting submarine would have been armed with. Parts had been too hard to obtain, and the fuel and warheads on the ones they'd received from the Soviet Union had gradually deteriorated into rusting piles of metal and toxic liquid. But mines—ah, now there was a weapon. Stable for decades with minimal maintenance, and capable of wreaking immediate destruction on anything they hit. Even the oldest Soviet models were still potent weapons.

Forty minutes later, they were done. A double line of mines ten miles long stretched out in the path of the *Arsenal*.

1900 Local (+5 GMT)
USS Arsenal

On the forwardmost portion of the weather decks, Seaman Fred Dooley took his lookout station. After a quick discussion with the sailor already standing the watch, he accepted the sound-powered phones, the binoculars, and the life jacket. At least the weather was clear, a great improvement over the previous week. He shucked his foul-weather jacket, tossing it over the anchor chain. He doubted that he'd need it tonight.

He turned forward and lifted the binoculars to his eyes. The cruiser was headed west, directly toward the setting sun. It dazzled him, and he tried to look to either side instead of gazing directly at the sun, to use his peripheral vision to pick up shapes and objects more clearly. Dooley was learning, just as the OOD was.

Something off to the right caught his attention, and he quickly focused the binoculars in on it, tweaking the small focus knob to sharpen the image. He tensed for a moment, wondering if he would be the one to spot the only survivor of the wreck.

Being first mattered on the USS *Arsenal*—and mattered to Dooley more than most. Joining the Navy last year had been the best decision he'd ever made in his short life. A job, training, a steady paycheck—and a way out of the grinding poverty of inner-city New York.

A few seconds later, Dooley's hopes were dashed. It was

merely a dolphin frolicking with a wave, trying in some odd fashion to complete a circle both above and below it. He watched it for a few moments longer, trying to decide exactly what sort of game the dolphin was playing.

Guiltily, aware that he'd let his attention be diverted by the eternal distractions of the sea, Dooley resumed his scan, carefully examining each area of the water in front of the ship. Another movement directly ahead caught his attention. A dolphin, he figured; nothing else should be moving out there.

He squinted, trying to make the object pop into view without refocusing the binoculars, which were set for dolphin length. The object was still unclear. Sighing, he focused again, then stared in horror.

It couldn't be—no, wait. He pressed the button on the sound-powered phone that hung around his neck, his eyes still glued to the object. "Bridge, forward lookout—mine, in the water; I say again, mine, dead ahead in the water. It's directly in front of us."

"He said what?" The OOD wheeled on the operations specialist manning the sound-powered phone. "What the— helm, hard right rudder. Lee helm, starboard engine back full, port engine ahead full."

Captain Heather shot bolt upright in his chair, hit the deck in one motion, and was at the quartermaster's side in a matter of seconds. He slapped down the collision alarm toggle switch, and seconds later the harsh buzz echoed throughout the ship. The bosun's mate of the watch took that as his cue, and began passing, "Stand by for collision. Mine to port—"

He never had time to finish the announcement. The cruiser heeled violently to starboard, throwing the entire bridge team across the pilothouse. The captain hit the bulkhead just next to the hatch leading onto the bridge wing.

The officer of the deck hurtled past him, cleared the bridge wing railing, and was in the water before the ship had even finished its downward motion.

The captain tried to scramble to his feet, only to discover that his legs wouldn't move. One of them, at least. He looked down, touched the raw, shattered bone protruding from his pants leg in horror, then groaned as he tried to twist around and survey the rest of the damage.

Six feet away, the bosun's mate of the watch was struggling to his feet. He looked dazed, disoriented, but at least mobile. "Boats! Get the TAO up here. Man overboard, port side." Captain Heather struggled to get the words out, relieved to see that the sailor appeared to understand. "And tell the exec—" As darkness overwhelmed him, he let the sentence slip away from his consciousness.

1000 Local (+5 GMT)
USS Jefferson

The conference room was oddly still and silent. In response to the blast, everyone from the Senate subcommittee to the Secretary of the Navy through the Chief of Naval Operations had ordered the battle group to a heightened state of alert and to withdraw outside the Cuban no-fly zone until the politicians could assess the fallout. On board the carrier, pilots and other flight officers flooded the passageways, restless without the constant overhead pounding of their aircraft spooling up, launching, and returning to the carrier. Both the 03-level Dirty Shirt and the more formal Officers' Mess on the third deck were crowded, not only with aviators but with the flight crews that supported them. Brunch had made a comeback, even on this weekday when normally the carrier wouldn't have been operating at flex-deck operation.

"So where do we stand?" Batman glanced at Tombstone and then continued with his line of questioning. "Somebody tell me this makes sense. We just shot a bunch of precision munitions at Cuba—Cuba, for God's sake—and shot up a soccer field. And maybe, just maybe, some missiles. Then the ship that shot them runs into a really high-tech threat—a mine. Now she's limping around like a wounded duck and we're hiding out a hundred miles south of Cuba." Glancing around the room, he saw agreement on every face, even as the men and women shifted uneasily in expectation of having to try to come up with an answer to the situation. "Admiral," Batman continued, turning to Tombstone, "anything to add?"

Tombstone shook his head. "No, that about sums it up. Once again, politics has played a nasty role in what should have been a tactical exercise." His voice grew hard. "And, for the record, there will be no further cooperation with any news media from this battle force. Is that absolutely clear?"

Once again, heads nodded, the gazes avoiding his. Tombstone shifted his inscrutable gaze back to Batman. "I'd be interested in hearing some options."

"You'll have them." Batman pointed at the chief of operations. "Get your brightest minds together. I want plans, options, and at least a decent idea of how you're going to defend this battle group both from a Cuban navy threat and from mines. You've got two hours." Batman stood and walked out of the room behind Tombstone.

The chief of operations stood as well. "Okay, people, let's get out of this birdcage and get back to our spaces. We've got some work to do."

Bird Dog headed straight back for his desk, excitement pounding in his veins. This was his chance, the evolution he'd spent the last year training for at the War College. Notional flight schedules, concepts of operational art and deception flitted through his head, each one vying for his immediate attention. It would be, he decided, his finest moment so far in the Navy. Even better than shooting down those MiGs in China, more exciting than flying over the harsh Aleutian terrain as he had in the past—no, this would be the one evolution that broke him out from the pack. Admirals would be fighting to get him on their staff, and *early* promotion to commander . . . well, that was another question, wasn't it? The war-game instructors back at the Naval War College had said he was a natural, after all.

He slid into his chair, scooted it up to the desk, and fired up his laptop, eager to get started on his plan to win the war. Just as he keyed up the word processing and planning outline, a stack of envelopes landed on his desk, knocking his mouse away from his fingers.

"Mail call, Bird dog." Gator's voice was sardonic, as always. "Looks like you've got some incoming fire from Callie. I thought I'd go ahead and read it first, but—"

"Asshole," Bird Dog snapped, grabbing for the light pink envelope Gator held just out of reach. "Give it to me, now!"

Gator scampered out of range and dodged behind the filing cabinet. "Only if you promise to let me read it when you're done with it. Though what that woman could ever see in you is a mystery to us all."

"Gator," Bird Dog howled, darting around the file cabinet and desperately trying to get his hands on his RIO's. "I swear to God, you're going to be puking your guts out in the back of that Tomcat when I get my hands on you. I swear it!"

"Looks like a damned kindergarten around here," the operations chief snapped. "Gator, damn it, give him his envelope. Let him drool over it a while so he'll eventually get back to work. You heard the admiral—we don't have time to fuck around with this."

Gator yielded up the pink envelope to his pilot, but only after running it under his nose and taking a long apprecia-tive sniff of the delicate scent. "It still smells like—"

"Gator," the chief of operations said warningly. "Don't you have to be somewhere else?"

"I guess I do at that," Gator answered mildly. He ambled to the door, and heading back down toward Strike Planning said, "Let me know when he's sane again, Captain."

Bird Dog held on to the letter with both hands and looked pleadingly at the chief of operations. "Could I—"

The chief scowled at him. "Fifteen minutes. Get the hell down to your compartment, read the letter from your honey, then get the hell back up here. And when you're back here, mister, I want your full attention focused on what we've got to do. You got that?"

"Yes, sir!" Bird Dog smiled and headed for the door. Callie's timing was perfect. A letter arriving just as he made a masterstroke in his career! How could she have known?

Bird Dog darted down to the compartment, dodging other sailors and leaping easily over knee-knockers. He flung open the door to his stateroom, made sure his roommate wasn't skulking in a corner, and threw himself down on the lower bunk. He paused to take a deep, appreciative sniff of the letter before he delicately teased the envelope flap away from the body of it. The smell of perfume grew stronger. He inhaled deeply, then drew out the two folded pages of paper. Only two sheets—he frowned slightly, then dismissed the feeling. Callie wasn't much for long letters, he knew, though he himself could have written ten or fifteen pages to her every night if he had the time, pouring out his need for her, his plans, and his description of the life they'd have together eventually. Still—

The first words stopped his breath. He read the first paragraph again, trying to understand what his eyes were seeing, at a complete loss as to understand why it sounded like his fiancée was . . . she was. Dumping him? How could she? Gradually, his heart started to beat again, though it had taken a dive to somewhere down behind his navel. The possibility that Callie wouldn't follow through with their plans, would find someone else while he was on cruise, had never even occurred to him.

He let the pages flutter from his hand and land on the worn, nubby carpet on his deck. This would take some time to think through, some planning to figure out just how to convince her that she was making a terrible mistake. Time he didn't have right now.

When Bird Dog walked back into the Operations Department only four minutes after he'd left, the rest of the staff looked startled, then maintained a cautious silence. There was no teasing, no joshing about what he'd been doing in those moments alone in his stateroom. Whether it was the short time span or the expression on his face, every single officer there seemed to know. Know, and commiserate. At least half of them had had the experience of receiving a Dear John letter while out on cruise. But the predictability of the event made it no less tragic for the officer involved.

Bird Dog seated himself at his desk, toggled his mouse to dissolve the flying-toaster screen saver into shards of color, and called up the beginning of his operational plan. Within minutes, he was immersed in the intricacies of it.

The noise level in the Operations compartment gradually returned to normal. Everyone left Bird Dog alone.

1045 Local (+5 GMT)
USS Arsenal

"We're still afloat, if that's what you mean." Captain Heather's voice sounded infinitely weary. "Damage control is still desmoking and dewatering the ship, but I don't think we're in any imminent danger of sinking. At least I hope we're not." He ran one hand over his face, rubbing wearily at the skin that seemed to sag off his cheekbones. His leg had been hastily splinted, and he held it out in front of him as he squirmed in his command chair. If the corpsman had had his way, the captain would be down on the mess decks with the other casualties right now.

The voice over the speaker was in marked contrast to the way the captain felt. Two days ago, it could have been him. There was a cool, calm note of command in it, the very choice of words and expressions denoting absolute confidence in the ability of the battle group to take this war to the enemy's homeland. "And your operational capabilities?"

Captain Heather forced down a small spike of anger. Admiral Magruder knew that there were dead sailors on his ship, men still waiting on the mess decks for medical attention. The admiral was just asking what he had to know, needed to know—and had a right to know: How capable was the Arsenal ship of being a part of the battle plan?

"Most of the electronics are fine," he answered, striving for professionalism. God, it was hard, when he'd just come back from visiting the wounded and dead on the decks below. "What was damaged we can bypass. The structural integrity of the launch tubes is another matter. I think we have some damage—we won't really know until we try to op-test them."

"I don't have to tell you we don't have time for you to return to port and do that," Magruder said slowly. The captain stared at the speaker as the admiral paused. "Give me your best guess. We'll plan around it."

The captain sucked in a sharp breath. "Admiral, the missile-launching capabilities of this are honeycombed together in the forward and aft parts of the ship—even along the gangplanks, in some cases. If one cell is defective, it could pose a major fire hazard for us. Without shipyard-level testing, I can't be sure."

"If you're looking for certainties, you're in the wrong business. And I don't think you are. There was a reason the Navy put you in command of *Arsenal*, and I suspect it's because you're superbly qualified for the position. This is why you get paid the big bucks, Captain. Or are you going to take the easy way out and declare your ship a total casualty?"

"I need to get back to you, Admiral," the captain said, his voice frostily neutral. "Give me two hours. I'll have a complete operational damage assessment for you then. And my decision as to whether there's any chance at all we can still launch safely."

"That will have to do," the admiral said. "Make it sooner if you can." The circuit dissolved into a smooth hiss of static, the connection broken. The captain slammed the receiver down and jolted upright in his seat, slamming his hand into his open palm. After a few minutes, his anger became determination.

As much as he hated to admit it, the admiral was right. The USS *Arsenal* was out here for one purpose—to demonstrate the operational capabilities of a platform so far advanced over anything else the Navy had ever designed that it would change the shape of battles to come. And if it couldn't survive a hit from the most primitive of naval weapons, an underwater mine, and continue fighting, then it might not be worth all the money that had been sunk into the program. It was up to him to demonstrate that now, one way or the other. He owed that to the men who'd died, to the men who'd lived, and to his country.

He could do it. He was convinced of that now. It was just a matter of making his crew believe that their ship could do it, too.

1300 Local (+5 GMT)
Fuentes Naval Base

She was getting tired of being tossed into rickety jeeps and
ferried about to obscure locations—and even more fed up
with the Cuban demands that she broadcast what they
wanted when they wanted. This was not the way reporting
was supposed to be, not at all. Where was her journalistic
integrity, her independence, her right to seek out the story
that her audience deserved? Not here—not under these
circumstances. The First Amendment and freedom of speech
simply had no application in Cuba.

As the jeep jolted over the potholed, muddy road, an
unwelcome thought intruded itself into her indignation.
Maybe there was a reason that Cuba was off-limits for
American citizens. Maybe the United States government,
and even the State Department, knew just a tiny bit more
about the situation in this country than she and her cohorts
did. Was it possible? Had she made a mistake?

No. The day she permitted the State Department to
determine where and when she might go anywhere in the
world was the day she might as well turn to narrating
documentaries instead of broadcasting combat reports. She
gritted her teeth, partially out of determination but more to
keep from biting her tongue as the jeep swerved on the road
to avoid a tank, and concentrated on the story. She turned to
her companion. "Where to this time? Are more SEALs
invading? Or do you have some other facility you want to
make sure the Americans avoid bombing? I'd give that last
reason some rethinking, if I were you. It didn't seem like it
did much good last time."

And so it hadn't. Even though they'd known she was present at the last missile site, the Americans hadn't been deterred from launching their precision strike weapons at it. She felt an odd rush of loneliness, of abandonment. Even amongst the cynical, hard-bitten reporters, there had been an unspoken article of faith that they were Americans, that if they really got into trouble, the Marines would come and get them—not launch weapons at them.

But wasn't that a reciprocal obligation? If it were, she'd violated it sorely by broadcasting photos of the SEALs coming ashore. She supposed she couldn't blame them if they were less than eager to come to her assistance now, since she'd almost gotten some of them killed. In a strange way, it hurt.

"Nothing quite that important this time, Miss Drake. Or maybe more so. You'll have to judge for yourself," Colonel Santana said cryptically. "It depends on what you define as important. This might meet that criterion."

Pamela's breath caught in her throat. "The actual missile sites?" she said softly. "It is, isn't it?" For a moment, the glimmering ethical reflections she'd had a few moments earlier were blasted into oblivion by the all-encompassing drive to get the story. She'd been thwarted once, twice, but not this time, she vowed. Oh, no, this time she would send the story home, all wrapped up in a neat, succinct package for her viewers, telling them what happened, why it happened, and how they, the viewers, ought to feel about it. She could do that. She'd done it too many times already not to be able to.

"Why the big hurry now?" she said suddenly, still feeling the rush of euphoria from the prospect of this story. "Something's not making sense about this."

He glanced at her, annoyed. "It would make perfect sense to you if you were Cuban."

"Why don't you try explaining it to me?" she wheedled. "That's why I came here, you know—to tell your story, not the one the American military establishment wants told. Why waste this opportunity to build support for your cause?"

"Mine is not a cause!" he said, his voice harsh. "Causes are what rabble-rousers have. I represent the legitimate, elected government of the nation state of Cuba. That is what Aguillar and even Leyta and his rabble seem to forget. They are nothing more than troublemakers, and have no concept of what the Cuban people really want—or need. We do."

"You certainly won a landslide victory at each of the last elections," she said carefully, "with a record voter turnout that the United States itself has never approached. Still, there was only one candidate on the ballot. Do you feel that weakens your position any?"

"The people wanted only one candidate. This was their opportunity to show their grateful support for our leader, not to engage in pointless bickering." The jeep ground to a halt unexpectedly, throwing Pamela sideways against the hard metal strake. She hit her head sharply, felt a flash of pain, then pushed it aside to zoom back in on the man she was questioning. "So if the Cuban people feel that way, in the majority, why is this revolution taking place?"

"It is not a revolution. It is treason." He smiled coldly. "And that, Miss Drake, is something you ought to understand."

"But how will missiles help you deal with an internal affair?" she pressed. "Surely if Cuba is capable of handling this issue herself, the last thing you need is the United States annoyed and intervening. Unless," she said, pausing as insight flashed into her mind, "you're having a problem with your Libyan masters. Are they holding out for more control over the legitimate government in exchange for quashing the rebels for you? Is that it?"

Bingo. She knew she'd struck gold by the flash of annoyance in his eyes. Exultation warred with an increasing feeling of uneasiness as she contemplated her position. She was in Cuba illegally, neither entitled to nor likely to get support from her own government, and trapped between three warring forces—the so-called legitimate government of Cuba, the Libyan "advisors" who were increasingly in evidence, and the guerrilla fighters whom Leyta represented on the mainland.

A hell of a story—if she survived it.

1315 Local (+5 GMT)
Washington, D.C.

"I don't know how you can expect me to keep this up," Admiral Loggins hissed. "There's absolutely no chance I can keep the aircraft carrier out of it. Not after what's happened down there. It's not only impossible, but it makes no tactical sense whatsoever. None."

"You're going to be lucky if you've even got any carriers left after I'm through with you," Senator Williams shot back. He pointed at the TV broadcasting ACN headlines in the corner of the room. "That footage of those SEALs is worth more during budget debates than five hundred pounds of briefings and testimony. You think they ever read all the material we send them? No—they make their decisions based on sound bites and shots like that. And you can bet they're going to be hearing from every Cuban constituent in every district over this one."

"What you're asking is unreasonable. With the Arsenal

ship damaged, if we need to take action against Cuba, it's
going to have to be with the carrier. There's no other way to
do this safely; there's just not—"

"'Safety' is a relative term. And you're going to be
thinking longingly about this conversation when the Senate
subpoenas you about your relationship with Miss Pamela
Drake and the film footage ACN broadcast. Don't cross me
now, Keith. You're in this too far."

Admiral Loggins slammed his hand down on the desk
and glared at the senator. "Don't you dare threaten me. Not
me, not Pamela—not ever. I've gone along with your plans
because they were what I felt was best for the Navy, but
you've gone too far this time. My relationship with Pamela
has nothing to do with her work, nor does she have anything
to do with mine. We're just private citizens, trying—"

"The hell you are!" Senator Williams shoved himself out
of his chair and leaned across the desk to glare at Loggins,
his hands planted and splayed on the blotter in front of the
admiral. "You gave up a private life the day you put on those
stars, and don't you forget it. Just the way I did when I took
my first oath of office in Congress twenty years ago. What
you do, who you screw, all of it—it's all career material.
And if you don't understand that, then you've already been
promoted two times too many. You got me?"

The admiral stood up from behind his desk slowly, his
shoulders slumped. He stared out the window that gazed out
across the Potomac, at the landscape spotted with fog and
pollution, at the distant white figures of the various memo-
rials scattered around Washington, D.C. There was truth to
what the senator said—but it wasn't the whole story. And if
it were, then what did that say about the twenty-five years
he'd spent in the military?

Duty, honor, country. Those were things that mattered,
not the pork-barrel electioneering that Williams was en-

gaged in. Not even his *own* career mattered more than duty. He wondered why he hadn't seen that before, what should have been so obvious to a man raised, educated, and tempered in the service of his country.

In the beginning, he'd seen the Arsenal ship project as something *good for the Navy,* an added capability that would give his country more options in coping with shattered nations and turmoil around the world. He'd been proud to be one of the prime backers of the project, eager even to show the political powers why this was the right project to back.

When had that changed? He stared at the slimy senator opposite him and wondered at what point and how he'd let himself be drawn away from the honorable path and into a pattern of careerism and self-aggrandizement. What had happened to his honor?

It might be too late for him personally, but it wasn't too late for the Navy. To do the right thing, the honorable thing—he felt a heavy burden lift as he reached his decision.

He straightened his shoulders and turned to glare at the senator. "No more private conversations. I've had it with you. And if it ruins my career, so be it. Three stars ought to be enough for any man—and they will be for me if that's what it takes."

"I'm not going anywhere until you agree," Williams snarled.

The admiral pushed a button located under the ledge of his desk. "Oh yes you are." He moved around the desk quickly and slipped a half nelson on the senator before he could even react. Loggins shoved the man's head down until he was half bent over, then wrenched the senator's arm up behind him. With the senator completely under his control, the admiral goose-stepped him across the deep blue carpet to the door, opened it with his free hand, and shoved him into his anteroom. "Come back when you can get a civil tongue in your head. And when you understand what your job for this nation really is."

The crowd of visitors, petitioners, and those with appointments waiting in the anteroom gaped dumbfounded as Loggins slammed the door to his office. One of them, a short, sandy-haired man carrying a large manila envelope, stood up slowly. His boss expected him to use his best judgment, and if ever it had been called for, the aide mused, it was this situation. The budget information, the requests for information on sailors, and the rest of the weekly packets the aide was bringing over for the admiral's attention could wait. He was certain that his boss, Senator Dailey, would be much more interested in what he had just witnessed in the anteroom.

1330 Local (+5 GMT)
USS **Arsenal**

Captain Heather leaned awkwardly against the missile tube, supporting his weight on his one good leg. Getting down here with the help of the boatswain's mate had been a bitch, but he'd done it; with this much on the line, there was no substitute for firsthand knowledge. He knelt down on the dirty deck, heedless of the damage it was doing to his sharply pressed khaki pants. He stared at the launch tube, only vaguely aware of the engineering and weapons technicians around him. He ran one hand over the smooth metal, feeling for damage. It was as though he could feel straight through the metal, ascertain the delicate condition and structural integrity of each tube without really seeing it.

"This one's fine," he said finally. He looked up at the chief engineer and the weapons officer.

The engineer nodded. "I think so, too. That makes the figure about eighty percent, Captain, maybe a bit more."

The captain straightened, winced as his splinted leg complained loudly. The pain was getting worse—sooner or later, he'd have to take the painkillers the corpsman kept handing him. For the first time, he noticed the grease and grime covering his khakis, evidence of the damage control battle that had been fought here the day before. "Guess I should have worn coveralls." The logistical problems of trying to get them over the splint would have baffled him.

The chief engineer followed his gaze to look at the spots, then dropped his gaze lower down to the splinted leg, the khaki pants hanging in shreds. "I could have reminded you, Captain."

The captain shook his head. "No." He glanced back up at the chief engineer. "I've already been reminded enough of the basics today."

1345 Local (+5 GMT)
USS **Jefferson**

Tombstone hung up the receiver after taking the Arsenal CO's report. His eyes met Batman's across the table, and he smiled slightly.

Batman nodded. Not many of Tombstone's staff members would have believed it, but he himself had seen the somber admiral smile on several occasions. This was one of them. "Sounds like the man's got his shit together, doesn't it?"

Tombstone returned the nod, the merest inclination of his head. "He does. So what now?"

"You're asking me? Hell, Tombstone, you're the one with two stars."

Tombstone shook his head gravely. "It doesn't make me infallible. Tell me what you think."

Batman stood and started pacing around the compartment. Finally, he looked back at his old flying mate. "I think this is a come-as-you-are war. No fancy preparations, no amphibious force standing by—hell, we're close enough to the U.S. to get anything we need on short notice. This is the O.K. Corral, and we're here, and the hell with how Washington wants the war to be won. I say we disable the remote controls on the Arsenal ship and shift targeting back to where it belongs—the captain. Factor him into our strike plan, get the aircraft back up in the air where they were meant to be, and let's go for it. We can turn those missile silos into glass, or at least shredded metal, in less time than it takes for the chaplain to say the morning prayer in Congress."

"We're getting rudder orders from D.C. I suspect they're going to insist that the Arsenal take the lead again in the attack." Tombstone's eyes were backlit with anger. "What's your take? You've spent more time in D.C. than I have."

Batman sighed. "If we propose a classic strike, they'll say no. By the time we could convince them, we may have missiles inbound from Cuba headed for the continental U.S."

"Agreed. So?"

"So fuck them—we don't ask. We just take care of business and our people and deal with the consequences later. That's why we're wearing the stars—to take the incoming fire."

Tombstone stood as well. He stretched, let out a long groan, then shook himself like a wet dog. "Do it. See how easy having two stars is?"

1400 Local (+5 GMT)
The White House

The President stared out at the Rose Garden from the Oval Office, his back to the two men standing at attention in front of his desk. Let them wait—it was one of the prerogatives of his office as commander in chief that he could keep the chairman of the Joint Chiefs of Staff and the chief of naval operations braced up for as long as he wanted.

He wondered what he would have said thirty years ago when he was a grunt on the ground in Vietnam if someone had told him he'd one day have this much power. He would have laughed, he suspected. Laughed and made some joke about somebody smoking too much pot. In country, where soldiers reckoned their lives by how many patrols they had left to do, a future devoid of artillery and snipers would have seemed an impossibility.

I blew it. Not only did I make the same mistake my predecessors did during Vietnam, but I have even less excuse than they did. I was there; I should have known better. At least I can fix it this time. And maybe the next President that's tempted to micromanage will know better.

He turned back to the two men, his face grave. "As of now we're out of the targeting business." He pointed his finger at the chairman. "You and me both."

"You," he continued, jabbing the same finger at the CNO, "call up your commander down there. You tell him that the Arsenal ship is hereby transferred to his complete command, as theater commander. Give him my objectives—and give him his head. You got that?"

The CNO nodded, a grim smile starting at the corners of

his mouth. "Aye, aye, sir. We'll get results—that I can promise you."

Even with the urgency of his information, it had taken the aide a good half hour to clear out the petitioners clogging Senator Dailey's anteroom. Finally, when his boss motioned him in, he had his chance. He described what he'd seen in Admiral Loggins's office, not bothering to supply his own conclusions. They'd discussed the Williams-Loggins link too often for this falling-out to have many surprises.

Senator Dailey leaned back in his chair and stared thoughtfully at the ceiling. "So it finally happened. That's what I was counting on. The Keith Loggins I knew when I was on active duty had more balls than to let somebody like Williams suck him into something shady. Wonder what they broke up over."

The aide shook his head. "I couldn't hear everything, Senator. Just enough to convince me it had to do with the battle group to the south. And we both know what side of the problem those two are on."

Senator Dailey unfurled himself from the angle between his desk and his chair, then reached across for the telephone. He paused, studied his aide thoughtfully. "Let this be a lesson to you. There's an old saying— 'The enemy of my enemy is my friend.' I think it's about time I called Admiral Magruder and gave him the day off." He began dialing the number from memory.

"The day off?" the aide asked, looking puzzled. "Why is that?"

The senator smiled broadly. "Because in about fifteen minutes, Admiral Tombstone Magruder is going to think it's Christmas. Santa Claus, played by little old me, is about to give him everything he ever wanted or asked for."

1615 Local (+5 GMT)
USS **Jefferson**

For the second time that day, Tombstone Magruder hung up the telephone and laughed. "Just when you're getting ready to mutiny, the elected Powers That Be come through for you."

Batman smirked. "I was just getting used to the idea of it myself. What did Senator Dailey have to say?"

Tombstone smiled back. "We've got everything we wanted and we're willing to do without authorization. Weapons free, aircraft free—everything. Evidently there's been a falling-out amongst thieves back in D.C., and we're back to being the good guys."

Batman dropped his feet off the desk and stood. "Hell, Tombstone, we always were the good guys. Sometimes they just forget that back there."

"Now that they've got it straightened out," Tombstone said, "let's see if we can make it clear to the Cubans."

1620 Local (+5 GMT)
Air Operations Office, USS **Jefferson**

Bird Dog double-clicked his mouse, transferring the contents from his rough drawing sheet into the cell on his war-game planning sheet. This plan had everything he

needed, everything he'd been taught to plan for during his
year at War College. He studied it again, trying to see if he'd
missed anything. No, it was all there—logistics support,
objectives, and finally a succinct explanation of the desired
end state to this conflict. He knew that was a little bit
beyond his duties as a carrier staff puke, but it didn't hurt to
show off a little anyway. Besides, this was going to be his
big move, wasn't it? No point in not showing the admiral he
had a little bit more on the ball than the average lieutenant
commander pilot. The sick uneasiness he felt over Callie
was merely a background throb of pain now, constant yet
submerged in his consciousness under the driving need to
finish the operational plan. He kept his eyes riveted on the
spreadsheet, not certain that he wanted to release it for
review by the Air Ops chief. Every minute he kept himself
distracted with that prevented him from having to deal with
the issue of Callie.

Finally, he noticed one small improvement he could make
on the plan, one that just might lift his spirits a bit. He
moused over to the relevant cell and added an additional
flight of aircraft, one he knew that the squadron was not
capable of providing on short notice—they simply didn't
have enough pilots. With a little cooperation from Gator, he
just might be able to pull it off. Now if only the Ops ACOS
didn't read the details too carefully. . . .

Staff work was demanding, but it was usually finished by
the time the aircraft went into the air. No point in not taking
the extra manpower into account when planning for strikes,
particulary since there were aircraft that would be sitting
empty on the deck otherwise. He smiled, wondering how
Gator was going to be feeling about that.

"No way." Gator's voice was cold and adamant. "I'm not climbing into a cockpit with you right now, not after that bitch just jilted you."

"She's not a bitch," Bird Dog said, defending Callie unwillingly. In truth, he himself thought that she might be. There was no other explanation for her complete lack of taste in dumping him in favor of a submariner.

Despite Bird Dog's intentions of keeping his pain to himself, Gator had wormed the story out of him in less than five minutes flat. After hearing it, and noting the anguish in Bird Dog's voice, Gator had flatly refused to fly with him again.

"I'm not unsafe in the air—you know I'm not."

"Even on the best days, you have an interesting interpretation of the standard rules of flight," Gator said caustically. "But now, with your heart down around your asshole, I'd be crazy to get in the cockpit with you. Plumb crazy."

Bird Dog tried again. "Look at it this way, Gator. Who's got more experience in combat than us? You and me, remember? The Spratlys? The Aleutians? Now that was a helluva ride, wasn't it? And if I can bring you back safely from that, flying twenty feet above ice with no radar and limited visibility, I can get you back from a normal, ordinary strike during daylight hours on a big island, don't you think?"

Gator shook his head. "You ain't been flying much, buddy."

"That's the problem—Gator, come on. I need to get back

in the cockpit, and I don't want to miss out on this one. That bitch dumped me—there's gotta be something more to life than that. Please?" With all the bravado dropped and his soul exposed bare for Gator to see, there was something terribly appealing about the young aviator. Despite his best intentions, Gator felt himself giving in.

"We'll get caught," the RIO said.

"No we won't. All pilots look alike in helmets and flight suits, and the squadron doesn't know the admiral grounded me. Even Tomboy doesn't have a clue."

"Bird Dog, of all the idiotic schemes you've gotten me into, this is—"

"Please?" There was quiet dignity and plaintiveness in Bird Dog's voice.

Gator sighed. "I'm an idiot. Okay, count me in."

Bird Dog smiled.

TWELVE
Tuesday, 02 July

0200 Local (+5 GMT)
USS Jefferson

"That's it, then." Tombstone Magruder scrawled his initials in the upper-right-hand corner of the message, releasing it for transmission. He leaned back in his chair, tossed the pencil on the table, and looked impassively at the men surrounding him. "If it doesn't work, I'll take the heat for it. You people are just following orders."

The SEAL OIC—Officer in Charge—shook his head. "That plan's got my name all over it, Admiral. With all due respect, I wouldn't mind getting hung for that one little bit."

"You may get your chance," Tombstone snapped. He glanced at the standard Navy-issue black clock up on the bulkhead. "And sooner than you want."

"Admiral, at the risk of sounding like an optimist," Batman broke in, "this is a damned fine operational plan. It's classic. We get our people out, take ownership of the airspace, then proceed inward to strike our objectives. They'll be studying this one at the War College."

"They study Grenada, too, for what it's worth." Tombstone shifted his gaze to Bird Dog. "They do, don't they? And Beirut as well."

Bird Dog nodded. "I think this one will work, Admiral."

Tombstone stood and started pacing back and forth. Had it been any other officer, Batman decided, it would have been a sign of nerves. But with Tombstone it was more an indication of the pent-up rage and anger seething through him, a physical release of that which kept him from exploding in temper. It was from such small physical activities that Tombstone got his reputation for being utterly unflappable and granite-faced.

"We need to get going," Sikes said finally. "If we want to leave on time." He glanced uncertainly from Batman to Tombstone.

Batman nodded slightly, giving permission. "Get your people ready." With another gesture, Batman cleared the room of the rest of the personnel, indicating that they should go to their racks and get some sleep while they could. When they were alone, he walked over to his old lead and said, "Don't sweat the load, Tombstone. You know this has got as good a chance of working as anything."

Tombstone wheeled on him. "If it were simply a matter of taking out those missile structures, do you think I'd be worried? Hell, even that damned Bird Dog could figure out how to do that! There's no mystery to how we operate." His mouth clamped into a thin, taut line.

"Yeah. What? What is it that's got you so wound up about this plan?" Batman pressed, already suspecting that he knew the answer. Should he say it? No, with a man like Tombstone, it was better to let him come to his own conclusions about when to publicly air a matter. If Batman mentioned Pamela first, it would simply drive his old lead against the wall, cementing his silence for good.

Batman felt Tombstone's eyes searching his face, looking for something there. The younger admiral willed himself into immobility. Finally, Tombstone nodded, and the tension seemed to drain out of his body. He flung himself down on the flat leatherette couch against one wall, onto his back, feet propped up on the far armrest. The sudden change in posture was as disconcerting to Batman as having Tombstone actually smile.

"Don't get diplomatic on me, Batman," Tombstone said finally. He turned his head and stared over at his old wingman, amusement tugging at the corner of his mouth. "We've known each other too long for this. You know what it is."

"Then you say it first, Tombstone," Batman challenged. "Anytime I bring it up, you start backpedaling on me."

"Pamela Drake." Tombstone pronounced the name quietly, neutrally. "That's what it is. And that downed pilot, too. Thor. Both of them—but especially Pamela."

"Can they get her out?"

Tombstone shrugged. "The SEALs seem to think so. And if they can't—damn it, Batman, you know I'll do it. I'm going to quit thinking with my dick. She's there illegally, against all U.S. policy, and interfering with our operations. If they can't get her out, I'll send a strike in anyway."

"And Thor?" Batman's voice was hard and cold. "What about him?"

Tombstone levered himself up and swung his feet back down on the floor. "Same answer, for a different reason. Major Hammersmith's paid to take chances. He's a Marine; he understood the risks he was taking. I'll try my best to get him out, but if I can't . . ."

"You'll go ahead with that strike, too." Batman had not realized how much he wanted to believe that wasn't true. Deep down, he'd known this was exactly what Tombstone would order, and why Tombstone had been sent up to the battle force. Even before he himself had suspected it, Batman's superiors had known that he might flinch from this last—and deadliest—military decision. He tried to feel resentment, but all he felt was relief. Relief that the decision was someone else's, an unwillingness to face the ultimate reckonings of life and death that took place in the correlation of forces.

"I think—I think I'm happy with one star, Admiral," Batman said slowly. He stood, walked to the center of the room, and offered a hand to his old lead.

Tombstone took Batman's hand, used it to lever himself up from the couch, then turned the grip into a warm handshake. "You never know what you'll do until you're there, shipmate. You know it's the right decision. It's the same one you'd make if you were in my shoes."

"Let's get some sleep, Stoney," Batman said. "If tomorrow is as long a day as I think it's going to be, we'll need it."

0200 Local (+5 GMT)
Fuentes Naval Base

Colonel Santana ran his hand over the .45 pistol holstered on his hip. The gun was smooth, gleaming—better cared for than 90 percent of the houses and people living in his country. But his life did not depend on people right now—it depended on this gun. And on the temper of the man seated opposite him.

Santana left his fingers resting gently on the butt as he glared at the Libyan. "Your plan is not working. The Americans are here in force and have already penetrated and destroyed our deception."

Kaliff Mendiria lounged lazily in the chair, seemingly unaware of the gun at Santana's hip. He lifted one hand and waved away Santana's concerns with a light flip of his fingers. "You think short-term, my friend. That is why our partnership is so good. You have experience and are excellent in executing the immediate, the tactical. But for the longer-range planning, you need an outside viewpoint to balance your impetuousness. Ah, that hot Cuban blood—it has landed you in trouble more than once, has it not?" The Libyan took a deep breath, then yawned. "It is growing late. I suggest we retire until tomorrow morning."

Santana jerked the pistol from his holster and slammed it down on the table, butt first. The nine-inch barrel pointed menacingly in Mendiria's direction. Not at him directly— no, Santana was not willing to make that threat just yet—but certainly in that direction. "What of the missiles! You promised them by now."

Mendiria frowned. "You threaten me, then demand concrete evidence of our friendship? Is this how Cuba thinks?"

"We had a deal," Santana said tightly. "A distraction here, so that you could proceed with your plans in Africa. We have drawn the American battle group away from the Mediterranean as you requested, and what good has it done us? Merely invited a missile launch that decimated an empty field."

"An empty field," Mendiria echoed. "And do you suppose that if we had already delivered the missiles to you, they would have been in that field? Undoubtedly so. You see, Santana, you simply must learn to look ahead."

Santana paused uncertainly. Was it possible? Had the swarthy African sitting across from him actually foreseen the American strike at Cuban soil, and planned around it? He studied the Libyan more closely now, cataloging his features. An ugly man, but one with a compelling sense of power about him that even Santana only rarely dared to brook.

Santana holstered the pistol and sat down in the chair

opposite the Libyan. "So. Enlighten me, then. Explain to me
how this is all a part of your plot, how every movement is
accounted for and proceeding exactly as planned. I'm ready
to believe, Mendiria—just not yet convinced."

The Libyan leaned forward on the table, resting his
weight on his elbows. His piercing eyes were half hooded
with sleepy eyelids, the mouth slightly slack and barely
covering the even row of white teeth. "And this is why you
keep me up so late at night?" He shook his head. "Let me
explain this to you one more time. Then either shoot me or
start cooperating, I don't care which one—but quit waking
me up in the middle of the night with your stupid nightmares.

"The Americans are here, occupied by what they perceive
as the Cuban problem. Your soil is vulnerable, my friend,
especially with reinforcements so close at hand. But now
that the Americans have actually conducted a first strike, the
balance of world opinion will shift in your favor. The United
States will find neither support nor approval for further
action against Cuba. And you—you have lost nothing.
Turned up a few dirt clods, perhaps missing a few agricultural workers, but that is it. And furthermore, you have this
excellent videotape of American Special Forces intruding
on your soil. That is bound to weaken support for America
within the Caribbean basin. This opens new opportunities
for you—and for us."

"But the missiles—," Santana began.

Mendiria cut him off with a wave of his hand. "Are on
their way, even as we speak. Do you think we would leave
them here for the American attack to destroy? Are you so
confident of your ability to hide them that you would risk all
in this matter?" The Libyan shook his head disapprovingly.
"No, we will keep you from such mistakes. As soon as
matters are settled in my country, we will off-load the

missiles to you. They are even now a bare three hundred miles away from here, nestled in the hold of a merchant ship."

"What exactly is happening in your country that requires the Americans to be otherwise occupied?" Santana asked bluntly. It was the question that had lingered unasked in every discussion he'd had with the Libyan, and one that the Libyan had never volunteered the answer to. Now, sensing the Libyan's willingness to reassure him, Santana asked for the first time.

Mendiria shook his head. "You have no need to know, but I will tell you this much: There are certain border disputes that are even now being resolved in a manner favorable to us. Certain . . . political considerations . . . that are being realigned to be more in keeping with a modern, powerful Libya."

"A coup?" Santana asked.

"A realignment," Mendiria corrected. He smiled, teeth flashing in the dim light. "There are many of us who believe that Libya should take a more active role in world affairs. With our natural resources, our strategic coastline—well, there are many opportunities for a nation such as Libya, especially under an enlightened leadership. If the United States is preoccupied with her backyard, it gives us a free hand in ours, the Mediterranean."

"The missiles," Santana insisted.

"In two days," Mendiria said finally, grudgingly giving up the delicate cat-and-mouse game. "We will unload them in two days. And then, you may make whatever use you wish of them."

0300 Local (+5 GMT)
USS Arsenal

The ship steamed back and forth in her firing basket like a caged tiger. Six knots on gentle seas induced a slow, hypnotic roll. The few sailors still in their racks were lulled into even deeper sleep, while three decks below complex fire control circuitry compensated for the motion in the targeting data it fed to the launchers.

Within the bowels of the ship, technicians eased themselves into the narrow interspaces between weapons, carefully making last-minute checks and adjustments to the warheads. A few of the tubes still showed smoke smudges from the earlier fire, but the delicate wiring and structural supports were undamaged.

An undercurrent of tension and excitement throbbed throughout the ship, a reflection of the eagerness of the new and untried crew to finally, after what seemed like decades of testing, make the boat demonstrate the capabilities of their platform. No ship in history, save perhaps the old-style battleships, had ever possessed such a massive load of firepower and deadly weaponry. And this was the crew that would make it work.

In Combat, the tactical action officer paced back and forth in front of his console, chained like a dog to it by the cord running from his headset to the internal communications system. He listened to the myriad reports rapping crisply out over the circuit, glanced around to make sure every station was manned, then turned to his captain. "All stations report ready, Captain." He hunched his shoulders a bit, distracted by a bead of sweat trickling down his back.

"Very well. Commence firing weapons package number eight-two-nine, at will." Captain Heather made it sound like a routine order, his voice calm and deadly professional, but the pain was clawing away at the edges of his self-control. Still, it evidently worked. His words had a steadying effect on the young TAO, who nodded.

"Firing weapons package number eight-two-nine, aye, Captain." The TAO turned back to his console, slipped into the chair, and turned his key in the lock. The SPY-1 computer took over from there.

For the next ninety seconds, being inside *Arsenal* was like rolling down a hill in a steel garbage can. The hull rang and shivered with multiple explosions as Tomahawk cruise missiles were ejected from their vertical launch tubes. Each missile came out impossibly slowly, seemed to hover over the deck for a few minutes, scorching the nonskid and gray paint with hellfire from its propulsion section, then picked up speed and darted out toward the horizon. Within moments of leaving the ship, the missiles were traveling too fast and far for the naked eye to follow.

But the SPY-1 system held radar contact on each one, sorting out the tiny pulses of returned radar energy, comparing them with the launch vector and destination of every missile, and assigning a serial number to each green lozenge blip on the screen. The launching went quickly, and completely without incident. When it was finally over, the TAO turned back to the captain. "Weapons package complete, Captain. All stations report no damage."

Captain Heather tried to grin. "Feels better when you get to do it yourself, doesn't it? Now let's just hope those men make it into shore."

"Men?" The TAO looked puzzled. For just a moment, he thought the captain might have finally lost his mind. But no, glancing at the self-satisfied visage, he knew better. TAO or not, there were still things the captain knew that he didn't.

0305 Local (+5 GMT)
Ten Miles West of Cuba

"Jesus! Will you look at that?" Sikes pointed toward the horizon. "Looks like they started their Fourth of July celebration a little early." He smiled, a cold, twisted line to his lips. The amusement never reached his eyes.

Behind him in the RHIB, three other SEALs shifted slightly to keep their balance as they also turned to watch. "Makes for a nice diversion, doesn't it?" one of them said to no one in particular. "Beats a helicopter gunship, anyway."

"Yeah, like you'd know anything about them," Huerta said mildly. "Boy, I was taking helicopter gunships into areas that didn't have any names while you were still sucking on your mama's tit. You use 'em right, there's nothing that beats it." He turned back to the horizon as three new far-off explosions echoed in the air. A trace of respect crossed his face. "Have to admit, though, this is nice."

"Let's see if it works first." Sikes's voice was still grim.

"How will we know if it works?" Garcia asked, more out of curiosity than any real need to know.

Huerta and Sikes exchanged an amused look. Huerta turned back to the younger sailor. "If there are people standing on the beach waitin' to offer us a friendly greeting when we show up, it didn't work."

Huerta smiled. "And it won't be the first time—nor the last—that that's happened to a SEAL."

0310 Local (+5 GMT)
USS Arsenal

"Lost contact over land," the TAO reported. He slipped one of the earphones off so that he could listen to the chatter inside the compartment. The sailors were starting to talk now, breaking into professional discussions of how the launch had been executed as well as exchanging congratulations.

"Good work." The captain's voice was warm. "Nice to have the first operational test out of the way, isn't it?"

The TAO nodded. "Sir, you mentioned some men . . .," he ventured.

The captain smiled, real relief crossing his face. "Let's just say that we're doing our part for a SAR mission and leave it at that."

0320 Local (+5 GMT)
One Mile off the Western Coast of Cuba

"Okay, gents, just like last time. You know the drill." Sikes touched his gear, verifying the tightness of the connections, then took a hard look at Garcia. Behind him, Huerta and Carter were performing similar services for each other. Finally, satisfied that all their gear was operational, they slipped into the warm water and headed for shore.

Twenty miles to the southeast, the other team was repeating the same maneuver. The diversion to the north, in the form of *Arsenal*'s cruise missiles bombarding isolated military targets, drew Cuban forces away from both landing zones, at least to the extent of available reserves. But, as Sikes had noted, there was always somebody who didn't get the word.

0400 Local (+5 GMT)
Western Coast of Cuba

"Helluva good swim." Sikes forced the words out, trying to disguise his urgent desire to suck in deep, gasping breaths. To his right, Huerta smiled slightly, recognizing the deception.

"You might start finding time from now on to break away from that paperwork for more PT," Huerta mused. He took the entrenching tool out of his backpack, unfolded it, and began digging a shallow hole near the base of one tree. He'd already taken his cammies out of the waterproof pack, carefully reversing the vent that allowed him to pump air out of the plastic container. He stood, stripped off his wet suit, and folded it carefully before putting it in the hole. He then slipped into his cammies.

The other SEALs followed suit, metamorphosing from waterborne warriors to land commandos. Versatility was one of the most critical qualities of any SEAL team.

After the preliminaries, they set off east, traveling in a widely spaced, snaking line toward their objective. Huerta took point and vanished into the shadows. Sikes caught an occasional glimpse of him, sometimes just the slightest hint of movement, but never saw the man in profile against the sky, or the slightest glimmer of equipment. It was as though he was a ghost, an unnatural presence stalking the land. Sikes tried his best to follow suit, knowing that in the arcane science of this type of warfare, he was hopelessly outclassed.

Finding the concrete building where their objective was supposedly housed was simple. At that hour of the night, men's spirits and attention spans are at their lowest. With the sun still hours away, even in the southern tropical climate, sentries around the world found it difficult to concentrate on the graduated shades of black and shadow around them. If anyone were still on watch, not drawn off to the north by the diversion, that is. The SEALs were counting on the Arsenal ship's evening the odds.

They clustered together under a small clump of bushes and conferred in soft whispers and hand movements. Their intelligence said that Miss Drake was hardly here against her will, although the Cubans might have been less than cooperative in letting her go. Too, given the prior incursion of the SEALs onto their island, it might be reasonable to expect a heavier guard on her. While they publicly hooted about any threat that a Cuban security force might pose to a team of SEALs, privately each man knew that an armed guard of any kind could pose a problem. That, and your luck going sour on you at the worst possible moment.

A few minutes of observing the compound did much to allay their fears. Although the base blazed with lights, there was evidently only one patrol, and he was a slackard at best, criminally negligent at worst. The Cuban patrolled at regular intervals, pacing his way easily around the compound in continuous circles. With a nightscope, Huerta watched him, noting how the man kept his attention centered on the lighted areas, never peering beyond the fence into the dark shadows surrounding the compound. The Cuban nodded, satisfied. It was doable.

With the arrival of the team outside the compound, leadership of the evolution had shifted to SEAL3. Sikes waited until he saw the hand signal, nodded acknowledgment, then darted silently forward. He was wearing the

nighttime version of woodland green cammies, a combination of burnt green and dark gray that made him part of the
night. He darted twenty feet across open land, then settled
down into the grass surrounding the fence. A few quick
experiments told him their intelligence was accurate—it
wasn't electrified, a relief, even though the SEALs had
come prepared to deal with that eventuality if necessary.

Garcia joined him moments later and pulled an insulated
set of wire snips out of his back pocket. Two minutes later,
there was a SEAL-sized hole in the wire fence.

Sikes and Garcia squiggled through it, found cover, and
waited for Huerta and Carter to join them. Operating in
teams of two, they proceeded leapfrog fashion through the
dark and shadows, blending in with the night when they
could, taking cover when they couldn't.

The security guard was almost painfully easy to avoid.

The cement building was locked from the outside by a
heavy padlock. Nothing fancy, nothing complicated, but
effective. They made a quick circuit of the building,
verifying that there were no windows in it, then turned back
to the problem of the lock. A shot from a pistol would have
destroyed it, but even their silencers would have been easily
detectable in the quiet Cuban night.

Garcia produced the snips that had dealt with the fence
around the compound and fitted them experimentally around
the lock's shaft. He bore down, squeezing the blades together,
but made little impression on the metal. Huerta watched
patiently for a few moments, then gently shoved him aside.
He took the handles to the snips in his two massive paws,
his hands enveloping them completely. Sikes watched in
awe as Huerta bore down, knots of muscles and blood
vessels popping out at odd angles all over his hands and
arms. The metal blades whined slightly as they bit into the
steel, complained, and suddenly met with a sharp click.

Huerta twisted the rest of the lock off the door and tossed it to Garcia. Sikes shook his head, then put his hand on the doorknob.

It is always difficult to tell how hostages will react, even more so when they are members of the media. There is a well-known phenomenon, the Stockholm Syndrome, in which hostages begin identifying with their captors, to the extent of even resisting rescue. Sikes wondered if such would be the case with Miss Drake.

He shook his head. No, no way. Their biggest problem would be getting her out without letting her catch it all on film. These reporters—just who the hell did they think they were? A spur of anger cut through his concentration, distracting him. She was here by her own actions, but her willful disobedience of her nation's embargo on Cuba was now endangering his life and that of his men, plus the team on the other side of the island headed for the downed pilot. Was it worth it? No, she probably wasn't—but the pilot sure as hell was.

He shoved the door open quietly and stepped into the room, still a ghost. It was stark, furnished only with a bed and linen. A door off to the right appeared to lead to a bathroom.

Pamela Drake was asleep. She was lying on her stomach, her head cushioned in one elbow, the pillow partially shielding her eyes. It also covered her ear, making it unlikely that she'd heard them enter the room. He motioned the other men in, out of immediate line of sight, then quietly shut the door so that it would appear normal from the outside. The only problem would be if the sentry came close enough to observe that the lock was now missing from the door. Given his brief observation of the man's performance, he doubted that was a probability.

Crossing the room in a few steps, Sikes knelt quietly by

the bed. He shook the mattress slightly, trying to rouse her without bringing her to full consciousness. Many times he'd found that actually touching sleeping hostages had startled them so much that they'd screamed, thus bringing unwanted attention to the rescue operation.

Pamela moaned and rolled over onto her back, and her eyelids fluttered. He shook the bed again.

Her eyelids slammed upward and she rolled to the right, freezing as she saw the man kneeling next to her bed. He felt her eyes travel over his uniform quickly, noting the lack of insignia.

"SEALs?" she finally whispered.

He nodded grudging approval of her quiet voice and quick grasp of the situation. Whatever else she was, this woman was no dummy. "Time for you to go home, ma'am."

Pamela sat up in bed, gathering the sheet around her defensively. "What makes you think I want to go home?"

Sikes rocked back on his heels. "The admiral thought—"

"Tombstone, was it?" Her voice was sharp and slightly louder. "Coming to rescue the fair damsel again, is he? Well, you just head back and tell the admiral that I think I can take care of myself. I got in here on my own, I can get out. Now go away. You're interrupting my beauty sleep." She lay down again and turned her back to him, pulling the sheets up around her neck.

Sikes sighed. This mission was becoming more of a pain in the ass every second. "Ma'am, I don't think I can let you do that," he said gently. "There's some things you need to know."

"Are you going to make me leave by force?" she asked, still not turning to face him.

"There's a strike inbound on the base. We don't recommend you stick around for it."

"I already survived one."

"You won't survive two." Sikes made his voice deadly certain. "Not from our weapons—they're as accurate as you report them to be. If they hit what they're supposed to, this area's going to be lousy with nuclear debris."

"We're shooting a nuclear weapon?"

He saw her go stiff under the sheet. "Not us. Conventional munitions only. But what's stored in those weapons is dirty weapons, ma'am, real dirty. Some nukes, maybe some biological. Certainly some chemical ones. And they're all capable of reaching the United States. You want to come back when it's all over, hell, I'll help you talk them into it. But for now, I think you're going to want to be out of here when it goes down. At least long enough to find out what's in those boxes."

"You saw my report?"

The question surprised him, but not for long. He forced himself to sound calm. "It was used for an intelligence briefing, ma'am. I figure," he said, an idea suddenly occurring to him, "that that's what you intended. That wasn't a mistake, was it? Getting all that in the background?"

Finally, she rolled over to look at him. The smile creeping across her face lit it up like a child's at Christmas. "You noticed that, did you?" There was no mistaking the self-satisfaction in her voice.

He nodded. "We all did. It takes a pro to keep their wits about 'em during something like that. That information will help save lives, ma'am." And so this is the way you skin this particular cat, he thought, wondering if he'd find his Psychology 101 classes more useful in this mission than any swimming skills.

"Dirty weapons?" she quizzed. "Could we—"

He shook his head again. "No, ma'am, the only thing we can do now is leave. There are a lot of people putting a lot on the line to afford you this opportunity, so I suggest you take it. You've done your part for the war, now let us do ours." He stood and held out a hand to her, suddenly uncertain as to exactly what she was wearing beneath the sheet, and wondering whether the SEAL team was really ready to transport a naked female out of the compound undetected.

She flipped her sheet back, and he was relieved to see her in a dark T-shirt and a set of sweats. A pair of blue and white fluorescent running shoes were peeking out from under the bed. She slipped them on quickly.

"Did you mean that? About getting me back in?" she asked as she tied her right shoe. She looked up at him, a winsome smile lighting her face. "I'd really like that if you did."

"I'll try, if the debris isn't too deadly. Best we get back to the shop and let them make that determination before you go back in, though. You've reported from some dangerous places, but I don't want one of them to be a plague quarantine hospital."

She looked slightly paler, but still determined. "We'll see," she said enigmatically, standing next to him.

Pamela grabbed her equipment bag and followed them to the door. She paused at the threshold, glancing around suspiciously. Sikes motioned to her impatiently. "Come on—we know what we're doing."

She stepped across the threshold and stopped again. "What about the pilot?"

The air between the SEAL team members crackled with tension. Was it possible? Of course it was—they should have suspected it, planned for it. "Pilot?" Sikes said, stepping close to her and whispering. The question wasn't necessary—he knew which one she meant.

Pamela pointed impatiently. "The Marine Corps pilot. I

saw him yesterday—I think they're keeping him over there."

Five hundred yards away, a small building blazed with lights. It was surrounded by another fence, and a mongrel-looking dog roamed restlessly inside of it.

Good thing we're downwind, Sikes thought. It's sheer luck that he wasn't alerted by our motion. If he'd caught our scent, he'd be barking his damned head off.

The SEALs held a hasty huddle. The SEAL team to the east thought they were heading to Major Thor's rescue, but clearly the Cubans had screwed that plan up. And since his team was already here, they had very few options. Come back with both hostages—or don't come back at all. While the admiral hadn't said it, that had been the secret resolve of each member of the team.

"So we go get him," Huerta said finally, settling the matter. "Dogs, lights—no big deal." He looked toward Sikes as though seeking permission—a courtesy, both men knew, but one that was appreciated. "You two head back toward the coast with Miss Drake. Sikes and I will go after the jarhead. That work?"

Sikes nodded. As much as he hated splitting up the team, it was the only course of action that made sense. They could not risk Miss Drake's life—no matter how much he despised what she'd done—by taking her on the rescue mission.

"No way." The objection came from the expected quarter. Although her voice was still a low whisper, Pamela Drake was livid.

"There's a good chance we won't make it," Sikes said calmly. He already knew it was futile to argue. He motioned to Garcia to key up his communications equipment.

"I think maybe I have more faith in you than you do." The

reporter regarded him solemnly, no trace of mockery or sarcasm on her face.

"Call the other team," Sikes said finally. "Abort their mission. We'll grab the pilot and scoot."

"When SEALs go out to get someone, that someone generally gets gotten. So let's go—we're wasting time." She pointed at the dog. "That's your first problem. Somehow, I don't think I'm going to want to be up close and personal for your solution."

0415 Local (+5 GMT)
USS Jefferson

"They should be back on the beach by now," Batman said. "This timetable is tight—too tight, maybe." He thought about the many SEAL operations he'd participated in, how the damnedest sure bets could go wrong at the worst possible time. The risk factor was enormously greater than that of a combat air patrol in an F-14.

"They designed the schedule, Admiral. I'm sure it's something they can live with." Lab Rat's voice sounded a good deal more convinced then he himself felt. "Anyway, there's nothing that we—"

"Commander?" An enlisted technician looked up from his bank of electronic monitoring equipment. "I think you'd better see this."

Lab Rat darted over to the console, checked the screen in front of the technician. "Oh, shit."

Batman joined him behind the technician. He studied the array of figures and scrolling information, incomprehensible to someone not inculcated into the arcane traditions of Intelligence. "What is it?"

Lab Rat shook his head. "Missile launch indications. They're getting ready. We should see thermal blooms any second, once the preliminaries are out of the way."

"Damn it all to hell!" Batman slammed his hand down on the console. "We need another two hours to get them back aboard. Launching a diversionary small-scale strike with men on the ground is one thing, but I don't want them there for the main attack. But if we're going to prevent a strike on the continental U.S., we'll have to move it up. Damn the Cubans—damn them!" He glared at Lab Rat for a moment, then the anger drained out of his face. "They're not going to make it, are they?"

Lab Rat shook his head slightly. "I don't know, Admiral. I just don't know."

THIRTEEN
Tuesday, 02 July

The flight deck was a maelstrom of noise, heat, and wind. For the last fifteen minutes, aviators had been kicking the tires and lighting fires on a wide variety of aircraft. EA-6B Prowlers were already spooled up and waiting on the catapult; their bulged cockpits and forward radomes, coupled with the distinctive pods mounted aft atop tail fins, marked them as EA-6B variants. The strange pods held both receivers and antennas for the SIR group, a systems integrated receiver for five bands of emissions. Other antennas were mounted on the fins, below the pods, enabling the aircraft to cover all electronic emissions from the A through the I bands.

The two J-52 turbojets flanking the fuselage were generating over eleven thousand pounds of thrust each, and each aircraft was straining at the tieback that held her shackled to the shuttle. The JBDs—jet blast deflectors—aft of the catapult shunted the wash from their engines to the side, although the gaggle of fighters clustered farther back on the flight deck was generating more than enough wind across the deck.

Each aircraft carried three jamming pods, one on either side on a wide pylon and one on the centerline fuselage hard point. Additionally, AGM-HARM antiradar missiles graced their wings from the other pylons. Each aircraft weighed in at slightly over sixty thousand pounds.

Overhead, two E-2 Charlie Hawkeye airborne early warning aircraft orbited, each under the protection of two F-A18 fighters. The Hawkeyes and their escorts had launched an hour earlier, and were keeping a close watch on the airspace in the vicinity of Cuba's coast. Should anything launch, either aircraft or missiles, the E-2 Hawkeye would catch it on its ALR-73 PDS radar and relay it instantly to the carrier Combat Information Center through a two-way Collins AN-ARC-34 HF or ARC-58 UHF data links. Since the installation of the joint tactical information distribution system (JTIS), the E-2 had become capable of controlling and vectoring the air picture for any combat aircraft in the U.S. inventory.

The catapult officer, a lieutenant who had been on board *Jefferson* less than six months, shook his head as he looked at the cluster of aircraft queuing up behind the JBDs. Even during workup operations, he'd never seen so many turning at once, never had an opportunity to appreciate the delicate ballet orchestrated by the handler and the yellow-shirted deck crew. Most of the plane captains had already scampered away from the hot tarmac, taking cover in the vicinity of the island to avoid being inadvertently sucked down the throat of one of the screaming engines.

"Get your head out of your ass, Cat Officer," his earphones thundered. The lieutenant glanced up at the tower and nodded his head at the air boss, invisible behind the dark glass. It all came down to this, the one moment when he, the catapult officer, released the first aircraft for flight.

Even from his position in the enclosed bubble protruding up out of the flight deck, he could sense the tension.

"Roger, sir." He made his words sound as calm as possible. In the present mood the air boss was in, it wouldn't do to irritate him unduly. Not that he blamed the junior captain ensconced above—hell, they were all nervous right now.

The catapult officer shifted his attention back to the flight deck and studied the Prowler straining at the shuttle in front of him. A plane captain held up a grease-penciled Plexiglas board to the pilot, showing the aviator his field state, weight, and weaponry. The pilot nodded, and the catapult officer saw the control surfaces on the Prowler waggle up and down. It was called cycling the stick, the last check of control surfaces that a pilot made before being launched.

"Now." The catapult officer authorized release of the aircraft on deck. He saw the yellow shirt come to attention, snap off a quick salute, and drop to his knees, pointing down the deck toward the bow. The pilot in the Prowler returned the salute, then leaned back slightly, bracing himself against the seat for the shot.

As always, it seemed to start impossibly slowly. The first few seconds of a cat shot were a study in tension as the massive aircraft slowly gathered speed. Soon, though, the expanding steam behind the shuttle overcame the aircraft's inertia and the Prowler accelerated from a leisurely roll to a thundering bolt down the deck.

Fourteen seconds later, it was over. The catapult officer stared toward the bow, watched the aircraft disappear from view as it briefly lost altitude, then saw it reappear as it struggled for airspeed. The angle of ascent was minimal at first, gradually steepening as the Prowler overcame gravity.

Seconds later, another Prowler shot off the bow cat, gained altitude, and joined its wingman as they ascended.

Two down twenty-seven to go. The catapult officer turned his attention aft. The JBDs were already lowered, and two Tomcats were taxiing forward eagerly.

It was going to be a long morning.

Thirty minutes later, the deck was still and quiet. The carrier had launched two Prowlers, fourteen Tomcats, and ten FA-18s. Additionally, another EA6 had gotten airborne to replace one that was experiencing difficulties with its CAINS system. Add to that total two KA 6 tankers, and the carrier had a full alpha strike package in the air. Back behind the carrier, a SAR helo kept station. The catapult officer glanced down at his schedule and frowned. One helo was already airborne—why did the schedule call for another? He wasn't entirely certain, but he suspected it might have something to do with the small boat launched in the wee hours from the carrier's aft deck. No matter—he hadn't been briefed on it; therefore, he had no need to know. All he did was launch 'em—it was up to someone else to decide the whys. He glanced up at the tower. And to get them back on deck.

The second helo's launch was markedly anticlimatic after so many jets. It quivered slightly on the deck, jolted once, then crept up into the air. It moved slightly to port, away from the carrier and over open water, and began gaining altitude. The catapult officer watched from his enclosed bubble as it headed out due west until it was merely a speck on the horizon.

Not that it ought to be flying at all, the catapult officer thought. As an F/A-18 pilot himself, he took it as an article of faith that a helicopter had no more right to be airborne than a bumblebee. Only problem was, no one had bothered to tell either the bug or the helo. A collection of one thousand parts flying in close proximity to each other. He shuddered at the old gibe—it was too close for comfort. No, give him speeds in excess of Mach 1 and two wings full of weapons over a helicopter anytime. Speed meant safety.

0440 Local (+5 GMT)
Fuentes Naval Base

"No, I didn't bring any doggy biscuits. So shoot me." Huerta's voice sounded sharp for the first time since the mission had begun. "How the hell was I supposed to know?"

"Well, do something," Pamela hissed. She gestured toward the east. "When does the sun come up, anyway?"

None of them bothered to answer the question. They still had some time. Not enough, but the covering darkness would last at least another hour. After that, the first traces of light would start illuminating the compound, increasing the danger of detection logarithmically.

"We're going to have to wait for a moment, then," Sikes said, his voice low and quiet. He glanced at his watch. "Another eight minutes, I think. Then we use the silencers."

"Why not use them now?" Pamela demanded.

Sikes saw the tension in her face, and saw her start to move before she even shifted her weight by much. He grabbed her by the elbow, his hand a steel band around her upper arm, and dragged her back down to the ground. "You shut up and stay under cover or you'll jeopardize the whole mission. I don't want you here—but we've got a job to do. You're not gonna screw it up, not like you did before. Now shut up."

"But what are you—," she began.

Huerta slapped one massive hand across her mouth,

anchoring her head in the crook of his arm. "You heard the commander," he said. "You stay quiet voluntarily or I crush your larynx." He smiled congenially. "I can do that, you know. Wouldn't even kill you, just make you mute for the rest of your life. You got that?"

Huerta felt her head move in his tight grip as she tried to nod. He rewarded her by loosening his hold slightly, while still keeping his hand lightly over her mouth. "We wait— eight minutes, like the commander said. When I want you to do something or say something, I'll tell you."

Garcia took out his silenced pistol and checked it for the thirtieth time, even though they all knew they were as ready as they would ever be. Eight minutes. They waited.

0450 Local (+5 GMT)
Tomcat 201

"Everybody's here, Bird Dog," Gator said impatiently. "What are you waiting for, an engraved invitation?"

"Nope," the pilot said cheerfully. God, it was good to be airborne again! And on a strike mission, too. Nothing could match the heady feeling of a Tomcat with wings dirtied, antiair missiles and five-hundred-pound bombs slung up under the wings on hard points, just waiting to be used. It made the Tomcat a bit more ungainly, true, but the added inertia during turns and maneuvers kept him conscious of the enormous firepower now under his command. "One more guy's gotta finish tanking—a Hornet, topping off his tanks, of course. I'm telling you, Gator, if I ever get out of the Navy, I'm going to invent a fuel line that spools out from the carrier and runs straight up to those bastards. Thirsty little motherfuckers—you can't even run a strike without giving them time to suck down the fuel."

"Lightweights," Gator agreed. "Can't even carry enough bombs to do any serious damage. But that's what we're here for. Anyway, you wanna get the rest of us headed in? The Tomcats are a little slower—we can start and the Hornets will catch up."

"Roger." Bird Dog flipped the communications switch to tactical. "Okay, people, let's make it happen." He heard Gator moan in the background. He'd catch hell back at the carrier later for his lack of circuit discipline, but for the moment, he didn't care. It was his plan, his mission, and he was about to see it work. One disgruntled captain—hell, even a pissed-off admiral!—couldn't change that.

Behind him, the Tomcats broke up into groups of two, flying a close formation in tight station-keeping circles. Once they left the sponge, the area where an attack force clustered to meet unexpected threats or to wait for ingress onto a target, they'd break into high-low pairs, one taking station at altitude to back up the lead down lower. It was a method of aerial combat that the Americans had perfected as no one else in the world had.

Finally, the last gas-sucking Hornet was ready. "Better get inborne before they have to go again," Bird Dog grumbled. He gave the signal over tactical.

Twenty minutes until feet dry, the transition from flying over water to flying over ground. But before that happened, it all went according to plan—

"Got the first one," Gator said suddenly. "Solid radar contact on contact breaking off from USS *Arsenal*."

"Good blackshoe," Bird Dog said approvingly. "Take your shot—we're next."

0448 Local (+5 GMT)
USS **Arsenal**

In addition to its vertical launch system for Tomahawks and antiaircraft missiles, the USS *Arsenal* had two four-missile Harpoon assemblies on either side of the ship. The long-range antiaircraft missiles, originally developed for launch against surface Echo 2–class Soviet missile submarines, were thick cylinders tapering into a pointed nose, wind and control surfaces folded during its storage in the self-contained launch box and popping out after it was ejected with pressurized air. It was controlled from Combat using the Harpoon shipboard command and launch control set (HSCLCS, pronounced "sickles"). It was a fire-and-forget missile, and a potent antiship threat.

"We've never fired one, except in tests," the captain remarked to no one in particular. No one answered. This was the first of many first launches for the *Arsenal,* and proving the operational capabilities of the Harpoon from it was almost as important as validating its land attack capabilities.

The captain watched the small camera screen mounted to the left of the large-screen display. It showed that the quad launcher was silent and passive. "Now."

The launcher shuddered once, then a thick cylinder emerged, its pointed nose slowly emerging, followed shortly by the seventeen-foot body. As it popped out, cruciform fins unfolded from both the centerline and the booster section. It seemed to take forever for the missile to launch.

As it cleared the launcher, the missile picked up speed. It

arced straight up, cleared the ship within seconds, then tipped over at a lesser angle.

"One away." The technician's voice was jubilant. "Successful launch; all stations report no damage, Captain."

"Very well." He waited for a few more seconds while the missile remained visible on the remotely controlled television camera, then shifted his gaze to the large-screen display. The potent SPY-1 radar had already picked it up as a target, and was tracking it on its northwesterly course. The SPS-64 surface search radar also held contact on its intended target, a small coastal command and control communications ship owned by the Cuban navy.

"I'll be on the bridge." The captain unbuckled himself from the seat and strode quickly forward and up to open air. He was just in time. A flare of light on the horizon, followed by a pressure wave of sound, washed over the ship. Fire spiked into the sky, then quickly died out as the sea ate the remains of both missile and ship.

"It worked," the OOD murmured. "Oh, boy, did it work."

The captain turned a stern eye on him. "You didn't doubt it would, did you?" From his superior's tone of voice, the junior officer could never have guessed that his captain was just as relieved as he was. "I'll be in Combat." The captain chided himself for his break from discipline in running out on the bridge to watch the first attack. Still, it would be his only opportunity—the rest of the missiles were after targets too far away to be observed by the naked eye. Any sense of achievement would come only after aircraft armed with TARPS overflew the land sites for battle damage assessment.

The Tomahawks took longer to launch, but six of them still left the ship in a rapid ripple of noise, fire, and smoke. The ship shuddered as tube after tube shot out the lighter, land attack missiles.

Each Tomahawk was of the TLAM-C variety, configured with a conventional warhead of high explosives. It was capable of achieving speeds in excess of five hundred knots, and cruised at an altitude of fifty to one hundred feet above the sea, making it a difficult target to detect at long range. It could be launched over two hundred and fifty nautical miles away from the target, and used a combination of digital sea mapping area correlator radar along with optical viewing of the target area for terminal flight. For these missiles, the target package took them on a slight detour to the east to insure that they cleared the inbound fighter raids.

"And now we wait." And if that were news, the captain thought. If there's one thing every sailor in every navy learned how to do, it was hurry up and wait.

0450 Local (+5 GMT)
Hawkeye 601

"The atmosphere's lousy with the shit," the E-2C radar intercept officer complained. "They've got more radars on that island, especially on top of that mountain range, than we've got on all the aircraft out here. Just try to get through that stuff."

"Well, we're going to have a little help this time. It's not all up to the Prowlers," the other RIO responded. "And here it comes."

His radar screen lit up with a barrage of sharp green blips tracking rapidly to the east, then veering in mid-flight back to the west. They were traveling at four hundred knots at first, then quickly adding another hundred to reach Mach .75. "Good thing we're up so high. We'd never see them otherwise."

"And the Cubans aren't going to see them until it's too late, either," the other RIO said. He leaned back in his chair and stretched his feet, trying to work a kink out of his neck. "Nice to have somebody else doing the nasty work for a change. Especially when it's not the Air Force."

"Especially not the Air Force," the first RIO echoed. Dealing with the Wild Weasel missions and antiradiation strikes by the Air Force always proved to be a complicated matter of coordinating communications and commands. Not that they were incompetent, mind you—just different.

"Deep dive," the first RIO announced. "And we should see . . . ah, yes. There it is." He toggled his ICS switch and called to the pilot. "Lost contact on all missiles."

"Roger." The laconic tones from the aviator in the forward half of the aircraft indicated what he thought of the traditional pilot disdain for his passengers. "Can we go home now?"

"Not yet," the RIO answered. "We still got the strike inbound, and the egress after that. Don't worry, that rack will be waiting for you when we're done."

0451 Local (+5 GMT)
Fuentes Naval Base

The missile streaked in over land and began comparing the terrain with the memory of its flight path stored in its fire control circuits. So far, a good match. It made one, minute course correction, then descended twenty feet to continue skimming forty feet above the gently rolling terrain.

One thousand meters from the target, it switched over to optical guidance, relaying a picture of what it saw through the nose camera back to the carrier. If necessary, the technician aboard the aircraft carrier could have made another course correction—but it wasn't. This Tomahawk knew exactly where it was going, and didn't need any help getting there.

Seconds later, it was over. The Tomahawk burrowed through the cement, pausing for two seconds after impact before it jerked the final firing circuitry. The warhead exploded into a firestorm of high explosives inside the concrete bunker, immediately blowing out all four walls and the roof. The contents were incinerated instantly.

Six hundred feet away, Pamela Drake screamed. Huerta clamped his hand hard over her mouth and threw her to the ground, landing on top of her. Debris rained down on him, partially blocked by the overhang of the roof they were under, but still splattering the walls above their heads. All four SEALs and their civilian guest were flat on the ground, heads tucked reflexively under their arms, waiting on the edge of life and death for the firestorm and downpour of shrapnel and debris to end.

The world went silent. Huerta shook his head, and kept his hand firmly clamped over Drake's mouth. Temporary deafening from being close to ground zero was normal stuff for him, but he could count on the civilian to panic. He could feel her lips moving beneath his hand as she tried to scream. He clamped down tighter.

Finally, he felt her body wilt. He eased his hand off gently and spun her around to face him. Her face was pale and beaded with sweat. She opened her mouth, and he raised his hand warningly. She nodded and fell silent.

Sikes flipped his hand toward the target compound. The dog had erupted in a paroxysm of motion. Probably barking its fool head off, Sikes figured. Not that anyone was within earshot to hear—they'd all be as deaf as the SEALs were. Still, best to put an end to this quickly before the acoustic shot wore off. Garcia lifted his pistol, sighting carefully, and nailed the dog through the skull with a nine-millimeter round. The dog dropped to the ground instantly and lay motionless.

Sikes gave the "go ahead" signal and led the way toward the small compound. The fence was partially torn from the nearby explosion, providing a convenient ingress point for the team. Huerta took the second position, his hand firmly clamped around Drake's wrist, dragging her along.

They were inside the compound in seconds, and Garcia put another round into the lock on the door. He burst through the door and saw a large, short-haired man in a green flight suit hunkered down under his rack. He motioned sharply at the man. "SEALs," he said, feeling the word leave his throat but still unable to hear it except as a vibration in his bones. He hoped the other man's hearing was better, but doubted it.

The pilot appeared stunned. He gazed at them blankly for a moment before comprehension began to dawn. He scrambled out from under the single bed and lurched to his feet.

Good. Uninjured. Sikes nodded approvingly, then spared two seconds to shake the man's hand. It quickly turned into a hard, quick embrace.

Getting out was just as easy. Whatever remaining Cuban forces had been in the compound were significantly distracted by the destruction raining down on them. Sikes tried to remember—the mission was briefed as a six-missile strike, all impacting their targets simultaneously. If things went according to plan, there would be no more inbound missiles to jeopardize the team's escape. Not that the SEALs should have ever been there in the first place—by now, they should already have been back in their boat and headed for the carrier. Still, the Cubans didn't know that more missiles weren't coming. There was a ten-minute window between the Arsenal attack and first strikes by naval aircraft.

He hoped it would be enough.

0455 Local (+5 GMT)
Hawkeye 601

"Oops. Here comes trouble." The RIO's voice over the ICS brought everyone back to full alert. On each screen, just at the outer edge of the detection capabilities, six small blips appeared. "Where the hell did they come from?" the RIO muttered under his breath. "It would be too good to be true if we had air superiority without a fight, don't you think?"

The second RIO reached for his mike. "I'm going to let strike leader know, if he hasn't already seen them on his AWG-9."

"Intercept time?" the first RIO asked.

"About six minutes." The second RIO left unspoken the obvious conclusion—there wasn't enough time for the inbound strike to dump weapons and disengage. They'd have to take the MiGs on while still fully loaded or dump their weaponry harmlessly in the ocean. A helluva choice to make, and one the E2C RIO was glad he didn't have to entrust to his pilot.

0455 Local (+5 GMT)
Tomcat 201

Bird Dog swore softly. Why the hell couldn't the MiGs have waited another ten minutes? By then, he'd be wings clean and at his most maneuverable. As it was, air combat maneuvering against the nimble Soviet-built fighters would be problematic, not only for the fighters but for the smaller Hornets accompanying them. And the EA-6Bs carried no antiair weaponry except the HARMs.

"Why didn't we have the *Arsenal* neutralize that land base and airfield?" Gator asked. "I would have thought that would be the perfect mission for them."

"You don't understand conflict, Gator," Bird Dog said hotly. "This is an operational air problem. This is a limited war—we don't want it spreading into a full out-and-out conflict between the United States and Cuba. See, if we conducted an attack on the other base, we'd be sending a signal that—"

"Maybe they don't read sign language, Bird Dog. Did you ever think of that? All your fancy operational art has gotten me so far is fighters inbound." Gator sounded tired. "Okay, let's figure out how we're gonna get out of this one."

"We outnumber them," Bird Dog observed. "You got the contacts relayed by the E-2?"

"Affirmative. We definitely outnumber them, but they're moving like greased lighting. Tight formation, good flight discipline. They should be—ah, there they go. High-low formation now."

"Let's give them something to shake up that tight discipline a little," Bird Dog said. He toggled over to tactical. "Red Dog Three, this is Red Dog Leader. Vector zero-four-five and take bogeys with Fox One. Hold them off for a while, Fred, until we can get rid of this load we're carrying."

"Roger. Coming right now." Two aircraft peeled off from the formation and headed toward the incoming MiGs.

"Fox One, Fox One," Red Dog Three announced seconds later, indicating that he had fired Phoenix missiles at the intruders.

The Phoenix missile was the long-range attack weapon of choice for the United States Navy. Designated the AIM-54, it was the most sophisticated and longest-range air-to-air missile in service in any nation. Over thirteen feet in length, with a diameter of fifteen inches, it weighed almost one thousand pounds and was capable of achieving speeds of up to Mach 5. With a maximum range of 110 nautical miles, it gave the F-14 Tomcat, controlling with an AWG-9 post—Doppler radar, an extended standoff engagement range.

The primary problem with the Phoenix was that it required continual guidance from the Tomcat and had a long history of unreliable fusing problems. But even with its shaky performance, the Phoenix had one big plus going for it—it made any intruder stop and think and go on the defensive. The expanding continuous rod and control fragmentation warheads did work sometimes, and when they did, the results were devastating. An adversary aircraft could not afford to count on the Phoenix's not working. It did, just often enough.

Bird Dog listened to the chatter of tactical engagement over the circuit as Red Dog Three sighted the missile in on the two lead aircraft. At the last moment, both MiGs jigged violently, shaking the Phoenix off. Hard thrust maneuvers coupled with chaff and jamming were often enough to confuse the post–Doppler radar terminal homing.

"Well, what did you expect?" Gator said when it became obvious the two missiles had missed.

"Yeah, but check their combat spread. It threw them on the defensive. Now Red Dog can close in with Sparrows and Sidewinders. Maybe take out a couple of them—hell, two Tomcats can take on six MiGs any day." Bird Dog tried to sound confident.

It was a bold statement, and one that had little basis in fact. The MiG was a smaller, more maneuverable aircraft.

At best, the Tomcats could possibly take out two MiGs each, and that was only if everything went well. The possibility that the MiGs would down a Tomcat was not even mentioned.

"Fox Two, Fox Two." The second call indicated that Red Dog Two had launched a Sparrow, a radar-guided, medium-range air-to-air missile. The Sparrow was not the dogfighting missile of choice, and was much more effective in a nonmaneuvering intercept. Though more reliable than the Phoenix, there were still problems with the solid-state electronics and the missile motors.

"Fox Three, Fox Three." And now the Sidewinders.

Bird Dog nodded in approval. It was every pilot's choice of weapon for a close-in dogfight. The annular brass fragmentation was wrapped in a sheath of preformed rods and used infrared homing to provide all-aspect tracking for the missile. It was a fire-and-forget weapon, one that could be off the rails and on target without distracting the firing pilot from critical evasive maneuvers.

"Got one!" Red Dog Three's voice was jubilant. "And there's another one—oh, shit, Fred, he's on my ass! Get him, get him!"

"I can't—" The transmission ended abruptly but without the noise blast and squeal that would have indicated a deadly shot on the Tomcat.

"Damn it, why aren't we in that?" Bird Dog swore. "We've got more combat experience than all of these other pilots put together."

"Don't even consider it, asshole," Gator snapped. "You're flight leader—your job is to get them in, all of them, and put ordnance on target. Not pick off fighters on your own. Get used to it, buddy."

"But I could've—"

"You don't know what he did until the debrief," Gator cut him off. "Get your head back in the ball game."

Gator was right. Bird Dog tamped down his temper and concentrated on the tactical mission around him. "Red Dog Four, roll off and assist Red Dog Two." An odd feeling of heaviness settled into the pit of his stomach. He hadn't expected this, being left out of the actual fight, ordering other crews off on an intercept. He knew he shouldn't feel so bad—so guilty. Still, sending men and women off to die in dogfights while he bore in on the grand target? It shouldn't be like that.

"They're down to three MiGs," Gator reported. "One Sparrow, two Sidewinders. Red Dog Four just took a Phoenix shot at the trail aircraft."

"Where are we?" Bird Dog demanded. In concentrating on the air battle going on to the east, he'd temporarily lost the big picture.

"Feet dry in ninety seconds," Gator answered.

Hearing the familiar voice of his RIO provided an unexpected amount of comfort. After all the missions they'd flown together, the MiGs they'd shot down over China and the hair-raising assault on the Aleutian Islands, it meant something to have the right man in the backseat. Or woman, he amended, one part of his mind worrying over that as another fought to regain the tactical picture. "I'm descending now," he said.

Gator clicked his mike twice in acknowledgment.

From five hundred feet above the ground, the terrain was suddenly familiar. God knows he'd studied the topography maps often enough, and it was starting to pay off now. It was like making a run on Chocolate Mountain in southern California, a familiar, predictable terrain.

The early morning sky suddenly lit up with fireflies. No, not fireflies, they were—

"Tracers," Bird Dog yelped. "Shit, Gator, we're taking antiaircraft fire!"

"Damn it, Bird Dog, don't lose it now. That was briefed— you knew about it. Just get us in on target."

Bird Dog fought the almost visceral urge to grab altitude and climb to safety. At five hundred feet, he had little room for error, and less for maneuverability. They were so close to the target point now that any twitch off course would put ordnance on the wrong targets—with his luck, probably a hospital or orphanage, more grist for the news media to castigate the American military establishment. He gritted his teeth, focused in on the terrain, and pressed on. Another seventy seconds until he could climb to safety.

Unexpectedly, he thought of Callie. His relationship was fucked up, but at least he'd do something right—something he was trained to do, something he'd practiced millions of times. And there was no chance the Cubans would send him a Dear John letter over this attack.

0456 Local (+5 GMT)
Fuentes Naval Base

"Those are ours," Sikes said, pointing up to the sky. "You can tell by the Tomcat engine."

Huerta nodded. "Are we clear?"

Sikes shrugged. "I don't know. It depends on how accurate they are."

They'd left the Fuentes Naval Base perimeter the same way they'd come in, dragging Pamela Drake through the hole in the perimeter fence. Suddenly, she'd seemed convinced of her own immortality, and had actually argued that she should remain in the compound during the air attack on the base. He shook his head. Women—and reporters. No sense at all.

"Let's put a little more space between us and the IP," he ordered. "I want to be on the beach in five minutes." He turned to the Marine Corps pilot. "Think you can keep up?" he asked, deliberately ignoring Pamela Drake.

The Marine major seemed to swell slightly. "I'm a Marine. You wanna race me to the beach?"

Sikes shook his head. "No, the real question is this—how well can you swim?"

0457 Local (+5 GMT)
Tomcat 201

"Twenty seconds," Gator said. "Almost there, Bird Dog— we're almost in." The backseater sounded like a football coach calling a routine play. "And hurry up!" The RIO's voice took on a new note of urgency. "We've got company."

Bird Dog's head snapped up. He'd been staring down at the terrain, tensing himself for the moment that he would release the five-hundred-pound bombs. "Where? And who?"

"Dead ahead. Ten miles. Looks like more—it is. MiGs, from the radar. Bird Dog, we can make it. Hold steady on this course, dump the bombs, then we'll take care of the MiGs." Gator's voice was insistently urgent.

"How many?"

"You don't wanna know."

"How many!" Bird Dog heard Gator sigh.

"About twenty so far. And the E2 says there's a second wave behind them. It looks like the six inbound from the east were just a diversion."

Bird Dog toggled his tactical circuit on. "Red Dog Flight, this is Red Dog Leader. You see it now, guys—MiGs, dead ahead. We've got time—just enough. Dump your ordnance, then combat spread. All flight leads acknowledge." A quick flurry of acknowledgments followed.

"No one flinches," Bird Dog said, a hard, deadly tone in his voice. "We finish their base, then we finish them."

0500 Local (+5 GMT)
USS Jefferson

"Damn it!" Tombstone slammed his hand down on the arm of his battle chair. "How the hell did they get away with that? And where did all those aircraft come from? That's more than Cuba has in her entire inventory!"

Batman clenched his fists and glared at the large-screen display. "Libyans. It's got to be. Five years ago, you and I would never have fallen for that feint."

"Five years ago, we wouldn't be on some wishy-washy presence mission constrained by political considerations in our own backyard," Tombstone snapped. "Damn it, Batman, we blew it. Face it."

Batman shook his head. "Not yet, we didn't." He pointed at the flight of Tomcats and Hornets inbound on their objective. "Do the time-distance problem. They've got time to dump their ordnance and engage. It ain't over until it's over, Admiral."

The use of his title snapped Tombstone back to reality. He shifted out of his emotional reaction to the sudden appearance to the inbound raid and focused strictly on the tactical scenario. What Batman said was true. And, with their ordnance dumped, he'd match his flight of Tomcats up against any raid of MiGs.

That the Cubans had surprised him frustrated him no end. Perhaps what he'd said in anger was true—maybe he was too old to be in command of operational forces. God knows he'd certainly had his taste of combat, in missions ranging from fighting the Soviets during the Cold War in the skies of Norway to his most recent foray against them, repelling a missile launch crew from the Aleutian Islands. Maybe it was time to step down, give the younger men a chance. Maybe it was—

"Admiral Wayne. We need to talk—now." Tombstone drew his old friend aside to a quiet corner of TFCC. He steepled his fingers in front of him and gazed at his old wingman, his dark, unreadable eyes now backlit with frustration. "What's the first principle of command, Batman?"

"Lead from the front," Batman said promptly. "Don't ask your troops to do something that you aren't willing to do yourself."

Tombstone nodded. "I'm glad you remember that. Maybe you won't think I'm completely crazy, then. Listen, it's your air wing—can I borrow a Tomcat?"

Batman's jaw dropped. "Hell, no, you can't have an aircraft! How long has it been since you've been behind the controls, anyway? Two years?"

Tombstone shook his head. "Not that long." He managed a grim smile. "A three-star draws enough water to catch an occasional refresher FAM flight, even in SOUTHCOM. Two weeks, max."

"But what the hell for?" Batman's voice had ratcheted up three notes. What his old lead was proposing was crazy—absolutely insane. Admirals didn't fly combat flights—they stayed in TFCC and kept the big picture, drawing on their experience and training to coordinate the myriad factors that could—and often did—go wrong in combat. "You're of more value right here than you are in the air."

Tombstone shook his head again. "No. We've got two admirals on board as it is. You and I both know that I should never have been ordered out here as task force commander. You're more than capable of running your own carrier group, whether or not it includes an Arsenal ship."

"But what do we gain by putting you in the air?" Batman asked, tacitly acknowledging the truth of Tombstone's statement. "I've got a dozen pilots sitting in ready rooms ready to man up those birds. I hate to say it, old friend, but they're a helluva lot sharper in the cockpit than you are now. You could have taken them back when we were both flying regularly, but not now." Batman shook his head. "No. I can't see any justification for this. With all due respect, Tombstone, no."

"Think about this, Batman." Tombstone pointed back toward the large-screen display, then fished in his pocket and pulled out a laser pointer. He toggled it on and then circled the symbols for the incoming raid aircraft with a red dot. "We've got what looks like Cubans inbound, right? Only you and I both know that they're probably Libyans. How the hell our satellite surveillance missed them is something we'll puzzle out later. But for now, there's a lot more on the line than merely air battles and losing aircraft. We've got a whole new foray by a foreign nation into our bathtub down here, and however this ends up, it's not going to be pretty. I'm not having my men and women face it alone—not when I can be out there with them. If there's going to be some shit hitting the fan over this, it's going to have to go through me to get to them. They're all good pilots, every last one of them, and they don't deserve to put up with the political bullshit that's going to be falling out from this. That's why I need to be there—I'm a shit shield, if it comes down to that in the aftermath."

Tombstone's face looked hard, weary. He was making sense, Batman had to admit, but not in a way he'd ever heard a three-star make sense before. They both knew that fighting a war and winning it tactically was only half the solution. It was the news reporting and diplomatic interpretation of the battle afterward that really made American foreign policy. But still, was the solution to risk a senior officer on a swan-song combat flight? He didn't think so.

Tombstone took a step closer to him. "I'm retiring after this tour, Batman. I've got three stars now, three more than I ever planned on." His voice took on a wistful note. "All I ever wanted to do was fly. The promotions, commanding a carrier battle group—that was the pinnacle. There's just more paperwork, more D.C. tours after this. I'm going to punch out while it's still fun."

"But Tombstone, there are other operational commands. And there's always JCS." Batman struggled to find more arguments to present to his old lead.

"Not for me." Tombstone's voice and face suddenly lightened, as though some terrible tension had been released inside of him. "This is it—one final mission, putting it on the line one last time and hopefully doing some good for this country. I owe the country that—and you owe me an aircraft."

Batman's throat seemed to close up slightly. "What's your mission?"

"BDA—bomb damage assessment. We need a firsthand look at it, from somebody who's got enough background to know what they're seeing. And those missile launchers—hell, these pilots are all too young to have seen the real thing. You and I would know what they were."

"I'll go with you." Batman was surprised to find how

exciting the prospect was. To be back in the air, to feel the smooth surge of twin engines pounding under his butt, facing off against the adversary in a nimble, deadly fighter— he wanted it, too.

"You can't. Someone has to stay in command here." What might have been a smile tugged at the corners of Tombstone's mouth. "And I'm senior, buddy. This is your battle group—you stay here and command it like I had to do in the Spratlys. I'll go out and get the BDA, help us plan our next move."

"Damn it, Tombstone—oh, all right. But you'll need a backseater." Batman's eyes looked unfocused as he considered the roster of naval flight officers on his staff.

"I'll go," a quiet, feminine voice said. Both men turned and stared at the small figure standing a foot away from them.

"Eavesdropping, Commander?" Batman said harshly. "Not a good way to get off to a good start with your new battle group commander."

She met his angry gaze levelly. "No, it's not. Just about as bad a way as letting a three-star admiral fly off this boat without the best damned backseater available going with him. Do you know what happens to this grandiose plan if he gets shot down and killed? All of this self-serving bullshit is for nothing—and you're left facing the long green table."

"Better to be judged by three than carried by six," Batman said.

"Better if neither happens. If Tombstone's taking a Tomcat on a strike or recon mission, I'm going with him. We've flown together before, and I know how he thinks. I might be able to keep him alive when no one else can." Her voice was firm and insistent.

"Following that logic, I ought to be on his wing," Batman countered.

"The admiral already shot down that idea," she pointed out. "And he's absolutely right—your place is here with the battle group. Not for me. I haven't relieved Henry yet, so I've got no formal role in this battle. My place as prospective executive officer is anywhere I'm needed. And right now, that's in the backseat of his Tomcat." She turned to Tombstone and shot him a withering glare. With all due respect Admiral, this is the stupidest idea I've ever heard you come up with. Sir."

"You're not going," Tombstone said. "End of discussion."

"Why?" she shot back. "Because I'm your wife? Damn it, Admiral—Tombstone—I was a helluva fine RIO before I ever met you, and I'll be a damned fine one after you retire. But there's one thing I won't be, not at this age—a widow. So if you've got good reasons for taking this flight yourself, you can just count me in. You got that? Sir?" She made a visible effort to rein in the temper that went with her fiery red hair.

The two admirals looked at each other, each slightly surprised to find that he'd been outflanked by the diminutive commander. Finally, acceding to the inevitable, Tombstone shrugged. Batman scowled. "Well?" Tombstone asked. "Do I get my aircraft?"

Batman nodded. "And my favorite RIO, as well. Take care of her, you old son of a bitch. I'll kill you myself if she gets hurt."

Tomboy snorted. "If you've both just about run the gamut of your testosterone-laden self-recriminations, could we get on with it? I've got a mission to brief." She turned smartly, then looked back. "I'll be in the Ready Room when you're ready to go, Admiral. I suppose you can still find the way by yourself?"

"And I thought the Cubans were getting good at outmaneuvering me," Tombstone said wonderingly.

"I need to talk to you—alone," Batman said abruptly. He pointedly looked away from Tomboy, who shrugged and left immediately.

"What was that about?" Tombstone asked.

"Just something she doesn't need to know about—hell, I wouldn't tell you except that you outrank me and you're going to be on the front lines out there. It's about *Arsenal*. She's carrying UAVs—unmanned aerial vehicles."

Tombstone was stunned. "Since when?"

"Since my last tour in D.C. I've still got sources there, Stoney. I heard about it from a shipmate who took the time to hunt me down last time I was there. They're playing this Arsenal program so close to the chest that need-to-know evidently doesn't even include me. But you can count on it—she's got them on board."

UAVs—one of the cheapest, most cost-effective assets in development. Tombstone had seen a few test films, had been impressed by the weaponeering and intelligence potential in them. Yet sadly, the program languished. Despite its tremendous benefits to all the services, there simply wasn't enough money involved to garner the political support to keep it funded.

At least not most of it. Evidently someone in Washington drew enough water to get them put on board the USS *Arsenal*.

"I'll keep that in mind," Tombstone said. "Though I don't know that it'll make any difference right now."

0508 Local (+5 GMT)
Tomcat 201

Bird Dog was only two hundred feet above the ground, screaming across the landscape at 450 knots. The pucker factor involved in low-level operations was second only to trapping on the carrier at night, and particularly so when dawn had not even started to make its first appearance over in the east. Luckily he knew from studying the maps that there were no obstructions on their ingress route, and as long as he stayed on course and at altitude, he should be over his target without encountering a hard, immovable object. Like a mountain. Or a building. Either one of those was guaranteed to ruin an aviator's day, along with the more minor hazards, less visible but equally deadly, of electrical lines and television antennas.

"Ten seconds," Gator said. "On course, on altitude—steady, steady."

The comments were unnecessary but reassuring. Bird Dog glanced down at the target track indicator on his heads-up display, followed the red pip displayed there. He could see himself that he was making a perfect approach on the target. The only problem, as far as he could see, was the inbound raid of MiG-29s. And those wouldn't be much of a problem as soon as he dumped the ordnance on his wings.

"Five seconds," Gator announced with all the emotional involvement of a stockbroker reporting an inactive share. "Four, three, two—now, now."

Bird Dog had already shifted the weapons selector switch to the appropriate station. He toggled it sharply and felt the Tomcat jolt upward as a pair of five-hundred-pound bombs left the wings. His airspeed picked up immediately, as did his altitude. Bird Dog slammed the throttles forward, cut sharply to his right, and kicked in the afterburners. The increase in thrust slammed him back against his seat, and he heard a sharp, involuntary gasp from Gator. Bird dog grunted and tensed his stomach muscles, forcing blood out of his torso and into his head to insure he kept consciousness during the high-G maneuver. It wasn't his preferred way to leave a target—sure, get away smartly, but this insane coupling of maneuvering and speed brought its own dangers. Graying out right now, less than five hundred feet above land, would be fatal. There was no room for error.

Still, there was no other option. With the MiGs inbound in a classical high-low combat formation spread, the Tomcat flight had to gain altitude. And fast. It would be an easier task for its lighter Hornet brethren, but the Tomcats would be the mainstay of any extended ACM. After the bombing run, heavily laden and traveling close to the ground, the Hornets would be burning fuel at an incredible rate. He figured they had no more than twenty minutes on station in ACM and violent maneuvering before they'd have to vector back to the carrier to tank. As formidable as the light aircraft were in ACM, easily outclassing the MiG in turning radius and maneuverability, their short legs were too often a fatal weakness.

Bird Dog watched the altimeter spool up past angels two. He eased out of the turn and felt the aircraft begin to gain altitude even more quickly. Finally, at ten thousand feet, he cut the afterburners and eased back to military power.

His wingman, Short Mahoney, was lagging behind. Bird Dog orbited, waiting for him to catch up.

"Six minutes," Gator announced in the same tone of voice he'd used to count down the bomb drop. "Within Phoenix range now."

"Right. If I had any." He'd selected a weapons load consisting primarily of Sidewinders, since carrying the five-hundred-pound bombs left little additional space on the wing hard points.

"Three minutes to Sparrow range," Gator added.

"Short, go low. I'll take high station," Bird Dog ordered over tactical. He ascended another two thousand feet and watched as his wingman dropped down to angels seven.

The MiGs were visible now in the eastern sky, no longer simply black spots on the horizon but sharp-angled sleek fuselages and wings. And the wings—dirty, he could tell even at this distance. What were they carrying? Probably a combination of short- and medium-range weapons, he decided. They'd known they were going to be in a dogfight, and wouldn't have bothered to carry the Soviet equivalent of a long-range standoff Phoenix. And since they hadn't had to carry five-hundred-pound bombs into target, they'd have more than enough weapons to spare, he figured. If they could catch the Tomcats, that is.

He watched the heads-up display adjust itself as radar homed in with the AWG-9 radar on the lead target, switching from search to tracking mode. A low growl sounded in his ears as a Sidewinder signaled that it had acquired a heat source sufficiently large to warrant its interest. Bird Dog took a quick, reflexive check on the position of the sun. It was something you always watched for with a Sidewinder, that you weren't taking a long-range shot at the sun with the short-range missile. No, it was still below the horizon. With all of his own aircraft safely behind him, he felt confident that anything the Sidewinder had acquired was a bad guy.

"Fox Three," he said as he toggled the weapons selector switch over to the appropriate station. He slammed his eyes shut for a moment as the aircraft shuddered, trying to save his night vision from being destroyed by the phosphorous white fire of the missile's ignition system. Even with his eyes closed he could see the red reflecting through his eyelids.

"Missile off the rail," Gator said. "Looking good, looking good—flares, Bird dog. He's got flares. Your eyes—" The warning came too late. The lead MiG shot off three flares from an undercarriage slot and the white phosphorous orbs shattered the darkness. Bird Dog swore as his pupils contracted down to pinpoints in reaction to it, effectively destroying his night vision.

The only consolation was that the MiG pilots would have been as blinded by the flares as he was.

0900 Local (+5 GMT)
MiG 101

Santana was concentrating on the radar picture and barely felt the flares shoot out from the undercarriage. The MiG-29, while a superbly engineered aircraft, had one major fault: It was a one-man operation. In a high-threat environment with this many adversary aircraft inbound, he would have preferred to have an extra set of eyes in the backseat to keep watch on the other side. It was always a danger in a single-seater aircraft, losing sight of the big picture. He concentrated on the scope, his own source of data now that the Willie Pete shots had ruined his night vision, and vectored in.

Which one of those mongrels had had the audacity to fire on him? There—that was the one. He marked the radar symbol with a target designation. As often as he'd trained for ACM in practice, Colonel Santana had never actually faced hostile air. It was one thing to take on a small private aircraft *mano a mano*. No challenge, that—like shooting ducks in a barrel, as the Americans said. He'd practiced this often enough that he felt comfortable with the tactics and fire doctrine, but there was still something intangibly different about the actual event. In practice, one could always call a time-out, pause and regroup, review one's mistakes, and, most important, brag about one's exploits afterward with the victim. Here, it was different.

The sudden, cold realization shook him. The air was no longer a friendly playground, something he'd earned the right to by virtue of his training, intelligence, and experience. It was a killing ground, and losing this battle meant more than having to put up with obnoxious bragging by the other side afterward.

And that aircraft, the one with the brilliant glowing red circle around it, was the one that had had the audacity to shoot at him. He felt a sense of relief, an easing of fear, as the threat to his existence became identifiable, distinct. No longer was it Death flying in the air around him, it was a single aircraft with a single pilot—and a RIO behind him, he realized—that threatened his existence. The odd conviction that if he could kill that one aircraft he would be safe overtook him. It made no sense, yet there it was.

Around him, he heard the rest of the flight calling out excitedly, each man claiming a particular target as his own. The designation popped up on his screen as the other pilots did as he did, made the enemy personal and singular instead of massive and unreal.

Before, it had been a matter of tactics. Now, it was personal. And someone would pay for that.

0510 Local (+5 GMT)
Tomcat 201

"Asshole's after us," Bird Dog snarled. The MiG he'd shot at had turned and was headed directly toward him. With a closure rate of one thousand knots, it would be mere seconds before he would be within knife-fighting range of the other aircraft. Bird Dog had an advantage, though—from what he could see, he had at least two thousand feet of altitude on the adversary. Altitude was safety, a fungible commodity in the air that he could trade for speed, for safety, or for any one of a number of critical flying factors.

He watched the MiG approaching, carefully calculating the angle between them. It would be a lead-lag situation in moments, particularly if the other pilot was not smart enough to avoid it. He wondered fleetingly how well the other pilots were trained. Not very, probably—not if the Soviets had had a hand in it. If the other pilot misjudged the situation, Bird Dog would be able to climb slightly and drop in behind him, a perfect position for a Sidewinder shot. The white-hot exhaust from the other aircraft's engine would render any flare deceptions virtually useless.

"Hang on, Gator, time for some airspace." Bird Dog slammed into afterburner again, tipped the Tomcat's nose up, and shot almost vertically into the sky. The maneuver decreased his speed over ground radically, and would, he hoped, confuse the pilot below him.

As the altimeter spooled past fifteen thousand feet, he said, "Come on in, buddy. I've shot down MiGs before. You won't be my first—and I doubt you'll be my last. If you think you've got what it takes, come on up and play with the big boys."

0511 Local (+5 GMT)
USS Jefferson

Tombstone ran his hand lightly over the familiar controls of the Tomcat, marveling at how it all flashed back to him every time he took the controls. He could hear Tomboy murmuring to herself behind him, quietly walking through her own preflight checklist. They were sitting on the catapult, already affixed to the shuttle, steam pressure satisfactory, just waiting for the signal.

"All done. Ready to launch, Stoney." Tomboy's voice sounded as coldly professional as ever.

"Ready up here—have been for hours." He forced a chuckle. "That's how it always is, isn't it? The husband waiting for the wife to get ready?"

"You're gonna pay for that one, big boy."

Tombstone's retort was forestalled by approaching launch. He wiped his control surfaces, then signaled his readiness to the plane captain. He glanced at the Plexiglas board the man held in the air, instantly absorbing the figures noted there. Finally, he held out a thumbs-up.

The yellow shirt came to attention, snapped off a quick salute, then dropped to one knee and pointed dramatically forward toward the bow of the ship. Tombstone returned the salute, dropping his hand quickly to rest it on the throttles. Seconds later, the seat slammed him from behind and the ejection harness straps bit into his shoulders. He gulped down a quick breath at the sensation, as familiar as every curve of Tomboy's body. More so, really—he'd spent more time in a Tomcat than in her.

The bow of the ship thrust forward quickly to meet him. Fourteen seconds later, he felt that sickening drop as the aircraft departed the carrier, that moment of sheer panic every pilot feels as gravity fights to suck the aircraft down into the sea. One of his own personal nightmares was a soft cat—a shot where insufficient steam power on the downstroke led to insufficient airspeed. The results were almost always fatal, unless the pilot were quick enough to eject before the Tomcat hit the water. And every time he launched, he was certain it had just happened. His fingers closed around the ejection handle.

As always, however, he felt the Tomcat grab for altitude

at the last moment. The engines screamed as they fought to overcome the relentless downward pull. Slowly, too slowly for anyone's comfort, the aircraft gained altitude.

One last mission, one last combat patrol, one last chance to stare the enemy in the face and find out who was the better pilot. He hoped it would be worth it.

0512 Local (+5 GMT)
MiG 101

Santana watched as the Tomcat shot up into the air. The American fighter had a higher thrust-to-weight ratio, as well as a higher wing loading factor, giving it greater power than the MiG but decreasing its turn radius. And just as he knew the capabilities of the American fighter, so he was certain that the U.S. pilot knew exactly what his MiG was capable of. Decades of planning and training to fight the Soviet Union had given the Americans an enormous lead in the arcane field of dissimilar fighter tactics.

The Cubans had been similarly diligent, drawing upon the expertise of their Soviet masters for research and advice.

The Tomcat's ventral side was a cold, gleaming silver in the sparse starlight. Already the sky had started to lighten almost imperceptibly, a foreshadowing of the dawn that would soon break. By that time, when the sun was finally visible, only one of them would still be in the air.

The best tactic for a more maneuverable aircraft such as a MiG versus a behemoth like the Tomcat is to fight an angles war, restricting the plane of combat to the horizontal as much as possible and preventing the larger craft from using its greater thrust-to-weight ratio to attain altitude—and therefore, potential airspeed—on the smaller one.

Santana assessed the Tomcat's rate of climb. It seemed that the pilot had not started his ascent soon enough, leaving some possibility that the angles fight could be turned to the Cuban's advantage immediately.

Santana put his MiG Fulcrum into a hard left turn, standing the nimble aircraft on its wing as he ducked underneath the path of the offending Tomcat. He knew what the American intended—to gain altitude, roll over, and drop in behind him for a killing shot. By forming a T with the ascending aircraft, he made that probability unlikely.

In a few more seconds, he would see if his plan was working. Then he could judge the geometry of the engagement and quickly correct the agile Fulcrum's course as necessary. The seconds ticked by inexorably.

0513 Local (+5 GMT)
Tomcat 201

"Furball forty miles to the east," Tomboy said. "Recommend we come left slightly to avoid it. That is, if what you really want to do is get the BDA you said you were after."

Tombstone clicked his mike twice in response, annoyed by Tomboy's insight. She knew as well as he did that what he really wanted to do was vector over to the furball, pick off a MiG, and go one-on-one as he had so many times before. Even the absence of a wingman to assist him in a combat spread didn't bother him. He'd fought solo against MiGs more times than most of these pilots had trapped on a carrier.

Instead, he eased the aircraft to the left, swinging wide of the engagement. Maybe later, after he'd had a chance to see what he'd come to see, and radioed the results back to the carrier. Maybe one last time—but duty first. Whatever else he might have felt about flying, his obligation right now was to the carrier. And to Batman. This aircraft had been released to him for one purpose and one purpose only—to obtain critical information for the carrier group commander—not to allow him to live out some boyish fantasy one last time.

"Feet dry in five mikes." Tomboy's voice was still coldly professional, empty of any trace of "I told you so."

Tombstone spared one last look off to the right, searching the sky for the aircraft that he knew were dancing deadly waltzes with each other at this very minute. Then he refocused his attention on the heads-up display inside. Duty first.

0514 Local (+5 GMT)
Tomcat 201

"Oh, you bastard," Bird Dog muttered. "You slimy little Cuban bastard." He craned his neck over and stared down, hoping to catch a glimpse of the aircraft darting underneath his flight path. He thought he saw it—the dim sparkle of starlight on hardened painted metal—but he couldn't be certain. For now, Gator and the radar provided a better picture of their relative positions than eyesight.

"Under you," Gator warned. "Still turning—Bird Dog, he's an angles fighter."

"Of course he is," Bird Dog snapped. "So would I be if I were flying a MiG against a Tomcat. Well, we're going to have to put the kibosh on that little scenario."

He jerked the Tomcat into a hard right turn, breaking off

the ascent. As he leveled off, he rolled the Tomcat through 180 degrees until he was standing on his port wing, pointing down toward the ground. The maneuver cost him altitude, which was just what he intended. He waited until he was approximately level with the MiG, then continued to roll, twisting twice more until he was head-on-head with the MiG.

And take that, you motherfucker. Nose-on-nose, you're mine.

"Watch him," Gator warned. "With his turning radius, he'll be out of here in a heartbeat."

"He turns, and I'll be on his ass," Bird Dog answered. "Which is just where I want to be for a Sidewinder."

0515 Local (+5 GMT)
Fulcrum 101

Santana snarled at the radar picture reflected in his heads-up display. He'd halfway expected it, hoping against crazy hope that his first maneuver in angles fighting would win the battle, but clearly the American was too well trained to fall for it. Still, he had started his ascent too late. Now, nose to nose with a closure speed in excess of Mach 2, the American would undoubtedly expect him to use his greater maneuverability to turn out of the confrontation.

The American had made one mistake—maybe he could be enticed into making another. Santana held the MiG on a steady course and bore in, waiting for the right moment.

0516 Local (+5 GMT)
Tomcat 201

"Inside minimums!" Gator screamed. "Bird Dog, you can't shoot now. It won't fuse."

The pilot swore, damning his overconfidence. He'd been so sure the MiG would turn. The MiG *had* to turn to take advantage of its aerodynamic advantages and maneuverability. It made no sense for the MiG to have continued on. Bird Dog had been waiting for the turn, intent on shooting a Sidewinder up the bastard's ass. Instead, he was facing the equivalent of two freight trains roaring toward each other on the same piece of track. And how he'd lost his opportunity— no way to take a Sidewinder shot now. Well, he'd have to pull out of this engagement, or at least go for the overshoot and come back for another maneuver.

What had made the Cuban undertake this game of chicken? Maybe they weren't as well trained as doctrine had taught, and didn't really understand how to use every advantage of the more nimble fighter in a furball. If that were the case, then he could count on the other pilot making another mistake sometime soon. And it would be his last one.

0516 Local (+5 GMT)
Fulcrum 101

"Now." Santana had already toggled the weapons selector to gun, and knew that this opportunity was just moments away. The American would still be expecting him to break, waiting for that moment to shoot a Sidewinder on the oh-so-attractive heat source flaring out of the engines. What he wouldn't expect was this.

Santana jinked the aircraft up, correcting his angle for approach on the Tomcat from a near miss to guaranteed collision. If the American wanted to play chicken, Santana would find out what he was made of.

Seconds later, he saw it begin. The angle on the Tomcat changed slightly, indicating that the American was attempting to maneuver away from certain midair collision. Santana grinned, jogged the MiG slightly nose up, and shot a brief burst from his 30mm GSh-301 gun in the port wing root. The depleted uranium pellets saturated the air directly in front of the Tomcat.

The American had no chance. The Tomcat streamed right through the barrage, and Santana saw, in the American's last moments, a delicate tracery of black holes spout up along the starboard wing and fuselage. Seconds later, the night flared into brilliance as the fuel streaming out of the wing tanks ignited. The light blinded him, just as his flares had earlier. However, a satisfying dull thud followed momentarily by a rocking wash of air over pressure told him the attack had been a success. The Tomcat exploded.

0516 Local (+5 GMT)
Tomcat 201

For five seconds, Bird Dog and Gator operated on instinct rather than training. Bird Dog saw the angle change, realized with a sickening rush of fear what the MiG intended, and reached for the ejection handle above his head.

Gator beat him to it. The older, more experienced aviator activated command eject. The canopy shot off, the explosive bolts severing the connection between hardened Plexiglas and steel fuselage. Bird Dog felt one gush of wind, a flash of heat as Gator's ejection seat shot away from the aircraft at an angle, then the hard, unconsciousness-inducing motion of his own ejection seat parting company with his aircraft.

He was less than fifty feet away from the aircraft, the seat already starting to respond to the inexorable pull of gravity, when he heard the soft *crump* of the Tomcat's disintegration. The fireball reached out for him, its outer edges clawing hungrily for the delicate canopy now unfolding from the ejection seat. If it touched even one of the thin strands, or licked a panel of the unfolding parachute, it wouldn't matter whether he survived the ejection. The fall alone, five thousand feet to the warm, blood-temperature sea, would kill him.

0517 Local (+5 GMT)
Fulcrum 101

As his night vision started to return, Santana rolled his aircraft over inverted and looked up at the canopy now pointed down at the sea, searching the sky for parachutes. There was no chance, really, that the Americans had managed to escape. Still, he wanted to make sure that the pilot who had dared to challenge him died with his aircraft. Even though the man had been fatally insolent in targeting his MiG, Santana wished him a good death. One in midair, inside the aircraft, not killed by the uncertain vagaries of ejection or smashed against the hard surface of the ocean below. He wished the man a good death, but a death nonetheless.

0517 Local (+5 GMT)
Tomcat 202

"Jesus!" Tombstone slammed his eyelids shut, too late. "Tomboy, lost my night vision. What's around us?"

"I thought you were going to stay clear of the furball," his RIO snapped back. "One straggler dogfight in the area, and you wander into the middle of it. Didn't I tell you to—"

"Where is the MiG now?" Tombstone demanded. "Give me a vector."

"He's breaking off and RTB," Tomboy reported after a slight pause. "The Tomcat—it exploded midair."

"Any chutes?" Perhaps his RIO's night vision had survived the fireball in front of him.

"I think I see—yes, one. No, make that two. I'd call it good chutes, but who can tell from here?"

Tombstone reported the engagement and the presence of two probable parachutes settling into the water below to the carrier. With any luck, *Jefferson*'s SAR would be on top of the aviators before Cuba could vector in any small boats to pick them up. Had he had the time, he would have stayed overhead himself, circling and providing cover from surface attack with his guns.

But he couldn't. Not if he intended to accomplish his mission and get the information back to the carrier in time to make a difference in this battle. He hoped the downed aviators would understand. He wasn't so certain that he would, in the same position.

Jefferson acknowledged Tombstone's call for SAR, and

reported that the Angel helicopter was inbound his location. Tombstone acknowledged the transmission with a brief click, then turned his attention back to his mission. Moments later, the verdant landscape of Cuba, now a dim watercolor engraved in black, rushed by below his aircraft. Feet dry.

FIFTEEN
Tuesday, 02 July

0600 Local (+5 GMT)
Western Coast of Cuba

By the time Sikes and his cadre reached the beach, the sun was already nibbling away at the darkness that had been their primary protection. Behind them, they could hear sirens and explosions. Whether it was a new attack by the American forces, one not noted in the original plan, or simply secondary detonations of munitions lockers and stored aviation fuel, they didn't know. And it didn't matter, really. What was important was that the chaos on the base was providing a needed distraction while they made good their egress. Sikes glanced back at Drake and Thor. The Marine was holding up as well as he'd boasted he would, and had not even broken a sweat on the quick run-jog back to the beach. Drake—now that was a different matter. She had guts, he had to admit. She was clearly exhausted, at the very edge of her endurance, yet was grimly putting one foot in front of the other as fast as she could. She had slowed down a little, but not much. Then again, sometimes "not much" was the difference between life and death.

When they reached the point where they'd stashed their wet suits, Sikes parked the two in deep cover while the

SEALs quickly slipped back into their gear. Minutes later, he rejoined them, his face mask hanging down around his chin. "As I asked earlier—how well do you swim?"

"Well enough," Drake answered immediately. She looked over at Thor.

He spread his hands out in front of him, palms up. "I'm a ground pounder, but I imagine I can keep up." Unlike before, there was a small note of uncertainty in his voice.

Sikes tried again. "Mister, play straight with me. I don't have time for games. Can you swim or not? If you can't, we'll just make other arrangements." He wondered exactly what those "other arrangements" would consist of, but put the matter off for a moment while he waited for the Marine's response.

"I can swim. Not real well, and I'll never win any speed records, but I can churn my way through the water and stay afloat, at least well enough to pass the water-survival flight test."

Sikes groaned inwardly. While every pilot had to demonstrate the ability to stay afloat for thirty minutes, and to use his or her gear to provide flotation while waiting for rescue, the test was hardly a grueling one. But if that was the extent of the Marine's water skills, so be it; it would have to be enough. He turned back to Pamela Drake. "You'll come with me. It's only about a mile swim, but it will feel like longer if you're not used to it. Especially after what you've been through today. Don't worry, I won't let you drown."

He assessed her candidly, noting the long, smooth muscles rippling beneath her flawless skin. Yes, probably a swimmer. She had the build and the musculature for it.

"Garcia and Huerta, you stay with the major," Sikes ordered. As hefty as the Marine was, it might take more than one man to keep him afloat if he needed help. He saw the Marine start to protest, and cut him off with a quick motion.

"My mission, my expertise, Major. You just do what you're told. We won't tell anybody when we get back to the boat, okay?"

There was no point in wasting any further time. Sikes turned, started down to the water with Pamela Drake in tow, and let the warm ocean slip over him.

0602 Local (+5 GMT)
South of Cuba

The first cramp in his gut brought him back to full consciousness. Bird Dog woke abruptly, coughing and sputtering, trying to eject the seawater from his lungs and to take a deep, shuddering breath. His brain was demanding oxygen, but the gray unconsciousness still lurking there was more than drowned out by the agonizing cramp in his gut.

He choked, came to his senses, and leaned back into the life preserver. It had done its job well, keeping his head out of the water, though not by much. At any rate, he hadn't drowned after losing consciousness, and that was good enough.

Gator. Where was he? He must be somewhere near—the two had punched out fractions of a second apart, although the RIO's offset angle of trajectory away from the cockpit might have led to some separation when they hit the water. Had Gator even survived? He tried to remember whether or not he'd seen his chute open. Yes, a chute. Had there been motion below it? If there had been, it had been indiscernible from the motion generated by swaying to and fro under the canopy. Whether or not his backseater was still alive was an open question.

The life raft—where was it? Seawater on the seat pan

would have activated it automatically. The theory was that the pilot would remain conscious and thus be able to swim over and grab it before it drifted out of range.

He hoisted himself up out of the water as he topped another wave and scanned the ocean around him. There was not a sign of the bright orange life raft, nor of his backseater.

They're coming for us, though. He was certain of it. He fished out his emergency radio and tried to raise the carrier. A voice immediately answered his transmission.

With the prospect of SAR helicopters immediately inbound his location, Bird Dog curled up in a ball, let the life jacket support him, and tried to massage the cramp out of his gut.

0615 Local (+5 GMT)
West of Cuba

Sikes heaved himself into the boat first, then reached over the gunwale, lying flat on his stomach, and grabbed Pamela Drake by the waist. He heaved back, dragging her over the rigid inflated side and onto the cold, clammy deck. On the opposite side of the boat, the other SEALs and Thor were executing the same maneuver.

They took a SEAL rest period, approximately two seconds of stopping, orienting themselves, and taking three quick, deep breaths to flush carbon dioxide out of their systems. The immediate influx of oxygen generated a temporary feeling of well-being, but Sikes knew that the draining effect of the swim out from shore could not be avoided indefinitely. They needed to get moving now, back to the carrier, back to safety.

As the small boat topped a wave, he could see the carrier

outlined against the rising sun to the east, just barely visible above the horizon. Fifteen miles, he decided—maybe a bit more. Twenty minutes to safety, if all went well.

But so often it didn't, not in the final stages of a mission. The prospect of safety, the illusion of relative security, tempted SEAL teams into mistakes. Mistakes that were likely to be fatal at this point.

Garcia slipped into the stern of the boat and gunned the muffled, sound-suppressed engine. It caught the first time. The other men settled into their accustomed spots in the boat. Drake and Thor sat on the deck, holding themselves steady by grasping the lines that ran around the gunwales.

"Let's get going before it's full daylight," Sikes ordered. The boat surged beneath his feet.

The unexpected struck when they were halfway back to the carrier. The massive floating airfield had grown from a gray, semisolid haze to the massive floating fortress that it was. Sikes could even catch glimpses of the combatants and escorts around her, identifying them mainly by their running lights.

The seas were running smooth, with the morning winds picking up, flecking the swells with whitecaps. Sea state two or three, he decided. Uncomfortable, but not dangerous.

Ahead in the water he noticed a log. No, not a log. He turned to shout at Garcia to throttle back. Whatever it was, they didn't need to run over it. If the impact didn't kill them, it would most assuredly toss them all into the ocean, thus necessitating rescue by the carrier.

As the boat slowed, he faced forward again and studied the anomaly carefully. It looked like part of a dry dock that had broken loose somehow and floated out to sea, or maybe the rusted remains of an old houseboat, or—oh, hell.

The rest of the submarine emerged from the sea, and

figures appeared on the conning tower. He noticed them scampering quickly up, mounting stanchions and machine guns on brackets on the conning tower, and quickly bringing the focus on the SEALs' boat. By the time he had turned to give the order to Garcia to get them the hell out of there, the submarine had them covered.

0618 Local (+5 GMT)
Tomcat 202

"Stoney, break off, break off!" Batman's voice was commanding.

"What the hell—?" Tombstone reached over to flip his communications switch to tactical. "Roger, copy RTB. What the hell?" Tombstone asked.

"Not RTB, but you've got a new primary mission. That SEAL team I sent in a couple hours ago—they've run into some problems on their way back to the carrier. I need you to get in there and cover them. Stoney, there's no one else close around—it's got to be you. We'll vector you back to the primary mission when you're done with them."

"A SEAL team? But what good will—"

"It's a guns mission. They were headed back to the carrier when the Cuban Foxtrot surfaced and held them off at gunpoint. Now there's two small Cuban boats inbound on them, and it looks like the Cubans are planning on taking them hostage. The SAR helo's still somewhere off chasing down Bird Dog, and I don't have anything else in the area. Here, I'll have the TAO give the coordinates to your RIO."

Tombstone wanted to scream. It seemed that everything in the world was working to prevent him from accomplishing his primary purpose for being there. But still, he'd left

Batman in command of the carrier battle group, and implicitly placed himself under Batman's command by undertaking to fly this mission. And if the battle group commander thought there was a more valuable use to be made of his aircraft, then it was up to Stoney to toe the line.

He sighed, then swung the Tomcat around in a hard, tight 160-degree turn as Tomboy fed him new fly-to points.

It took only three minutes to cover the distance between him and the SEAL boat. At once, in his first overflight, he saw the nature of the problem.

The SEAL boat was bobbing uneasily in the stiffening wind, held at gunpoint by the submarine-mounted machine guns to the west. Two small boats were approaching from the east. Cuban patrol boats, no doubt unreasonably pissed off after the destruction of their communications, command, and control vessel earlier that day. If the Cubans got ahold of the SEALs, Tombstone wouldn't give a plug nickel for their chances of survival.

He stayed high on the first pass, five thousand feet, staring down to assess the scene before making his decision. Batman had been right—this was a guns-only mission. Good thing he probably wouldn't need them for the rest of it.

He swung the Tomcat around and dove for the deck, picking up speed as he descended. He stayed to the west of all participants, hoping to avoid silhouetting himself against the rising sun. He stopped his descent barely one hundred feet above the churning ocean, made a small course correction, and arrowed in toward the submarine.

Four hundred feet away from the Foxtrot, he fired his first short burst, made another small course correction, then walked the guns in toward the submarine. There were men running around the fo'c'sle frantically, trying to clear the conning tower and decks in response to his gunfire. How-

ever, a Tomcat traveling at three hundred knots covers a lot
of ground quickly. The first of them had barely started down
the ladder into the interior of the submarine when the rounds
stitched their way down the submarine's hull. He saw two
men crumple and fall to the deck and another one topple off
the narrow flat surface into the sea.

With the decks cleared, the SEAL boat immediately
kicked it in the ass and took off for the carrier. Tombstone
watched them go, made sure that the submarine crew stayed
out of sight long enough for them to escape, then turned his
attention back to the approaching small boats.

The SEALs could probably outrun them, but there was no
point in taking chances. Two low-altitude passes, four sharp
sparks of gunfire, and the small boats were out of action.

"Mission complete," Tombstone radioed back to the
carrier. "Now, may I please get back to my original mission?"

"Permission granted," Batman said crisply. "And when
you get back to the boat, I think you're going to find there
are a couple of SEALs on board who want to buy you a
beer."

0630 Local (+5 GMT)
South-southwest of Cuba

Her face slammed into the side of the boat as an unexpectedly rough portion of chop caught the small rubber craft
sideways. She yelped, then quickly stifled herself. Huerta
had taught her the value of silence. She wondered if she'd
ever be able to scream again without experiencing an
anticipatory dread of that steel-banded hand closing over
her mouth.

No, her time with the SEALs on this mission had been

singularly unrewarding. They'd done nothing but abuse her, gag her, try to run her into the ground and drown her, and now, batter her against the side of a small boat that had no business skimming across waters as quickly as it was. She felt anger well up—and something else.

For a moment, Pamela paused, her hand gingerly resting on her aching cheekbone, her body a mass of lactic acid—laden muscles and bruises, and thought. What was it that she actually felt about this? Hate for SEAL? Yes, that certainly—but something more. Underlying it all was a grudging respect, the beginnings of an understanding as to why these men were the way they were, and what their purpose in the world was. She didn't like their tactics—to be honest, she didn't like their tactics when they were applied to her—but after watching them in action, she was beginning to understand the necessity for them.

She glanced across the boat at Thor. He was large enough to brace himself arthwartships, his ribs resting on one side of the craft, his feet planted snugly against the opposite side for security. The pilot—he would have been dead by now, had it not been for the SEALs. And would she herself have survived? She tried to believe that her Cuban captors/friends would have freed her from her cell, would have warned her of the incoming attack.

Tried, and failed. In the three days she had been in their country, they had shown no more concern for her safety or well-being than a spider does for a struggling fly caught in its web. They'd used her, steered her toward sights and sounds they wanted broadcast to the world, tried to subvert her from her true purpose of getting the facts out.

And she'd let herself be used, she admitted. She had thought she'd be able to play the delicate cat-and-mouse game with them, pretending to do what they wanted while managing to sneak such shots to her audience as her cunning and wile would allow. In the end, they'd come out almost even, she suspected.

She suddenly realized with a chill that if she'd stayed at the compound she would have been dead by now. The SEALs had saved her life, and more than that, earned her grudging respect.

Not that that meant they'd be getting favorable coverage for this little episode. Oh, no, far from it. But she'd find a way to bring some balance to the picture, to show the necessity for such men in a world like today's, and to explore the political considerations and checks and balances that held their deadly power in leash.

She turned to Sikes suddenly. "The dog—did you kill it?"

He gazed back at her, eyes a dark steel blue, face carved out of granite. There was no way that she could make him answer, none at all. But something must have shown in her face. Finally, he nodded his head frantically. "Didn't like to do it, but there was no other way."

She settled back against the rigid gunwale and thought about it. Why should she judge them harshly for killing a dog, when Cuba had made few bones about murdering thousands and thousands of its countrymen? Should Americans be held to a higher standard of honor than foreign nations? And if so, how does one fight rogue nations like Cuba, those barely civilized hordes of hotheaded fascists now in possession of some of the world's latest technology?

Fire with fire, she decided. That's what it would have to be. But some part of her mourned the death of that dog.

0635 Local (+5 GMT)
Fuentes Naval Base

The Cubans hunkered down in the command bunker twenty
feet below ground had escaped the bombardment with
minimal damage. Plaster had crumbled off the walls as a
result of the vibrations bombarding the center, and a few
chunks of ceiling had detached themselves from the steel
beams overhead and shattered on the concrete floor below,
but everything was still operable.

Santana wished he could say as much for the launchers
above. How had the Americans managed to locate the
underground launch tubes? A satellite, he supposed, or
perhaps one of those damnable reconnaissance flights. No
matter—he glanced at the weapons status indicator panel
again, and was relieved to see it was unchanged.

The rows and columns of idiot lights looked like Christmas. At least half of them were glowing steady red,
indicating that their components were beyond reinitializa-
tion or repair. Another half was blinking red, clamoring for
operator attention to either reset critical parameters or
simply clear something obstructing a launch hatch. Finally,
on the far right-hand side of the board, three columns of
lights glowed bright, steady, reassuring green. At least three
missiles were still operational, if the damage indicators
could be trusted. Three chances to strike, either at the
mainland, or at the battle group poised to strike from the
south.

The mainland, he decided finally. That had been their
intent all along, and the first hint of attack against their
landmass would no doubt send the Americans sputtering

and sniveling to the United States. That alone would tie up their forces for days, while Cuba negotiated a massive aid package in exchange for an apology from the United States for their uninvited incursion into a foreign nation. The fact that Cuba had retaliated all out of proportion to the alleged violation would be ignored, as it always was. In terms of politics, the Americans were the perennial patsies.

The crew in the command center was still alert and coherent, although some of them appeared shaken by the man-made earthquakes they'd experienced in the last five minutes. He thought he could count on them—he would have to count on them, at least until relief crews could be brought in, the rearming process could be started, and his country could begin working back toward full military power.

In the meantime, only one thing mattered—getting off that one shot at the U.S. mainland that would show them just how capable Cuba was, and how serious it was about its sovereignty.

He gathered the technicians around him, soothed them with words about their courage and the greatness of the act they were undertaking, and sent them back to their stations recharged and energized. As their missiles would be shortly.

0637 Local (+5 GMT)
Tomcat 202

"Tombstone, get the hell out of the area," Batman snarled over tactical. "No argument, just do it. Now!" Puzzled, Tombstone flipped the Tomcat into a tight turn, slinging it around like David lining up against Goliath. It was an article of faith among aviators that when the air traffic controller insisted on immediate obedience, you obeyed first, questioned later. That the man directing his tactical disposition was another admiral made little difference to Tombstone. Surely Batman had good reasons for it, although it frustrated the hell out of him to be taken off his mission once again. What was it about this island? Would he ever get a damned look at the BDA?

"Roger, coming right to one-eight-zero now, angels ten and ascending." Tombstone waited for a moment, then asked, "What now?"

"The UAVs," Batman said. "I need you well away from the ground site."

"Why not send me in?" Tombstone asked. "I've got five-hundred-pound bombs on the wings, and I think I still remember the basics of strike warfare. We can be in and out before—"

"No time," Batman said. "Tombstone, the Cubans are getting ready to launch. I don't want you anywhere near that area when the first missile heads out toward the United States. Your electronic emissions, the fire control radars that are lit off—buddy, get your ass out of there, Buster. I'm going in with everything I've got in one last try to blast those burrowing moles out of the ground. I don't want you anywhere near the fireball."

Tombstone switched his microphone back to the ICS. "You listening?" he asked Tomboy.

"I am. And there's something missing from this equation," she said thoughtfully. "Surely the UAVs don't carry tactical nuclear warheads?"

"I don't think so," Tombstone said, although suddenly he wasn't nearly as certain as he'd have liked to be. "Deploying tactical nuclear weapons in my theater of operations— even that would be going too far. Sure, they might put UAVs on the Arsenal ship without my knowledge, but to get us involved in a nuclear conflict—no, I don't think so. It was bad enough that they tried to micromanage the targeting, but surely they wouldn't—"

"What if the Cubans have them, and the U.S. knows it?" Tomboy persisted. "And Batman's so worried about us being close in—it's not the blast, it's the EMP he's worried about. What else could it be?"

EMP—electromagnetic pulse—was the first and most devastating effect of a nuclear explosion. The deadly forces unleashed by the weapon disturbed the electromagnetic field of the earth, shorting out sensitive microelectronics and transistors for miles around. Cars would stop, computers would fail, and the delicate instrumentation of the fly-by-wire Tomcat would immediately cease to function. He'd be left with only manual hydraulics, if that. And no electronics whatsoever. That meant he couldn't fire missiles—hell, he'd be lucky if the EMP didn't trip something in the fire control circuitry and inadvertently ignite something while they were on the wings.

"Nukes. My God. And if they miss, or don't fire?" He let his voice trail off.

"Then we're in the middle of the biggest political cluster-fuck in twenty years," Tomboy finished. "Tombstone, that command center—it's gotta be destroyed. And we can't trust a UAV that's never been tested in combat to do it."

His RIO—his wife—was making eminently good sense. There was no longer any question in his mind about BDA. What he needed now was complete and total destruction of the command center before it could launch weapons—possibly nuclear weapons—at the continental U.S. Furthermore, he needed to make that happen before the United States was tempted to use its mobile nuclear arsenal, now circling, he suspected, in the skies over Cuba.

"You're right," he said softly. He paused for a moment, then asked, "Are you up for this? You know it's dangerous."

Tomboy's voice was calm and level. "You know I'm in. We're all in this together, Tombstone. This was our role in life before we met each other, and right now it's more important than anything I've ever done. Except maybe—no, let's go on," she concluded firmly.

Something in her tone of voice bothered him, but he let it pass, pressed as he was by the need for an immediate decision on the mission. As pilot in command, he had the ultimate say-so in where the Tomcat went and how she executed her mission. And in this case, that would include disobeying orders from the rightful battle group commander. He flipped the switch back over to the tactical circuit. "Batman, you're coming in weak and broken. I can't read you at all." He felt oddly amused at that old, hoary trick that pilots and aviators used everywhere for avoiding complying with directions from the ground they didn't like.

Batman knew the ploy, too. "Damn it, Stoney, don't you pull this crap," he roared, his rage clearly evident over the crystal-clear circuit. "You're not having radio problems. Don't you even—"

"Switching to secondary," Tombstone announced calmly. "Home Plate, this is Tomcat Two-zero-two, switching to secondary. Primary circuit is weak and broken, possibly from some form of, uh . . . sunspot interference. Yes, sunspots—I do believe that's it." Tombstone switched the radio off.

"What will he do?" Tomboy asked softly. "I know he doesn't believe you."

"You're *almost* right—he doesn't believe me about the radio, but he does believe I'm going to ignore his orders. It's up to him now. Give me a vector back to the command post."

Tomboy spieled off a series of numbers, directions, and speeds, and Tombstone jerked the Tomcat around in a tight turn. He finished off with a barrel roll just for the hell of it, not bothering to let Tomboy know about it beforehand. Her yelp from the backseat registered her protest.

"Ten minutes," Tomboy said, her voice still a few notes higher than normal. Among other things that he'd have to pay for the barrel roll would be among them.

"See if you can find that UAV for me," Tombstone said. "It's probably over water, though I gather it's inside the twelve-mile territorial limits. If it weren't, Batman wouldn't be as worried as he is about us bustering out of here—we'd have a little bit more time."

"No sign of it," Tomboy said promptly. "I've been scanning for it in tracking mode ever since Batman mentioned it. Those little bastards are hard as hell to find, Stoney. I wouldn't count on our gaining contact."

Unless we're both inbound on the same target area and our separation decreases dramatically, he added silently. That may be the first time we'll get contact on it—as we're both launching at the target. And if that little bastard is nuclear, God help me. And Tomboy. Again, something in her comments over the last few minutes, coupled with an odd sense of resignation in her voice, nagged to be understood. He let his thoughts linger on it for a moment, on how he'd met her on board *Jefferson* during a cruise, how they'd gradually come to know and respect each other, first as aviators and then as lovers. And on the impact she had made on his life, in marked contrast to that of Miss Pamela Drake. What had he ever done to deserve such a wonderful woman? A superb, giving lover, tender and supportive spouse, and dynamite bulldog tactical officer in the air—if he'd made up his own wish list of what he wanted in a wife, he would have sold Tomboy far short.

But her voice . . . he pushed the thought aside, and concentrated on the land coming into view ahead. By now, the sun was nearly half visible over the horizon, and streaks of rose and orange striped almost the entire sky. Night was no longer a protecting cloak.

As the minutes passed, Tombstone could feel the tension mount in the cockpit. It was a familiar sensation, but still fraught with all the fear and anxiety that going into combat always brought. He and Tomboy had been here before, done this time after time together, both over the Spratlys and the Aleutian Islands. Why should this occasion be any different? It wasn't, he suspected; it was just the fact of their marriage that made it seem odd.

An odd silence hung in the cockpit as well, unalleviated by any tactical chatter from the secured radio or communication with other pilots. According to the radar, the furball to the southeast was still in frantic action, American pilots chasing the nimble MiGs across the sky, periodic flashes of increased radar detection indicating that another airplane had exploded into a massively reflexive ball. American or Cuban—there was no way to tell until the flash settled down and Tomboy could verify whether or not the surviving blip showed IFF transmission.

As far as he could tell, it looked like the Americans were winning. An EMP would change that, knocking both the American and Cuban aircraft out of the sky more effectively than the smartest air-to-air weapon in either inventory.

"Tombstone. I think I've got it." Tomboy's voice sounded forced, but calm. "Look out at zero-nine-zero; see if you can see anything. It's an intermittent blip on radar. Could be the UAV."

Tombstone turned his head right and stared into the rising sun. Just occulting in front of it was a small, dark blip, barely more visible than a pinprick. The UAV—he was almost sure of it. It was all the wrong shape, had all the wrong movements for a fighter aircraft. "I've got it. Yes, I think that's it."

"Good. I hold it inbound toward the same target area. Speed Mach one-point-two, altitude five thousand feet."

Tombstone nodded. That matched his visual identification. "So Batman's going in with it."

"Maybe. Remember, he's still holding us on radar as well. Did you secure the IFF?"

"No. So he's at least got that to break our radar blip out of the pack. He knows where we are, and he knows his newest play toy is headed dead for us. This is one decision I can't make for him."

"Feet dry," Tomboy announced, refocusing him on the mission. Tombstone nosed the Tomcat down, heading for the deck. He'd make his initial run at five hundred feet, see what intelligence he could gain from his first pass. Then, time permitting and depending on what Batman did with the UAV, he'd vector back in on a bombing run.

The command post was reportedly located under twenty feet of dirt, but the five-hundred-pounders at least had a chance of damaging it. Maybe fatally. It was better than losing all the aircraft currently airborne to EMP if the UAV held the warhead he suspected it did.

"Two minutes," Tomboy said. She suggested a tiny course correction, which Tombstone promptly adopted.

Again, the odd silence descended on the cockpit. With nothing else to do except watch for antiaircraft fire and wonder if some prehistoric idiot armed with a Stinger would be sitting on a hill waiting for them, Tombstone found odd pictures flashing into his mind. Tomboy, the first time he'd seen her, climbing into an aircraft. Her face at their wedding, brilliantly radiant. And later, Tomboy in bed, the small, voluptuous frame responding to his every touch, her passion rising to meet and exceed his. He shook his head, let his mind linger one last time on the lush curves and smooth swells of her body, and then—"Tomboy? You're not pregnant, are you?" There was horror in the voice, as much as he hated to have it there. If she were, and she hadn't told him, then flying this mission was perhaps the most foolhardly thing she had ever done in her life. Her condition would require an evaluation by a flight surgeon before she could remain in flight status.

"No, you idiot, of course I'm not pregnant. What in the world gave you that idea?" Tomboy's voice was lightly amused. "Jesus, Tombstone—get your head in the game."

"Okay, I just wanted to—never mind." Now was not the time; then again, there might never be a decent time to discuss it, not after the blunder he'd just made with his new bride. "Where did you say that UAV was?"

"There." Tomboy inserted a special target designator in his heads-up display. "Our only chance to keep Batman from using the UAV is to go after the target ourselves. You know that, I know that—let's get moving." Her crisp tone of voice brooked no argument.

Tombstone corrected his course and bore in on the Cuban naval base.

"Trouble," Tomboy announced calmly. "Stoney, I'm getting targeting indications from the carrier. I think they're talking to our little unmanned friend over there. Now if I see—there it goes. It's changing course, Stoney, climbing, getting some altitude."

"How far behind us is it?" he asked.

"Ten miles now."

He shook his head. Not enough time. Air distance, in this case, though in the arcane geometry of the sky, time, and distance seemed to merge into a single lethal pucker factor. How much fuel did the UAV have left on board? Would it be able to accelerate to a max cruising speed of Mach 3, or would it have to choose a more fuel-efficient speed?

That depended on how long it had already been in the air, and whether he'd be required to make any other moves to avoid detection. Two other factors he didn't know.

Damn it, Batman, you could have told me. It might have given me an edge—might even have talked me out of this last-ditch effort. As it stands now, I have no choice about it. If I can stop you from making a possible nuclear strike on Cuba, I have to. The EMP—we'll kill more of our own pilots than the Cubans can.

"You know, there's one other possibility," his backseater said. "This UAV may not even be under Batman's control. Remember the arguments on installing that remote targeting and firing option on the Arsenal ship? Sure, they would have needed some cooperation from *Arsenal* to launch UAV, but what if all targeting and deployment control is directly under JCS now? *Arsenal* may have some relay communications gear or some other way to override, but I doubt it. That's what the politicos would have wanted— direct control over the missiles once they're launched. That turns the whole carrier battle group into just a remote control weapons launch platform, doesn't it? Next thing you know, they'll be able to fly an F-14 off the deck with the pilot sitting in it like a monkey. I don't like this one little bit."

Tombstone considered the matter. "It's possible, I suppose." Even as he admitted it, Tomboy's explanation seemed more and more probable. "If Batman's not controlling it, you can bet he'll be on the circuit telling JCS we're inbound on the target. Might make them abort the launch."

"I guess we'll find out," Tomboy answered. "The hard way."

0650 Local (+5 GMT)
South of Cuba

The water was almost blood temperature. It soothed his strained muscles like a hot tub, coaxing the pain and soreness out of his back and legs. Bird Dog gradually relaxed into the flotation device, letting it carry his weight. It was over now for him—at least for this battle.

And maybe permanently for Gator. Every time Bird Dog crested a wave, he scanned the sea around him, looking for the distinctive orange color that would pinpoint his backseater's location.

There was no trace of him.

He felt his mind starting to drift, lulled into an odd state of relaxation by the warm water and the release of tension following his violent ejection from the aircraft. It felt so odd, to float so peacefully on the water while to the east the rest of the squadron still battled off the Cuban aggressors. He could hear his blood pounding in his ears, a gentle rhythmic *whop-whop* that—he jerked violently upright in the water, shifting his gaze from the sea to the air. That was no heartbeat—he recognized the sound all too well, although he'd never heard it from exactly this angle.

An odd, ungainly insect was hovering mere inches above the water—at least at first glance that's what it looked like. As he refocused himself out of the temporary euphoria that always followed unexpected survival, the shape resolved itself into the ungainly figure of the SAR helicopter.

He felt a wild surge of hope, a reorientation toward reality. From that altitude, he'd have an excellent view of miles and miles of surrounding ocean. They'd be able to spot Gator immediately.

At least, one part of his mind said, they would if his backseater's seat span had deployed properly. And if Gator hadn't impacted the canopy on the way out of the aircraft.

And if—Bird Dog shoved away the myriad possibilities of what could have gone wrong with Gator's egress from the aircraft. It didn't pay to think about it—not now, not with the helicopter inbound. He hoped if they saw Gator, they'd vector over and pull his backseater out of the water first. He watched for any jink in the aircraft's course, hoping it would veer away to pursue some other target. But no, it bore steadily in on him.

Five minutes later, the rescue swimmer plunged into the ocean beside him. The water was spread out flat around Bird Dog, evidence of the powerful downdraft from the helicopter's blades. As he horse-collared up into the helicopter, Bird Dog was already shouting questions to the pilot. He fumbled with the catches, flung the rescue device away from him, and stumbled to the edge of the open hatch. A crew member grabbed him, slapped a safety line on him. "You're not going back into the water. Not after I just hauled you out of it."

"Leave me alone." Bird Dog scanned the water frantically, then darted to the other side of the cabin and peered out the small window. Miles of ocean stretched out before him. Blue, solidly blue except for tiny scraps of white topping the waves.

There was no sign of Gator.

SIXTEEN
Wednesday, 03 July

0655 Local (+5 GMT)
Washington, D.C.

"You're out of options, Admiral." Senator Williams swiveled away from the tactical display. His presence here in the Joint Chiefs of Staff war room was unusual, but not unprecedented. As a member of the military subcommittee, he had access on a need-to-know basis. This, Williams figured, was the most need-to-know opportunity that had arisen since the original Cuban Missile Crisis incident.

Admiral Loggins's voice got tight. "Jesus, you are insane! Nuclear weapons? And in Cuba? If we use the UAV option, the fallout alone will have consequences in the United States."

Williams shook his head. "Not so. If you've been listening to the experts, the chances of radiation reaching American soil are minimal."

"I have pilots in the air right now," Loggins thundered. "What do your so-called experts say about them? Are they in any danger? You know as well as I do that the EMP is liable to knock them all out of the air! I'm not taking that chance—not today, not ever. They don't deserve that."

"Hard choices require hard men," Senator Williams shot

back. "You think it was easy for my predecessors, deciding to leave those POWs in enemy hands after each war? To sacrifice men and women in combat? Do you think we're that heartless?"

And that, Admiral Loggins realized, was essentially the question. Did he really think that the good faith on the part of men such as Senator Williams was sufficient for him to entrust the safety of the men and women under his command to them? Would Williams make good decisions, decisions that would strengthen the nation rather than weaken it? Or did the larger picture—"national strategy," as Williams was fond of referring to it—outweigh the safety of the men in the air, and his commitment to keep them alive?

"It's set up now, isn't it?" Williams asked.

Loggins nodded. "We've already programmed the vector to the command post. And the link between *Arsenal* and the missile is working well. All we have to do is authorize the divert and it'll be on its way. But I think we ought to—NO!" Admiral Loggins grabbed at Williams's hand, which was poised over the execute switch. The admiral's fingers grazed the back of Williams's hand as the senator quickly flipped the lever into execute position.

Four rows of green lights flickered on Loggins's console as the UAV ran its self-check—verifying what it had known all along, that everything was in working order—and commenced executing its last given instruction. As an additional safety precaution, the UAV was programmed to lock out further orders after it received a go signal, to prevent the possibility of enemy jamming or cryptological deception making it deviate from its course.

Loggins watched in horror as the UAV gently rolled out of its orbit, shuddered, and pitched its deadly rounded snout up. He saw the exhaust spit a whiff of black smoke, then steady into a clear, turbulent blast of hot gas. Seconds later, the missile was no longer under visual observation and could only be tracked by its small blip on the radar scope. That, too, was intermittent, given the Stealth technology of the missile.

"Dear God, what have you done?" Loggins gasped. "You had no right to—"

Williams leaned back in his chair and smiled, an ugly, twisted parody of a pleasant expression. "If you had the guts, you'd have done it yourself. Remember that, Loggins. Remember that."

0657 Local (+5 GMT)
Tomcat 202

"Stoney, it's starting a rollout!" The first trace of excitement entered Tomboy's voice.

"I see it, I see it—I've got it now." Tombstone identified the UAV's green blip on his heads-up display. "How long?"

"Minutes. Stoney, if that missile detonates on target, we don't have a chance. Neither do those men in the air to the south."

"I know it." Tombstone jammed the throttles forward into full afterburner. "It should be accelerating—keep giving me range and bearings to it, Tomboy, as well as a vector to intercept. There's going to be a very small window when it's within range."

"Sidewinder," Tomboy suggested.

Stoney clicked the mike twice. "Roger. It's the only one reliable enough to trust for one shot."

And one shot is all he'd have. One chance to knock the missile out of the air, to send it tumbling helplessly to land before the nuclear warhead armed, to detonate it into a conventional explosion in the atmosphere without invoking the deadly hellfire contained in its nose cone. One chance, one shot.

0700 Local (+5 GMT)
Washington, D.C.

"You're insane," Loggins blurted out. Suddenly, the sheer lunacy of their position struck him full force. How had he gotten involved in this, one part of his mind wailed. To wander so far from the traditional honors and values of the United States Navy, to allow political control to assert itself over the very targeting decisions the military made? If anyone ought to know better, it should be you, he chided himself. *After Vietnam, you swore you would never let this happen again. Not only did you let it happen, but you're part of it.*

"They'll think you did it, you know," Williams said softly. "Some sort of post-traumatic stress syndrome—you should be able to blame it on that. They might even let you keep your retirement." The senator smirked. "I'll say I tried to stop you, but if they compare our records, they'll know who's really behind it. You were—all the way; it was all your idea."

"No," Loggins said, his voice strong and firm. "I don't think so. You see, if nothing else, war has taught me a little bit about being prepared." He leaned forward, pushed a button on the speakerphone. "Senator, did you hear that?"

"I surely did," Senator Thomas Dailey said. The strong Midwestern drawl was unmistakable. "So did the rest of us, Admiral."

"And *Arsenal* is taking the appropriate action?" Loggins

said, a savage good humor fighting its way up out of the depression that had plagued him for the last several months. He glanced at Williams, saw the man wilting visibly in the chair. "Has it?"

"The chairman gave the order three minutes ago," Dailey said. "The warhead is disarmed. Too bad they didn't build a self-destruct function into it. As it is now, it will impact the target as strictly a conventional warhead."

"Thank God for the pickiness of nuclear triggering circuitry," Loggins said.

"You knew all along," Williams said, his voice defeated. "Where did I screw up? What made you think I'd really do it?"

"Just a promise I made to myself a long time ago," Admiral Loggins said softly. "And whatever else happens, those men and women on the front line will know I kept the faith."

0702 Local (+5 GMT)
Tomcat 202

"It's below us," Tomboy warned. "Altitude, two thousand feet."

"Roger." Tombstone nosed the Tomcat down slightly, quickly trading altitude for speed. Lower altitude, lower speed, as the air created more friction. The airspeed he'd gained by descending would be quickly bled off fighting the thicker air. Still, it wasn't as though he had much time. Or choice.

He craned his head aft, searching through the clear bubble of the canopy for some sign of the weapon. According to Tomboy's radar picture, it was almost on them, less than one

mile aft. He'd matched altitude with it, though he had no
hope of ever matching its speed.

"Twenty seconds." Tomboy began counting down the
time to intercept. Tombstone kept his hand glued to the
weapons selector switch. There it was, a tiny black speck on
the horizon, barely discernible to the naked eye. His gut
tightened down into a thin hard knot, and more intimate
parts of his anatomy attempted to snug up to the rest of his
body. The thought of the sheer destructive power contained
in that tiny object that could've been a dirt speck on the
canopy was overwhelming.

"Ten seconds." The moments clicked by inexorably, the
missile growing larger with each ticktock of eternity.
Finally, he could see it all. The slim, almost graceful-
looking fuselage of the missile. White, with cruciform fins
standing out from the body. It was moving fast, so fast—
had he ever encountered anything so awesome in the air?
Even normal air-to-air combat weapons couldn't match the
sheer grace and power of this devastating land attack
missile.

It was by him in a flash, almost too quick to see. His
retinas shone with the afterimage of it, white against the
brilliant sunrise behind him.

"Two seconds," Tomboy said.

Tombstone's finger tightened, then initiated launch. Two
Sidewinders leaped off the wings, one from each side, and
started streaking out into the empty air in front of the Tomcat.
Although the missile was still behind him, there was no way
he would ever catch it once it was past. No, the only option
was to shoot before it got to him and hope he'd calculated
the intercept correctly. It was a long shot, maybe the longest
one he'd ever taken. And the most important.

As the missile shot through his field of vision, he
automatically toggled the weapons selector to guns and

ripped the atmosphere apart with a continuous barrage of
pellets from his gunport. It had little chance of downing the
titanium-cased missile, but there was a chance the impact
would jar some delicate triggering mechanism inside it,
maybe prevent it from detonating—or maybe detonating it
early, it suddenly occurred to him. If that happened, he'd
never know it. For a moment, the thought of the hellfire
fireball that would erupt so close to the Tomcat shook him.

An instant later, he was certain that was what had
happened. A brilliant flash of white light filled the air,
brighter than the rising sun 180 degrees offset from it. He
yelped, slammed his eyelids down, too late. The fiery
incandescent ball seared his eyes, immediately invoking a
protective flood of tears. He dabbed at his eyes ineffectually
with one hand, wondering why it was taking so long to die.

"You did it!" Tomboy's voice was jubilant. "Damn it,
Stoney, I don't believe it—you hit the intercept dead-on.
That was the Sidewinder igniting, not the missile—those
poor suckers on the ground below," she finished, suddenly
quiet. "Shit, I hate to see what happens to anything
underneath those two."

"It didn't detonate," Tombstone said wonderingly. "I
thought it might—"

"It was a chance we took," Tomboy said quietly. "You
made the right decision. Again."

Tombstone drew a deep, shuddering breath, suddenly
filled with a joyous exhilaration. He was alive, still alive—
he'd just faced down the deadliest weapon known to
mankind and survived. After this little encounter, the Cuban
command and control center would be a piece of cake.
"Come on, shipmate—we've got a mission to finish."

"Lost video," the lieutenant commander manning the weapons tracking console announced. He glanced uneasily at the two civilians and the one admiral standing next to the command console. He hadn't tried to overhear, God knew he hadn't. But duty inside this war-fighting center of the most powerful nation in the world occasionally made him privy to discussions that no lieutenant commander should ever hear. So far above his pay grade that he couldn't even begin to breathe in the rarefied air of power filling the unexpectedly small compartment. Would he survive this tour? He shook his head, not knowing. Junior officers who happened to overhear discussions not intended for their ears sometimes found themselves with an immediate, high-priority posting to a billet as fuel officer in Adak, Alaska, there to languish out a three-year tour waiting to be passed over for promotion. No one ever said it, but there were ways that the admirals and generals had of communicating their desires to the promotion boards.

A flurry of angry shouts and enunciations filled the air behind him. The lieutenant commander hunched down behind his console, desperately wishing he were somewhere else.

Finally, it was over. He heard feet moving rapidly behind him, a harsh, barked order from a Marine sentry, then silence. One set of footsteps started toward him, paused, and finished the short trip over to stand behind him. He didn't dare look up.

A hand landed on his shoulder, squeezed it reassuringly;

then a familiar voice said, "Son, none of this happened today. You understand that?"

The lieutenant commander nodded. "Yes, Admiral Loggins. Nothing happened."

"Look at me."

It was definitely an order, and the lieutenant commander obeyed. He tore his eyes away from the green spikes and blips still streaking across his console and gazed into the hard, craggy face of Admiral Loggins. Senator Dailey was standing two paces behind the admiral, looking grim. His urge to jump to his feet was almost overwhelming.

"You just saw me keep faith with an entire battle group out there on the front line," Admiral Loggins said. His voice was soft and ragged. "I know what you're worried about— hell, I sat in that chair when I was a lieutenant commander. For the record—and I have a witness—," he said, nodding at Senator Dailey, "I take full responsibility for the actions that took place here. You understand?"

The lieutenant commander struggled to find his voice. "Yes, Admiral. Although," he dared, "nothing happened today. I'm sure I wouldn't know what you're talking about."

The admiral's face cracked into a small grin. "I didn't think you would."

"Some things never change, do they?" Senator Dailey added. He shifted his gaze to the admiral. "Still build 'em like they did when I was in the Navy. Admiral, I see a lot of potential in this man. I think I'll be taking a personal interest in his career from now on. You hear that, son?" the senator queried the young officer.

The poor lieutenant commander struggled to find his breath. One wrong move, the wrong interpretation, and—

"Quit messing with him, Tom," the admiral said good-naturedly. "I'll take care of him. We always take care of our own in the Navy. You remember that."

As the two senior officers walked away, the lieutenant commander drew a shaky breath. He looked back down at his screen, and stopped in mid-exhalation. "Admiral—I think you might want to see this." Damn it, it was the right thing to do, call the admiral back, as much as he'd been relieved to see the two men step away from him. "That Tomcat—it's inbound on the Cuban command center."

From some yards behind him, the admiral's voice said, "I know that, son. The senator and I are going to watch the last part of this from my console. When it's over we'll tell you what actually happened. You got that?"

"Aye, aye, Admiral." The lieutenant commander hunched back up to his controls and settled in to wait.

0710 Local (+5 GMT)
Tomcat 202

The prior air strike had silenced most of the antiair batteries on the ground. A few sites spat up tracers, but the Tomcat avoided them easily. Antiaircraft fire was no big deal when there were no overlapping fields of fire and when the Tomcat owned the air.

"Time to rejoin the world." Tombstone reached out and flicked on the communication circuitry. His earphones immediately filled with the loud tactical chatter from the furball still going on out to the east. From the sound of it, the Americans were continuing to dominate. Not surprising— though he wished he were there himself to see it. Still, maybe that's what getting more senior earned you—going head-on-head with UAVs instead of MiGs. If that was true, he was damned sure he didn't want that next star! What would *that* entail—taking on a satellite single-handedly? Maybe a space shuttle? Surviving near death always brought with it its own sense of giddiness.

"I've got a visual," he said, surveying the landscape ahead of him. The Cuban naval base was easily visible in the sunlight now pouring out from the east. Brilliant white buildings set against the lush tropical foliage, some of them partially concealed by towering palm trees. A thin line ran around the compound, undoubtedly a fence of some sort. Tombstone could see people moving around, the damaged building still smoldering from the strike the day before, and heavy construction equipment invading the open field that had contained the alleged missile silos.

Farther to the west, he established a visual on his target. From the air, the command center looked innocuous—a single-story building no different from its fellows. But according to intelligence, it burrowed deep into the earth, and the actual command center was cut off from the Potemkin village structures aboveground.

"Home Plate, this is Tomcat Two-zero-two," Tombstone said into his microphone. "Commencing bombing run."

"Stoney!" Batman snapped over the circuit. "Goddamn it, one of these days I'm going to—"

Tombstone cut him off. "Listen, shipmate, I don't have time to talk right now. I'm gonna blast this bastard back to the Stone Age. As for the details—well, if you come clean with me when I get back to the ship, I'll fill you in on them. Otherwise, you're permanently out of the loop."

"Not on the circuit," Batman snapped. "Jesus, don't you think that I—"

"I'm betting you didn't do anything," Tombstone interrupted again. "You remember a certain conversation we had in the Flag Mess two days ago? About Vietnam and what we learned from that?"

"Yes." Batman's voice was wary. "You've been thinking about that?"

"You bet. And I think I know how this whole thing developed—and how to keep it from happening again. We'll talk about that when I get back, but the priority right now is preventing Cuba from launching on the U.S. Quick now—I'm almost in—is there any later intel?"

"It's as we suspected, Stoney," Batman said. "It's that command center we ID'd from the photos. We believe the complete command staff is down there and they've got tactical control of every weapon on that island. If you damage them, even take out all their antennas, they've got no way to launch. Not unless they've got a remoted capability to each of their silos that we don't know about."

Tombstone sighed. "If we don't know about that for certain, we'd better assume the worst case. I want vectors back to the silos, the ones you know about. I'll drop a few HARMs at the command center and save the five-hundred-pounders for the three silos we identified. Are there any others?"

"No new reports of them. But Stoney, you'd better hurry," Batman said, his voice taking on a new note of urgency. "We've got targeting indications."

"On my way. Just keep the Libyans and the Cuban air power occupied to the east for a bit while I take care of business, okay?"

"You got it." Tombstone could hear Batman giving a series of orders to someone in the background. Finally, he came up on the circuit. "Think you can manage a little air-to-ground attack strategizing?"

Tombstone chuckled. "After what I've been through today, I think I probably can. But if you try sending me up against a satellite, you can forget it."

0712 Local (+5 GMT)
Fuentes Naval Base

"All systems green," the senior missile officer reported. He glanced up at Mendiria. They'd done this so many times as a drill—surely this wasn't the real thing? The echoes of the bombs that had exploded around him yesterday still rang in his ears. Yes, he conceded, his hands suddenly sweaty and shaky: This was it. The moment they'd been training for, the decisive point in the battle that their Libyan advisors had been coaching them for for the last two years. One strike, they'd all agreed, and the U.S. would crumble. They'd never be able to stand the political pressure at home following an attack from the Cuban mainland.

He wished he were as certain about that as his superiors. He laid his hand over the launch button, and tried to stop his finger from trembling.

0713 Local (+5 GMT)
Tomcat 202

As Tombstone bore in on the target, he rolled the Tomcat over and stared downward at the ground through the canopy. Land streaked by in a haze of brown and green, the colors almost indistinguishable at this speed. He watched for a few seconds, craned his head to get an accurate visual on his IP, then rolled the Tomcat back over into level flight.

Four seconds later, he was over the command center bunker. He flipped the weapons release switch, felt the Tomcat leap up into the air as missiles left its rail, then jerked the aircraft away to the right in a hard, screaming turn.

The two HARM missiles seemed to hang in the air. Suddenly, something seemed to catch their attention—the invitingly enticing scent of electromagnetic radiation. Rocket motors kicked in, seeker heads aligned on the emissions, and the missiles dove in on the target.

When they were seconds away from impact, the radiation suddenly ceased. No matter—they were too close now, too certain of a kill, to disarm or detonate harmlessly. The two missiles exploded, the first one half a meter in front of a delicate microwave communications assembly and the second at the base of a high-frequency antenna whip.

The microwave structure exploded into a hail of shrapnel, shredding two guards located outside the front of the command center. The destruction of the high-frequency antenna was less dramatic, but equally telling. The thirty-foot whip exploded up out of the ground as though it were a javelin, arcing across the compound to clatter to the ground just outside the officers' club. Wires that were ripped out of the ground and out of the power supply trailed around it before settling into awkward, half-described circles on the ground. The base structure sputtered once, then shorted out in a spray of sparks.

"Commander! We've lost data link with the launch site." The senior missile officer felt a vague trace of relief, then felt guilty over it. It was wrong to be relieved that a commander's strategy had been foiled, entirely wrong. Nonetheless, if he hadn't known better, he would have sworn he was grateful for it.

0714 Local (+5 GMT)
Tomcat 202

"Come right, steady on zero-one-five," Tomboy ordered. "Twenty seconds to IP."

The Tomcat groaned as it took the high-G turn, racing between ground targets like a car negotiating a set of orange pylons on a test track. The Hornet, while it would have done better on the quick turns and maneuvers required to hit the missile launcher sequentially, couldn't have carried enough armament to take out everything. Not that and the command center as well.

The first target was an easy one. Tombstone didn't even bother with the rollover maneuver to take a visual sighting on his target, but simply followed Tomboy's direction in. By now, her ESM indicator was screaming about launch indications from the farthest-away site, and that had to be the top priority. Still, he doubted there was time to take that one first and then come back for the others. No, they would do them in sequence, the way they'd planned.

The first five-hundred-pound bomb hung up on launch. Tombstone swore, dropped the Tomcat down into a hard dive, then jerked it up. As the Tomcat pulled up violently, he toggled the launch button again. The sudden change in force vectors shook the bomb loose from the rack and sent it hurtling toward its intended target. The decrease in weight increased the Tomcat's angle of attack. The massive aircraft stuttered for a moment, momentarily approaching stall speed, then grabbed hard at the air for lift.

"Now, due north, Stoney," Tomboy coached. "Longer this time. Thirty seconds. Counting now—" Her quiet voice ticked off the moments.

This time the five-hundred-pound bomb fell smoothly away from the Tomcat. Again, the shudder as its weight left the fuselage, the sudden extra lift and speed he felt take the aircraft afterward.

"Fish in a barrel," Tombstone said cheerfully. "What's that last vector?"

"Zero-eight-zero, the last one." Tomboy glanced down at her ESM indicator. "And Tombstone—it might be a good idea if we hurry."

Tombstone slammed the Tomcat into afterburner again, taking note of his fuel status. The high-speed race in, the battle with the UAV, and carrying a full load of heavy weapons onto target had taken their toll. The Tomcat was sucking down fuel like a Hornet. Much more of this, and he'd be lucky to make it back to the boat. He switched his circuit over to tactical. "Batman, get some gas in the air. I think I'm gonna need it."

"Already there, buddy." Batman chuckled. "You think I'd forget how you abuse the afterburner?"

"Tell him to expect me in ten mikes," Tombstone said. "I'm going to need to make it on the first approach."

"Five seconds." Tomboy's voice sounded relieved. "Stoney, it's the last one. Let's make it a good one."

This time, Tombstone rolled over inverted for another look at the target. Smoke and fumes were boiling away from the hole in the ground, indicating that launch preparations were under way. There was not a person in sight—they'd all taken cover, not wanting to be exposed to the poisonous fumes and gases generated by a launch. Even more important, if there were an accident no one would have any chance of surviving a misfire by a nuclear weapon on the ground.

Not that they'd survive what he was about to do if they were anywhere in the vicinity. He rolled back into level flight, bore in for the last five seconds, then jerked the Tomcat up sharply as he released the final bomb. The motion of the aircraft, coupled with the weight of the bomb, acted like a slingshot, lofting the weapon through the air and toward the launchers.

He peeled out in a hard starboard turn, taking a quick glance back at the bomb. It was still in the air, now descending, smack-dead on target. He watched it go, occasionally glancing forward to make sure his flight path was clear, and saw how deadly accurate his shot had been. Just as the bomb approached the launch structure, a thin, poisonous gray spear emerged from the ground. It was traveling slowly, still being boosted out of the silo by compressed gas in a small igniter rocket. That would soon change as the main battery kicked in, sending it arcing toward the mainland.

The deadly javelin was halfway out of the ground when the five-hundred-pound bomb hit. It landed immediately next to the missile, instantly crushing one wall of the silo. The silo collapsed, pinching the missile at its waist and holding it in position. Tombstone saw the silo shudder, then break in half. Its forward portion had not even hit the ground when the area erupted in an orange fireball.

Tombstone jinked the Tomcat away from the scene, satisfied. Three up, three down.

"Good shooting, Stoney," Tomboy said. "Glad I came along for the ride."

"I'm glad you did, too, love," he said softly. "I wouldn't have had you miss it for the world."

"How about we grab a quick drink and buster back to the carrier?" Tomboy suggested.

"Next stop, Texaco," Tombstone said. He felt his spirits lift with the Tomcat as they rose into the air.

0715 Local (+5 GMT)
Washington, D.C.

"That's it, then." Senator Dailey's voice sounded relieved. "At least until next time." He turned to the admiral standing next to him. "What about you, Keith? I'm not going to forget what you did here today."

Admiral Keith Loggins shook his head. "I was stupid, criminally stupid." He glanced up at the senator. "Ambition, personal power—I forgot the oath that I took so long ago to protect this country. Those things . . . well, maybe that's okay in your world, Senator—no disrespect intended, sir. But for us there's got to be a higher purpose in life. We're here to prevent wars, not start them. If we let personalities get in the way of that, let our own personal ambition override our sound operational thought, then we deserve what we get." He looked back toward the console from which Senator Williams had launched the weapon. "You understand that. He never would have."

"Maybe our worlds aren't all that different, Keith," the senator said. "Or at least, they shouldn't be. If you've got a moment during the next few days, I'd like to spend some time talking about what happened. Maybe we can work out some ways to avoid its happening again, some approaches toward preventing the command and control structure from getting in the way of the operational commander. I think we've both learned a lesson out of this one."

"I'd like that, Senator, although how much longer I'll be in the service I couldn't say." The admiral shrugged, then felt a weight lift off his shoulders. "It might be time to retire. Hell, three stars is enough for any man, don't you think?

And Pamela—well, it might be fun to spend some time alone with my new wife."

Senator Dailey looked startled. He quickly rearranged his face into a look of congratulations. "Well, that is good news. When's the big date? I will be getting an invitation, I hope?"

Admiral Loggins smiled. "I haven't asked her yet, Tom. But now—well, I'm starting to see things in a different light. And yes, if she'll have me, you can count on an invitation. We'd be honored by your presence."

The two men shook hands, the grip hard and certain. The disaster they'd diverted today had cemented their friendship.

0718 Local (+5 GMT)
Fulcrum 101

Santana heard one last yelp on the tactical circuit connecting him with the Cuban naval base, and then the hissing silence that indicated the transponder on the other end was destroyed. He swore, jinked his MiG around in an impossibly tight curve, and nailed the Hornet that had been glued onto him like a leech with a withering barrage of gunfire. He was so close he caught a brief glimpse of the other pilot's face, partially masked by helmet and visor, before the entire cockpit disintegrated into a scathingly hot ball of metal, flames, and flesh.

The base! That was the key. There was no point to this losing air battle if he and his compadres didn't buy enough time for the missiles to ripple off their launchers. The air battle was not winnable, not in the long run. There was too much firepower massed off the coast, too many fighters waiting in the wings to relieve their battle-weary front line.

Not that it looked so injured, he had to admit. Results thus far had been startlingly disappointing. Even though they had practiced MiG on MiG for the last two years, growing increasingly efficient in pinpointing each other's weaknesses and exploiting the high maneuverability and low wing loading factor of the MiG, they'd had no real adversary aircraft to train against. Not like the Americans, who since World War II had made it a practice to carefully maintain adversary air for the credibly trained force.

Had he actually gone up against the Hornet one-on-one, he would have known that the wing loading factors he'd read about in *Aviation Weekly* were illusory. With the fuselage providing a good deal of lift, the Hornet was considerably more nimble than its specs would warrant. As with the Tomcat, the lack of credible intelligence on the performance capabilities of these two aircraft flown at the edge of their envelope by pilots who knew them like their family car was astounding.

And meaningless. If the missiles didn't launch . . . Santana peeled away from the furball and put out the call over tactical. RTB—return to base. If there was anything left to protect, that was their place now, not holding off this force so far away.

0719 Local (+5 GMT)
USS **Jefferson**

"What the hell are they doing?" Batman grumbled. "Just when we're winning, they want to turn tail and run." He switched his gaze back over to the far left-hand side of the screen, where the small blip representing Tomcat 202 was just going feet wet. "At least Stoney's out of the area."

But maybe he'd spoken too fast. As he watched, the gaggle of remaining Cuban fighters turned toward the southern boundary of the air base. The American fighters milled about in the air uncertainly for a few moments, awaiting direction from the carrier. Taking on Cuban fighters in the air was one thing—chasing them back down to their home base over Cuba was another. Absent orders, they'd remain where they were.

Batman snatched up the microphone. "Get on them!" Within moments, the small blue blips turned to follow the MiGs back toward Cuba. "It's what you want to do anyway," he muttered. He glanced at Tombstone's aircraft symbol. The tanker was only thirty miles away, patiently circling with an anxious fighter aircraft. If he had any sense of how his shipmate flew, Stoney would be sucking fumes in another twenty minutes. Batman always did like the afterburner.

"Stoney, you've got a load of Cuban MiGs inbound on your nine o'clock. They're at altitude, and the rest of the wing's giving chase. You might want to vector to avoid them until you can tank." Batman knew how much Tombstone would hate doing that, but it was the only sensible thing to do under the circumstances.

0720 Local (+5 GMT)
Tomcat 202

"Nothing to come home to, boys," Tombstone said to the incoming MiGs. "Nothing at all. You might as well park those puppies on the tarmac for all the good they're gonna do from here on out."

"Tombstone, there's one out in front of that pack,"

Tomboy's worried voice reported. "He's got a big lead on the Hornets and Tomcats—Stoney, he's gonna be here before they are."

Tombstone glanced down at his fuel gauge. It was dropping perilously low, far out of the acceptable range for beginning a dogfight. And the tanker with its fighter escorts was too far ahead to provide cover for them. He sighed—it was always like this. Just when you thought it was over, the fat lady failed to sing.

"Been a while since our last dogfight, my love." He slewed the Tomcat violently back toward the incoming raid and grabbed for altitude. "Let's get up where we can get a good look at what's going on." And where I'll have some reserve altitude when this bird runs out of fuel, he added silently. Altitude was safety, safety and reserve airspeed and maneuverability. With it, he might have a chance. But without it, the starving Tomcat was no match for a MiG.

0723 Local (+5 GMT)
Fulcrum 101

Santana tweaked his radar, looking in vain for the flight of attack aircraft he'd been so certain were outbound from his home base. Regardless of his delicate twiddling of the knobs, the radar insisted on showing only one air contact—a Tomcat, according to the ESM gear that had made it an AWG-9 radar in search mode.

But where were the others? There should have been at least three other Tomcats in Bombcat configuration, along with some fighters armed with antiair missiles for protection, not one lone Tomcat straggling off toward the boat. No, he corrected, not straggling—already alerted to what was happening around him, and climbing for altitude to gain a superior fighting position.

It was inconceivable that only one aircraft could have so fatally damaged Cuba's master plan. Inconceivable—and unacceptable. The Tomcat pilot was probably congratulating himself right now, dreaming of the awards and medals he'd receive for such a daring mission. Even more unacceptable.

Santana pulled the nose of the MiG up and headed for the sky. He needed some altitude, something to force this into a horizontal-plane battle of angles as he'd had earlier with the last Tomcat victim. For if he had anything to say about it, this particular Tomcat pilot was going to see his dreams of glory turn into his worst nightmare.

0723 Local (+5 GMT)
Tomcat 202

"Not so fast, buddy," Tombstone murmured. He was concentrating on the attack geometry between the MiG and the Tomcat, seeing in three dimensions the advantage that the MiG was trying to obtain. "If you're like the other MiG pilots I've been up against, you have a much better idea of what your aircraft will do than mine, although my former squadron may have given you just a little refresher course on it very recently. Still, I'm betting that you're a lot more familiar with MiGs than you are with Tomcats. Let's just see, shall we?" Tombstone kicked on the afterburners again and watched the fuel gauge spiral down. The Tomcat seemed to stop in midair, ceasing all forward movement to turn into a flaming arrow launched toward the sun. "Can you match that rate of climb? I don't think so—not with

your low thrust-to-weight ratio. You may have the maneuverability, but I've got the power."

At least until I run out of gas. He winced to see how far
to the left the arrow pointed. There wasn't going to be time
to try this twice—it would be a close-in-knifefight, first-
punch-wins engagement. And after that . . . well, he'd try
to make it to the tanker, and if not . . . well, it wouldn't be
the first time he'd ditched an aircraft.

He radioed Batman and asked that the tanker be brought
in as close as feasibly possible. "Already on it," Batman
said. "And he's got two fighters buster with him, just aching
to get a piece of a MiG."

"Not a chance. This one's mine." Tombstone brought the
Tomcat into level flight, now at thirty-five thousand feet.
His fuel consumption rate was much lower this high, but not
sufficiently economical to make up for the gas he'd sucked
up on afterburners. Still, the MiG probably didn't know that.

He watched the MiG ascend, climbing at a shallower
angle, but still impressive. He vectored toward it, intending
to cut him off before he reached Tombstone's altitude. One
of the purposes of gaining altitude was to force the MiG into
playing Tombstone's game, into trying to match the Tomcat's rate of speed. He couldn't—all the MiG could do
would be to gain altitude while losing speed. With any luck,
he'd be going too slow to maneuver quickly out of Tombstone's way.

The second reason for taking the MiG now was to avoid
an angles fight. It was a battle that the Tomcat pilots were
trained to avoid at all costs. Never play the adversary's
game—make him play yours. The key to successful fighter
tactics was an aggressive, heads-up attitude, exploiting the
adversary's weaknesses while playing to your own strengths.
For the Tomcat, that strength was power. The MiG had the
corresponding weakness.

Tombstone flipped the Tomcat over to watch the MiG ascend, then nosed down still inverted to meet him. He heard the low growl of a Sidewinder insisting it had acquired an interesting target. Tombstone was headed east, right into the rising sun. Did the Sidewinder have the MiG—or was it going to begin one of its famous solar attacks, veering off in the atmosphere toward the rising sun until it ran out of fuel? There was no way to tell, not with the angle as it was between the two aircraft. He would either have to let the MiG proceed up a bit farther and gain some separation from the sun, or take a chance on losing the missile.

What the hell—he had two. In fact, in relative terms, he had more missiles than gas. Tombstone toggled off a Sidewinder, crying "Fox Three, Fox Three" into the ICS.

0724 Local (+5 GMT)
Fulcrum 101

Santana glared suspiciously at the Tomcat loitering above him, inverted in the air. When it nosed down to point at him, still inverted, he slewed the MiG around to put the Tomcat directly on his nose. Too far away for guns, but the Tomcat pilot might not know that. At any rate, seeing the tracers might distract him. He fired off two quick bursts.

A missile leaped off the Tomcat's rails, headed almost directly for him. Almost—Santana watched with something that approached amusement as the missile vectored determinedly away from his aircraft and toward the rising sun. His confidence slowly returned. Perhaps he'd overestimated the Americans—even he knew better than to take an eastern shot at the sunrise with the Sidewinder. He glanced down at the airspeed indicator, saw the MiG was still struggling to ascend. He swore quietly. Soon he'd have to either pull out of the climb or resign himself to ambling through the sky like a wounded turkey. At any lower speed, he'd be too easy a target for the Tomcat. He'd lose maneuverability, and his low speed vector would be no problem for the Tomcat to overcome.

He reached a decision, dropped nose down, and plummeted one thousand feet within seconds. His airspeed picked up satisfyingly, and he quickly rolled back around to face the Tomcat.

He was on the Tomcat's six now, with a beautiful view of the Tomcat's glowing tailpipes. He toggled off his own missile, another heat-seeker, satisfied that the angle might be almost sufficient to distinguish between the aircraft and the sun. Had the American made that same assumption, he wondered, studying the Tomcat's undercarriage. Three more Sidewinders hung there, more than enough to waste one shot as the pilot had done earlier. Suddenly, he wasn't quite so certain that the Tomcat pilot had been foolish.

0725 Local (+5 GMT)
Tomcat 202

Tombstone heard the shriek of the missile indicator before Tomboy's voice cut through the ICS, warning of it. He swore, slewed the Tomcat around to virtually pivot in midair, and pointed nose down at the MiG. The heat-seeker came on, clearly fixed on the Tomcat rather than the sun. The Cuban pilot had taken the same chance he had, with better results. Fortunately, he hadn't touched his countermeasures so far.

The Tomcat shook lightly as three packets of flares were ejected from the undercarriage. They burst into brilliant white phosphorescent fire, easily outshining both the sun and the heat signature of Tombstone's exhaust. Later-generation heat-seekers were trained to ignore targets that were too good, thus correcting for the tendency to vector on a flare rather than an exhaust and reducing the probability of its racing off toward the sun. Tombstone was betting that the Cubans used an earlier version of the missile, given to them by their Soviet master of their new friends, the Libyans.

"Got it—acquiring the flare," Tomboy said. "Tombstone, he's coming around."

"I've got him. I've still got altitude on him—he's not going to like this."

0726 Local (+5 GMT)
Fulcrum 101

Santana was already setting up for his next shot as his first heat-seeking missile exploded harmlessly into a flare. He hardly spared it a thought—he was too busy trying to coax the Tomcat into descending into an angles fight. He could understand the other pilot's refusal to take the bait, but he was determined not to fight it out in a wild yo-yo of shifting altitudes that would inevitably provide the Tomcat with a marked advantage.

Now what the—he watched as the Tomcat nosed over and headed down toward him, surprised to see the pilot descending. Would he actually do that? Enter a horizontal battlefield, knowing that it would put him at a disadvantage? Well, he'd seen the pilot make one mistake. Perhaps it *had* been a mistake, and not a calculated chance. At any rate, this was the battle that a MiG excelled at. And if it was a mistake, it would be his adversary's last.

0727 Local (+5 GMT)
Tomcat 202

"Stoney," Tomboy gasped. "What the hell are you doing?"

"The only thing I have time to do before we run out of fuel," Tombstone said grimly. "Start the preejection checklist. If this doesn't work, we're going for a swim."

0728 Local (+5 GMT)
Fulcrum 101

The Tomcat was indeed descending to his level. Santana smirked. It was as he'd thought—Americans were not nearly as well trained and proficient as they pretended to the rest of the world to be. Here, in the sky, *mano a mano,* there was no disguising their foolishness. He swung the MiG around, calculated the intercept, and bore in for the kill. In the last twenty minutes, he'd discovered a real taste for knifefights.

0739 Local (+5 GMT)
Tomcat 202

"I see what you're up to, buddy," Tombstone said. "It worked on that youngster you splashed, but I've been around guys like you too often. Your kind always does like the close-in fight. That's because you treat those funny little things hanging on your wings like your balls, protecting them and not using them like you should. Well, if you want to learn some knifefighting, I'm not above teaching it to you." He watched the MiG bore on in until he was almost within range. The Cuban pilot would be running the geometry through his mind, calculating the exact intercept. To encourage him to continue thinking the American had made a mistake, Tombstone toggled off another Sidewinder. He knew it was well inside the minimum range for shooting one, but he hoped the Cuban would think he didn't.

It seemed to work. The Cuban MiG didn't even flinch from its course, continuing to bore on in toward him. Tombstone felt his eyes go squinty and a muscle in the side of his jaw start to jump. One more kill, one last kill—that would be it.

Just as the vectors approached range and optimum angle for firing, Tombstone did three things simultaneously. First, he swept the wings of the Tomcat forward, overriding the automatic angle configuration that selected appropriate sweep angle for speed. Moving the wings forward decreased his lift, rendering the Tomcat slightly more ungainly in the air, but from this angle was also an almost imperceptible way of draining off airspeed without the other pilot's noticing. Second, in one quick motion, he popped the speed brakes and dropped his landing gear. Dirtying up all of his airflow surfaces peeled one hundred knots off his airspeed almost instantaneously. Instead of a graceful, powerful fighter, the Tomcat was now a lumbering aircraft configured for landing.

An ugly turkey in the air—with a MiG right in its sights.

Third, Tombstone switched the selector over to guns, pressed the buttons, and heard the delicate beelike hum of the gun in his port wing firing. It was almost anticlimactic at first, watching the delicate line of bullets trace their way down the fuselage. He jinked the Tomcat slightly to the right, watching the tracery elevate up and penetrate the other aircraft's canopy. An explosion of glass and body, followed shortly by a fireball.

"Fuel," Tomboy insisted, for all the world sounding as though she'd completely ignored the knifefight going on in front of her. "Stoney, vector three-two-zero. Now!"

Tombstone did as ordered, then said, "No comment? Aren't you going to congratulate me on that last kill?"

"If it is your last kill, you idiot," she snapped. "The next one will be us if you don't get some fuel into this bird."

The tanker was waiting only one mile away. Tombstone vectored straight in on it, and pulled off the most remarkable plug of his entire aviation career. The probe slid in smoothly, as if the basket had been coated in Vaseline. Two other fighters hung nervously off his port and starboard bow, acting almost as though they could somehow buoy him up should his fuel tank suddenly run dry.

Ah, but the luck was flowing his way now. A smooth plug, fuel good at probe tip within minutes. The tanks sucked the fuel in, and within moments he felt the Tomcat start to grow heavier. He corrected automatically, keeping the probe centered in the basket while the sun rose behind him.

Fifteen minutes later, they'd topped off enough to make a run on the boat. Tombstone thanked the tanker crew, then peeled away from the formation.

"Now about that last kill . . . ," he said casually. "Not bad for an old guy, huh?"

Tomboy was silent for a moment, then said, "It was brilliant for any pilot. And that it was you just makes it that much better."

A grin crept across Tombstone's face. Nothing like having your new bride admiring your latest kill.

Four minutes later, he dipped quickly into the starboard marshal, then was vectored in toward the ass end of the carrier to make his approach. The trap went smoothly, as professionally done as anything he'd ever executed in his life. He followed the yellow shirt's direction across the flight deck, moving the Tomcat into an unoccupied spot right behind the island. He popped the canopy and waited for the plane captain to safe the seat and assist him in unfastening the ejection harness.

"Really something, Admiral," the airman said as he climbed up the side of the Tomcat. "I heard about that MiG—sir, I mean, it was—I mean, Admiral—" The airman's voice trailed off into a confused panic as he realized who he was talking to. Behind him, Tombstone could hear Tomboy chuckling.

Finally unstrapped, Tombstone sauntered back into the carrier and headed for Flag Plot. Bird Dog might have thought he was hot shit flying JAST birds back at Pax River, but he was willing to bet that he'd earned bragging rights after today's kill.

Tombstone strolled into TFCC and was greeted by a wave of cheers. He started to wave in a self-deprecating manner, ready to display the traditional false modesty over a daring aviation exploit. Then he realized that none of the cheering men and women were even looking at him. Batman clapped him on the back. "Good news, Tombstone! An American sailboat just outside of Cuba's territorial waters just picked up one of our aviators. You probably remember him— Gator, Bird Dog's RIO. That damned ejection seat of his must have had an extra forty pounds of charge or something. He was way the hell off where he ought to have been."

Tombstone tried to smile. "That sure is good news. Hey, about that MiG—"

"Hold on, old buddy. I need to get some SAR on this boy, then we'll talk."

Tombstone stood silent for a moment in the middle of the roiling pack of aviators, each one celebrating Gator's rescue. Finally, he chuckled and headed off for his stateroom. It was always dangerous, getting too damned impressed with oneself. He'd be better off going to the Dirty Shirt and grabbing a quick slider than looking for a pat on the back.

1000 Local (+5 GMT)
United Nations

Ambassador Sarah Wexler smiled as she walked into the crowded subcommittee meeting room. In the last twenty-four hours, there had been more than adequate proof that Cuba was in possession of nuclear weapons and intended to use them against the United States. While all of the island nations might not feel completely supportive of everything the United States had done in this scenario, neither were they willing to have that capability—so easily retargetable and so deadly to the flora and fauna of the Caribbean basin—unleashed against them. They would side with her, of that she was certain. The behind-the-scenes discussions with each of them had confirmed what she'd already known. The tiny island nations that crowded the Caribbean basin would insure that the United Nations sanctioned every action the United States had taken. War on this scale, involving weapons of mass destruction, was far outside of anything they ever saw their nations playing a role in.

She surveyed the ambassadors and assembled staffs, favoring all of them with a calm, confident smile. There were times during the last two days when that smile would have been a lie, and victory was all the sweeter for having been uncertain. In the delicate balance of international politics, sometimes appearances mattered more than reality. Reality: The United States could have smashed Cuba into a glowing ember, had it wished. Illusion: The United States was a force for stability in the region. Result: Smaller nations would flock to America's side, providing training opportunities and much-needed votes on the main floor—and, she had to admit, a bigger drain on the State Department as they demanded money and technical assistance as their just due.

No matter. In the long run, it was better for those nations to be allied with the United States than to be open to foreign influences such as Libya. She sighed, and wondered if this entire scenario could have been averted had the first Cuban Missile Crisis been handled appropriately. What would it have taken to tempt Castro away from the Soviet yoke? Money? Would that alone have been enough? She doubted it, and there was no point in second-guessing President Kennedy at this point. What mattered was that Cuba was once again a nuclear-free part of the United States' backyard.

She took a deep breath and began her address. "My fellow ambassadors, I know you will join with me in expressing deep remorse over the industrial accident that occurred in western Cuba just this morning." She turned a sympathetic gaze on the Cuban ambassador. "Sir, my staff tells me that you have recently discovered a large coal deposit on the westernmost tip of your island." She noted with pleasure the puzzled expression on his face. "What a tragedy, to have such a massive cave-in so soon after you began exploiting those resources. Perhaps, if the offer would not be taken amiss, I could suggest that we render some technical assistance and support to your nation? If it

would be acceptable or desired, of course." Ball in your
court, she thought, watching the range of emotions flit
across his face. Will you reject the offer here, in front of so
many others who have taken advantage of our generosity? I
suspect that you have the authority to do absolutely nothing,
and will initiate the appropriate stalling measures until you
can confer with your grand supreme leader. For just a
moment, she wished that the Cuban president had been
visiting the naval base when the American firepower had
rained down on it. How much easier it would have been for
everyone had he simply ceased to be alive.

But no, those consequences would have been unacceptable as well. Assassination was not a part of American
foreign policy, as evidenced by the Coalition restraint
during Desert Storm and Desert Shield. In earlier centuries,
nations such as Cuba—and, of course, those of the Middle
East—had found assassination to be the quickest way to
clarify difficult questions of sovereignty and succession.
But in the modern world, even the collateral damage of
killing a nation's leader while pursuing a valid military
objective would have been looked at askance by the world
community.

"Of course, I will have to ascertain the status of the rescue
operations before replying," the Cuban ambassador managed finally. "Your gracious offer will not be forgotten."

She glared back. "See that it's not. It remains available,
since you have need of it." She turned back to the chairman.
"And now, on to other business. I understand that the
representative of the Bahamas is having a birthday today.
May I be the first to extend my congratulations?"

And so the business of international diplomacy churned
on, a tangled web of personal relations, illusions, and
political power. As she watched the nations struggle through
the morass of conflicting loyalties and orders, she marveled

that the august body, conceived with such good intentions, could ever accomplish anything.

1100 Local (+5 GMT)
The Pentagon

Pamela Drake stormed past the secretary and barged into Admiral Loggins's office. She was pale, still drained-looking, although a quick shower and change of clothes at her hotel in Crystal City had washed away most of the dirt and grime from her Cuban adventure.

"What the hell were you doing? What were you thinking?" she raged, pounding her fist on his desk. "How dare you criticize Senator Williams after all he's done for the military!"

Keith Loggins leaned back in his chair, steepled his fingers in front of him, and realized that he'd just arrived at another point of no return. For the past day, he'd been daydreaming about his next meeting with Pamela, fantasizing about how masterfully he would ask her to marry him, imagining her ecstatic and eager response. It would have been, he was certain, a marriage made in heaven. With the right planning and dreaming, they could have metamorphosed into the most powerful couple in Washington outside the White House. Her connections, her inside knowledge of the political process, and his background in the military would have—well, no matter. He studied her carefully, seeing the anger boiling close to the surface.

"I see you've heard about Senator Williams's indictment," he said neutrally. He pointed to a chair. "I think you'll have to talk to Senator Dailey if you want any details."

"I did." Her rage seemed to seep away, and she collapsed into the chair he'd offered. "His staff said that you were responsible for providing most of the information leading to the indictment, and that you were present when he was taken into custody. Oh, Keith, how could you? Do you know what that man has meant to my career?"

He shook his head. "Do you know what he almost did to mine?"

She leaned forward. "Tell me. Let's see if we can salvage anything out of this situation."

He took a deep breath. He started to explain about duty, about a higher cause, and about the service that a man or a woman offers to the nation while in the military. He saw her eyes glaze over and a sour expression cross her face.

"I've heard this speech before, Keith," she interrupted. "You're starting to sound like Tombstone, you know. He was always on about that sort of stuff as well. I thought you had more sense."

"I do. Enough sense to know that what Williams wanted for this country was bad. Political power is one thing, Pamela. That belongs to the politicians, the men and women who are elected to represent the people of this country, not to a military officer. We exist to serve, not to rule. What Williams wanted was to transform the Pentagon into a uniformed version of the Senate." He shook his head ruefully. "And I almost fell for it, too, Luckily, at the last minute, I came to my senses." He looked up, pinned her to the chair with a stern glance. "I have no regrets about what I did, Pamela. Quite the contrary. If there's any way I can make up for what seems to me now to have been bad judgment, I will. And, if the Navy thinks that includes retiring, that's what I'll do." For a moment, his voice took on a more hopeful note. "Pamela, I thought that if I was no longer in the service, that we might be able to—"

It was her turn to look grim and shake her head. "Keith, I thought you understood how the world worked. I've already been in one relationship with an idealistic Navy officer. I don't need another." She stood, offered him a hand. "Call me if you come back to your senses." He took her hand, feeling the smooth skin, noticing the broken nails and grime still embedded beneath her fingertips. What a woman—that she would dare the trip to Cuba, stand in the middle of bombs to get her story. In so many ways, they were so much alike.

But there was one critical difference between them. Regretfully, he realized that that quality was honor. He shook her hand, resisting the impulse to pull her close, then showed her to the door.

He sat down at his desk again and glared at the seemingly endless pile of paperwork crowding his in basket, reflecting that virtue was sometimes its own reward. And no more than that.

1800 Local (+5 GMT)
Battaglio's Restaurant, Miami

"So there we were, at five thousand feet," Bird Dog continued, maneuvering his hands to indicate the relative positions of the aircraft. "He was on my six, see? I was trying to shake him, but—"

"Bird Dog, give it a rest," Gator said wearily. He glanced at the young lady standing between them. "I think she's heard enough about your air battles."

The young woman shook her blond head vigorously. "Oh, no, I think it's fascinating! In fact, it reminds me a lot of my dad's stories. He was in Vietnam, and he was a pilot." She paused doubtfully, and studied Bird Dog carefully. "You look like him, too. How old did you say you were?"

Gator almost choked. He took a sip of his beer to disguise his amusement, then started laughing again as he saw Bird Dog's expression. "Face it, Bird Dog—you're getting older, buddy."

"I'm just thirty," Bird Dog protested. "Hardly an old man. Not like you."

Gator studied him for a moment. "Come on, let me introduce you to someone," he said abruptly. He set his beer down on the bar and led Bird Dog off toward a table at the back of the room. Three women were sitting there, sharing nachos and mixed drinks. "Mind if we join you?" Gator asked politely.

"Hey, Gator," a striking brunette said. "What you been up to?"

"Not much," he said, taking the proper chair and gesturing Bird Dog into the other vacant seat. "Like you to meet a friend of mine—Bird Dog, a pilot."

The brunette shot him an appraising look. "Tomcat?"

Bird Dog was slightly taken aback by her knowing smile. He nodded, at a loss for words.

She stuck out a hand. "Me too. Name's Chris Hansen."

"Lobo." Bird Dog stared at her, awe dampening the first tricklings of lust tickling him in the normal places. "Weren't you the one who was—"

Lieutenant Chris "Lobo" Hansen—Lieutenant Commander Hansen by now, he figured. On a previous cruise, *Jefferson* had confronted the Russians on the Kola Peninsula. Lobo had been shot down during a mission over the Polyarnyy submarine base and been taken prisoner by the militia in control. She'd been tortured, gang-raped, and finally rescued by the Marines. Rumor had it she'd finally made a successful recovery from the mental and physical havoc the experience had wreaked on her and been declared fit for duty.

She cut him off. "Yeah, that was me." She grimaced. "Being a POW isn't all it's cracked up to be. I'd advise against it as a career path. But that was then. I'm back in the cockpit now."

Gator studied the two of them with amusement. During the last two tours, he'd watched Bird Dog chase more women across the landscape than any other pilot he'd ever seen. Following Bird Dog's engagement to Callie, Gator had seen the first traces of maturity begin to show in the young pilot's character. Now, he figured, it was time Bird Dog met a real woman, one who could probably outfly him.

Lobo and Bird Dog. Gator sat back to watch the fireworks.

ACKNOWLEDGMENTS

So what do we do about Cuba? And how are newer, smarter, and more deadly weapons going to influence our choices? Will we repeat our mistakes of the last century—or make new ones?

Regular *Carrier* readers may notice a difference between this book and earlier ones. *Arsenal* is longer, going into more depth on the battles and conflicts we'll be fighting in the next decades. Let me know if you like the longer style.

My thanks, as always, to the following:

Jake Elwell and George Wieser, the finest agents in the world. John Talbot, the next-finest agent and superb new writing mentor. Tom Colgan, my editor, who'd make a great fighter pilot. Captain Bud Weeks, USN, my first CO on USS *Jouett* (CG 29). Cyndy Mobley and Ron Morton, technical advisors and war consultants. Lynette Spratley, who types faster than I can talk and reads my first drafts. Bobby, the guy that cuts my hair and knows about Cubans.

And finally: to the men and women who go to sea in the service of our country—BRAVO ZULU.

I like to hear from *Carrier* readers. Drop me an E-mail at KFDouglass@aol.com (the F stands for Francis) or write to me at:

Attention: Tom Colgan
The Berkley Publishing Group
200 Madison Avenue
New York, NY 10016

STATE OF

EMERGENCY

A NOVEL BY

STEVE PIECZENIK

PUTNAM